Curtiss Ann Matlock

Cold Tea on a Hot Day

MIRA®

MIRA

Recycling programs
for this product may
not exist in your area.

ISBN-13: 978-0-7783-2549-9
ISBN-10:   0-7783-2549-0

COLD TEA ON A HOT DAY

www.MIRABooks.com

Printed in U.S.A.

ACKNOWLEDGMENTS

I am grateful to many people who sustain me each day, in my writing and in my life:

Leslie Wainger, Dianne Moggy and Kathleen Adler, who have encouraged me and brought my books to the bookshelves.

Writer friend Cait London, who has taught me "Life moves on," whether we're ready or not.

Dear friends Lou and Barb, and my long-lost sister, Sue, most especially on those days I would rather have stayed in bed and covered up my head.

And the readers whose kind letters embolden me to keep writing.

Thank you all.

One never knew about the deep secrets
of ordinary lives.
—Tate Holloway

One

Another Day in Paradise

In the hazy glow of first morning light, a gleaming red Mercedes, a Roadster with its top up, sat on the side of the blacktopped county road. The engine idled gently, and headlights shone on the patchy grass and weeds.

The driver was slumped in the seat, comfortably, as if taking a nap. He was dead.

A dog lay with his head upon the man's thigh. He had lain there for some time, out of loyal respect to a friend.

In a nearby tree, a meadowlark gave out a shrill morning call.

The dog, perking his ears, sat up and then went over to poke his wet nose out the window, fully open because the man had been driving along in the cool spring night with the passenger window down so that the dog could enjoy putting his face in the wind.

Fairly certain the man would no longer notice being

abandoned, the dog hopped through the window with graceful ease and landed on the dewy wet grass.

After a moment of the sniffing the damp, pungent air, the dog trotted off in the easterly direction that the car had been heading. It was pleasant in the cool first light. A little way along he came to a fresh armadillo run over in the road. He sniffed it, but he was yet far above the depths of eating roadkill. An owl perched on a fence post was kind enough to tell the dog that a town, where likely he could find breakfast, was just over the hill.

Sure enough, when he topped the hill, a town lay before him. The dog sat and looked at it. The morning sun was just beginning to peek over the horizon and cast its pink glow upon this world of humans. Where families of buffalo once wallowed and great herds of cattle once crossed on their way to the rowdy markets in Kansas, there now existed a place springing out of the prairie with tree-lined streets and brick buildings and clapboard houses.

The dog had come to the town in the same manner that he went everywhere and to each of his humans, following the direction led by his heart. The day he had come to the large concrete parking lot and to the man with the glasses, he had known that was the place for him and the human for his dog's loyal work of companionship.

Now, looking down on the town, he knew this was a new place for him and a new human awaited his ministrations.

The dog started down the hill, taking in the lay of the land and ready for any opportunity that presented itself.

* * *

The garbage trucks were starting on their first runs, and early risers all over began tuning kitchen radios to the morning weather report and going out on front porches to hang up flags in support of the campaign to keep Valentine's distinction as the Flag Town of America.

Fayrene Gardner, who had come into the Main Street Café a half an hour early because she had been unable to sleep due to the excitement of expecting a visit from her first ex-husband, came out the café door and set the United States flag in its holder.

A few yards down the sidewalk, at the doors of *The Valentine Voice,* Charlotte Nation was doing likewise. Charlotte, who was a little dismayed to see Fayrene had beat her to it, thought it important for the *Voice* to get their flag out first, as they were a leader in the community.

Setting the pole in the slot with some haste, she hurried back inside to get a cup of coffee for Leo, Sr. before he got off on his deliveries. Since their circulation manager quit three weeks earlier, Leo had been handling the job. Charlotte was thrilled, as now Leo was there early each morning, like herself. He got all the other deliverers off, and then was the last to leave on a route of his own.

"Thanks, Charlotte," Leo said, taking the cup she handed him and sipping. "Well, I gotta get goin' now."

"Yes…you do." She followed him to the doorway and stood there as he slipped into the delivery van and drove off down the alley, watching with the eyes of a woman in love with a man she could never have.

Up on Church Street, Winston Valentine was glad to

be able to manage the job of getting out the front door of his house with the aid of a cane, while carrying two folded flags under his arm. One of his lady boarders, a piece of toast jammed in her mouth, came after him.

He told her with poorly tempered impatience, "I'm all right, Mildred…you cain't help me and eat toast at the same time!"

She had already dropped jelly on her ample bosom; Winston didn't want her to get jelly all over his flags. He felt guilty for having the thought that she could in that minute drop dead and he would gladly step over her. He was relieved when she got more concerned about her toast and jelly than about helping him.

He got himself down the front steps and over to the flag pole in the front yard, where he raised the Confederate flag, followed by the Stars and Bars. He could still raise his flags, and once more all by himself, thank God, and he wasn't yet pissing in his pants, so the day looked good.

Across the street, his neighbor Everett Northrupt, younger by better than ten years, was raising his flags, too, only the Stars and Bars of the U.S. of A. was on top and a lot bigger. Everett was from up North.

Both men stood at attention as music, a mingling of "Dixie" and "The Star Spangled Banner," blared out from speakers from each man's home. Winston, not wanting Everett to have anything on him, stood as straight as he could and saluted the flags and the day.

Then, as most days, he saw Parker Lindsey jogging down the street. Parker, a single fellow who no doubt had plenty of pent-up energy, would jog from his veterinary

clinic at the edge of town, cut through the school yard and
behind houses along a path that came out east of the
Blaine's house, then go down Church Street to Porter
and make several jogs to get to the highway and back east
to his own place. It was a distance of five miles. Winston
played a game of judging the younger man's state of
sexual energy by how hard he was running when he went
past.

"G'mornin', Doc," Winston called to him, remembering what it was like to be a virile man in his prime. He
admired Parker Lindsey, who was going at a pretty good
clip this morning.

"'Mornin'." Puffing, Parker raised a hand in a wave
and kept on going.

From the opposite direction came Leo, Jr., pedaling
past with his teenage legs on his Mountain Flier. "'lo, Mr.
Winston!" he said and sent a rolled newspaper flying into
the yard and landing two feet away.

"Bingo!" Winston called back with a wave.

He bent carefully to get the paper, considering it
exercise. When he came up, he saw a woman in bright
pink on a purple bicycle pumping along toward town. It
was his niece, Leanne, who sometimes jogged and sometimes rode a bicycle. A professional barrel racer, Leanne
worked to keep her legs strong.

"'lo, Uncle Winston!"

Winston waved back, while averting his gaze from the
sight of her. Leanne wore the skimpy attire so popular
with women these days, and being her uncle, Winston did
not consider it polite to stare. Leanne was a fine specimen
of a woman. It was a little too bad she liked to display

that around a lot. Winston felt women today had forgotten mystique. He liked to watch women on exercise shows on television, though.

Walking stiffly, but grateful to be walking, he went around the side of the house, where he clipped blossoms from his dead wife's rosebushes. *I'm keepin' on, Coweta.* He would miss his wife until his dying day.

Further up Church Street, Vella Blaine, wearing a lilac flowered apron and a big straw hat over her greying hair, was out in her backyard, snipping fresh blooms from her own rosebushes. She held each to her nose to inhale the delicious, soothing scent. Her very favorite were the yellow Graham-Thomas blossoms. She was so proud of her roses this spring.

Hearing a car, she looked up to see her husband behind the wheel of his big black 80s Lincoln as it chugged away, carrying him onward to his twelve-hour day at his drugstore.

Perry had not bothered to tell her goodbye. Again.

Gripping the stems of the cut roses so tightly that the thorns pricked her hands, Vella walked purposefully up the back steps and went inside to prepare a fresh pot of coffee for herself and Winston, who had, with the arrival of balmy spring, begun once more to join her for an early-morning chat. She got out the blue pottery mug Winston seemed to favor. In the mirror hung on the inside of the cabinet door, she paused to put on lipstick.

Down on Porter Street, the sun had risen high enough to shine its first golden rays on the roof of a small house dating from the forties that Realtors called a bungalow.

In bed in the back bedroom, Marilee James, who was definitely not a morning person, was awakened by her eight-year-old son.

"Maa-ma…"

Marilee managed to crack an eyelid.

"Maa-ma…" He peered into her face, his blue eyes large behind his thick glasses.

Marilee tried to focus enough to see the clock. Willie Lee simply had no sense of time at all. He woke up when he woke, and slept when he slept, never minding the rest of the world…or his mother, who had not had a decent night's sleep since Miss Porter had suddenly and fantastically thrown the newspaper management into her hands and run off with a husband.

Was that red numeral a five or a six? She was going to have to get a bigger clock. The thought caused her to close her eyes.

"Ma-ma, can I have a dog?" Willie Lee spoke in a whisper and slowly, carefully pronouncing each word, as was his habit.

"Not right this minute," Marilee managed to get out with as hoarse a voice as she used to have when she smoked a pack and a half a day of Virginia Slims.

She gathered courage and stretched herself toward the clock. The red numerals came in more clearly. It was 6:10. Giving a groan, she rolled over and thought that she could not get up. That was all there was to it. She *would not* get up.

"I want this dog in this pic-ture." Willie Lee shoved a book in her face.

Marilee, who could not respond in any way, shape or

form, stared with fuzzy vision at a picture of a spotted dog in one of her son's picture books.

Willie Lee, not at all bothered by not being answered, sat back on folded legs and said, "I will ask God for this dog."

Marilee's sleepy gaze came to rest upon her son, upon his head bent once more to study the picture book. His short white-blond hair stood on end in all directions, as was usual.

Her Willie Lee, who had put up a mighty struggle to enter the world and ended up with brain damage that cast doubt still upon his future ability to lead anything resembling a normal life without someone to watch over him.

Her heart seemed to swell and her heartbeats to grow louder…*thump…thump…thump*…echoing in her ears, broken only by the clink of dishes from the kitchen, where Corrine was no doubt readying the table for breakfast, as she had each morning since coming to stay with them.

With the aroma of coffee floating in to reach her, Marilee pictured the slight figure of her young niece at the counter. Likely she had to pull a chair over and stand on it in order to fill the coffeemaker.

Two of them, two little souls, depending upon only her, Marilee, a mere woman alone.

The idea so frightened her that in an instant she had flung back the covers and gotten to her feet, moving in the manner of generations of women before her who had struggled with the overwhelming urge to run screaming out of the house to throw themselves in front of the early-morning garbage truck. The saving answer to that urge was to propel herself headlong into the day of taking care of those who needed her.

"Let's get you dressed, buster," she said to her son, scooping him up, causing him to giggle.

"Time to get go-ing," he said, mimicking her usual refrain.

"Yes…time to get going."

When focusing on the needs of those around her, she did not have to face the needs clamoring inside herself.

"Here they are," Corrine said and brought Marilee the car keys she had been searching for, as the child did each morning at seven-thirty—or any other time, really.

"Thank you, hon…now, let's get goin'…."

The children trooped before her out the front door, and they all piled into the Jeep Cherokee for the five-minute drive to school, where Marilee let them out on the wide sidewalk in front of the long, low brick building.

The two, taller and very thin Corrine and shorter, slight Willie Lee, did not run off with the other screaming and laughing children but stood there side by side, forlornly watching her drive away.

Marilee, who caught sight of them in the rearview mirror, felt like a traitor abandoning her delicate charges.

Pressing firmly on the accelerator, she focused on the road and reminded herself that she was a working mother, just like a million other working mothers, trying to keep a roof over all their heads, and that her children needed to learn to deal with real life.

As she whipped the Cherokee into its accustomed place in the narrow lot behind the brick building that housed *The Valentine Voice*, she realized that she had been doing the same thing for most of seven years. *Where did the years go? When had twenty-one turned into forty?*

It was Miss Porter running off into a new life who had caused this unrest, Marilee thought with annoyance, hiking her heavy leather tote up on her shoulder. The next instant, having the disconcerting impression that she was beginning to resemble Miss Porter, she dropped the bag to her hand.

"My computer is down," Tammy Crawford said immediately when Marilee came down the large aisle of the main room.

"Call the repairman." Marilee threw her bag on her already full desk and picked up the day's edition of the *Voice*. She had not had time to read it at home. She had not had time for weeks.

"Mrs. Oklahoma is going to visit the high school this mornin'," Reggie said. "Principal forgot to call us...I'm goin' right over there."

"'kay." Marilee didn't think everyone really needed to report to her.

Charlotte strode forward with a handful of notes. "Here's the first morning complaints of late papers...and Roger, that new guy they've hired up at the printer, wants you to call him...and here's a note from the mayor for tomorrow's 'About Town' column. City hall has lost those flags they thought they had left."

Marilee took the notes and sank into her chair.

June, who was now working on their ad layouts since their top ad layout person had quit last week, came over and said, "I can't read this note Jewel put on this ad. Do you think that is supposed to be a two or a five?"

"Call the Ford dealer and ask. I don't think they would appreciate us guessing."

"Okay. I can do that." June generally needed to convince herself of action.

Marilee, giving a large sigh, fell into her chair and flopped open the paper to see how it had come out, and if she would need to be making any retractions and groveling apologies. She thought she was learning to grovel quite well.

"Another day in paradise," she said to no one in particular.

The Valentine Voice
About Town
by Marilee James

For the one or two people in town who have not heard by now, Ms. Muriel Porter, former publisher of *The Valentine Voice,* and Mr. Dwight Abercrombie, who met last year on a Carribean cruise, were married yesterday afternoon in a small ceremony at St. Luke's Episcopal Church. Immediately afterward the two left on a world tour they estimate will take them upward of eighteen months. Following their world tour, the couple plan to settle in either Daytona Beach or possibly Majorca, Spain. Ms. Porter-Abercrombie wanted everyone to know she will always remain a Valentinian, however far she may roam.

"Valentine will always be my home," Ms. Porter

stated. "My ties there are as necessary to my life as cold tea on a hot day."

The new publisher and editor in chief of *The Valentine Voice,* Tate Holloway, will be arriving this weekend to officially take over the paper. Mr. Holloway is Ms. Porter-Abercrombie's cousin and a veteran newspaper journalist with thirty years experience on a number of the nation's leading newspapers.

An open house will be held in honor of Mr. Holloway on Monday at the *Voice* offices. Cake and coffee will be served courtesy of Sweetie Cakes of Main Street. Come by and welcome Mr. Holloway, or address to him your complaints.

Until Monday, I will continue as managing editor. All news stories should be reported to me, and you can call me at my home number, 555-4743, afternoons and until 8:00 p.m. Please save all complaints for Mr. Holloway on Monday.

Other important bits of note:

The first meeting of the Valentine Rose Club will be held tonight, 7:00 p.m., at the Methodist Church Fellowship Hall. Vella Blaine will head the meeting and wants it stressed that all denominations are welcome and there will be no passing of a collection plate.

Jaydee Mayhall has formally declared his candidacy for city council. Thus far he is the first candidate to declare intentions of running for the seat being vacated by long-time member Wesley Fitzwater, who says he is tired of the thankless job.

Mayhall invites anyone who would like to talk to him about the town's needs to stop by to visit with him at his office on Main Street.

Mayor Upchurch has ten Valentine town flags left at city hall, for anyone who wants to fly one outside their home or shop. The flags are free; the only requirement is a proper pole high enough that the flag does not brush the ground.

Two

Looking in the Wrong Direction

"How long has he been missing?" Principal Blankenship demanded of the teacher standing before her.

"Since lunch recess," Imogene Reeves answered, wringing her hands. "I don't care if he is retarded and looks like an angel. He knows how to slip away. He is not just wanderin' off."

The principal winced at the word *retarded* spoken out loud. There were so many unacceptable words and phrases these days that she couldn't keep up, but she was fairly certain the term *retarded* fell in the unacceptable category. She checked her watch and saw it was going on one o'clock.

She headed at a good clip out of her office, asking as she went, "Has anyone spoken to Mr. Starr…checked the storerooms?"

It could very well be a repeat of that first time, she thought, calming herself. It had been Mr. Starr, the custodian, who had found Willie Lee the first time. That time the boy had been all along playing with a mouse in the janitor's storeroom. This had been upsetting—a little fright that the mouse might bite and the boy get an infection—but it was better than the second time, when the boy had gotten off the school grounds and all the way down to the veterinarian's place a half-mile away. That time Principal Blankenship had been forced to call the boy's mother, because the veterinarian was a *friend* of the boy's mother.

Oh, she did not want to have to tell the mother again. Marilee James wrote for the newspaper. This would get everywhere.

Imagining what her father, a principal before her, would have said, would have *yelled,* Principal Blankenship just about wet her pants.

The storeroom had been searched and the custodian Mr. Starr consulted; involved with changing out hot water heaters, he had not seen Willie Lee since the beginning of the school day. The closets were searched, and the storerooms a second time, and the boys' bathrooms.

At last the principal resorted to telephoning down to the veterinarian's office.

"I haven't seen Willie Lee," the young receptionist at the veterinarian's told her. "And Doc Lindsey has been out inoculatin' cattle since before noon."

The principal, with a sinking feeling, went along the corridors of her small school, peeking into each classroom, searching faces, hoping, praying with hands clasping and unclasping, for Willie Lee to appear.

In her heart she knew that Willie Lee had escaped the

school grounds a second time, but she did not want to think of such a failure on the part of one of her teachers. Or herself. And truly, she didn't want anything to happen to the child.

She did wish he could go to another school.

At last, with pointy shoulders slumping, she broke down and spoke over the school intercom: "Attention, teachers and students. Anyone who has seen Willie Lee James since lunch recess, please come to the office."

In Ms. Norwood's fourth-grade class, Corrine Pendley heard the announcement of her cousin's name. Face jerking upward, she stared at the speaker above the class-room door. Then she saw all eyes turn to her.

Her face burned. Bending her head over her notebook, she focused her eyes on the lined paper in front of her and concentrated on being invisible.

The teacher had called her name several times before Corrine was jolted into hearing by Christy Grace poking her in the back with a pencil. "She's callin' you."

Corrine looked up at the teacher, who asked if Corrine had seen Willie Lee. Corrine said, "No, ma'am." She wondered at the question. Maybe the teacher thought she was a little deaf. Or else she thought Corrine would lie.

Why didn't everybody mind their own business and quit looking at her?

Bending her head over her math problems, she made the numbers carefully, trying to concentrate on them, but thinking about her cousin. Willie Lee was only eight, and little for his age.

He was slow, but this did not mean he didn't know

about some things. *One thing he seemed to know was how to get away when he wanted to.* Corrine wished she had gone with him.

Her anxiety increased. She felt responsible. She should have been looking out for him. She was older, and he didn't have any brothers or sisters, just like she didn't.

All manner of dark fantasies paraded through her mind. She hoped he didn't get run over. Or fall in a muddy creek and drown. Or get picked up by a stranger.

Her pencil point broke, startling her.

Carefully, she laid the pencil down, got up and walked as quietly as possible, so as not to become too visible, to the teacher's desk to ask in a hurried whisper to go to the rest room.

In the tiled room that smelled strongly of bleach, she used the toilet and then she washed her hands. She kept thinking about the front doors. When she came out of the rest room, she turned left instead of right and walked down the hall and right out the double doors. She did this without thinking at all, just following an urge inside.

All the way down the front walk, she felt certain a yell was going to hit her in the back. But it didn't. Then she was running free, running from school and then running from herself, scared to death to have done something that was very wrong and would make everyone mad at her.

She would have to find Willie Lee, she thought. If she found him, no one would be mad at her. The sun felt warm on her head and the breeze cool to her face.

At that very instant, when finding her cousin and being a hero seemed totally possible, she looked down the street and saw her Aunt Marilee's brilliant white Jeep Cherokee coming.

The Jeep's chrome shone so brightly, Corrine had to squint. Still, she saw Aunt Marilee behind the wheel. Corrine stopped in her tracks, and her life seemed to drain right out her toes.

Likely she was going to get it now. And she deserved it. She never could seem to do things right.

The vehicle pulled up beside her, and the tinted window slid down. Aunt Marilee said, "Where are you goin'?"

Corrine, who could not read her aunt's even tone or blank expression, said slowly, "They announced 'bout Willie Lee being missin'. I was goin' to find him."

Her aunt said, "Well, that makes two of us. Get in. I have to go see the principal first."

Corrine opened the door and slipped into the seat in a manner as if to disappear. Carefully, she closed the door beside her. In the short drive to the school parking lot, she tried to read her aunt's attitude but could not. She had never seen her aunt look like this. She thought desperately of what her aunt might be thinking, in order to be ready for what to say or do.

But all Aunt Marilee said to her when they got to the school was, "Come on back in with me. You'll need to get your stuff from class."

Aunt Marilee went to Corrine's class with her and told Ms. Norwood that she was taking Corrine home early. Corrine, who was used to moving from an entire apartment in just a few minutes and therefore was not in the habit of accumulating needless trifles, stuffed all her books and notebooks from her desk into her backpack in scarcely a minute. As she lugged it to the classroom door, she could feel everyone looking at her, but it didn't matter. She was leaving, at least for today.

The heels of Aunt Marilee's Western boots echoed sharply on the corridor floor all the way back to the principal's office, where Aunt Marilee said to her, "Sit right here. I don't want to lose you, too."

Without a word, Corrine sat. Aunt Marilee disappeared into the principal's office.

The secretary, who had bleached blond hair teased up to amazing heights, looked at her. Corrine looked around the room and swung her feet that only brushed the floor.

Aunt Marilee had not fully closed the door, but even if she had, the voices would probably have been heard. Aunt Marilee had the furious tone she used when she and Corrine's mother got into their fights. Corrine imagined her aunt was standing how she did when she meant business: feet slightly apart and eyes like laser rays.

Aunt Marilee wanted to know how people supposedly educated in child development could not manage to keep track of one little boy who was diagnosed as learning disabled and not able to think above five years old. The principal answered that the school was not a prison and did not have guards.

"We are trying to mainstream Willie Lee to the best of our ability," the principal said. "We do not lose normal children, who are taught to participate."

Corrine held her breath, afraid that her Aunt Marilee was going to reveal finding Corrine halfway down the block. And maybe, since she had gotten away—since she had even *attempted* to leave—maybe she was not quite normal.

"We are doing the best we can with your children, Mrs. James," the principal said in a low tone.

Corrine saw the big-haired secretary's eyes cut to her, as if thinking, You're one of those troublemakers. Corrine swung her feet and looked at the wall, feeling the empty hole in her chest grow until it seemed to swallow her.

"Arguing will not find Willie Lee. I apologize. Now, tell me when and where my son was last seen." Aunt Marilee's voice, sounding so very calm and firm, enabled Corrine to draw a breath.

"I'll tell you," Aunt Marilee said when they got back in the Cherokee, Aunt Marilee slamming the door so hard the entire vehicle rattled. "Willie Lee knew exactly what he was doin'. I don't care how dumb people think he is."

"He is only dumb in some things," Corrine said.

Aunt Marilee didn't seem to hear her. She started off fast, gazing hard out the window. "Oh, Willie Lee," she said under her breath, and for an instant Corrine thought her aunt might cry. This was very unnerving to Corrine, who instantly turned her eyes out the window, looking hard, thinking that she just had to find Willie Lee. She had to make everything all right again for her aunt.

They drove slowly down to the veterinary clinic, looking into yards as they went. They went into the veterinarian's office, where two people waited with their dogs, a yippy little terrier and a trembling Labrador.

The girl behind the counter told them that Doc Lindsey had been out most of the day, was at that moment tending a sick horse at some ranch but was expected back any moment.

Dr. Lindsey was Aunt Marilee's boyfriend. Parker Lindsey, which Corrine thought was a lovely name. He was so handsome, too. Clean and neat, and he smiled at her and Willie Lee. He smiled at just about everyone, and had very white, even teeth. Sometimes, although she never would have told anyone on this earth, Corrine imagined having a boyfriend just like Parker Lindsey.

Aunt Marilee did not want to take the office girl's word that Willie Lee wasn't there. Corrine, who never took anyone's word for anything, was glad to accompany her aunt and search along the outside dog runs and look into the cattle chutes and pens. Corrine even called Willie Lee's name softly. He might come to her first, she thought, because Aunt Marilee was getting pretty mad now.

They got back inside the Cherokee and drove around a couple of streets surrounding the school. Aunt Marilee said that they should be able to spot Willie Lee's blond hair, because it shone in the sun. They stopped and asked a couple of people they saw in yards if they had seen Willie Lee. At one falling-down house, a man sat in his undershirt on the front step, drinking a beer. Aunt Marilee got right out of the car and went up to ask him about Willie Lee, but Corrine stayed rooted in the seat, watching sharply. She made it a point not to talk to men with beers in their hands.

Then Aunt Marilee headed in the direction of home, saying out loud, "Maybe he's on his way home."

Corrine, who was beginning to get really scared for her

cousin and for her aunt and for her whole life, scooted up
until she was sitting on the edge of the seat, looking as
hard as she was able.

It was a long walk to home, but only about a five-minute
drive. Maybe Willie Lee knew the way, and he wouldn't
have to cross the highway or anything. Still, no telling
where he might go, and again all sorts of fearful images
began to race across her mind, such as cars running over
her cousin's little body, and snakes slithering out to bite
him, or maybe a black widow spider like in the movies, or
maybe a bad man would get him, or a bunch of big, mean
boys.

At one point she said, "Willie Lee doesn't like school.
Some of the kids tease him and call him dumb and stupid,
and it's hard for him to sit still all day." She didn't want
her aunt to make Willie Lee go back to school.

Aunt Marilee said, "I know."

"I don't like school, either," Corrine said, quietly, in
the manner a child uses when she has to speak her
feelings but does so in a way and time that she believes
the adult might not hear. Then her throat got all thick, and
she hated herself for being so stupid as to risk making
Aunt Marilee mad. She would die if Aunt Marilee got
mad at her.

Aunt Marilee, her gaze focused out the windshield,
said, "We'll talk about it later." And a moment later, she
whispered, "God, help us find Willie Lee."

They searched the streets on the way home, following
the route Aunt Marilee took when driving them to and
from school. Again Aunt Marilee questioned several
people who were outside.

A man who was roofing a house said, "Yeah, Marilee, I saw him over there on the corner. I'm sorry, I didn't recognize him as your boy. And I didn't see what direction he went."

At least when the man had seen him, Willie Lee hadn't been dead yet, Corrine thought.

Aunt Marilee drove the rest of the way home, where she went immediately to the backyard and checked to see if Willie Lee might be there with his rabbits or up in his tree fort. Corrine climbed the ladder to look in the fort, even though no one answered when they called. "He's not here," she called back to her aunt.

Aunt Marilee went to the front yard and hollered, "Willie Lee! Willie Lee!"

There was no answer.

Aunt Marilee unlocked the front door and went inside and straight to the answering machine on her desk in the corner of the living room. There were no messages. Aunt Marilee immediately picked up the telephone and called the school, asking if Willie Lee had been found there. He had not. Next Aunt Marilee telephoned the sheriff's office to ask for help.

Afterward, she snapped the receiver back on the hook and looked at Corrine. "He's all right. God watches over all of us, and most especially little ones like Willie Lee."

Corrine, who had reason to doubt God watched over her, thought her Aunt Marilee was speaking to calm herself. She felt guilty for the thought.

"Well, we've done all we can," Aunt Marilee said, rising straight up. "We'll wait here and let God handle it."

Aunt Marilee let God handle it for about the length of

time it took to make a pot of tea and fix a cup with lots of sugar for Corrine, and search for a pack of cigarettes, which she didn't find, and then she went to telephoning people.

From the chair at the table, where she could look clear through the house to the front and watch her aunt hold the phone to her ear while pacing in long strides that pushed out her brown skirt, Corrine felt helpless and desperate.

Three

Your Life Is Now

Tate Holloway drove into Valentine from the east along small, bumpy roads because he had taken a wrong turn and gotten lost. He never had been very good at directions. A couple of his city desk editors used to say they hated to send him out to an emergency, because he might miss it by ending up in a different state.

He slowed his yellow BMW convertible when he came into the edge of town. He passed the feed and grain with its tall elevator, and the car wash, and the IGA grocery. Anticipation tightened in his chest. Right there on the IGA was a sign that proclaimed it the Hometown Grocery Store.

This was going to be his own hometown.

Driving on, he entered the Main Street area and spied *The Valentine Voice* building. He allowed it only a glance and drove slowly, taking in everything on the left side of the street, turned around at the far edge of town and took in everything on the opposite side of the street.

He had seen the town as a child of nine, and surprisingly, it looked almost as he remembered. There were the cars parked head-in on the wide street. There was the bank, modernized nicely with new windows and a thorough sandblasting job. There was the theater—it had become something called The Little Opry. There was the florist…and the drugstore, with the air conditioner that dripped. The air conditioner was still there, although he could not tell if it dripped, as it was too cool in April to need it. He imagined it still dripped, though.

There were various flags flying outside the storefronts: the U.S. flags, the state flag of Oklahoma, what appeared to be the Valentine City flag, and a couple of Confederate flags, which surprised him a bit and reminded him that people in the west tended to be truly individualistic. There was a flag with flowers on it at the florist, and at least one person was a Texan, because there was a Texas flag flying proudly.

Tate thought the flags gave a friendly touch. He noted the benches placed at intervals. One thing the town needed, he thought, was trees. He liked a town with trees along the sidewalks to give shade when a person walked along.

Back once again to *The Valentine Voice* building, he turned and parked the BMW head-in to the curb. Slowly he removed his sunglasses and sat there looking at the building for some minutes. It sat like a grand cornerstone of the town, two-story red brick, with grey stone-cased windows and The Valentine Voice etched in a granite slab beside the double doors.

Emotion rose in his chest. Tears even burned in his eyes.

There it was—his *own* newspaper.

It was the dream of many a big-city news desk editor to become publisher of his own paper, and Tate had held this dream a long time. A place where he could express his own ideas, unencumbered by the hesitancies and prejudices of others less inclined to personal responsibility and more concerned with being politically correct and watching the bottom line dollar. Newspaper publishing as it once was, with editors who spoke their fire and light, drank whiskey from pint bottles in their desk drawers and smoked big stogies, with no thought of the fate of their jobs or pensions, only the single-minded intent to speak the truth.

The good parts of the old days were what Tate intended to resurrect. Here, in this small place in the world, he would pursue his mission to speak his mind and spread courage, and to enjoy on occasion the damn straight wildness for the sake of being wild.

Yes, sir, by golly, he was on his way.

Tate alighted from the BMW, slammed the door and took the sidewalk in one long stride. A bell tinkled above as he opened the heavy glass front door and strode through, removing his hat and taking in the interior with one eager glance: brick wall down the left side, desks, high ceiling with lights and fans suspended. Old, dim, de-teriorating…but promising. A city room, by golly.

"Can I help you?"

It was a woman at the front reception desk, bathed in the daylight from the wide windows. A no-nonsense sort of woman, with deep-brown hair in a Buster Brown cut and steady black eyes behind dark-rimmed glasses. Cheyenne, he thought.

"Hello, there. I'm Tate Holloway." He sent her his most charming grin.

"You're not."

That response set him back.

"Why, yes, ma'am, I believe I am." He chuckled and tapped his hat against his thigh.

She was standing now. She had unfolded from her chair, and Tate, who was five foot eleven, saw with a bit of surprise that he was eye to eye with her.

"You aren't supposed to be here until Saturday."

"Well, that's true." He tugged at his ear. He had expected to be *welcomed.* He had expected there to be people here, too, and the big room was empty.

"But here I am." He stuck out his hand. "And who might you be, ma'am?" he drawled in an intimate manner. It had been said that Tate Holloway could charm the spots off a bobcat.

This long, tall woman was made of stern stuff. She looked at his hand for a full three heartbeats before offering her own, which was thin but sturdy. "Charlotte Nation."

"Well, now…nice to meet you, Miss Charlotte."

She blinked. "Yes…a pleasure to meet you, Mr. Holloway." She wet her lips. "I'm sorry I didn't say that right away. It's just that Marilee said you weren't coming until Saturday." There again was the note of accusation in her voice. "We aren't prepared. We are…" She looked around behind her at the room and seemed to search for words. "Well, everyone is busy working for the paper, just not here."

"I'm glad to see that," Tate said. "I didn't expect a welcoming committee."

A spark of suspicion about that statement shone in her eyes, before she blinked and said, "I'm assuming you know that Chet Harmon, Harlan Buckles and Jewel Luttrell have all quit in the last month. June Redman has taken on the layout, and she's out gettin' her mammogram this afternoon. She used to just work part-time, anyway. Imperia is out on some sales calls. Leo and Reggie and Tammy are on stories, and Marilee's had to go find her little boy." She paused, then added, "Zona's here, of course."

"Marilee James? Her little boy is missing?" He recalled the woman's voice on the phone, deep and soft, like warm butter. He had been anticipating seeing her and felt a bit of disappointment that she wasn't here. Actually, saying that he didn't want a welcoming committee was a fib, as this woman recognized. Tate had anticipated being greatly welcomed…at least, he had expected to be received with some enthusiasm.

The woman nodded. "Willie Lee. He's wandered off from school again. He's eight years old but learning disabled."

"I see."

"He is sweet as the day is long, but he tends to drift away. And he is not afraid of anybody in this world. That's the worry…so many strangers come down here these days from the city."

He felt vaguely guilty, since he had just driven in from a city. "Well, I'll just have a look around."

The woman blinked, as if surprised.

Just then a door from an office down on the left opened. A person—a small woman—appeared, saw Tate, and stepped back and shut the door. It happened so quickly that the only impression Tate had was of a small, grey-haired mouse of a woman. The office had window glass, but dark shades were drawn.

Tate looked at the brown-haired woman, who said, "That is Zona Porter—no relation—our comptroller."

Tate waited several seconds to hear more, to possibly be introduced to this woman, but just then the phone on the desk rang, and the brown-haired woman immediately snatched it up.

"*Valentine Voice,* Charlotte speaking." She gripped the telephone receiver. After several seconds, she told whoever was on the other end, "I'll have Marilee call you back about that. She's had to go out after Willie Lee. He's wandered off from school again." Her eyes lit on Tate. "Oh, wait! Mr. Holloway, the new publisher, is here. You can talk to him. Hold on a minute while I switch you over to another line…yes, he's the new owner, Ms. Porter's cousin…. I know it isn't Saturday, he came early. Now I'm switching."

She said to Tate, "It's the mayor. They've landed the detention center after all, and he wants to give you the story."

He stood there staring at her, and she stared back. Then a ringing sounded from a room behind Ms. Nation.

"Go on and get it in Ms. Porter's office," the woman ordered, shooing him with her hand. "I have to keep this phone clear in case anyone calls about Willie Lee."

Tate turned and strode down the wide reception area to the opened doorway, the office he remembered as his uncle's. Two long strides and he reached the enormous old

walnut desk. Almost in a single motion, he tossed aside his
hat and answered the phone, at the same time pulling a pad
and pen from the breast pocket of his brown denim sport
coat.

His journalist's instincts had kicked in. He was a newspaper owner, by golly.

The mayor, a meek but earnest man with extremely
thin fingers and hair, drove Tate out to see the site for the
new detention center that would employ a hundred people
right off the bat.

There was a lot of controversy over the center, the
mayor admitted. He stuttered over the word *controversy*.
Tate listened to the man's explanations and read a bit
between the diplomatic lines. Many people didn't want
what they thought of as a prison in their midst.

The mayor drove him all around, giving him a guided
tour of the town and surrounding area. He took him into
the Main Street Café and introduced him around, and then
over to Blaine's Drugstore and introduced him to Mr.
Blaine, the only person in the store at the time and who
seemed reticent to break away from his television. His
only comment on the detention center was, "They'll need
a pharmacy, those boys."

After that Tate walked with the mayor, who shyly requested being called Walter, up and down both sides of
the street, the mayor introducing him to various shop
owners, who all said more or less, "Hey, Walter," and
slapped the mayor's back fondly and got a warm back-
slapping in return. The mayor was generally beloved,
Tate saw.

When he finally begged off from a supper invitation by the mayor and returned to the newspaper offices, Miss Charlotte was on her feet.

"I'm glad you are back. It's after five o'clock, and time for me to go home. Leo took the disks for the mornin' edition up to the printer. We didn't think we could wait for you," she added in the faintly critical tone Tate was beginning to recognize. "Harlan used to handle it. Since he quit, we're all just sort of filling in for the time being." There was an air of expectancy in that comment, too.

"That's just fine. I didn't realize it was after five. I'm sorry to hold you up."

"I waited because I wasn't sure you had keys. I didn't want to lock you out." She pulled a purse as big as a suitcase from beneath the desk.

Tate felt a little embarrassed to tell her that he didn't have any keys. She strode out from behind her desk, and he stepped out of her way, having a sense she might walk right over him. She continued on into his cousin's—*his*—office, reached into the middle drawer of the desk and pulled out keys that she handed over to him.

She was through the front door when he thought to ask, "Did they find Marilee James's little boy?"

She looked over her shoulder at him. "No. I'm going over to her house now and take some fried chicken."

The door closed behind her, and Tate watched through the big plate glass window as she walked away down the sidewalk and turned the corner. Miss Charlotte wore an amazingly short skirt and high heels for a prim-and-proper woman. And she didn't walk; she marched.

* * *

He went out to the BMW that he'd left right there with the top down, his computer in full sight. He had figured a person could do that in Valentine.

Making a number of trips, he carted the computer, monitor and then a few boxes into his new office. After he'd set the things down, he stood smoothing the back of his hair. That he ought to be doing something to help in the search for little Willie Lee James tugged at him. He felt helpless on that score. There didn't seem anything he, not knowing either the child or the town, could do.

He left the boxes in a stack and started to connect up his computer, but then decided he was too impatient to see his new home. He wanted to get a look around while the light was still good. He locked the front doors and was one step away when he stopped, remembering the small grey woman he had earlier seen appear. Was she still in there?

He didn't think she could be, since Miss Charlotte hadn't said anything about her. Still, the thought caused him to go back inside to check.

On the door glass of the office was printed: Zona Porter, No Relation, Comptroller. He did not hear sound from beyond the walls. He knocked. No answer. Very carefully he turned the knob and stuck his head in the door. The office, very small and neat, even stark, was empty.

Well, good. He felt better to have made certain.

Back at the front door again, he locked the door of *his* newspaper, wondering if one even needed to bother in such a town. Whistling, he strode to his BMW, where he jumped over the door and slid down into the seat. He backed the BMW out of its place and had to drive the length of town and turn around and come back to the intersection of Main and Church Streets. His cousin Muriel's house, which he had bought sight unseen since he was nine years old, was on the second block up Church Street, on the corner. He heard Muriel's clipped tone of voice giving him the directions.

The town was pretty as a church calendar picture in the late-afternoon sunlight that shone golden on the buildings and flags, houses and big trees. Forsythia blooms had mostly died away, but purple wisteria and white bridal wreath were in full bloom.

It struck him how he knew the names of the bushes. He had learned a few things from his ex-wife, he supposed. He experienced a sharp but brief stab of regret for what he had let pass him by. He had not cared about houses and yards during his married years; he had not valued building a home and a family.

Then he immediately remembered all that he had experienced in place of domesticity, and he figured his life and times had been correct for him. In fact, that was what Lucille had told him: "You need to be a newspaperman, Tate, not a married man."

Funny, he hadn't thought of Lucille in a long time. Her image was fuzzy, and her voice came only in a faint whisper from deep in memory. She had been a rare woman, but neither of them had fit together in a marriage. Set free, she had blossomed as a psychologist, mother, political activist.

To everything there is a season, a time for every purpose under heaven, he thought as his gaze lit on the big Porter house that came into view—the *Holloway* house, he mentally corrected.

He thought of his season now, as he pulled the BMW to a stop in the driveway just outside the portico. His season had come to put down roots. He had reached that point, by golly, finally, at the age of fifty-one. It was a fact, he thought, that might daunt a lesser man.

His strides were long and swift. He took the wide front steps two at a time and unlocked a door that needed re-finishing. It creaked loudly when opened.

He stepped inside, into a wide hallway. There was a pleasant scent of old wood. He walked through the musty rooms, the oak flooring creaking often beneath his steps as he gave everything a cursory, almost absent look, noting the amazing fact that Muriel had pretty much left everything just as it was.

When Muriel had decided to leave, she had definitely decided to *leave*.

He poked his head out the back door, the screen door that definitely needed replacing, then walked more slowly around the kitchen that had not been painted in twenty years. His cousin had not been a domestic type, any more than he had been. On into the dining room, where he unlocked the French doors and stepped out on the wrap-around porch. By golly, he *liked* the porch! He was going to sit out here on hot afternoons and smoke his cigars and drink iced tea thick as syrup with sugar.

Just then his gaze fell on the wicker settee, where he saw a little boy asleep.

A little boy, a dog, and a big orange cat who regarded Tate with definite annoyance.

Four

Vast Stretches of the Heart

When Parker's blue pickup truck, with the white-and-gold Lindsey Veterinary Clinic emblem on the side, came pulling up in her driveway, Marilee went running out to meet him. There was in the back of her mind the idea that he would be bringing Willie Lee.

She saw immediately that he had not.

"I heard about Willie Lee. Is he home yet?" Parker strode around the front of his truck toward her.

"No…all this time, Parker…" Her arms pried themselves from her sides, and she reached for him.

He took her against him and held her tight. Then, as he walked her back into the house, with his arm around her shoulders, Marilee told him of her conversation with the principal, of having searched the neighborhoods, of calling Sheriff Oakes, and of the helplessness of just having to wait. She did not mention the fear that was rising to choke her throat, that maybe this time Willie Lee was truly gone, a fear that had haunted her since the night she had delivered him early, blue and choking for breath.

"He is just out diggin' in a ditch for crawdads or explorin' ant trails or something that boys do," Parker said with perfect reasonableness.

Recriminations for having felt the burden of being a mother echoed in her brain, bringing shame and self-loathing.

"He'll turn up, Marilee. It'll be okay," Parker whispered in her ear as he again drew her close.

What was great about Parker was his solidity in any crisis. Probably it had something to do with being a veterinarian, facing life and death on a regular basis. He was not daunted by a crisis, but was, in fact, better in a crisis than at normal times. He could offer himself in a crisis, whereas during normal everyday times, he withheld himself and kept his affability around him like a shield.

"Did you bring any cigarettes?" she asked.

"No. Why would I have cigarettes?" He looked startled.

"Parker, don't you keep any, just in case?"

"I quit three years ago, and so did you, remember?" he said with a righteousness that Marilee thought uncalled for in the situation.

Annoyed, she almost asked him to go get her a pack, but then the phone rang.

Phone calls had been coming in from people as they heard about Willie Lee. Each time Marilee would jump to answer, hoping it was the sheriff calling to say Willie Lee was found. After three more such calls, she waved at Parker to answer.

Then Charlotte Nation drove up in her little red Grand

Am. Marilee, sitting at the window, watched Charlotte unfold her long legs out of the car and come swiftly up the walk, her arms loaded with brown bags. Charlotte had brought containers of fried chicken and potato salad from the Quick Shop that had put in a delicatessen.

Marilee looked at the food and felt sick; it was like funeral food.

Charlotte reported that June had managed to correct both the Ford and IGA ads in time for Leo's delivery of the disks to the printer for tomorrow's edition. And that their new publisher, Tate Holloway, had arrived before schedule.

"He did?" Vaguely, Marilee tried to be concerned about this.

"Don't worry about him," Charlotte said, giving a dismissive wave. "He took it upon himself to come early, so he had to take what he got. And when Willie Lee comes home, you are going to be worn out, so sleep in tomorrow morning and just come on down when you get ready."

When Willie Lee comes home…

As Charlotte's Grand Am pulled away from the curb, Marilee, who felt the need to keep vigil out the front window, was dismayed to see her mother's Cadillac pull in. The car bore a front license plate that said CCoopers, which was advertising of a sort for the discount appliance store owned by her mother's second husband—Carl Cooper—one of those stores that plastered the television with cluttered and tasteless ads. What this did for Marilee's mother, however, was give her the fame she craved.

Watching her mother, a small woman with Lady Clairol blond hair who walked in short, quick strides,

Marilee had the thought to run and hide, but like one inextricably caught, she kept sitting there.

Her mother had come to talk about Marilee helping her get new tires for her Cadillac, because her husband could not be counted on to do this to her satisfaction.

"Carl won't take the time," she said, having launched immediately into her request. "He insists on just goin' down to the discount tire warehouse and getting the cheapest ones slapped on there…and he doesn't pay attention if they balance them or not."

Marilee jumped in to say, "Mother, I can't talk to you about this now. Willie Lee is missing."

Upon being told of her grandson's disappearance, her mother became very agitated. Her entire countenance became one of doom, so much so that to look at her made Marilee have trouble breathing.

Her mother then launched in with comments of a dire sort. "Anything could happen to him out there, all these perverts in the world." And, "The boy is too friendly, doesn't know a stranger. I hope he didn't get in a car with somebody." Then, "You never should have sent the boy to school anyway. He isn't capable of regular school," and, in a whisper that really wasn't one and that Parker heard very well, "You should marry Parker, and then you could stay home with the boy."

Invariably her mother called Willie Lee the boy.

"He has a name, mother. It is *Willie Lee*."

"Well, I know that," her mother said, looking confused and hurt and more fearful than ever. Marilee felt like a toad but did not apologize.

Parker, who could stand no conflict, said, "Norma, would you like more coffee?"

Marilee turned and went and shut herself in the bathroom, where she stared at her reflection in the medicine cabinet mirror for a long minute, asking all sorts of unintelligible questions of herself and God.

Finally, her spinning brain settling somewhat, she opened the medicine cabinet and began a thorough search. Surely she had some pills left in here from the time when Stuart had walked out on her. Surely she did. Oh, Lordy, she felt like she was coming apart.

A knock sounded at the door. Marilee, wondering if word had come of her son, whipped the door open to see standing there her tall and sturdy Aunt Vella.

"Hello, sugar. I'm sorry, I'm not Willie Lee." Her eyes, all sympathetic, went beyond Marilee to the sink strewn with the stuff out of the medicine cabinet. "What are you doing?"

"Looking for any of my old pills. I don't have any, though. I threw them all out."

"Well, yes, you did. I was here that day. Now, I've brought you what you need—a big chocolate shake."

"Chocolate?"

"Yes, sugar…it's in the kitchen."

"Bless you." Marilee threw herself on her aunt, who hugged her tight and then kept an arm around her all the way to the kitchen, where her mother saw and frowned. There had always been animosity between Marilee's petite mother and her statuesque Aunt Vella, who was her father's sister.

Marilee disengaged herself from her aunt and sat

down, taking up the large paper cup and spooning the thick shake into her mouth. Her Aunt Vella and Uncle Perry owned Blaine's Drugstore and Soda Fountain, and Aunt Vella knew exactly how Marilee liked her chocolate shakes, with an extra squirt of chocolate syrup.

Then Marilee saw that Corrine had her own shake, too. Corrine's black eyes met Marilee's for an instant, in which Marilee summoned forth an encouraging smile from the place mothers always keep them. She had forgotten about her niece and wanted to make up for it. The child had enough of being forgotten in her life.

Corrine quickly looked away, though, as if needing to protect herself.

"Well, I have to go," Marilee's mother said. "I have to get Carl's supper."

"That's okay…there's nothing you can do here." God forbid Carl's supper be interrupted. Marilee breathed deeply.

"You call me as soon as you have news…and I can come back down." She was edging toward the door, and turned and told Parker, "Good seeing you, Parker—you call me if Marilee needs me."

Parker nodded politely, wisely not committing himself.

"Vella, it was good seein' you."

"Norma…"

Different as night and day, the two women managed to tolerate each other.

For a second Marilee's mother hovered uncertainly, and then she patted Marilee's arm and stroked Corrine's dark hair away from her forehead, saying, "Honey, can't you clip your hair out of your eyes?"

Marilee saw Corrine quietly keep sipping her milk shake, while beneath the table her legs swung about ninety miles an hour.

"Well, I'll get with you this weekend about the tires," Marilee's mother said before leaving.

Marilee played the straw around in her milk shake and suffered guilt at the thought of telling her mother to cram the tires up her ass.

Vella, feeling the need to be polite and thoroughly cover the annoyance she always felt in the other woman's presence, hopped to her feet and escorted her ex-sister-in-law to the front door. And needing to make certain the woman did indeed get out the door. It was, Vella thought as she saw her ex-sister-in-law get into her car, a great failing on her part that, after all these years and the death of her brother, Norma Cooper should still have the power to irritate the fire out of her.

When she returned to the kitchen, Parker was massaging Marilee's shoulders and joking with Corrine, producing a rare smile from the child. Although she had always found Parker Lindsey vaguely wanting, Vella thoroughly admired the way he could lighten a moment when he put his mind to it.

Marilee said to her, "Don't you have the Rose Club meeting tonight?"

"Yes. And I'm going. There's plenty of time. Perry can get supper over at the café, and I can go straight to the meeting from here." Perry always took himself off to the café, if he came home and she wasn't there and no supper was on the table. Then he would come home, turn on the television and fall asleep in his La-Z-Boy.

She went to the counter to unpack a grocery sack from the IGA, where she had bought chocolate cookies and bananas. In her estimation a person could live on bananas for a meal and cookies for desert. She noted then on the counter a big bucket of fried chicken and a container of potato salad. With a small slice of alarm over possible food poisoning, she put the potato salad in the refrigerator.

The phone rang, and all of them jumped. Parker was the first to reach the receiver hanging on the wall. "James house," he answered in an uncharacteristically clipped tone.

They all stared at him, not a breath being breathed. He said, "Hmmm…okay," and hung up then said, "That was Neville. He said they haven't found Willie Lee, but they have talked to five people who saw him this afternoon. He was definitely heading this way home."

Marilee wished she had talked to the sheriff herself. Hearing his voice would have been something. Then she imagined the sheriff telling her that they were searching all the drainage culverts.

"Where *is* he?"

They all stared helplessly at her. She swung around and pushed out the back screen door and down the steps to the yard, hardly realizing what she was doing.

Please, Lord, bring my baby home. I will do anything. Please, Lord…just please. How will I bear it if you take him from me? If anything happens to him…

Thankfully, those in the kitchen knew her well enough to let her go alone. She went to the foot of the tree that housed the little fort Marilee and Willie Lee had built together and looked upward. She did not cry. She never cried in a crisis. As she saw it, crying had never changed anything, and if she cried, then all would be lost.

She went to the rabbit cages and realized it was way past time the two rabbits inside were fed their evening meal. She got their food from the garage and filled their dishes, changing their water, too. She thought how Willie Lee loved animals. He seemed more comfortable with them than with people.

As she stood gazing at the rabbits, a squeal sounded... the familiar squeal of the gate in the back fence.

She whirled around to see a man coming through the gate. A tall man...Charlotte had said Tate Holloway...

Then she saw, standing beside the man, her much smaller son.

"This boy says he lives here," the man said.

"Oh, my...*Willie Lee!*"

It was not until that instant of seeing the small boy's figure and then her eyes falling on his upturned face that she realized she had truly begun to believe she would never see Willie Lee alive again, and that what she had been wrestling with all these hours was the inner imagining of his limp little body being pulled from some muddy ditch.

But here he was, his blond hair standing on end and his blue eyes peering out from his thick glasses, regarding her calmly.

"Hey, Ma-ma."

She had scooped him against her. He pushed away and put a hand on her cheek, looking deep into her eyes.

"Why are you cry-ing, Ma-ma?"

"Because I missed you…" She was crying so hard that she could hardly speak. "I didn't know where you were, and I've been so scared, because you were lost."

She hugged him close again.

"I was not lost," he said, again pushing away to look at her with his dear blue eyes blinking behind his glasses. "I was com-ing home."

"Oh, honey…" She caressed his dear, unruly hair, so glad for the feel of it. "It is a long way from school. You shouldn't come home all by yourself."

"I was not all by my-self. I had Mun-ro with me."

For an instant of confusion, Marilee thought he meant the man, but then he was reaching to bring forward a dog. A shaggy, spotted small type of shepherd.

"Mun-ro," Willie Lee introduced happily.

The man was Tate Holloway, which was a little surprising, but not so much, because Marilee had recognized his deep Southern drawl. He explained that he had been looking around his cousin's house and had discovered Willie Lee sleeping on the wicker settee on the porch, with the dog and a big orange cat that had, as Mr. Holloway put it, "skeddaddled faster than a hog skatin' on ice."

Tate Holloway's voice was as it had been when Marilee had spoken to him on the phone, all deep and smoky, and he drew his words out like he purely enjoyed each one on his tongue.

"Bub-ba," Willie Lee said, turning concerned eyes up to her. "I was going to feed Bub-ba, but his food is all gone, and he ran away from us."

Understanding dawned as to what had brought Willie

Lee home by way of the back gate. "We've been going through the gate each night to feed Bubba on the back step," Marilee explained. "Bubba is—or *was*—Ms. Porter's cat. We've been feeding him until you came. She said you got the cat with the house."

Willie Lee said, "Bub-ba needs food."

"We'll let Mr. Holloway take Bubba some of this chicken," Marilee told him.

They all sat around the big oak table in Marilee's kitchen, eating the meal friends had brought earlier. It was very much like a party. Marilee kept Willie Lee sitting on her lap, where she could repeatedly touch him. On one side, within touching distance whether she wished it or not, sat Corrine, who seemed to grin an awfully lot for her, and on the other side, with his arm often on the back of Marilee's chair, sat Parker. Aunt Vella hovered, a good hostess attending everyone. Marilee soaked up this time of contentment, of safety after threat.

"I was going to call you," Tate Holloway said, having gone over the story a second time and embellishing with how *Miss* Charlotte had taken him to task for coming before his scheduled Saturday arrival and how surprised he had been to see a boy on his settee.

"I had your telephone number, but Willie Lee here—" he winked and pointed at Willie Lee with a chicken leg "—said he would show me the way over. I sure wondered where he was goin' when he led me into those cedar trees, but by golly, there was the gate right in the midst of those ramblin' roses, just like he said."

Marilee, putting warm chicken meat in her mouth with

her fingers, watched the man and her son grin at each other. Tate Holloway had a charming grin.

"I knew the way. I was not lost," Willie Lee said. Then he looked at Marilee, squinting with one eye behind his thick glasses. "Well, oncet I was lost, but Mun-ro led me home."

Taking a roll from his and Marilee's plate, he slipped from her lap and went to feed it to the dog lying on the spiral rug in front of the sink, as was the right of a dog who had protected her son.

Marilee, approving of how gently the dog ate from her son's hand, felt a sinking feeling. "Honey, Munro may belong to someone. He has a collar."

Willie Lee said, "No...he was look-ing for me, to come live here. I told God I want-ed him. Re-mem-ber?"

Marilee glanced at Parker.

"I don't think I've seen that dog before," Parker said. "But not everybody 'round here brings me their pets. Most, but not everyone. And he doesn't have any tags... may not have had a rabies shot," he added as caution.

Everyone looked at the dog, who blinked his kind eyes.

Tate Holloway said, "You just can't separate a boy and a dog, oncet they've chosen each other," and winked at Willie Lee. "Plain secret of life is a good dog."

Now Marilee knew where Willie Lee had picked up saying "oncet."

"How come you to name him Munro, Willie Lee?" Aunt Vella asked.

"That is his name."

At this good sense, all of them chuckled, except Corrine, who had begun to help Aunt Vella clear the table and who informed them, "It says Munro on his collar."

When they all looked at her, she added, "It's printed in white. M-U-N-R-O."

Parker took a look, pulling the collar out of the dog's hair. "Yep. Munro." He petted the dog.

"Who told you his name?" Marilee asked.

"Mun-ro told me," Willie Lee said practically, stroking the dog.

"Did he tell you if he has had his shots?" Parker wanted to know, giving Marilee a wink.

Willie Lee looked at the dog and then said, "He does not want shots."

They all chuckled. Marilee looked closer at the dog, who smiled happily back at her. She had to admit the name fit him perfectly.

The sheriff and friends and neighbors and Marilee's mother had been alerted that the crisis was over, and Willie Lee had been returned home safe and sound. Vella, who had made a majority of the telephone calls, left to go to her Rose Club organizational meeting. Now that all was safe and sound, she was in a hurry, backing her Crown Victoria with racing speed.

Tate Holloway decided he would walk home on the sidewalk. "Think I'll see a bit more of the neighborhood," he said.

Parker went with Marilee to see their new neighbor out the front door. It occurred to Marilee that in all the years she had worked for Ms. Porter and lived just beyond the rose-lined fence from the big Porter home, the woman had never even once visited her home. Here, in the first hours of his arrival, Tate Holloway had not only visited, he had returned her beloved son and eaten a celebration meal with them.

Streetlights were on now, sending their silvery glow up and down the street and casting shadows into yards.

"Thank you for the delightful meal," Tate Holloway said, stopping at the foot of the steps and turning to look upward at Marilee and Parker on the edge of the porch. "And for this fine fare for Bubba," he added, lifting the plastic bag containing the leftover chicken pieces.

Marilee said, "Thank *you*, Mr. Holloway, for returning Willie Lee."

Tate Holloway grinned. "Well, now, I think it would be more accurate to say that Willie Lee led me over here."

He gazed at her with that grin.

"And I'd prefer it, Miss Marilee, if you would call me Tate," he said in his deep, slow East Texas drawl.

His eyes that seemed to twinkle, even at this distance, rested on her. There was a contagious inner delight in Tate Holloway.

"All right. Tate. I'm glad to meet you."

"I'm glad to know you, Marilee James, and your family. I won't be a stranger…you can count on that."

Marilee gazed down at the tall man who grinned up at her, until Parker slipped his arm around her and said, "We are sure grateful for you bringing Willie Lee home, Tate."

Tate's eyes shifted to Parker. "Ah…yes, well, sir…I'm just glad things turned out so fine. Good night." With another glance at Marilee and a wave of the little bag of chicken, he was off down the walkway.

Marilee's eyes followed, seeing that his fine, white-blond hair caught the light and shone like sun-warmed silk, and that his shoulders were strong, his torso lean, and his strides long, in the way of a man who is all muscle and purpose.

Then Parker was turning her from the sight. They walked back into the house with his arm around her shoulders. Just inside the closed door, in the dimness, he drew her to him and kissed her.

"Your Willie Lee came home safe and sound, just like I said," he reminded her.

"Thank you for being here, Parker." She was very grateful.

He pulled her against him and kissed her neck. She felt him wanting a lot more, but she could not give any thought to it right now. She was too busy clutching to her what she had feared she had lost. There was no energy left at this moment to consider her relationship with Parker.

She tucked Corrine and Willie Lee into bed.

"Honey, we will have to run an announcement in the paper about finding Munro," she told Willie Lee, taking off his glasses and setting them on the night table.

"He is my dog now." He put his hand on the dog, who lay beside him.

"He has a collar with his name on it. That means someone bought it for him. Someone who cares for him. What if you had lost him? Wouldn't you want whoever found him to do their best to get him back to you?"

Willie Lee frowned, and his lower lip quivered. "Munro found me. I did not find-ed him."

"We will run an ad in the paper for two weeks. That is the right thing to do, the most we can do."

Willie Lee turned on his side and clutched the dog to him.

Marilee kissed him and considered not running the ad. Maybe just the Sunday paper.

She kissed Corrine and turned out the light, then went to the kitchen to prepare the coffeemaker for the morning. She thought it a wise course to tone down the strength of the brew that Corrine made. Maybe lessening her caffeine intake would help her nerves, which seemed so on edge these days.

At the moment of stretching her hand to the light switch, her eye came to rest on Willie Lee's picture book lying on the edge of the table. The book he'd had that morning, when he had been trying to show her the picture of the dog.

She took it up and thumbed through the pages, until she came to the one with the dog picture that jumped right out at her.

She scanned the print below, which was a description of the dog. An Australian Shepherd, it said, bred for herding sheep. The dog in the picture had his tail bobbed. Marilee had seen similar dogs in the rural areas.

Taking the book, she went to the open door of the children's room, where the dog lay on the rug beside Willie Lee's bed. The dog opened his eyes and looked at her. His tail thumped.

In the dim light cast from the bathroom, Marilee consulted the book, then looked again at the dog.

She would check again in the clear light of day, she thought. So many wild things could occur to a person in the night and be cleared up in the light of day.

When the morning came, Marilee found that Munro did look remarkably like the dog in the picture book, although, he *was* darker.

Her eyes followed the dog and her son walking through the kitchen. No matter the dog's appearance, she thought, her son had asked for a dog and been given one. She wondered what she would ask for…and wished she could believe it would be given.

Five

The Beauty of the World

It was bare first light of his first full day in his new town when Tate, dressed in brand-new, grey sweatpants, brand-new, bright-white T-shirt with the words *Just Do It* emblazoned on the front, and brand-new top-of-the-line jogging shoes, came out on his very own front porch.

Tate had jogged intermittently off and on for years, and had profited from it, too, but now he wanted to really make it routine. He was in the prime of his life and wanted to honor that by making the most of himself physically and mentally. That was the spirit!

Stretching his arms wide, he sucked in a deep breath. Ahh! The brisk morning, quite different from the heavily humid air of Houston.

He jogged down the steps and out to the sidewalk of the quiet street. As he turned along Porter Street, in the direction of Marilee James's house, the yellow cat, Bubba, streaked out from beneath a lilac bush and joined him, bouncing along behind Tate, looking like an orange basketball with a tail.

Tate wanted to see Marilee's house clearly in the light of day. He wondered if she was an early riser.

He had a sudden fantasy of her being on the porch and seeing him, jogging along manfully, her waving and him waving back. He smiled at his fanciful notion, although he did experience a little bit of disappointment when his gaze found her front porch, white gingerbread trim, and empty.

Not only was all quiet at the James house, but along most of the street. At the house on the corner, a young man wearing a UPS uniform was chinning himself with bulging arms on a beam across the middle of his porch ceiling. He dropped to his feet, headed for his car at the curb, casting Tate a wave as he came. Friendly fellow! Tate waved back.

Turning up First Street, heading for the commerce area of Main, Tate slowed. He had begun to breathe quite hard. He sure didn't want to have a heart attack on his first day in town. He glanced back and saw that Bubba had deserted him.

Tate continued on, a sort of jog, meeting two ladies who were race walking, pumping arms, talking at the same rate they were walking. They exchanged swift hellos with Tate.

On Main Street, a woman was unlocking the door of her shop—Sweetie Cakes Bakery painted across the window. She nodded and slipped in the door. Further down the street, he looked across at *The Valentine Voice* building. By golly, it was his!

He was walking now.

Just then Charlotte came through the front doors of the *Voice,* surprising him somewhat, and put up the flag, setting it quickly and returning inside before Tate got close enough to holler a good morning.

He was perhaps breathing a little too hard to offer a hearty good morning.

For the past two weeks his attention and time had been taken up with his move to Valentine; that he had not been routinely jogging was telling on him now.

At the corner of the police station, from where he thought he smelled coffee brewing, he turned up Church Street, heading for home. The golden rays of the sun now streaked the horizon.

Funny how he had not realized that the street went up a hill.

Ah, there was another jogger coming toward him. Tate felt the need to push himself into a jog. Didn't want to be out jogging and not doing it.

A minute later he was sure glad he was jogging, because the young man coming toward him turned out to be not quite so young, and to be Parker Lindsey. By golly, he looked all youthful male in a sleeveless shirt and jogging shorts that showed tanned hard thighs.

The two approached the intersection.

"Good mornin'." Tate raised his voice and refused to sound breathless.

"'Mornin'," Lindsey returned, cruising along at a good clip. He even wore a sweatband around his forehead, like a marathon runner.

Tate put some strength into his jog. He might have a

few years on Lindsey, and a lot of grey in his hair, but
where there was snow on the mountaintop, there was a
fire in the furnace. He thought of the old saw as he continued on across the intersection toward his driveway,
intent on at least jogging around to the back of the house,
out of view.

Just then he saw, coming along down the hill, a shapely
blond young woman in a skimpy exercise outfit, jogging
and smiling at him. He might have stopped to talk to her,
but the young woman's attention was captured by Tate's
older neighbor on the opposite corner, who came from her
house in walking shorts and shoes, waving and calling the
blond woman by name.

The town was a haven for health enthusiasts!

He continued up his driveway, which had much more
of an incline than he had before noted, and around to the
back steps, where Bubba now lay, sunning himself. The
cat gave Tate a yawn.

"I feed you…no comments."

Tate dragged himself in the door and sank down upon
the floor, going totally prostrate on the cool linoleum.

Marilee sat holding her coffee cup in both hands and
thinking that she should have made it stronger. She had
gotten used to Corrine's brew and seemed not to be able
to function well on a weaker variety.

Across from her, Corrine, looking for all the world like
she was about to be shot, played with her food. Willie Lee,
who ate slowly, asked if Munro could go to school with
him.

"He will be lone-ly with-out me," he said.

Marilee, watching Corrine play the fork over her egg, thought, there are only three weeks left to the school year.

"I think we can have the ending of our school year today," she said, suddenly getting up and taking her plate to the sink. "You two do not need to go back this year."

She looked over her shoulder to see their reactions.

Willie Lee's eyebrows went up. "I do not have to go to schoo-ool to-day?"

"No, not today, and no more until fall. We'll see about it then."

Corrine was looking at Marilee with a mixture of high hope and sharp distrust on her delicate features.

"I'll call Principal Blankenship and see what we can do about you finishing your work at home," Marilee told her.

The relief that swept the girl's face struck Marilee so hard that she had to turn away and hide her own expression in her coffee cup. She thought of her sister, Anita. Corrine's mother. She had the urge to toss the coffee cup right through the window.

Then Willie Lee was at her side and tapping her thigh. "Mun-ro needs breakfast."

Looking into his sweet face, Marilee smiled. "He does, doesn't he."

"I can give him my egg," Corrine said.

"Please, make him toast, too, Ma-ma."

"Yes, darlin'...I'll make toast for Munro." She looked at the dog, now eating the egg very gently from Corrine's plate.

Marilee's reasoning mind told her to force the children to go to school and face what they would have to face sooner or later, a regimen and self-control, and those few cruel and mean and inept people one will come across on many an occasion. Life was a tough row of responsibility to hoe, and the sooner the children, even Willie Lee, learned this, the better.

She all but took out a gun and shot her reasoning mind. It wisely shut up.

Thinking of both the principal and her new boss, who she would now ask to let her work at home, she got herself dressed nicely in a slim knit skirt and top in soft blue, accented with a genuine silver concho belt from her more prosperous days of no children and a husband who earned quite good money as a world-renowned photojournalist. She managed to talk herself into doing a thorough makeup job and brushed her hair until it shone.

Then she sat at her cherry-wood desk to telephone Principal Blankenship and secure from the woman the promise that Corrine would be kept with her grade. The principal was surprisingly agreeable, even eager, at the idea of releasing the child, whom she all but labeled troubled straight out.

"Corrine has perfect straight A's," the principal said. "Her grades are not a question. She is a very bright girl. That is not at all her problem in class. I'm sure we can accommodate you in order to help Corrine have the rest she needs." Then she tacked on, "Ah…I have the name of a child therapist you might want to consider."

For Willie Lee, the principal promised to consult his teacher about work that might possibly help him. Marilee, who had from her teenage years been unable to shake her faith in her own mental capacity, told the principal not to bother Mrs. Reeves. "I'm going to pick out a curriculum for Willie Lee."

The principal definitely disapproved of this action, labeling it risky, but stopped short of pressing, no doubt fearful Marilee would change her mind and bring the children back to school.

Marilee thanked Principal Blankenship for all her help and hung up, sitting there for some minutes, her hand on the telephone, gazing at nothing, until she realized she was gazing at a pattern on the Tibetan rug that fronted the couch. She remembered, then, buying it in Calcutta, on one of hers and Stuart's trips. Her gaze moved about the room, noting a painting on the wall that had been purchased in New Orleans, and a pottery vase picked up in the Smoky Mountains.

Her eyes moved to the small picture of her ex-husband that she kept, still, on her desk.

Stuart James grinned at her from the photo. She picked it up, remembering how handsome she had found him the first time she had laid eyes on him, remembering how wonderful he had made her feel when he touched her body. Stuart was a man who greatly enjoyed making love.

Into these deep thoughts came the sound of childish voices. She blinked and got up, following the sound to the back door.

Willie Lee and Corrine, with the dog between them, sat on the back stairs in the dappled morning sunlight that shone through the trees. They did not hear her footsteps, and she was able to watch them for some minutes through the screen door.

Corrine was talking to the dog, right along with Willie Lee. And she was actually smiling.

"Ma-ma…Mun-ro needs to come, too." He spoke as if scolding her for not remembering the dog.

Marilee looked at her son and then the dog. "Okay, Munro…get in."

As she backed the Jeep Cherokee from the drive, she gave thanks for the all-purpose vehicle. She supposed she might as well accept that the dog was destined to go everywhere with them. He could, in Valentine, America.

A new vehicle, a yellow convertible BMW, was parked in the block of spaces behind *The Valentine Voice* building. The top was down, and with a raised eyebrow, Marilee peered into the vehicle, noting the soft leather seats. Obviously, coming from Houston, Tate Holloway was unaware of how serious dust could be in this part of the country.

The two-story brick building that housed the newspaper had changed only marginally since it was first built in 1920. The back area of the first floor, which had once housed the printing press, had been converted into a garage and loading area. Printing was now done by a contract printer who did a number of small-town newspapers; *The Valentine Voice* was one of the last small-town dailies in the nation.

The front half of the first floor was pretty much as it had been built. The original bathroom had been enlarged and a small kitchen sink area added. Several offices had been made by adding glass partitions, one of which had dark-green shades all around and a door with a dark-green shade. The name on the glass of the door read: Zona Porter, No Relation, Comptroller. Everyone respected that Zona preferred privacy. One could go in and speak to Zona in the office, but Zona rarely came out. Had a bathroom been installed off her office, Zona would not have come out at all. She had her own refrigerator, coffeemaker, cups, glasses, tissues. She did not care to touch things after other people.

E. G. Porter's original office remained at the right, with tall windows that looked out onto the corner of Main and Church Streets.

Entering through the rear door, Marilee felt a little like she was leading a parade, with the children and the dog Munro trailing behind her.

Leo Pahdocony, Sr., a handsome dark-haired Choctaw Indian who wore turquoise bolas, shiny snakeskin boots and sharply creased Wranglers, was pecking away at the keyboard of his computer and talking on the telephone at the same time, with the receiver tucked in his neck. He gave her a wave and a palm-up to Willie Lee.

His wife, Reggie, a petite redhead who handled news in the schools, churches and most of the photography, popped out of her swivel chair and came to greet them with delight. Reggie, who had for the past five years been trying to conceive another child, extended her arms to capture the children in a big hug. Corrine managed to sidestep her way to Marilee's chair and sat herself firmly, but Willie Lee, always loveable, let Reggie lift him up and kiss him.

"You gave us a scare, young man, running off," Charlotte told him, coming forward with messages for Marilee.

Willie Lee said, "I did not run off. I was coming home."

"Uh-huh. Good thinking." Charlotte turned her eyes on Marilee. "Tammy phoned. She's got a horrible tooth-ache."

Marilee saw that Charlotte was thinking the same thing she was: that Tammy had a job interview elsewhere. Without Miss Porter's money pouring in, no one expected the newspaper to continue much longer than a year, if that.

A pounding sounded from the office of the publisher. Marilee looked at the closed door and noticed that Muriel Porter's name plaque was gone, leaving a dark rectangle on the oak.

Pounding again.

"He's hangin' pictures," said Imperia Brown, smacking her phone receiver into the cradle. "It's drivin' me crazy. I'm outta here." She grabbed up her purse and headed for the front door.

Charlotte strode over to the large, gilded frame of the newspaper's founder's portrait now propped on the floor against the copy machine, and said to Marilee, "He took down Mr. E. G. first thing." Charlotte definitely disap-proved.

"Might be one of us next," Reggie said.

Marilee and Charlotte cast each other curious glances, and Reggie said she wondered if Ms. Porter might not be feeling her skin crawling at the removal of her daddy from the wall.

"I've been halfway waitin' for the wall to cave in, E.G. having his say from the grave," she said.

"The walls are apparently holding," Charlotte said, "and he's hanging them with all sorts of pictures. He has one of him with President Nixon. I don't know why he'd want to advertise it," she added.

"He has one of him with Reba," Reggie put in with some excitement. "He did a feature piece on her for *Parade Magazine*."

Reggie had every one of Reba McEntire's albums. She suddenly grabbed up a pen to hold in front of her mouth like a microphone and began singing one of Reba's songs. This was something she often did, pretending either to be a singer or a television commentator. Reggie was every bit pretty enough to be either; however, she could take clowning and showing off to the point of annoyance, as far as Marilee was concerned. Right then was one of those points, and Marilee felt her temper grow short as Reggie kept jutting her face in front of Marilee's and singing about poor old Fancy.

"Reggie, would you keep an eye on Corrine and Willie Lee for me?" she said, thus diverting the woman to more quiet childishness, while Marilee went to their publisher's solid oak door and knocked.

The sound of hammering drowned out her knock, and she had to try again, and when still no answer came, she poked her head in the door. "Mr. Holloway?" She was unable to address him as Tate, being at the office.

He turned from where he was hanging a picture. "Marilee! Come in…come in. Just the person I've been waitin' for. You can come over here and help me get this picture in the right place."

It was a picture of him with Billy Graham, black-and-white, as all the photographs appeared to be. He placed it against the wall and waited for her instructions, which she gave in the form of, "Higher...a little to the left...a little lower. Right there."

Having, apparently, a high opinion of her ability to place a picture, he marked the spot and went to hammering in a nail.

In a flowing glance, Marilee, wondering how an accomplished journalist of Tate Holloway's wide experience would manage in tiny Valentine, took in the room. The sedate, even antiquated office that had belonged to Ms. Porter was gone. Or perhaps a more accurate description was that it was being *moved out,* as pictures and books and boxes full of articles, a number of them antiques, were in a cluster by the door. Next to that, in a large heap, lay the heavy evergreen drapes, which had been ripped from the long windows, leaving only the wooden blinds through which bright light shone on the varied electronic additions: a small television, a radio scanner, a top speed computer and printer, a laptop computer, and one apparatus that Marilee, definitely behind the electronic times, could not identify.

The major change, however, was to the big walnut desk, which had been moved from where it had sat for eons in front of the windows, facing the wall with E. G. Porter's portrait. Marilee had always had the impression that Ms. Porter would sit at the desk and look at her father on the wall and worship him. Or maybe throw mental darts at him.

Now the desk sat in front of that wall, looking away

from it, and behind, where E.G.'s august portrait had hung, was an enormous black-and-white photograph of Marilyn Monroe in the famous shot with her dress blowing up.

After eyeing that for a startled moment, Marilee's gaze moved on to the clusters of photographs already hung—the ones of Tate Holloway with Reba and President Nixon, and ones of him receiving awards, and with soldiers, and a curious one of a boy plowing with a mule. She stepped closer for a better look at that one. Next to the faded snapshot of the boy and the mule was one of a lovely blond woman in the front yard of an old house, her arms around two boys.

"That's my mother," Tate told her, coming up behind her. "With me and my brother, Hollis. I'm the older, skinnier one."

"And that's you, plowing with a mule?"

"Yep. Farmin' in East Texas in the fifties. My mother took that picture. Mama liked to take pictures."

He had come to stand very close behind her. Close enough for his breath to tickle her hair.

"This is Mama in front of the house me and Hollis bought her." His arm brushed her shoulder as he pointed at another photograph. "And this is how my daddy wound up."

He tapped a photograph of a mangled black car stuck to the front end of a Santa Fe Railroad engine.

"I like to see where I've come from and how far I've journeyed and remind myself where I don't want to go," he said with practicality. Then, the next second, "You smell awfully good, Miss Marilee."

That comment jerked her mind away from the horror of the mangled car. She turned, and her shoulder bumped his chest, because he didn't move but stood there gazing at her with a light in his clear, twinkling blue eyes that just about took every faithful breath out of her lungs.

His gaze flickered downward, and hers followed to stop and linger on his lips.

The next instant she stepped quickly away from him and said as casually as possible, "And just what does that picture mean in your journey?" She gestured at the photograph of Marilyn Monroe.

"Well—" he sauntered to the desk and laid down the hammer "—I like the touch Marilyn gives the place."

"What touch are you going for, exactly?"

"Oh…I think a photograph like that sets people off balance, for one thing." He folded his arms, and his strong shoulders stretched his shirt. "And it is lively. I might come in here feelin' a little too serious about myself and things in general, and I'll look up there at that beautiful woman—" he looked up at the picture and grinned "—with a laugh like that and those legs goin' to heaven, and it makes me remember the true secret of life." He gave a little wink.

Marilee took that in and took hold of the solid walnut back of the visitor chair, feeling the need to have the chair between herself and Tate Holloway.

She looked at him, and he looked at her in the manner of a man who was intent on having what he wanted. It was both flattering and unsettling.

Breaking the gaze, she said, "I need to discuss my job here."

His eyebrows went up, "Well, you go ahead, Miss Marilee…as long as you aren't about to tell me you're gonna quit."

Marilee reacted to this with a mixture of gratification and annoyance. There was something very commanding in the way he spoke, as if he would not *allow* her to quit.

"Do you want a raise?" he asked before she could speak. "I can spare twenty more a week—okay…I'll go to thirty."

"I don't want a raise…but I'll take it."

"I won't force it on you, if you don't want it."

"I want it. I only meant that a raise wasn't what I was going to discuss, but now that you've offered, I will take it."

"Well, since it isn't a question of a raise, there's no sense in talkin' about it."

"But we *are* talking about it now, and I'll take it. My workload has greatly increased since Harlan and Jewel left."

"Okay, twenty dollars a week it is."

"You said thirty."

He cocked his head to the side and regarded her. "What was it you wanted to discuss about your job, Miss Marilee?"

Keeping her hands pressed to the chair back, she told him of her decision to remove her children from the final weeks of school and therefore her need to work from home. That she had been so bold as to take the raise before explaining this, and the glint in his eye that showed admiration, gave her courage.

She explained that until this year, when she had

enrolled Willie Lee in school, her arrangement with Ms. Porter allowed her to often work from home, and she had managed very well.

"I have made arrangements with a high school girl to help me in the summer," she told him, "but until school ends, I will only have her occasionally in the evening hours."

"Well now, I don't see any problem at all with you workin' from home," said her new boss and publisher. "I already have laptop computers coming for everyone, and we'll be installing a networking system so that any of us can work from anywhere in town, or in the nation, if need be."

Marilee thought that *The Valentine Voice* was suddenly on a rocket, being blasted into the twenty-first century.

Moving purposefully, her boss went to stand behind his desk, placed his hands on it and leaned forward. "I want you to keep this to yourself for a few days. I'll tell everyone shortly, but for now, I'm just telling you." He paused. "We're going to have to cut the paper to a twice weekly."

She took that in.

He said, "I don't imagine that comes as any shock to you."

"No…it doesn't." It saddened her, but it was no surprise. Everyone knew that Ms. Porter had been subsidizing the paper for years, and Marilee, having taken over for Ms. Porter, had consulted a number of times with Zona and knew the great extent to which that subsidizing had run.

Tate Holloway eyed her with purpose so strong that he

leaned even farther forward. "It is my intention to get this paper to be payin' for itself. I'm out to build somthin' here, Miss Marilee. And I'm going to need your help to do it."

"I'll do what I can."

"I'm countin' on that, Miss Marilee…. I sure am."

Gazing into his twinkling baby-blue eyes, Marilee kept tight hold on the chair back, as if holding to an anchor in the face of a rising, rolling sea.

Six

Maybe She's Human

Marilee came out of Tate Holloway's office and closed the door firmly, then held on to the doorknob for some seconds. Behind her, through the door, the low tones of music began—Charlie Rich singing from Tate Holloway's stereo.

Pushing away from the door, Marilee wrestled with high annoyance at her new boss. Tate Holloway was way too full of himself.

The next instant Reggie was sticking a pen in front of her face, saying, "Tell us the news, Ms. James. Are we all goin' to be swept out to make way for new employees to go with the new publisher?"

This had been a major worry of Reggie and Leo's, both being employed at the same place. Mainly it appeared to be a great worry of Reggie's, since Leo wasn't given to worrying over steady employment. Before coming to work at *The Valentine Voice,* he had held various positions in automobile sales, insurance, cattle brokering, photography, trucking and a half-dozen others, several for no more than a week or two before either quitting or being fired. While Reggie defended her husband as trying to find himself and being a victim of too much feminine attention, it had been fact that he had not been able to keep a job of any secure endurance, until he had landed the one of sports reporter at the *Voice.* He proved excellent at it, and the one time he had shown any inclination to quit, Reggie had come in behind him and finagled a job of her own, thereby being on the scene to make certain he kept his position.

A part of Marilee's brain tried to be sensitive to all of this, but seeing everyone's eyes, even Willie Lee's and Corrine's, turned in her direction made her very irritated.

"Don't put that thing in my face, Reggie. I need both my eyes." She pushed Reggie's hand aside and strode to her desk and began shuffling through files to take home.

"Okay. So are you pissed off because you do not want to tell us that we are all about to be fired?"

The breathlessness of the question struck Marilee, and she looked up to see Reggie's thoroughly uneasy eyes. The precariousness of all their positions came fullblown into her mind, and she felt sorry for her short temper.

"Of course we aren't all going to be fired. Who would he get to replace us? The paper can barely pay for itself now." Just a mild fib. "He can't afford to be hauling in a whole new crew of Pulitzer prize winners to Valentine. Right now he's dependent on us. We are all he's got."

She felt as if she were withholding from her friends,

being unable to tell the entire truth about the change from a daily to twice weekly. Darn him for confiding in her.

Turning from this dilemma, and from Reggie's searching eyes, she said, "He said it will be fine for me to work at home," and went on to briefly explain about Willie Lee and Corrine not going back to school. "I want to be home with them, like I used to be with Willie Lee, and this will work fine, because Mr. Holloway is getting us all laptop computers and a net-working system."

"Wow," Reggie said. "Guess there's more money than we thought."

She jumped from Marilee's desk and went over to hug Leo, who said quite practically, "Doesn't mean money. Just good credit."

"I finally got my machine working how I like it," Charlotte said, frowning. She had gotten so furious with the technician who had first set up her computer that she had refused to allow him to touch it again, read the manual front to back and now knew enough to maintain her machine herself.

Marilee, who was gazing at her typed up notice for Lost and Found, crumpled up the paper and tossed it into the trash. The dog was Willie Lee's now, she figured, and she was going to let it be.

"Let's go get some ice cream," she said to the children. "You, too, Munro," she added, when Willie Lee opened his mouth to remind her.

With Willie Lee holding one hand and Corrine the other, and Munro running along beside them, Marilee headed directly to where she went whenever she felt her spirits in disarray—to her aunt and uncle's drugstore.

Blaine's Drugstore and Soda Fountain had been in business for over seventy years, in the same spot on Main Street. There was a rumor that the outlaws Bonnie and Clyde had once gotten lemonade and bandages from the distant relative of Perry Blaine who had opened the store in 1920. Perry had taken over from his father in '57, when he had come home from Korea. Things had been booming in Valentine in the fifties, with oil pumping all around, and farming and cattle going okay. That same year Perry had installed the sign with the neon outline that still hung between the windows of the second story.

Ever since the fateful summer of '96, when it had been featured in both the lifestyle pages of the Lawton paper and then on an Oklahoma City television travel program, Blaine's Drugstore had received visitors from all over the southern part of the state. People, enough to keep them open on Friday and Saturday evenings in the summertime, came to order Coca-Colas and milk shakes and sundaes in the thick vintage glassware. Some of the glasses were truly antiques, and to keep the visitors coming, once a year Vella drove down to Dallas to a restaurant supply to purchase new to match. She would covertly bring the boxes into the storeroom and place them behind the big boxes of napkins and foam to-go containers.

When taken to task by her daughter Belinda for perpetrating a hoax, Vella said with practicality, "People like thinkin' the glasses are old, and they would rather not be apprized of the truth. Besides, they *will* be antiques in another fifty years—and I sure pay enough for them to be looked at."

As Marilee and the children entered the store, the bell above the door chimed out. Immediately Marilee was engulfed by the dearly familiar scents of old wood, simmering barbecue and faint antiseptic of the store that had not changed since she was a nine-year-old child and so often came running down the hill to escape the sight of her father sitting in his cracked vinyl recliner, beer in hand and glassy eyes staring at the flickering television, and her mother in the kitchen gone so far away into country songs on the radio that she would not speak.

"We have come for ice cream," Willie Lee said as he went directly to his Great-Aunt Vella, who was sitting at the rear table, with glasses on the tip of her nose so she could more easily read the IGA ads in the newspaper spread wide before her.

"You've come to the right place then, mister," said Winston Valentine, who was sitting across from their aunt and who nudged an empty sundae dish that sat in front of him. Being yet spring and midmorning, the place was empty except for these two.

"Hel-lo, Mis-ter Wins-ton," Willie Lee said.

"Hello, Mister Willie Lee."

Willie Lee extended his hand, as Winston had taught him, and Winston shook the small offered hand with great respect.

Marilee saw that Winston's big, gnarled hand, when it released Willie Lee's, shook slightly. The blue veins showed clearly when he used that same hand to push his tall frame up from the table.

"If you ladies and gentleman will excuse me," he said, polite as always, "I have to walk on home and make sure Mildred has not drowned Ruthanne in her bath this mornin'. The nurse has the day off." He checked his watch. "They ought to be done by now."

Mildred Covington and Ruthanne Bell, two elderly ladies, shared Winston Valentine's home. Since Winston's stroke the year before, a home health nurse came in to check on all three of them three times a week. Aunt Vella had once told Marilee that on the days the nurse did not come, Winston, after making certain the women had breakfast, tried to leave home at midmorning, so as to not be present when the women were getting bathed and dressed; Mildred seemed to have a penchant for running around naked in front of him whenever she had the chance.

"Winston's really aging now," Marilee said, watching the old man lean heavily on his cane as he went out the door. He was eighty-eight this year, and only since his stroke had he slowed any.

"There's more life in him than many a man I know," Vella said, and in a snapping manner that startled Marilee a little. It only then occurred to her that her Aunt Vella was not getting any younger, either; no doubt it was distressing to her aunt to see a dear friend declining and heading for the border.

Marilee found the fact depressing, as well. She felt as if her life were going down a hole, and she could not seem to find the stopper.

"Now, what's this about my darlin's wantin' ice cream?" Aunt Vella asked.

"We want sun-daes," Willie Lee told her and scampered over to haul himself up on a stool at the counter.

"We'll have three chocolate sundaes, please," Marilee said, slipping onto a stool.

She set herself to getting into a better mood. Children learned by example and picked up on things easily. She did not need to add to any of their numerous wounds by being in a poor mood.

"Me and Mun-ro want va-nil-la," Willie Lee said. "Cor-rine says dogs should not ev-er have choc-o-late."

Marilee only then remembered the dog and looked down to see him already curled beneath Willie Lee's feet, as if knowing that he would need to be quiet and unseen to remain.

Aunt Vella took a cursory look around the end of the counter, then said, "We surely can't leave Munro out."

"No, we can-not," Willie Lee said.

"Is your choice chocolate, too?" Aunt Vella asked Corrine.

Corrine frowned in contemplation.

"I'll give you another minute." Aunt Vella went about lining up four dishes and making the sundaes—cherry for Corrine, it turned out. While doing this, she threw conversation over her shoulder, telling about the Rose Club meeting held the previous evening— "We had ten people!"—and how they had already voted as a first project to plant roses around the Welcome to Valentine signs at each end of town.

"Winston and I are goin' up to Lawton tomorrow to buy bushes," Vella reported, feeling increasing excitement with the telling.

She had been very pleased with the respectable turnout of people for the first rose club meeting, and felt a glow that her idea of a rose club had proven out. Especially after Perry had rather pooh-poohed the idea as frivolous. She almost had not pursued the idea, after his attitude, but it had turned out that a number of people, such as their mayor's wife, Kaye Upchurch, had liked the idea immensely. While Kaye Upchurch could be on the frivolous side, she was truly knowledgeable about what was good for the town. Her enthusiasm for the Rose Club's place in the community was heartening.

Vella was also becoming more and more excited about going up to Lawton with Winston. She had never been anywhere with Winston, outside of her own backyard or here at the store.

"We'd like to get the bushes in the ground soon. It's already so late to be planting," she added, bringing her thoughts back to the moment. "We could very well get a repeat of last summer and all that heat. Winston thought we could install some sort of watering system by the welcome signs," she said, focusing on a plan. "If the city doesn't want to pay for it, Winston said he would."

In Vella's opinion, Winston was a little free with his money, and this was both quite amazing and refreshing. Her husband Perry pinched a penny until it gave up the ghost. Vella thought she needed to take lessons from Winston in being more free and easy. She did not want to spend her remaining years being as controlled as she had spent her entire life to this point.

Marilee, only halfway listening to her aunt's conversation, other than to observe that the Rose Club seemed to make her aunt very happy, watched the loose skin at the back of her aunt's arm wiggle, while her biceps worked sturdy and strong. Marilee had lately been trying to exercise the backs of her own arms, which were the first thing to go on a woman; she was amazed that her aunt was so strong, though, despite the sagging back of her arm.

Then Marilee found herself looking over the counter, at the age-spotted long mirror, the shelf of neatly lined and glimmering tulip glasses, the modern licenses in dingy frames, and the yellowing menu with the Dr Pepper sign at the top. The drone of Uncle Perry's television reached her from the back room of the pharmacy, where her uncle would be sitting in his overstuffed brown chair.

Aunt Vella brought a dish of ice cream around the end of the counter and set it down for Munro. "I didn't think he needed whipped cream or a cherry," she said, then stood there, watching the dog, as they all were.

"I sure hope this doesn't give him a headache," Vella said, as the dog began to lick the cold sweet ice cream with some eagerness.

"He likes it," Willie Lee pronounced quite happily.

"Hmmm…"

Aunt Vella went back to put the finishing touches on the people's sundaes; they definitely got whipped cream and a cherry. She then set the children's sundaes on the granite counter, with a "There you go, sugars," pronouncing the word as *shu*-gahs in a way that caused a particularly strong pull on Marilee's heart.

As her aunt scooted a sundae across toward her, Marilee looked at it and suddenly realized she was sitting on the last stool at the far end of the counter, right where she had always sat as a child when she came running into the drugstore, dragging Anita by the hand. Aunt Vella would lean over the counter, dab at Anita's tears and ask, "What can I get for my two *shu*-gah girls today?"

Marilee would be choking back tears but would manage to get out quite calmly that she and Anita would like chocolate milk shakes, please. Her Uncle Perry always called Marilee a little lady because she never yelled or screamed or cried. There were so many times when she wished she *could* yell and scream and cry.

Now, as then, she took up the long-handled spoon and smoothed the chocolate syrup around on the vanilla ice cream. She liked to let the ice cream get a little soft and then mix it with the chocolate syrup. She would have to admit to being addicted to chocolate, but after having taken tranquilizers for too long after her heartbreak with Stuart, she thought chocolate a fairly harmless aid to getting along in turbulent times. Chocolate tasted good and felt good going down, and it did not make her brain so fuzzy as to spin out of the world.

As she spooned the chocolate and vanilla ice cream onto her tongue, she looked across and caught hers and Corrine's reflections in the wide old mirror. Corrine's dark eyes, for a moment, met hers in the mirror, before looking down at her sundae. Marilee watched Corrine's reflection, the bend of the dark head, the way she tilted it slightly, looking for all the world like her mother at that age.

Marilee's gaze returned to her own reflection. It struck her quite hard that here she was staring at middle-age and still employing the same coping skills she had employed as a ten-year-old girl.

"You've been workin' way too hard," Aunt Vella said. "You just need a little boost. You should take a potent mixture of B's for three months, and it wouldn't hurt for you to start taking calcium...you need to start thinkin' about keepin' your bones. Every woman's bones start to fade after thirty-five."

Marilee had followed Vella over to the pharmacy shelves, where her aunt perused the bottles of vitamins and herbs, while the children occupied themselves twirling on the stools at the counter. Actually, it was Corrine being twirled by Willie Lee. She held on to the stool with her thin little hands, while Willie Lee got a kick out of spinning her around. Corrine was always so patient with Willie Lee. She displayed strong mothering instincts with him, and very often she did things for him that he was capable of doing for himself. Willie Lee allowed this, in the pleasing way he always went along with people.

"You worry about them too much. They'll be fine. They have God, just like you do. He cares for you. Trust Him."

At her aunt's statement, Marilee looked over to see that the older woman had noticed her wandering attention.

"Then who looks after the children who are abused and forgotten all over the place?" Marilee asked, more sharply than she had meant to.

"I don't know," her aunt answered in the same fashion. "I'm not smart enough to know that. I only know what I know, that there is a God who cares for us, and that worrying never solved a thing. Change what you can, accept what you can't, and leave off worrying. It just wears you out."

Marilee sighed, her mind skittering away from a discussion she didn't wish to get into.

"I couldn't stand it anymore," she said. "I took them out of school for the rest of this year. Corrine looks like she's going to face the firing squad each day she goes to school, and Willie Lee just keeps runnin' away. Maybe I'm not even addressing the true problem…. I know I'm not…but it just seemed the one thing I could do."

"Good. You changed something. And there aren't enough days of school left to worry about it, anyway." Vella was peering at the labels on the vitamin bottles through her reading glasses at the end of her nose. "Do you have the kids on vitamins?"

"Dailies."

"Not enough."

Marilee watched her aunt set about deciding which vitamins would be sufficient for the children. She felt an anger well up inside.

"Can vitamins fix a brain damaged by birthing?" she asked. "Or a heart broken by an irresponsible mother who prefers to drink rather than take care of her daughter?"

Vella's dark eyes came up sharply. "No one prefers to drink. Anita is sick, Marilee, just like your daddy was."

Marilee could not address this. She felt guilty for feeling so angry at her sister. Even as she thought about being angry, the anger began to ebb and slip into sadness and guilt, which she hated worse. The guilt threatened to consume her. She kept thinking there ought to be something she could do to help her sister, but everything she had tried had failed. She could not look at it anymore.

"Mrs. Blankenship thinks Corrine needs a therapist," she said, the words falling out almost before she realized.

"Half of America needs a therapist," Aunt Vella said, "but where do you find a sane one?"

Marilee had to chuckle at this, said so seriously. She gazed at Corrine, who was now twirling Willie Lee on the stool. "I think a therapist is worth trying, but I just don't know how I can afford it."

"Children have an amazing ability to survive. Don't discount it."

"That's another question," Marilee said, her gaze coming back to her aunt. "What's goin' to happen if Corrine gets really sick? How will I pay the doctor bills? My doctor charges sixty dollars a visit." The limit of those could plainly be seen. "She isn't my daughter, so I can't put her on my insurance."

"Oh, my heavens, don't go makin' up worries that likely won't happen."

Marilee looked at her aunt.

Her aunt looked back and said, "We'll help you, Marilee. You know that."

"I know it, but how far can we all go? You know perfectly well a catastrophe could bankrupt us all without insurance."

Aunt Vella said very quietly, "Have you thought about adoption?"

"I've thought about it." Marilee felt guilty for admitting what seemed a very bad thought. "But I don't think Anita would willingly go along with it. I could press it. I could take her to court and prove she isn't able to care for Corrine, but what would that do to her?"

"You can't take on Anita's burdens for her, Marilee. She has to own up to being responsible for her own actions. If she's going to be a drunken sot, she'll have to take the consequences. You don't help her by letting her off. Maybe if you pressed, Anita would have more reason to try to get herself straight."

Marilee clamped her mouth shut. Discussing this was making her too depressed. She did not have faith in Anita, certainly. And now she was having doubts about having faith in herself. She was sinking into a full decline when the bell above the front door rang out.

It was Fayrene Gardner entering the store. She came swiftly toward the pharmacy counter and presented Aunt Vella, who stepped forward, with a prescription. Fayrene, sniffing loudly, was clearly distraught.

"We'll get this straight away," Aunt Vella said and immediately stepped through to the back room, calling, "Perry…we need this filled. Perry!"

Fayrene noticed Marilee, who just then found she was staring, feeling connected by her own distress.

"Are you all right, Fayrene?" Marilee asked, feeling the need to say something, and hoping Fayrene wasn't about to confess to having fallen victim to some horrible disease.

"Men," Fayrene said vehemently. "I wish they'd all drop dead."

Marilee wasn't certain what to say to that, and became

more uncertain when Fayrene's face crumpled and she went to crying into a tissue. Feeling comfort was required, and needing to give it, Marilee reached out a hand to possibly take hold of the woman and provide what assistance she could.

But Fayrene pulled herself up tight and called, "Vella, I'll be back to get it after lunch," then pivoted and strode out of the store, again holding a tissue over her mouth to block a sob.

"Well, mercy," Aunt Vella said.

"I don't think I have ever seen Fayrene in such a state," Marilee said.

"I haven't, either."

"What was the prescription? Is she really sick?"

Vella stepped back to the pharmacy area, then returned and said, "Tranquillizer. A good one," she added with approval.

Marilee felt quite fortunate in that instant. Or perhaps it was more accurate that she no longer felt quite so alone, after having witnessed another person in despair. It reminded her that life was difficult, and this was a plain fact that, once recognized, made living if not smooth, at least not quite so shockingly distressing. It pointed up that people did continue to live on, no matter how often the will to live seemed to be challenged.

And at least she herself was within the control of chocolate. Her eye fell to a Hershey bar in front of the prescription counter, and she quickly grabbed it and threw it in with the vitamins Aunt Vella was now sacking.

"I might need that tonight," she said. She thought maybe she ought to take a chocolate bar over to Fayrene.

* * *

When they came out of the drugstore, Corrine went skipping over in the direction of the florist next door. In fact, to Marilee's eye, it seemed Corrine was drawn to the tubs of colorful spring flowers on display outside as if by a cord. But when just a foot away, the girl suddenly stopped and turned back to Marilee, in the manner of correcting a wrong action.

Marilee, who had herself entertained a first thought that flowers were an unnecessary extravagance, said with purpose, "Would you like some flowers? I think I would."

As she spoke, she walked to the tubs of mixed bouquets that a few weeks ago Fred Grace, Jr. had begun setting out in front of his florist shop.

"If it works for Wally-world, it's sound," Fred told everyone, referring to the big Wal-Mart chain of stores. Within a week he gleefully reported that impulse buying had doubled.

"Which ones do you like?" Marilee asked the children.

Corrine, not quite meeting Marilee's gaze, shrugged her small shoulders. Her eyes slid again to the flowers.

"I *need* some daisies," Marilee said, reaching for a bouquet. "Absolutely need them."

One thing she intended to teach Corrine was a hard-learned lesson she herself had experienced, and that was that beauty was a necessary part of life. She felt society in general had forgotten this, and that fact might just be a major cause of wars. Often, against every cell in her body that told her to be frugal, she would buy flowers or a pretty picture, because she felt her very life might depend on it.

"You can both choose a bouquet for yourselves," she told the children as she examined the bouquet she had chosen, peering at little purple things that looked suspiciously like weeds.

Willie Lee wanted Marilee to pick him up so he could see better, which she did, and he gleefully pulled a bouquet of red carnations from one of the tubs.

"Cor-rine, you like yel-low," he said.

Corrine chose very slowly and reverently a bouquet of yellow daisies and white carnations.

"Oh, those are lovely, Corrine."

"Mun-ro needs flow-ers, too."

"He can enjoy ours," Marilee told her son.

Her son sighed heavily and bent to let the dog sniff his flowers.

Pulling a twenty-dollar bill out of her purse, she had Corrine help her figure out the total cost of the three bouquets, which Corrine did with amazing speed. Then Marilee handed the bill to Corrine and told her to go inside and pay Mr. Grace.

Corrine hesitated, and Marilee wondered if she had asked too much of the painfully shy girl, but Willie Lee spoke up and said, "Mun-ro says he will go with you, Cor-ine," and indeed, the dog stood ready at the girl's side.

Corrine turned, and Marilee watched her niece's oh, so slight figure disappear into the store. She felt like hurrying after her, to be there beside her, guarding for any type of hurt that might come her way.

Then, peering through the window while trying not to appear to be peering, Marilee saw Corrine walk up to the cash register and hand up the money to Fred Grace. Munro stood right at Corrine's leg, his head next to her knee, looking upward, too. Fred handed down Corrine's change, and then out Corrine and Munro came, a smile playing at the girl's lips.

"Thank you, Aunt Marilee," she said softly, depositing the change in Marilee's hand.

"Thank you, Corrine. And Munro." She and Corrine grinned at each other.

The three of them, accompanied by the dog, started down the sidewalk. Marilee, seized by a warm happiness, felt certain they were all walking straighter and marveled at the power of a handful of colorful flowers. The few people they passed along the way smiled, and one man tipped his ballcap.

The colorful flowers gave way to a spontaneous idea.

"Let's grow our own." Marilee looked at the children. "Let's have a garden."

Willie Lee gave back an enthused, "Yes," and Corrine raised an eyebrow, as if wondering if it could be done.

At the temporary plastic greenhouse set up at MacCoy's Feed and Grain, they ran everywhere at once, picking out flats of pansies and the biggest marigolds in the world. Corrine liked the blue cornflowers. Then the tomato plants looked so perky, and the idea of sweet homegrown tomatoes seemed so inviting, that Marilee got a half dozen of them.

The revolving stand of crisp and colorful seed packets caught Willie Lee's attention. When Marilee went to pull him away, she selected several packets.

Into the back of the Cherokee went containers of perky little plants, seed packets, bags of fertilizer, a new shovel for Marilee, and two small-size shovels for the children, all paid for with the ease of a card. Felt like she wasn't even spending money.

They sped home, where the first business was to get their cut flowers into vases of water. Marilee, determined to make everything a learning opportunity, showed the children how to cut the stems slanted to soak up the water and taught them as much as she knew about how flowers took water up their stems.

Afterward they trooped out to the backyard and hauled out shovels and their tender plants and seed packets. Watching Willie Lee attack the ground the best he could with his small shovel, Marilee found her hopes resurface for being able to teach her son simple skills that would enable him to function on a more or less adequate scale with everyday living in the world. Perhaps he would not ever be able to read or to count sufficiently, but learning to plant and grow and cut, and to clean up after himself, would see him a long way when his mother was no longer available to care for him.

Seven

Points of View

"What's for supper?" Parker asked after giving Marilee a kiss on the cheek.

"I have no idea."

Sprawled on the couch, having been gazing blankly at the television news, she felt incapable of any endeavor involving getting up and moving around.

"We dug a garden today. Shovels, half the backyard." At least it had seemed like half.

"Why didn't you go rent a tiller?" He shifted her legs over and sat beside her.

"I didn't plan to make it fifteen by fifteen. I just wanted a small garden for the children to grow some flowers, but then I saw the tomato plants, and they came in a container of six, and then Willie Lee saw the cantaloupe seed packets and wanted to grow those—they always put seeds in packets with beautiful pictures of perfect fruit, without all the hard work and bugs. I was just as bad as Willie

Lee—I got carried away and bought zucchini seeds because of the picture, and I didn't remember the awful bugs until I was on the way home. Anyway, I figured before planting the seeds, we needed to get the ground turned and let it sit there for the grass to die.

"I don't know. It just seemed to…mushroom," she ended lamely.

She really was unclear as to how she and two children had gotten into digging up a good portion of the backyard. Thinking of it now, she was amazed at the accomplishment, and as Parker began massaging her legs, she told him all about the activity with the children, painting word pictures of their funny antics for him. She had enjoyed digging in the dirt, had gone at it with a vengeance, for which she was now paying.

"Why weren't the children in school?" Parker asked, having now worked himself upward to leaning over and nuzzling her neck.

Marilee, vaguely aware of his scent and the warm, moist touch of his lips on her neck, realized she had not told him of her decision to remove the children from school.

"I took them out of school for the remainder of the school year," she said, now experiencing a rising certainty for the decision.

Parker quit nuzzling her neck and sat up. "You took them out of school?"

"Yes, there are less than three weeks left of the school year anyway." Seeing the disapproval bloom on his face, her certainty faltered. She realized two things at once: she had counted on his approval, and she had not been paying sufficient attention to his manly attentions moments earlier. No man was ever happy to have his advances ignored.

She felt at fault and annoyed at the same time. She was tired and not in the mood to deal with his male needs, nevertheless, this seemed a poor attitude on her part, so she sat up and tried to work up the stamina required of her.

"I believe that more than anything they can learn in the few remaining weeks of school, the children need to be secure and reassured," she said. "They need to be home for a while."

"What about your job?"

She saw he was determined to focus on obstacles, instead of swinging immediately into support.

She went on to explain her reasoning for her actions, which had begun to sound truly logical and reasonable when she had told it all to Aunt Vella, yet, in the light of Parker's expression now, Marilee had to work hard to keep on track.

"Tate doesn't have a problem with me working at home. He's giving us all laptop computers. Hooking them up on a network. I had already planned to try to work half days at home during the summer, anyway."

She thought that despite whatever Parker might be thinking behind his frown, her enthusiasm to proceed with what she saw as a viable healing endeavor for her children remained intact. She became more annoyed at Parker for not immediately grasping this concept.

"I know there is a curriculum available," she said, continuing to explain her plans for educating the children, "and I've heard of some support groups that I want to investigate. I'm going to draw up something for them to study every day. Especially Corrine. She is really smart, and one of her problems at school may have been boredom. Would you discuss ideas with me over supper? I want to start putting a plan in place for the summer."

If she could get Parker involved, he would come around. And, while she considered herself fully intelligent, she thought Parker better at critical, organized thinking. He could be, if he would apply himself, a great deal of help.

Parker, however, gave a remote shrug that Marilee did not find at all an acceptable reaction. She told herself not to be surprised. Parker could get into a very remote mood, as could every man of her experience.

But here she was more or less inviting him into her life, and he was not responding with any small bit of gusto. She supposed she wanted too much from him, and she felt at fault but couldn't figure out why, other than that her plans had brought on his disapproval. She felt herself getting all jangled inside, and angry because of it.

When the telephone rang, she grabbed it, as if grabbing some remedy for the conflicting moment. Unfortunately, she heard her mother on the other end of the line.

"Marilee? Marilee, this is your mother." Her mother had the habit of saying her name twice.

"Yes, Mom."

Her mother wanted Marilee to take her car for new tires tomorrow.

As Marilee listened to this, Parker stepped close and whispered, "Ask her to take the kids for the evening."

Marilee, amazed that he would suggest such a thing,

scowled at him. "I can't do it tomorrow, Mom. I can on Saturday."

Why couldn't she take it tomorrow, her mother wanted to know.

"Ask her…" He encircled her from behind and whispered in her ear about how they could drop the kids off at her mother's house.

She wiggled away from him and tried to think of how to put her mother and the tires off until Saturday without getting into a long explanation of having taken the children out of school. She finally got the arrangements straight, promising to go up to Lawton on Saturday morning for tire shopping.

"I have to go fix supper now, Mom. I'll see you Saturday." She hung up with a hard click and looked at Parker, who had turned from her and was stroking the back of his head.

"You know I do not leave the children with my mother. She does not want the care of them. She won't half watch them, and I am not going to leave them up there at her house, with her husband drinking every night." She wondered what in the world had gotten into him to suggest such a thing.

"Marilee, I want us to go out to dinner. The kids will be okay at your Mom's for a couple of hours. So what if Carl gets drunk? He doesn't bother the kids."

She gazed at him for several seconds, knowing he could not understand that taking them to her mother's was the same as setting them adrift for a few hours on a vast, turbulent ocean. The thought of it scared the daylights out of her.

"Corrine has had enough of that," she said flatly.

She averted her gaze, biting back all manner of words she was certain she would regret. She could not sort out what she truly felt. Likely she was overreacting, as was her habit. She just had to get some sort of control of herself.

"How 'bout gettin' a baby-sitter for the kids, then?" Parker asked.

"I am too tired to shower and dress, much less call to get a baby-sitter on last-minute notice," she said, unwilling to move in body or mind. "Besides, I have my pieces for Sunday's issue to write tonight." She would have to be writing more at nights now, and she thought him short-sighted not to get this point.

"But I can make hamburgers," she offered, swept with the urge to make up for her stubbornness, "and you can sit at the table and talk to me while I cook."

This would mean energy spent on cooking, which she should save for her writing job. How much easier if he would have been just as pleased with a can of soup thrown on the stove.

But hamburgers were Parker's very favorite food, as long as there were buns to go with them—Parker would not eat a hamburger on plain bread. Marilee was fairly certain she had buns in the freezer, and she wanted him to talk with her about the children. She wanted him to understand. She wanted him to share.

He did not fall into the plan with enthusiasm, but he did fall in and follow her into the kitchen, where he went straight to the refrigerator and pulled himself out a canned cold drink, while she peered out the back door to check on the children, who were playing in the dirt at the corner of their newly turned garden. At least Willie Lee was digging in the dirt for some reason, with Munro lying in it and watching. Corrine was sitting nearby in a yard chair; Corrine was a neat person who seemed to avoid dirt.

Seeing the children thus apparently contentedly occupied, and finding hamburger buns in the freezer, Marilee's spirits revived somewhat, and she had hope that she could set everything right with Parker by serving up both a good meal and the correct, upbeat attitude.

She set about winning him over as she went about preparing supper. She told him of her plans for the summer with the children. She hoped to better prepare them for school in the fall, and to enable herself to take a more forward part of their education, even when they went back to school. She felt she had been expecting too much from the school, a place made for the masses, to deal with the special particulars of her children's needs. It was her responsibility as a parent to see to those particular needs.

Parker, who had settled himself at the table with his cold drink, waiting for his supper to be served, replied to her remarks with "Hmms" and "Yes, I guess you can do that," all basically cautionary in nature, and all much less than satisfying.

Finally Marilee said, "Parker, I really would appreciate some support here."

To which he replied with raised eyebrows, "I'm listening."

"But you do not seem to be putting forth helpful ideas," Marilee said. "I do want your ideas, Parker."

"I don't think you want my ideas. You already have your mind set."

She gazed at him, telling herself not to overreact. One thing that she felt always got her into a lot of trouble was her habit of getting so emotional. Both Stuart and Parker had often accused her of this, and she determined at that minute not to give Parker ammunition.

"One thing you need to think about," Parker said, "is what Anita might think of you takin' her daughter out of school."

"Anita wasn't seeing that Corrine got to school half the time," Marilee answered, stung to the core. "And I don't see that she is here, making any of the decisions."

"Anita is still her mother. You're makin' all these plans for a child that isn't yours. You're gettin' way too involved, Marilee. You are referring to Corrine as your child. What if Anita shows up tonight at the door and wants to take her daughter with her? What are you goin' to do then?"

"I don't know," Marilee said. "I'm just tryin' to deal with 'right now' the best I can. I won't worry about 'then' until it happens."

Now that he had brought the concern to the front of her mind, she experienced fear of exactly that happening. This made her angrier at him for making her more fearful.

"And I don't know what you expect me to do. Should I just drop Corrine? Not look after her to the best of my ability? Well, who *is* goin' to do it, then?"

Clamping her mouth shut, she turned to the stove to remove the hamburgers from the hot pan before they burned. She herself was burning pretty good and didn't want to say something she would regret.

Parker didn't say anything more about it, and Marilee found this good thinking on his part.

The atmosphere at the supper table proved strained, despite all Marilee's good intentions for happiness. She and Parker were patently polite to each other in front of the children. Corrine's dark eyes moved from Marilee to Parker in a furtive fashion, and seeing this, Marilee brought up the subject of their gardening and the fun they had enjoyed. She managed to get Corrine to smile.

It had been a good idea, Marilee realized. The children had rosy faces. They had been outside, where they needed to be in the spring, and she had the sudden inspiration that tomorrow she would keep them outside most of the day. There were a lot of things she could teach them outside. So many things that must be experienced and could not be found in books. Being stuck at desks in school had no doubt been a major problem for them. They were souls who at this time needed to be out in the sun. And she could give them that.

The thought so pleased her that in a flush of warmth for everyone, she looked at Parker and smiled. He saw and smiled in return.

Marilee and Parker were alone in the lamplight in the living room. After supper Willie Lee had, with the innocence of an untroubled mind, simply lain down on the kitchen rug beside Munro, closed his eyes and gone instantly to sleep. Marilee had put him to bed in his underwear and simply wiped his hands with a damp rag; he had not awakened. Corrine was in the bath.

Parker wanted to make out.

"Corrine will be coming out of the bathroom any minute," Marilee said, pushing away from him after a particularly stimulating kiss that in truth she was reluctant to end. But the idea that Corrine might see them in a sexual encounter, even one with all their clothes on, was unnerving.

"We'll hear the door," Parker said, trying to pull her back against him. He had a very insistent manner this evening that aroused in Marilee both desire and irritation.

"Parker…I am not going to make love with you on this couch."

"Don't tell me you don't want it," he said in a sultry tone, moving his hand to her breasts.

She did not like his crude phrase, a dislike made even more annoying because, unfortunately, she wanted it very badly and even responded to his touch.

"Parker…I have the children to consider. Corrine could come in here at any moment."

His pushing the matter made her resolve return, and she was able to extricate herself from his embrace.

Parker gave a sigh of clear irritation. He had been sighing a lot that evening.

"What are you tryin' to show Corrine?" Parker wanted to know. "Don't you think you should be more honest? We are goin' together, Marilee. Most adults goin' together do have a sexual relationship. Corrine should be aware of this."

"She is eleven years old and aware of the facts of life, and I have little doubt that she's seen way more than she needs to see. Heaven only knows what she has seen with Anita." In Marilee's view, her sister changed men about like she changed underpants.

"She doesn't need to deal with any further information

about sex right now," Marilee said. "And I'm not ready to deal with it with them." This was closer to the truth than was comfortable.

Deep inside Marilee, where even she could not clearly see, was a child who longed still for the loving, nurturing mother she had not experienced. Could she have articulated her vision of a mother, she would have ended up describing Snow White. A way to get this fantasy mother was to *be* such a mother to these children given into her care, and that left little room for any type of sexuality.

"How long do you expect me to go on like this, Marilee?"

Marilee gazed at him. "I have never believed that a man and a woman could not control themselves until both of them were emotionally ready to handle the complications of sex."

"It isn't only that. When was the last time we had time for just us—you and me?"

Marilee could not answer him. She averted her gaze.

"Marilee, I want some time with you. Is that some sort of crime? I like the kids fine, but there is a time and place for grown-ups…that's us. You and me."

"I have the children. That isn't going to change." She thought Parker tended to remain on the childish side, too.

He sighed again, with clear irritation. "If you would marry me, we wouldn't have so many complications. We could sleep together, and you wouldn't be havin' to work at night but could be spendin' that time with me, and you could be free to do whatever it is you want to with the kids during the day."

A number of things went through her mind, the last being how he said *do whatever it is you want with the kids,* as if her daily endeavors in raising children were flights of fancy.

"Are you serious about marriage, Parker?"

Parker, never one for any confrontational question, regarded her carefully before saying, "I guess I'm the one who has brought it up, more than once."

That did not quite seem an answer to her.

"Yes, you are," she said. "And I suppose I've thought you were speaking in the passion of the moment. And marriage isn't like that. Passion fades, Parker, but everything else remains…the dirty laundry, the headaches and backaches, and the children."

She paused, giving him time to say something to that. He did not.

"I'm a woman with a handicapped son who will always need my greatest attention and a niece who will always have a part of my life. Marrying me means that suddenly you will have a wife and two children."

He nodded slowly. "I guess my life has included that for the past two years now, and I'm still here."

He guessed a lot.

"Yes, but there is a world of difference when you cannot simply walk out that door."

He blinked at that.

The rest of her doubts got all blocked up inside of her. She would have preferred some response on his part to her last statement, but he remained silent and did not jump in there with passionate proclamations of readiness right that minute to take on her and her children. This did not surprise Marilee. And she could give him credit for using his head and not thinking with his needs.

Consistently using one's head could be the secret of life, she thought, remembering Tate Holloway's use of the phrase.

Corrine, dressed in her yellow pajamas and having carefully combed her wet hair, went to tell her Aunt Marilee that she was ready for bed. She went quietly and with some hesitancy, a little fearful of being an interruption to her aunt and Parker.

She paused in the opening from the hallway. Her aunt and Parker were at the door, kissing. She ducked behind the wall and then peered out, watching until Parker left. Then she stepped back into the bathroom, shut the door silently and counted to ten, then stepped out again.

"I'm ready for bed, Aunt Marilee."

Her aunt was now standing at her desk, looking over some papers. Her head came up, and she smiled at Corrine. Corrine felt glad she had not let Aunt Marilee know she had seen her and Parker. Her aunt might have been mad at her. Aunt Marilee didn't get mad as fast as her mother did, but still, Corrine figured it best not to take chances. She liked when her aunt smiled at her, and the way her aunt always came with her after her bath, to pull back the sheets on the narrow bed and then tuck them around Corrine.

They would have to whisper, because of Willie Lee already being asleep. Although her aunt said, "I don't know why we bother to whisper—a two-ton cannon goin' off under his bed won't wake him." And then Aunt

Marilee would chuckle. Aunt Marilee was beautiful when she smiled or laughed.

Smiling now, her aunt said, "I sure had a good time planting today. Did you?"

Corrine nodded. She had enjoyed herself, but even if she had not, she would have nodded, because she knew instinctively she was supposed to have had a good time.

Aunt Marilee leaned down and said softly, "Bless and keep Corrine, Lord. Thank you." Then she kissed Corrine on the forehead, adjusted covers that didn't need adjusting, turned out the light and left.

Corrine lay awake for a long time, as she normally did. She generally had a hard time sleeping, and she figured something was wrong with her, since other people, like Willie Lee, just went to sleep, while she could not. Sometimes her legs ached, and they did tonight. Sometimes her feet cramped up painfully, and if she could not get this to stop, she would have to get up and put on a shoe, to keep her foot from balling in a cramp.

Tonight, however, it was only her legs, and only a little bit, so she just lay there and watched the moonlight come and make patterns in the room. She thought about when they had bought tomato plants and chosen seeds. It had been late for the plants, so the man at the store had said, but Aunt Marilee said she didn't see why that should stop them. Corrine had liked picking the plants and seeds more than turning the dirt in the garden. Dirt was dirty. But she did like the smell of the dirt.

She guessed she liked the whole thing of making the garden, but she didn't want to like it too much. The things she liked too much were frequently taken away. She usually tried to pretend to the world—and whatever governed Bad Luck—that she did not like anything very much, because that way the Bad Luck wouldn't know she did like it and then take it from her.

Thinking all of this, she was awake when the telephone rang. Likely it would have awakened her anyway, because Corrine slept lightly and awakened with the smallest sound. She knew immediately that it was her mother. She couldn't have said how she knew this, only that she knew it positively. Maybe because a phone call in the night meant trouble, and trouble meant her mother, and indeed, she heard her aunt Marilee say, "Hello, Anita."

Corrine's heart leaped, and she almost jumped out of bed to run to the phone. Her mother had remembered her! But then she registered the tone of her aunt's voice, which was sharp.

"It is nearly eleven o'clock, Anita." Then her aunt's voice dropped, and there were footsteps—her aunt going away into the kitchen.

Heart pounding, Corrine slipped out of bed and crept to the edge of the living room entry. She could see into the kitchen, only she couldn't see Aunt Marilee. She could hear, though, listening really hard.

"Anita…no. I'm not goin' to do that."

Corrine saw her aunt come into view. Her aunt was talking while she strode around the kitchen.

"I know you haven't spoken to her in two weeks, but that's your own doin'. It is eleven o'clock, and I'm not going in there and waking her up for her to talk to her drunk mother."

At *drunk mother,* Corrine put her head down. She could hardly breathe.

"Okay, you aren't drunk, but I can tell you have been drinkin'." Aunt Marilee spoke in a hushed, angry voice. "I'm not trying to keep you from Corrine…I'm just tellin' you that I am not going to go wake her up. Why don't you call back in the morning?"

Corrine's heart pounded.

"Around ten o'clock would be a good time." Aunt Marilee walked out of view over toward the sink. "Call collect…it's okay, Anita…you're my sister."

Aunt Marilee's voice fell, and Corrine could only hear the tone, which was sad. Then her aunt came back into view at the table, where she laid down the phone. Her head came around, and she stared into the hallway. Corrine drew back into the deep shadow and bumped into something that almost made her scream. She clamped her hand over her own mouth and saw that she had bumped into Munro. He licked her face. She pressed against the wall, not daring to move for fear Aunt Marilee would see her there and guess she had been spying. The memory of what had happened once when her mother had caught her spying came full into her mind, and her stomach turned. Corrine thought for a horrible minute that she was going to throw up.

After several long moments of holding her breath, Corrine dared to peek out. There was Aunt Marilee in the kitchen, having sat at the table, with her head in her hands. Her body was shaking.

Aunt Marilee was crying.

Corrine scampered back to bed so fast she forgot about

trying to be quiet. She pulled the covers up tight. Tears were coming out of her eyes now, and her chest felt like it would burst, but she did not want to make a lot of noise and have Aunt Marilee come see. Then Munro was there, licking her face. She put her arms around him, buried her face in his hair and wished she could disappear. She wished she had never been born. Everyone would be a lot better off if she had never been born. She had heard her mother say that once to Aunt Marilee.

The Valentine Voice
About Town
by Marilee James

The new publisher and editor in chief of *The Valentine Voice,* Tate Holloway, has arrived. Don't forget the open house to be held on Monday, here at the *Voice* offices. Cake and coffee will be served courtesy of Sweetie Cakes of Main Street. Everyone is invited to come by and welcome Mr. Holloway.

Other important bits of note:

Ms. Porter-Abercrombie, who as of this writing is somewhere in Tangiers, has sent in her first travel report, an overview of the Miami airport. Look for it in the travel section of Sunday's edition. Anyone who plans to pass through the Miami airport will find Ms. Porter's report invaluable.

The upcoming race for the city council post being vacated by longtime member Wesley Fitzwater heats up with G. Juice Tinsley throwing his hat into the ring. Mr. Tinsley, owner of the IGA, says that his platform rests on being for everything that Jaydee Mayhall, his opponent, is against.

Motorists and pedestrians, beware of a sinkhole on First Street, near the Methodist parsonage. Pastor Stanley Smith discovered it when the front right tire on his car, parked in front of his house, sank up to the hub. It had to be towed out of the hole. The City Works Department has put out a caution sign until they can get this hole repaired.

The mayor retracts his offer of city flags. There are none left.

Eight

Bright New Day

Tate walked the length of Main Street so that he was able to jog at a fresh pace homeward on Church, where he expected to and did meet Parker Lindsey just as the sun popped up.

"Mornin'," Lindsey said, coming to a stop.

"Good mornin'," Tate replied, a little surprised at Lindsey stopping.

"So, how's it goin', Editor?" Lindsey began a series of leg-stretching exercises.

Editor. Tate liked that, although he was a little annoyed at the way Lindsey said it.

"Goin' mighty fine," Tate said. He decided he could do stretching exercises, too. As he bent, he saw Bubba sitting like a fat Budda in his yard, watching with squinting eyes.

"I imagine you come into town to take advantage of the paved streets for jogging," Tate said. He knew the veterinarian's house and clinic were on the outskirts of town.

"Yep," Lindsey answered. "I jog in. Five miles a day."

Sounded like bragging.

"I guess I like reading better," Tate said. "Expands the mind."

"And the gut," Lindsey returned.

Oh, boy. He had stepped in there with that one, trying to be too smart.

When Winston came into his kitchen through the back door, bringing the day's supply of rose blossoms, both Mildred and Ruthanne were sitting at the kitchen table. That both women were rising early these days was a high annoyance. They were cutting into his solitude time.

"I can't find a one of those cheese-and-crackers samples we got up at the Wal-Mart the other day." Mildred was emptying the contents of her large purse on the table.

"I think you ate them all on the way home." Winston filled a jelly glass with water for the rose blossoms.

"Oh, really? That nice man gave me extra ones.... I was just sure I saved one or two." She was now raking out her purse and covering the table with everything imaginable: comb, hair spray, mayonnaise packets, sugar packets, tea bags, loose change, little box of Sugar Smacks cereal. "Oh, here's one!" She held it up with triumph.

Winston, who decided there was no room on the little table for the flowers, noticed that Ruthanne had not said a word, not even hello. Her eyes were closed.

He looked closer, seeing that she had her normal angelic countenance.

"She's asleep," Mildred said in a loud whisper.

"Oh."

Yes, she appeared to be breathing. He was relieved. It was something; she was sitting right there in the chair, only slumped a little bit. She was falling into an instant sleep more often these days, and he doubted that could be a good sign. He experienced increasing discouragement at the inevitable fact that Ruthanne, whose mind had never been fully with them, was now slipping away in body also.

As everyone did sooner or later, he thought with a large sigh.

He put a hand on Ruthanne's shoulder and called her name.

Ruthanne's eyes came slowly open. "Good morning, Winston. Is it time for me to get up now?"

"You're up, Ruthanne."

"Oh, how nice." One thing about Ruthanne, she was easily happy.

"Winston, let's have fried potatoes for breakfast." Mildred dug a cracker into the plastic square of cheese as she spoke.

"I was visitin' with my Mama," Ruthanne said and smiled at Winston.

"Fried potatoes with those Vidalia onions Charlene brought over," Mildred said, her mouth full of cracker.

"You're havin' cheese and crackers," Winston pointed out. "I'm goin' on down to Vella's for coffee."

"Oh, this is just a snack." She pointed at the cheese with a cracker. "A real breakfast would be so nice...and you know Marie won't make us fried potatoes," she added, her bottom lip quivering.

Marie was their day help, who came at noon to make one hot meal a day and to pick up for an hour. Marie was dedicated to nutrition, and anything fried was off-limits.

"I'm goin' on down to Vella's for coffee."

By durn, he had to get out of there. He felt a little guilty, thinking of the possibility that Ruthanne could die while he was gone, but he guessed it would happen when it happened. And mostly he wanted to live until he died, and not be smothered by Mildred Covington's love of food.

"Winston, you are mean not to make fried potatoes."

"I'll make 'em for you tonight." He was getting out the door.

"What you are makin' right now is a spectacle of yourself with that Vella Blaine," Mildred threw at him.

"I'm just goin' for coffee." He had stopped in the doorway, surprised at the accusation.

"Uh-huh."

"I'm eighty-eight years old, for Pete's sake."

Mildred started crying, but he knew if he stopped to comfort her, he would not get away. "Have toast and jelly, and I'll make fried potatoes tonight," he told her as he went down the steps.

He started across the yard, which was a little soft, so that his cane tip sank in. He knew he was hurrying away to a woman, but it was not what anyone could understand. It had to do with a longing for his wife, and for life as he once knew it, and the desire to get away from where he found himself, old and declining.

There was no running away from old age, he thought angrily. But he guessed he had better do whatever he could to enjoy the current moment, because he could wake up dead tomorrow.

The phone rang while Corrine was rinsing their breakfast plates. Willie Lee was coloring at the table, and said, "Get it, Cor-rine."

Corrine turned off the water and grabbed a towel as she ran to get the telephone.

"Hello," she said hesitantly.

"Corrine? Oh, Corrine, honey, this is Mama."

"Hello, Mama." Her heart beat very fast. Her mother had called her! And she sounded fine!

"I know it's early. Have y'all been up long…is Marilee up?"

"Aunt Marilee is in the shower," she said slowly, cautiously judging what to tell her mother, who easily could get angry at her aunt. "We've had breakfast," she added quickly, wanting her mother to know that they had not been lazing in bed.

"Well, that's good. I was afraid I might wake you up, but I needed to call while I'm on break. I got a job, honey—I'm workin' at the Tarrant County Court House."

"That's good." Corrine wished she could think of more to say.

"Yes, it is. It's a real good job. I'm a secretary, and I dress up every day."

"That's neat," Corrine said, pleased to have thought of the word.

There was a bit of silence, and then her mother said, "Well, honey…how are you doin' up there?"

"Okay."

Another pause and what sounded like her mother puffing on a cigarette. "I talked to your Aunt Marilee last night. She said she's taken you out of school."

"Yes." She answered cautiously, then thought to add quickly, "I'm still doin' my school work, though. I'll pass."

"Your Aunt Marilee is teachin' you, huh?"

"Yes."

"Well, she's good at that, I imagine." It was a question.

Corrine had a panic about which way to go with this. Finally she said, "Yes."

"Don't you miss goin' to school with the other kids? You can go back to school, if you want. I'll tell Marilee to take you back."

"I don't want to go back."

"Well, okay. I just wanted you to know I'd get you back in, if you wanted to go."

"I don't."

"All right. There's only a few weeks left of school anyway, and it won't be long until I can get you back down here with me. I'm makin' good money, and I have health benefits and everything. I'm savin' to get us a nice place, with your own room. Won't you like that?"

"Yes, Mama."

"Oh, honey, I sure miss you."

"I miss you, too, Mama."

"You do?"

"Yes."

"Well, it won't be too long now, and I'll be straight again and can come get you."

"Okay."

Aunt Marilee came in just then, and Corrine said, "Here's Aunt Marilee. You want to talk to her?"

"Yes, just real quick. Here's a kiss from Mama." A smooching sound came over the line.

"Here's one back," Corrine said quickly and did a faint smooching sound that made her feel silly, then handed the phone to her aunt.

Having no inclination to hear any of her aunt's end of the conversation, she went hurriedly to the back door and out into the sparkling sunshine flitting through the trees. She was quickly followed by Munro and then Willie Lee.

Willie Lee said the strangest thing. "Cor-rine, Mun-ro says you need a hug." And then he threw his arms around her middle.

Corrine about jumped out of her skin. "Stop that, Willie Lee." She pushed him away. "Come on, let's go up in your tree house."

She jumped up and took hold of the steps and then the branches, enjoying the feeling of strength in her body. She could climb trees. Someday she would be able to do everything and wouldn't need anybody to take care of her.

The Valentine Voice
Sunday, April 30
Today's Highlights:

—The *Voice* goes to twice weekly. Beginning May 7, *The Valentine Voice* will be published on Sunday mornings and Wednesday evenings. Story page 1.

—Controversial detention center becomes major campaign issue in city council seat race. Story page 1.

—Death proves of natural causes, but identity of man found dead in his car on the outskirts of town turns to mystery. Story page 2.

—Rose Club to plant bushes to beautify town. Open invitation to join the fun. Story page 3.

—Sinkhole on First Street grows. Warning sign falls in. Story page 4.

Nine

Come Sunday Morning

Spring had sprung and summer was taking over. Lilacs were gone, so were most of the irises, and Doris Northrupt's newly potted dahlias were poking out of the soil.

Young Leo Pahdocony, who was working to save money for the university next year, was mowing lawns in his spare time. He was getting so much business that his father was urging him to start a lawn maintenance business instead of going away to school. Leo, Sr., said he could handle the business end; Reggie was determined her son was going to get an education and her husband not handle anything.

Charlotte Nation was putting flea repellant on her terrier, and Parker Lindsey was working his butt off giving animal vaccines, so that come Sunday he turned off his alarm and slept in.

Winston went out later on Sunday morning to put up

the flag. There wasn't anyone out early anyway on a Sunday, so he and Everett Northrup had an agreement to do their respective flag raising one hour later.

This Sunday Winston worked up a damp sweat doing his patriotic duty. Northrup yelled over after they had finished the ceremony, "Hot!"

"Yep," Winston returned, thinking, What did the man expect at this time of year? Northrup was originally from up in one of those Northern states, like Indiana or somewheres.

Going around to the back door of his house, he checked the thermometer fastened there on the corner. The dawning sun rays had not yet hit it, and the needle pointed to seventy degrees. That did not look good. He didn't think he would wear a sport coat to church. He couldn't stand heat in his old age, and besides, he didn't need to impress anyone.

"The fella at the national weather channel says just a bit dry, is all," Perry Blaine reported to his wife Vella from where he sat in his easy chair, catching the early-morning television report. All week long, Perry got up at the same time, 5:00 a.m., but on Sundays he remained at home until the drugstore opened at noon, to serve the church crowd soft drinks and ice-cream sundaes. Perry did not ever work the soda fountain—they hired two high school kids for Sundays—but he opened the pharmacy, since the store was open anyway. Most of the time he could sit back there and nap and watch John Wayne movies. People didn't like to get sick on Sundays; it cut into their weekend time. He did a heck of a business on Mondays, though.

If they had another hot summer, that meant they would

make another killing with ice cream, he reminded Vella, who was pulling on her floral smock and straw hat.

At least this year they were having sizeable amounts of rain, and that meant war with leaf molds on the roses. Vella didn't make a breakfast on Sunday, but threw some jellied toast at Perry and went out to spray her bushes in an attempt to stave off powdery mildew and black spot.

Her roses were starting off better this year than last, she thought, clipping several long stems of fragrant Chrysler Imperial blossoms and carrying them inside to put in a vase for the preacher at that morning's services. She intended to get to church early. She always intended this, and seldom made it. Perry said she'd been born late and kept it up.

Sunday morning was the only morning Marilee got up early and with some anticipation. A long time ago, during one of her trips with Stuart, she had met an old black man sitting on the front porch of one of the tiny grocery stores that in those days inhabited dozens of small towns of Tennessee. He had offered her a cold drink and some wisdom. She had at the time been very annoyed with Stuart for going off on a story and leaving her flat at this grocery store; knowing Stuart as she did by then, she had been concerned with finding a ride back to their hotel. The old man had observed this.

"Me," he said, "I allow all week for worryin', but not on Sunday. Worryin' is a lot of work, and man is supposed to rest on Sunday so he'll be able to go fresh in the new week. Anything comes up on Sa'dy night, I just put it aside 'til Monday, when I'll be refreshed from a day of rest. Anger…frettin'…stewin'…it all waits. And sometimes, while it waits, it just seems to disappear."

When Stuart had decided he needed to be free, and she was going crazy with the idea of being alone and raising a handicapped son, she had remembered this bit of advice. Since then, Sunday was her No-Worry Day. Sunday morning she would make herself a cup of coffee thick with sugar and real cream—the only day she allowed herself cream, because she wasn't worrying about fat and cholesterol—and would go out on the front porch and sit in the swing. Even in winter, unless the weather was too inclement, she followed this routine, wearing heavy wool and wrapped up in a blanket, the warm coffee mug in her hands.

This was her time to simply be. A time to let go of striving and struggling to be something and think what needed to be thought. A time to listen to the stillness of the world, and to her own heart, and to the possible whisper of the Lord inside. A time to savor peace from the normal turmoil of her emotions.

Sometimes she would nod off, as she did this morning, until Leo, Jr. passing and the newspaper landing smack-dab on her porch woke her. She caught a glimpse of Leo, Jr. peddling on, then, right behind him, came a jogger.

It was Tate Holloway. She recognized him with a jolt of surprise. And here she was in her bathrobe.

He waved, and she waved back.

Okay. She snapped open the newspaper. As she was reading, her neighbor across the street came out in his pajamas to retrieve his newspaper, and on the corner, Buddy, the young man who worked for UPS, pulled his Mustang to the curb, in from an all-nighter, which was the liberty of the young and single. Apparently his mother didn't quite see it this way. She met him at the door, and her angry voice, if not the words, echoed down to Marilee.

When she went inside, she was curious at the quiet—no television cartoons. She heard hushed voices and splashing water in the bathroom. Corrine and Willie Lee were hanging over the side of the tub, bathing Munro.

"Mun-ro has to go to church with us," Willie Lee said.

Corrine became very still and did not look up.

"I suppose he should come," Marilee said, wondering at her sanity.

She and the children, and Munro, who smelled like a wet dog, had a leisurely breakfast, after which the humans dressed, and Marilee spritzed Munro with perfume. After a ten-minute wait on Parker—he sometimes joined them for church—she and the children and the dog walked down the block to First Street, then turned south for two blocks to the Methodist Church, where they viewed the sinkhole in front of the parsonage. The Sunday school classes had let out, and the pastor was giving a tour of the sinkhole, now about the size of a family dinner table. A big yellow caution sign sat inside it, just barely visible at the top. The City Works had now strung yellow tape around the hole.

Inside the sanctuary, Marilee directed the children into the rear row, moving from their customary second-row seats, in order to have Munro lie at Willie Lee's feet. The few people who noticed the dog only smiled. Munro was smart enough to keep a low profile.

Their change in seating, however, proved quite flustering to Aunt Vella, who invariably came after the first hymn had begun. This morning she came racing in to take

advantage of everyone standing and singing, blew past
Marilee and the children on up to set a bud vase with a
red rose on the corner of the pulpit, and then returned to
the second row, where she stopped, perplexed at finding
Imogene Reeves and her husband and grandchildren
taking up the pew.

"They're back there, Vella." Norm Stidham leaned
over from the opposite side.

"What?"

Iris MacCoy raised her voice over the singing. "In the
back, honey…Marilee and the kids are in the back."

"Oh…my…"

"They have a dog," Minnie Oakes said.

Marilee was in the aisle, motioning her aunt, who put
a hand to her pillbox hat and hurried back to join them.
She lifted an eyebrow on sighting Munro, and then went
right into the middle verse of "In the Garden."

The light came through the golden glass windows and
shone warmly on the walls and the congregation. On
Marilee's left side, Aunt Vella, smelling of Avon powder,
sang out the old hymn with feeling. On her right, Willie
Lee repeated, "Dew on the ro-ses…" and Corrine held her
hymnal open on the back of the pew in front of them; her
mouth moved but made no perceptible sound. Munro lay
with his eyes closed, either in misery or prayer.

Oh, Lord.

She was surrounded by blessings. In that moment, for
a slice of time, it was as good as it gets.

"Is the paper really goin' to twice a week, Marilee?" It
seemed as if the facts of the newspaper article could not

be taken seriously. People had to hear it confirmed from her lips.

"Durn shame."

"I knew Ms. Porter leavin' was goin' to be the death of the paper."

"Well, I'm paid up. What will happen to my money? Can I get a refund?"

Marilee repeated, almost word for word, because she had written the article, what it said in that morning's newspaper, that the change would save the paper and enable it to continue operation, that the editions would in time grow in size, and that accounts would be adjusted.

By the time she left church she found her No-Worry Day seriously invaded. On the way past the sinkhole she made Willie Lee and Corrine hold her hand, having a vague apprehension that the hole would reach over and grab her children.

On Monday morning Tate drew on new jogging shorts and a muscle shirt and checked himself out in the mirror. His legs were white. He could stand it, though, but he could not go that muscle shirt, no-sir.

Changing into a T-shirt, he thought maybe he would buy one of those sleeveless T-shirts. He could go to that, he decided, and was annoyed that he had not bought one at the sport shop. He was further annoyed that he was feeling the childish need to compete with Lindsey.

Ah, well, if he were perfect, he wouldn't have any need to be on earth.

The phone rang as he went out the door. He left it and jogged down Porter, with Bubba bouncing along behind him like a meandering basketball. Passing the James house, he looked at it with his usual fantasy and was startled to see a figure on the front step. A little dark-haired figure in yellow pajamas.

He waved, and Corrine gave a hesitant wave in return, then hopped up and skedaddled in the front door.

At the corner the young UPS man chinned himself three times on the porch beam, hopped down and, with biceps bulging, came to his car parked at the curb. "My mother sure is irritated at you for cuttin' the paper to two days," he said.

"I'm sorry." He might have wished for better first words between them.

He continued on, turning toward Main Street. Bubba dropped out of sight, as had become his habit. As if the cat was hesitant to be seen in public with him, Tate thought.

He came abreast of the walking-talking ladies. Their morning nod to him seemed decidedly cool.

The bakery lady's car was out front, but the door to the shop was closed, and all quiet there. All quiet on the entire street. Halfway along he had to drop to a walk. The calf of his right leg twinged, and he shook it out.

Turning east at the police station, with the aroma of coffee that stirred his taste buds, he saw Lindsey in the distance, coming down the hill right on time.

Okay. Get moving.

Pushing himself into an energetic pace, he met Lindsey at the intersection. Thankfully Lindsey came to a stop, so Tate could, too. His chest was burning.

"Mornin', Editor," Lindsey said, stretching his legs. "Hell of a change in the paper."

"Everythin' changes," Tate said, stretching his legs and trying not to pant.

Just then, here came the young blond woman, this time on a bicycle, wearing bright-blue short-shorts and a yellow halter top, showing lots of smooth, tanned skin. She slowed a fraction. "Hello, y'all," she said and cruised on past between Tate and Lindsey as they both offered hellos.

Tate's head turning as if on a swivel, he followed her with his eyes, seeing her lovely rounded rump undulate as she pumped the bicycle, heading east on Porter. Nothing wrong with appreciation, Lord. He was not lusting. He doubted he could keep up with such a woman.

Then he saw Lindsey had been watching, too.

Tate said, "If you hurry, maybe you can catch her, you bein' in such good shape and all."

Lindsey grinned a slow grin. "Why, I got a girl, Editor."

Tate thought a half a minute and said, "I don't think you have much more than I do…we're both out here joggin' our brains out."

Lindsey kept his mouth shut and headed off at a rate designed to show Tate what he did not have.

Tate pushed himself to semijog up his drive and around the back of his house, where he didn't bother to go inside but collapsed on the step. Bubba came and sat down to stare at him.

"Remember, I feed you," Tate told the cat.

Behind him, through the screen door, came the ringing of the telephone.

Another complaint about the changes in the paper, he surmised, remaining right where he was.

* * *

He met Marilee at the intersection of their respective streets. Seeing her face behind the Cherokee windshield, he tooted his horn and waved out the window, going so far as to holler, "Where are you goin' so early?" It was just eight-thirty.

Corrine's small head poked out the passenger window of the Cherokee. "To get doughnuts for the paper." The girl's voice came thinly across the distance.

Tate pulled his BMW through the intersection and up alongside Marilee. Her window and the rear passenger window, where Willie Lee poked his head out, came down at the same time.

"Hi, Mis-ter Tate."

"Hello, Willie Lee…hello, Munro," he added to the dog, who brought its head alongside the boy's.

Then he shifted his gaze to Marilee. Big dark glasses hid her eyes.

She said, "We're goin' to get doughnuts to take down to the paper."

"I thought we were going to have some cakes delivered." He tried to see through the dark lenses. It was disconcerting to be talking to emotionless dark glasses.

"Too early. Bonita isn't deliverin' the cakes until around ten, and the office is already filling up with people…who all pretty much want to smack you for darin' to change an institution of the town."

"I know." How well he knew. "Phone's been ringin' since yesterday. I got a call this mornin' before I even got my shower." Annoyance crawled over him, and he focused it on Marilee's sunglasses. He considered reaching out and yanking them right off her face so he could look her in the eye.

"Charlotte called to ask me to bring my tea maker," she said, "and to go get another three dozen doughnuts. She brought in a dozen herself, and they're gone."

"I'd best scoot down there, then, and give her a hand with crowd control." He could not believe the uproar over the tiny newspaper.

"Yes, you had better."

"Get me some jelly doughnuts," he thought to sling out the window as Marilee drove on.

He put his vehicle in gear and headed down the street, thinking that he should have anticipated a strong objection to changing the paper from a daily. Such outcry should be a cause for celebration on his part; it showed a lot more people than he had imagined read it.

He suspected, though, that the outcry had less to do with the number of people who read the paper and more with the simple fact that human beings did not take readily to change, even to change that meant improvement.

He shook hands and offered a friendly welcome and an attentive ear, which he had long ago learned was the best way to deal with complaints. Most people were content, once they had been heard out. There was not much more he needed to offer than a true listening ear.

The place had cleared out, and Tate had made it to his office, when a short but ramrod-straight grey-haired man in a dark cardigan, plaid shirt and creased khakis appeared at his door.

"Charlotte isn't out here," the man said to Tate. "No one is out here."

"Well, now, I'm sorry. Charlotte was just here." Tate came to the door and looked out at the empty room where only minutes before at least three women had been working at their desks.

"I guess everyone has stepped out. Can I help you?"

"Hmmm…Everett Northrupt," the man said, sticking out his hand.

"Nice to meet you, sir. I'm Tate Holloway."

"I figured." The man's eyes narrowed. "I want to know how you will handle my account. I'm paid up for a year of dailies. I expected to receive them. I have received them for eight years, since I moved down here. Always paid on time. I tip the boy ten dollars, twice a year, Easter and Christmas."

"I'm sure the young man appreciates that, sir. And we appreciate you as a customer. Don't you worry about your account. It will be adjusted. You won't lose any money."

"I paid for a daily. I expect a daily." The man stared intently at Tate.

"Well, sir…we can give you a refund." Tate pulled at his ear.

"I don't want my money back. I want my daily paper. I paid for a daily, and I expect a daily."

Tate saw Charlotte out of the corner of his eye, coming out of the rest room. She looked his way, but he did not think he should wave her down for help.

"Sir—" he felt compelled to sir the man "—as I explained in my editorial, I am sorry for the disappointing change, but it is my hope that by going to a twice weekly, we can save this important institution and turn it into even a grander paper than it has been for many years."

The man's mouth got tighter. "So then you'll go bankrupt, and I'll lose my payment anyway."

The man had a definite negative outlook.

Tate took hold of the man's elbow. "Would you like a cup of coffee, Mr…." He was embarrassed to have forgotten the man's name.

"Northrupt. I've had my coffee this mornin'."

"Well, sir, I find I'm in need of several cups this mornin'." He decided it was time to get Charlotte's help, no matter how blatant the request appeared. But she was busy at her computer. It was nearly impossible to get Charlotte's attention once she determined to focus on the computer screen.

Thank heaven, there was Marilee! She came through the door with the children, each carrying a white doughnut box and going over to the long, white-linen-draped table.

"Well now, here's doughnuts," Tate said. He hauled Northrupt along by the elbow. "Just look at this spread… fresh doughnuts…fresh coffee. Thank you, Miss Marilee."

Marilee, opening the boxes of doughnuts, said to him, "I have to go back to the Jeep for the tea maker and distilled water."

Tate was left there with his irritated customer, staring at Marilee and Corrine's backs disappear out the door.

"Hel-lo, Mis-ter North-rub."

It was Willie Lee, with Munro beside him, standing there looking up and holding out his hand for a shake.

Mr. Northrupt shook the boy's hand. "Hello, Willie Lee."

Willie Lee gave his hand to Tate for a shake, too.

Then Northrupt looked expectantly at Tate.

"How about a doughnut, Mr. Northrupt? Let's see, there's glazed, chocolate covered, cinnamon…and jelly. Jelly doughnuts are a secret to life, you know."

"I want a jell-y dough-nut," Willie Lee said.

"You betcha', son. Here you go." Tate handed a doughnut to the boy. "What kind would you like, Mr. Northrupt?"

"I have diabetes," Mr. Northrupt said.

"I'm sorry to hear that. You look fit, though, sir." He had a sudden disturbing vision of a newspaper headline that read: Editor Kills Man With Doughnut.

He filled a foam cup with steaming coffee and held it toward the older gentleman.

Mr. Northrupt looked at the cup. "I said I've had my coffee. And I don't drink from a foam cup, anyway. Tastes bitter."

Tate withdrew the cup, brought it to his lips and sipped. He didn't like foam cups, either.

"I don't see how goin' to a twice weekly paper delivered at fifty cents each can make you more money than a daily at forty cents each," Mr. Northrupt said.

"Cut down on outlay. Paper costs dearly these days. Over all, we'll cut down on paper costs, printing costs and delivery costs."

The man's frown deepened.

"I believe it will be a better paper. We'll have a lot more in each issue. We'll be adding two pages to start, another two in two more months, as well as special inserts from time to time."

"You're set to do this thing, then."

"Yes, sir, I am. It's gotta be done." He looked down to see Willie Lee standing there, jelly on his face, and his eyes behind his thick glasses intently looking up at them. The dog sat at his feet, doing the same thing.

Just then Marilee came in bearing the tea maker and a sack, and Corrine came right behind her, lugging two gallons of distilled water. Tate jumped to take the heavy gallon containers from the small girl.

"You have met the *Voice's* senior editor, haven't you, Mr. Northrupt?" Suddenly he realized the need to give her the title. Her eyes came quickly to his. "This is Marilee James."

"Everett and I have known each other for quite a while. Hello, Everett. How is Doris doin'? I heard she took first prize for her watercolor at the Spring Fair."

"Yep, she did." Northrupt turned to the table and took up two napkins. "I think I'll just wrap up a couple of these cinnamon rolls and take them with me."

"What about your diabetes?" Tate said, a little alarmed.

"I'm takin' these to Doris. I need to get some of my money back." He left with a napkin-wrapped cinnamon roll bulging in each pocket of his cardigan sweater.

For a few minutes—dare he hope for the rest of the day?—the visitors had stopped. Feeling frazzled, Tate got his ceramic cup, now appearing very dear to him, and poured himself a cup of coffee from the pot that sat on the cloth-covered table.

Marilee, who was adding fresh doughnuts to the plates, said, "I'll take twenty dollars more a month as senior editor."

"That is what the thirty was for. I just forgot to mention it."

"If I had known, though, I would have asked for fifty."

"When the paper makes money."

"Good enough. I'll remind you."

"Would you mind stayin' a while? I think we really need a hostess for this open house."

Charlotte didn't appear inclined to leave her desk, and if she did, Tate thought she seemed more intimidating than welcoming. He realized he felt a little desperate, and this made him feel silly, yet he still cast Marilee a hope-filled look.

"You're the boss," Marilee told him in that smooth, snappy way she had of speaking.

Her eyes looked very blue. He could never tell for certain when she was joking. He liked this about her—admired it, a trait he admired in himself.

"I doubt that very much where you're concerned, Miss Marilee," he drawled, relieved and happily taking up a jelly doughnut.

"I think I'll do a lot better to ask you, rather than to tell you," he added, and bit into the doughnut, raspberry, his favorite.

Her gaze was on him. He smiled, keeping his full mouth closed, savoring the jelly on his tongue and the sight of her blue eyes. Enjoying the electricity between them.

By golly, he wanted powerfully to kiss her. This struck

him so hard that for an instant he forgot to chew his doughnut and almost choked on it.

Then she had lowered her eyes and was saying cooly, "I'll stay until noon. Then I'll need to get the children home for lunch, and Willie Lee generally takes a nap."

Tate, inhaling a deep breath and allowing his gaze to drift downward over her body, her back now turned to him, thought, Marilee James is one heck of an attractive woman.

He had experience attending parties to welcome some pretty prominent dignitaries, however, he had always been in the capacity of observer. He knew how to blend in and watch others pay welcome and receive welcome, pay homage and receive homage. He had never been the one stuck out there in the thick of it.

He smiled until his smile felt pasted on, and shook hands until he thought his arm might be permanently stuck into position. Every third minute he was blinded by flashes from Reggie's camera.

"Let's get one of you and the mayor shaking hands," she said, going so far as to physically position Tate and Mayor Upchurch in front of the big spray of flowers sent over by Fred Grace. "Free advertising for town merchants never hurt anything."

"Wait! I want in the picture," said Kaye Upchurch, the mayor's wife, who bustled herself over, slipped her arm through Tate's and smiled at the camera.

Reggie snapped the picture, then told them to hold it. "I always take two shots, just to make sure."

Reggie took two shots of Tate with Sheriff Oakes and

Jaydee Mayhall, who was a prominent—not to mention the only—local attorney, and then two of him with Adam and Iris MacCoy, who owned the feed-and-grain store and were building a senior living community, and two of him with Winston Valentine, who presented him with a key to the Senior Citizens' Center.

"Let's get a shot of the publisher and his staff," Reggie commanded, assembling everyone who had returned to the offices—except Zona, of course, who might or might not have been holed up in her office behind the pulled shades.

"Marilee, you get there in front of Mr. Tate—" Reggie sighted through her camera "—Imperia, you get on his left, and, Tammy, you right here. June, get there beside Marilee, and, Charlotte, you stand behind his right shoulder, you're so tall…get in close. And, Leo, get closer in with Charlotte.

Tate caught a sweet citrus scent from Marilee's hair. He put his hand on her waist and felt her jump. A flash went off. Marilee moved away, but then Reggie made them all get back together for another shot, after which she enlisted Bonita Embree of Sweetie Cakes Bakery to take a shot with Reggie squeezing in.

"Nobody move! Take another one, Bonita, just to make sure."

Tate paused to look at the room for a minute. In his mind's eye, he constructed how he wished the room to take shape. He would hire a new layout manager and assistant as soon as he could find them, and two more staff writers. Two more desks along there, updated, pleasant partitions, maybe of blue…modern, while leaving the antique brick walls. They had to have new lighting, but he didn't intend to install a lowered ceiling, no, sir.

He was sinking all he had in the world into this place.

He turned out the lights and went out the front door to the curb, where he had begun parking his BMW in an effort to avoid what dust he could. He jumped over the door and into the seat, in the manner he liked to do to keep himself fit, or to display his fitness to himself and anyone else who might notice, and simply for the fun of it.

Backing out, he headed down the street drenched with early-evening sunlight. It rained a lot more down in Houston than here, and he was enjoying the dryness. He enjoyed seeing the play of golden setting sunlight on the buildings and trees as he drove the few blocks to his house.

When he saw the Victorian house, he reminded himself that it was his new home.

He pulled beneath the portico, got out and slammed the door, went easily up the stairs and in through the side door that wasn't locked. He didn't see a reason to lock the house. Most everything he owned was still in taped boxes that had been delivered on Saturday, which would make robbery pretty easy, he thought, glancing into the rooms at the stacked boxes. Although he figured that people exiting his house with boxes would likely be noticed and questioned in Valentine, America, where his neighbor across the street was often sitting on her porch and watching everything like a hawk.

Even when he had lived in the big city, though, Tate never had been much for locking anything. Lucille used to say he didn't lock doors because he had nothing worth stealing, not outside himself nor in.

Funny how he thought of Lucille these days. As if he was seeing a review of his life in order to see clearly the mistakes, so as not to make them again in the future.

The silence of the house engulfed him, and he had the dreary thought that he had not successfully built up riches of the spiritual sort, either. He had for too many years kept people at a distance, kept himself running after a journalism career so hard that he did not have time or energy to face the nagging bite of emptiness in his soul.

It was only when he had been brought to an abrupt halt, when he was face-to-face with the emptiness that was on the brink of swallowing him, that he had attempted to change his life. Sometimes, like right then, he wearied of the attempt.

Living life took a great deal of fortitude.

He thought of all this as he opened the refrigerator— a five-foot, curved-top vintage fifties Kelvinator that revealed his cousin's total lack of concern with either the house or modernization. Or perhaps it stood as a testament to solid craftsmanship from another era. Tate found himself reluctant to part with it.

He wished for a good glass of sweet iced tea, but having none made, he took the easier route of pulling a small bottle of Coke from the wire shelf, then slammed the door. He popped the cap from the bottle, shook five cat treats from the container on the counter, and walked out the back door, where Bubba had already learned to wait for him each evening.

"You're a pretty smart boy," he said to the cat, as the

animal sat up to receive each treat. "You take the good things of life immediately."

Immediately after the final treat, Bubba gave him a satisfied look and then turned and ambled away.

"Got what you wanted, and now you're off," Tate said to the cat's retreating behind. "I feel used."

Straightening, he drank deeply from the cold bottle.

The big, blooming lilac bush buzzed with bees. He was going to have to get a mower for the lawn. He had never owned a power mower. He had never owned a lawn. He'd *had* a lawn once, with Lucille, but he didn't think it could be called owning one. He had paid a lawn maintenance crew to handle it for the five months or so they had lived in the house.

Just then he heard childish voices, laughter and a dog's bark. A woman's voice cut in. Marilee's voice, from her yard just beyond the cedar trees.

His spirit perked up, and he started toward the sound, drawn along as surely as if by a cord. Through the break in the trees and to the gate in the fence covered with rambling rose vines, letting himself through the gate even before being invited by Marilee, who stood in front of a smoking grill, while Willie Lee and Corrine raced around with Munro in the shadowy yard.

"Well, you already have your drink," Marilee said to him, her eyes on the bottle in his hand. "Would you like to join us for hot dogs?" Her eyes came to his, and her smile was warm.

"Yes, ma'am, that sounds right fine," he replied.

He allowed himself the enjoyment of studying her womanly beauty, even when she looked away. Tate had always considered it one of his finest traits that he could appreciate the delicacies of a woman.

"My mama always said there was nothin' like these little Co-Cola's," Tate explained. "The Coke in them tastes better than in the bigger bottles. Lots better than in plastic."

They were sitting on the back concrete steps, eating their hot dogs and beans off plates in their laps. Marilee had said she once possessed a picnic table and benches, but that during a power outage in a bad winter storm, she had burned them and had never replaced them.

Tate was in the midst of explaining how his mother used to take him and his brother down to the corner grocery every afternoon to get a cold drink out of the cooler of ice. "We didn't even have 'lectric in those little country stores when I was a kid," he explained to the children he doubted could imagine not having electricity.

"Is it dif-fer-ent?" Willie Lee asked, breaking into Tate's tale.

"What different?" Tate asked. "Not havin' electricity?"

"What is in the bot-tle?" Willie Lee was looking at the now empty bottle in Tate's hand.

Marilee said, "It's all the same Coke, Willie Lee. Just some people think the little bottles taste different."

"They do taste different," Tate stated.

"Matter of opinion," Marilee returned.

Tate took exception to an opinion he found poor, and into this Corrine inserted with a hesitant voice, "The little bottles are glass. The bigger bottles are plastic."

Tate and Marilee regarded her, and then Tate said, "We should do a taste test." He grabbed the idea with enthusiasm. "We'll gather the different bottles of Coke and taste each one to see if there is a difference. It will be a great experiment. You can give the children points for a science project," he added to Marilee, thrilled with himself for thinking of a way to contribute to the children's education, and thrilled even still further at the bright smile that came across Marilee's face.

"I think that's a super idea," she said.

"Well, by golly, then…come on and finish up those dogs, kids, so we can get to it."

Ten minutes later, he was a little surprised when Marilee threw him the keys to her Cherokee and told him, "It's your idea, so you go buy the Cokes. I'll stay here and get the kitchen cleaned up."

"Okay. You kids want to go with me?"

"Yes," Willie Lee said immediately.

Tate saw Corrine looking uncertainly at Marilee, and noticed that Marilee hesitated.

"Yes, you guys can go," Marilee said.

"Mun-ro, too." Willie Lee put in.

"You bet, Munro, too," Tate said, pleased that Corrine was joining them as they went out the door.

It had been many years since he had been alone with children. He had on a number of occasions, years ago, enjoyed his brother's three children, but they were long grown. This experience with Willie Lee and Corrine somehow struck him as quite special. He realized he felt pretty important and grand, helping to improve children's spirits with an openness about life.

He supposed he was getting a little carried away about a short trip to the IGA, but nevertheless, there was something about being a man of his ripe age with children that enabled him to jump back into his own childhood. He supposed he'd had to grow up enough to be childish again.

He took an index card from his pocket and jotted a note on it. Then he noticed Corrine looking at him curiously.

"Just jotting down a thought I don't want to lose," he told her. "That's what newspapermen do." He thought maybe she should know that trait; it might prove helpful to her in the future, should she get interested in a newspaperman.

At the checkout counter, Tate told the young clerk, who looked quizzically at the array of Coca-Cola in the different-size bottles, and some in cans, too, "We are conducting an experiment. I have with me budding scientists—" he put a hand on each of the children's shoulder "—who might in another twenty years possibly develop soft drinks that can feed the world."

"Yeah, whatever," said the clerk, who was young enough to know everything.

Eager to get back to Marilee and share the fun of the experiment with her, Tate zoomed along the streets at a good clip. His mind was zooming on ahead, too, in the manner of a man who is powerfully attracted to a woman. That he had not been so strongly attracted to a woman in years came to him. Maybe it was simply the new changes in his life, he thought. Maybe the attraction would pass.

Still, Marilee James excited him, by golly. Each time he came into her presence, he felt like a man in a manner he had somehow forgotten along the way. His mind took off with a strong fantasy of drawing her to him, slowly and seductively…hoping he hadn't forgotten how to do that. He imagined kissing her.

It was at this part in the fantasy that he was brought to an abrupt halt, in both mind and vehicle, by the sight of Parker Lindsey's truck sitting in Marilee's driveway.

"Parker's here," Corrine said, as Tate pulled the Cherokee to the front curb. Her delight was apparent, and irritating.

"Yes, he is," Tate said, carefully, mindful that Corrine's young eyes had turned on him with some curiosity.

"Hello, Parker. Good to see you." Tate put the sacks of Coca-Cola on the table and held out his hand for a shake.

"Hello, Tate."

The man's grasp was very firm. Parker Lindsey was an inch taller than Tate and a good ten years younger, maybe, but Tate judged himself to be on the high end of any comparison with the man. He let Lindsey see this in his eyes.

"Marilee says you all are about to run an experiment," Lindsey said.

"Guess we're intent on havin' fun, too."

Tate lined the can and various bottles of Coke on the counter. Marilee brought glasses for each of them, and they began to taste.

"Better rinse with water between each taste," Lindsey advised.

Tate had been going to say that.

The one opinion everyone shared was that the cola in bottles, either the plastic or the small glass, tasted different from the canned cola. Everyone but Willie Lee, whose concentration went to the bubbles in each glass he was handed. He liked how the bubbles tickled his nose when he stuck his nose in the glass. At one point he inhaled too many bubbles and choked, causing Marilee to retire from the testing to keep an eye on him, as he wanted to continue experiencing the bubbles tickling his nose.

"Yep," Tate said. "These smaller bottles of Coke taste a whole lot better."

"I like the canned," Parker said. "And I really doubt you could tell the difference in Coke out of the small bottle or the big one, if you weren't lookin' at it."

"Try me. I won't look."

Tate, aware of being on the childish side but unable to stop himself, handed Lindsey his empty glass, picked up his water glass and swished water in his mouth, then turned his back.

Corrine was looking up at him, a curious expression on her small, heart-shaped face, and he winked at her. "You keep track of what bottle, missy, so there aren't any mistakes." Then he smiled at Marilee, who raised an eyebrow.

Lindsey handed him a glass with a couple of swallows of cola. Corrine watched him as he drank from it.

"Small bottle." Tate handed his glass back to Lindsey.

"Lucky guess. Three tries."

There was the sound of liquid splashed in a glass.

Lindsey gave Tate the glass again. Tate tasted, then tasted again. "One liter."

"Okay."

Lindsey disappeared with the glass behind Tate's back. Tate took a quick swish of water, and repositioned himself for the final taste.

Lindsey handed him the glass with several swallows of brown liquid. Tate drank deeply, swished the cola around his tongue. Lindsey and Corrine gazed at him. Marilee, holding a droopy-eyed Willie Lee, suppressed a grin.

"Small bottle," Tate said.

"You're a good guesser, I give up," Parker said.

Marilee chuckled aloud, which was Tate's reward.

Tate looked at black-and-white photographs of the prairie on the living room wall, while Lindsey, on the sofa like he was used to being there, flipped channels on the television. They were alone. Willie Lee was put to bed, and Marilee was helping Corrine in her bath.

"Why don't you go on home?" Lindsey said suddenly.

Tate looked around. "Why don't you?"

"I belong here."

"Do you?"

Lindsey gazed at him. "Marilee and I are engaged."

"Oh? I hadn't heard that."

He let himself survey Lindsey, and saw the man gearing up to say something more, but just then Marilee and Corrine appeared out of the hallway. "Corrine's ready to say good-night."

"Well, good night, missy. I sure enjoyed our taste testin'." He always fell into a deep Southern drawl with young ladies.

"Good night, Corrine." Lindsey did not have much of an accent.

"Good night," Corrine responded in a faint, shy voice.

Marilee disappeared with Corrine, and reappeared a few minutes later. She looked uncertain, and Tate figured he would do best to take the initiative of making things easier on her. People always greatly appreciated the person who made things easier.

"I'd best be goin'," he said. "Thanks a lot for the dinner and the company. Good seein' you again, Parker."

At the door, he looked long into the deep pools of Marilee's blue eyes and wondered if he dared kiss her.

"Thank you for an evenin's hospitality. I enjoyed it mightily, Miss Marilee."

"I did, too.

"Good night." He leaned over and kissed her cheek.

She became very still. "Good night, Tate."

He turned and walked away. When he reached the sidewalk, he briefly looked back. Marilee was standing there, gazing after him. He waved, and she waved. As he continued on walking beneath the streetlights, he mulled things over and decided Marilee was not thoroughly engaged as yet. And what he needed to do was give her a proper kiss. A kiss would reveal the possibilities between them.

The Valentine Voice
View from the Editor's Desk
by Tate Holloway

I would like to start this new era of *The Valentine Voice* off with a public thank you to all the people who have made me welcome and voiced support for the newspaper. An anonymous gifter left a basket of homemade jams and fruit on my front porch. Thank you. It was all *Delicious*. I wouldn't mind if you left another.

In speaking with people these weeks since my arrival in this beautiful town, I've been asking questions and compiling a number of concerns from the citizenry. I thought I would share the main ones with you here.

Mr. Winston Valentine says, "I think the town needs more public benches. We have a few on Main Street, but we older people don't live on Main Street. We need benches on the streets where we live and walk."

It was reported that Lucy Kaye Sikes felt faint during a recent walk and had to sit to rest on the curb of East Porter Street, and would still be there if Winston had not come along to help her to her feet.

Miss Julia Jenkins-Tinsley, our postmistress, says, "I would appreciate people paying attention when the wind is up and close the post office door behind them. It gets caught in the wind every couple of months, and that thingamajig that's supposed to close the door gets ripped right off. If people would read the sign I put up, it wouldn't keep happening."

Mr. Jaydee Mayhall, who is a candidate for city council, says, "I don't like a prison in our midst, and if I had been on the council when the matter came up, we would not be having to deal with it now. Vote for me."

Mr. Juice Tinsley, who is also a candidate for the city council, had this to say in response to Mr. Mayhall, "For one thing, it is a detention center, not a prison, and it will bring jobs and more people spending money in this town. I'm all for it, and I intend to support it, if elected or not."

My own suggestion to the city council is for planting trees along the sidewalks of Main Street. I'm heading up a petition for signatures of citizens who would like to see these trees, and I'll be taking the petition to next month's meeting of the council.

Please come by the *Voice* offices and sign the Tree Petition, or simply come by to visit and give us your views on what improvements you would like to see in your town, or what it is you like about your town. We want to be your voice in the community. The coffee is always hot and the door always open.

Charlotte, given the dubious honor of editing her boss's work, did not approve of the editorial. She thought it way too familiar in tone, and that he was opening them up for all sorts of kooks and weirdos and just plain time wasters. She thought the paper should set a more formal standard of leadership and not *mingle*. Ms. Porter, who everyone knew was a kind and compassionate soul, nevertheless had known the wisdom of retaining her place as a leader, not a mingler.

Charlotte brought this argument up to her boss and

suggested he might want to rework his editorial, especially the last paragraph.

But Tate Holloway was a man set on his own way. "Keep an open mind, Charlotte, or you get old. Change can be good."

"You could put down a time we are open for visitors," she suggested, motioning with her pencil. "Maybe Wednesdays, after noon." That was going to be their least busy time from now on.

"People won't remember that." He gazed at her and then said, "How 'bout you just check my spellin' and punctuation and let it go?"

"You were the one who gave it to me to edit," she pointed out, tapping her pencil on the paper. "You have spell-checker on your machine."

"Yes, but it makes mistakes. Won't catch *there* and *their,* you know, and I interchange those a lot."

"Do you want *delicious* capitalized?"

"No…that was a mistake. Glad you caught that."

"There isn't such a word as *gifter,*" she pointed out.

"Well, hmmm…" He knotted his eyebrows and rubbed his cheek. "I guess we should change that. Put *citizen* in place of *gifter.* I don't like it, but we have an educational standard to uphold."

She was glad he had some standard, even if she found it lacking.

"If you decide to reconsider about inviting all and sundry to come in here, I will be able to change it until 10:00 a.m. tomorrow." She placed the editorial in the layout, with a reminder to check before sending it to the printer.

Ten

Life's Unexpected Moments

Munro lay on the rug in front of the kitchen sink. His children sat at the table, doing something that caused them to speak in low voices and every once in a while laugh.

His lady came in to speak to the children. Munro liked her voice, most especially when it held a smile. Lying there, his eyes contentedly closed, he listened to his humans; that was how he thought of them, as *his* humans.

"I made a gir-affe, like in my bo-ok," Munro's boy said.

"Well, it sure is. Good job, honey. Did Corrine help you?" It was his lady's voice; it made Munro's tail twitch happily.

"No." This was Munro's girl, her voice soft, slow and true, like a sun-warmed creek in summer. "All I told him was to use the yellow clay, that giraffes are yellow with brown spots. He made it all by himself, though."

"He did?"

"Yes, I did."

"Well, my goodness…this is really something…."

Quite suddenly, Munro's ear detected another sound, and his head came up. Someone was at the front door. *Someone was opening the front door.* Instinct had him up and at the kitchen door, peering around the jamb and through the house. The person entering the front door was a stranger.

Munro went in a silent, streaking motion toward the door.

"Marilee…Marilee!" The stranger's eyes fell on him and went wide. "Yeeaaw!" A bulging brown bag came flying at Munro, and the woman's scream ripped the air.

Munro ducked the bag, at the same time seeing the contents—which were nothing but cloth—spill out across the floor.

"Mother? What is the problem?" It was his lady, her footsteps clicking, her voice now filled with alarm.

Munro, peeking out from around the big chair, watched and listened to the two humans, trying to judge if he might need to defend his charges or hide himself.

"That dog just about attacked me." The stranger pointed at Munro and her voice was sharp enough to cause him to wince.

"Munro?"

His lady's voice held a question. He looked upward to see eyes searching him. Then she smiled in a way that made him feel he'd done a good thing after all, even if he had not been going to attack this silly woman. He had been ready for attack, though, and he knew he had done right with that.

"Well, I guess he didn't realize…since you let yourself in. He doesn't know you, Mother. It's okay, Munro. She can come in." His lady patted his head, causing his heart to swell up in the right place.

Although still a little embarrassed, and quite annoyed with this stranger, Munro returned confidently to his rug in the kitchen.

"You should watch that dog," the woman with the sharp voice said. "He slips around, and he could have a vicious streak. You don't know…."

She went on in that sharp voice, and Munro thought maybe she would profit by his giving her a bite on the ankle.

Corrine went into Aunt Marilee's room to try on the clothes her grandmother had brought her: two dresses and a skirt and blouse. They all came from the secondhand thrift store, and so did the red plastic car Willie Lee played with in their room. The car looked brand-new. The clothes did, too. But they weren't.

Wearing the first dress, Corrine looked at herself in the mirror. She wondered if the dress was supposed to look like this on her. She wanted to tear it off and stomp on it. But doing that would make everyone mad at her.

Slowly she opened the door and went out to display herself to her aunt and grandmother. She was in sock feet, and they did not hear her.

Her grandmother was saying, "She's dating a lawyer from the district attorney's office. He's taken her out three times in a week."

Aunt Marilee said something in a low voice.

"Well, Anita says he is quite a big-wig…and he drives a Jaguar."

Corrine, not wanting to hear another word about her mother having a boyfriend, entered the room.

"Well, now…" Her grandmother's head came around. "That looks really pretty. It's a little big, but she'll grow into it."

Corrine jerked her eyes over to Aunt Marilee to judge what was the truth, seeing immediately that the dress was not right.

"Mom, she isn't goin' to grow into that until next year."

"Well, then it'll last her. Turn around, honey, let's get a good look."

Corrine did as she was told. Her eyes coming around again to her Aunt Marilee, she had the urge to run and throw herself into her aunt's arms.

"It's not that big. Children grow."

Corrine headed back to Aunt Marilee's room. Just inside the door, she stopped, hearing her grandmother and Aunt Marilee.

"Mom, why can't you buy her something new? Something that fits now?"

"You have to buy big for children. I always did for you girls. You and Anita grew so fast at that age, I couldn't keep clothes on your back. It's no sense buying new, when she'll be right out of it before you know it."

Corrine pushed the door closed and went to the bed, ripped off the dress and took up the second one. It was green and looked like a melon.

Then she plopped on the bed and brought her legs up and clutched them, wishing to make herself very small. She wished she could just disappear and not be any more trouble to anyone.

Marilee walked her mother to her car in the driveway.

"I don't think Corrine liked the dresses." Her mother was hurt.

"She thanked you for them, Mom." This was the best Marilee could think to say.

"She should wear dresses more. Anita hasn't taught her, and now you have to teach her, Marilee. You need to teach her to wear dresses and fix her hair, to be ladylike. Pretty is as pretty does. If you let her keep on wearing jeans and overalls—" her voice dropped "—she'll turn out strange."

"Oh, she will not, Mom. She's only eleven, for heavensake. What do you want—her to paint her fingernails and start dyin' her hair?"

Her mother said with a knowing air, "Eleven is a lot older these days than what it used to be when you were a child."

Marilee wanted to say that eleven had been quite old enough when she had been there, but she stopped all the resentful thoughts that tried to crowd into her mind.

"There is plenty of time for Corrine to grow up," she said. "She needs to just be a child and not think anything about growing up."

"Life doesn't allow us much *not* thinking about tomorrow," her mother said primly. "And that is what Anita is doing. She's looking down the road for some security, and it is a fact of life that she will be more secure with a husband who has a successful career than she will be alone, trying to make it on a secretary's salary. You need to think about that with Parker. Don't throw away what Parker could give you, Marilee. There's nothing wrong with finding a man with a future."

Marilee took a breath. "How are the tires doin'?"

"Oh…they're fine, I guess. Carl thought they were too expensive. I was afraid of that when you picked these." She looked at the front tire and frowned.

Marilee looked at the tire and held her lips together.

"Well, I guess I'd better go." Her mother cast her that rather helpless expression, as if knowing things were not right between them but not having a clue as to what to do about it. Marilee felt the same.

Marilee hugged her mother. At least she could do that. "Goodbye, Mom. Drive careful."

She stood politely in the drive, thinking she was glad to give her mother a daughter who watched and waved as her mother drove away in the gleaming Cadillac with the brand-new, too expensive tires.

Willie Lee and Corrine were both in their bedroom. Marilee went on to her own room and saw the clothes Corrine had left neatly spread upon the bed. Corrine was the neatest eleven-year-old Marilee had ever seen.

She held up one of the dresses, and then the other, and then the skirt and blouse, looking them over, shaking her head at both the colors and the large size. Painful memories of her childhood flitted across her mind. For a long time Marilee had believed that all children stuffed newspaper in the toes of their shoes to keep them from flopping off at the heel. There had been that black coat that she had hemmed two full turns; she had thought that made it the correct size, but then someone had pointed out how it hung off her shoulders. One day she had glanced at her image in the girl's bathroom mirror at school and seen a child's face in an old-lady's coat. She had been seventeen when she finally realized that she was not likely to wear a large in anything, because she wasn't going to grow much further.

Hearing a sound, she turned and saw Corrine in the doorway.

"Do you really like any of these?" Marilee gestured to the clothes.

"They're okay." Corrine's expression, as usual, was carefully guarded.

"You don't have to like them. You did the polite thing by thanking your grandmother, but you don't have to wear any of these."

Marilee tried to read her niece but couldn't. She wanted very much to shake the child and say, "Speak up. Tell me what you want."

Corrine gave a small shrug.

"Well, they're too big for you right now. We'll store them in my closet for a while." She reached into her closet for hangers, and her eyes fell on a bit of fur peeking out at the end of the closet rod. Beginning to chuckle, she wrestled the piece from the press of clothing and held it out for Corrine to view.

Corrine's eyes went wide.

"This was a present from your grandmother."

Marilee held the pink robe with the fake fur collar up in front of her and then sashayed a two step. "Can't you just see me wearing this when I take out the garbage?"

She was rewarded by Corrine's grin.

"Your grandmother tries to please. It's just that her ideas don't quite match ours. But still, it is the thought that counts. This is the only way she knows to show her love."

Her niece's heart-shaped face relaxed with understanding, and she nodded.

Marilee put the robe and Corrine's dresses in the back of the closet.

"You know, all of us really do need some summer clothes. Let's go shoppin' tomorrow." Now, there was an outstanding idea!

"Okay," Corrine said, and there seemed to be a glimmer of eagerness in her face.

Anita telephoned late that afternoon. She spoke for five minutes to Corrine and then wanted to speak to Marilee.

"I'm in a hurry," her sister said, sounding somewhat breathless. "I got a date, and he's pickin' me up in half an hour. He's an attorney."

"Mom told me this afternoon. She brought Corrine some clothes."

"Oh, Lordy, are they like what she used to buy us?"

"Pretty much." Marilee felt a warm connection to her sister flow over her. "Corrine does need some new clothes. She's grown quite a bit. I'm going to take her shopping tomorrow." Marilee thought how much fun it would be if her sister could join them in shopping.

"Okay. I'll send you some money from my next check."

The fantasy of them shopping together disintegrated. "When are you comin' up to visit?" she asked.

"I don't know. I can't get any time off, with just startin' and all."

"There are weekends."

"I'm tryin' to save money, Marilee. It takes money to get a nice place and everything. And I really don't think my car will make it up there and back."

"Corrine needs to see her mother, Anita." Marilee was aggravated at herself; she sounded as harping as her own mother.

"Look, things are really goin' good for me right now. I got this new job, and I've met Louis, and he's so great. I'm gettin' myself together, and who knows—maybe soon I'll have a new daddy for Corrine. I'd just love to do that for her. Oh…Louis is here. I gotta run. Kiss my baby for me."

"Anita! She likes the cards you send. Don't stop." Marilee wasn't quite certain why she felt the need to say that. She was feeling a strange panic, as if she needed to reach through the phone and grab hold of her sister to keep her with them and safe.

"Great, I won't…bye now." Then she was gone and the line went dead.

Marilee hung up and stood there for a long minute trying to believe that her sister would actually send money, and experiencing the strong urge to run down there and get Anita.

She always felt the need to save Anita, only she was not exactly sure what from.

As she checked the cabinets and tried to drum up interest in making supper, wondering if Parker might find

Chef Boyardee canned spaghetti acceptable, it came to her that it had been almost two weeks since she had promised Parker to consider marrying him.

Receiving this thought with some alarm, she checked the Stidham Texaco calendar hanging on the kitchen wall beside the telephone and saw that this was exactly the case.

Guilt assailed her. She had not given the question much thought at all. It was not that she did not care, but so many other things seemed to have taken pre- cedence since then. Researching and developing lesson plans for teaching the children, planning their days to include stimulating activities, adjusting to new conditions at the paper and new working arrangements—all of that left little time to consider meals, much less marriage.

And Parker had been very busy these last weeks, too, as he always was with each springtime. She had seen him only on brief occasions, and a number of days they had only spoken on the telephone. In fact, Parker had not made one tiny mention of the marriage proposal in these weeks.

While she remained uncertain about marrying Parker, Marilee did know that she did not want to lose him alto- gether. She and Parker had enjoyed a good friendship; they knew each other quite well in ways that some people could only imagine.

Certainly Parker deserved much more than the ne- glectful attention she had given him of late. And now that her guilt was working on her, she began to berate herself for foolish behavior in throwing away something dear and precious that she had with Parker.

She reached for the telephone and dialed his number at the veterinary clinic. Parker himself answered.

"Would you like to come to supper this evening?" she asked straight away, thinking maybe she should have identified herself. It was possible he had forgotten her voice during these days of little communication.

"Ah…yeah, that'd be great." He seemed surprised but eager as he explained he had surgery on a dog to complete before he could get away.

"That will be fine," she said, pleased to accommodate him. "We will have lasagna."

She hung up and threw herself into motion.

Eleven

A Woman Like Her

It was growing dark when Marilee spread the cream-colored linen cloth over the small table in the dining area. She set two tapered candles in crystal candlesticks in the middle of the table, then stood back to observe the look, wondering if she was getting carried away.

She was not trying to get Parker all worked up. It was just that she felt she owed him something for her recent neglect of him, for disappointing him in the sexual department, and for his patience in waiting for her to make up her mind about his marriage proposal. He deserved repayment for putting up with her indecisiveness.

She had, since phoning him about supper, been trying to decide about marriage. The question had lodged like a splinter in her brain, and she had not been successful in working it to one side or the other. She simply could not bring either a yes or a no to the forefront. What she hoped to accomplish tonight was to be able to work herself more in the direction of yes, and to keep Parker over on that side, too.

She was gathering silver and the good china plates when there came a rap at the back door. Tate smiled at her through the glass. She was not all that surprised. Had she been thinking of it, and not so much about her dilemma, she would have expected him; he had been dropping by for brief visits every few days since moving into the big house beyond her fence.

"Hello," he said when she opened the door.

"Hello."

She stepped back, letting him enter, glad to see the appreciation in his eyes as he looked at her, glad to know that she could get a man's blood up.

Then all this gladness produced a great anxiety. She was, of course, dressed for Parker, so she did not need to be so glad to see Tate. Of course it was simply a normal thing, pleasure at a man's appreciation. But she had everything planned out here. She didn't need Tate Holloway interrupting.

"Wow, it smells good in here," Tate said.

"Lasagna." Then she hurriedly added, "I'm having Parker for supper."

Tate's eyebrows went up. "You are? Does that mean you cooked him…or you're havin' him…here, I mean?"

"Parker is coming to supper," she stated, ignoring his innuendo and heading into the dining room with the plates and silverware.

Tate, of course, came right on her heels. Setting the two places and folding the linen napkins, she refused to look at him. It paid to be cautious around Tate Holloway, who was such an unpredictable man. He seemed to awaken tendencies that she did not need to have. She hoped he left quickly. She had already experienced the awkwardness of trying to deal with the two men together. They had been a handful together the previous week, during the Coke taste-testing episode.

"Well, looks like a romantic dinner for two," Tate said.

"Yes." She felt his intense gaze and didn't want to meet it. Best not to encourage him.

He followed her back into the kitchen.

She told him that she was sorry she didn't have time to visit with him, but Parker would be arriving any minute.

He pulled out a chair and sat down anyway. "I wanted to let you know that a new notebook computer will be delivered tomorrow…probably in the afternoon. A technician will bring it and make certain it is all set to work on the network. I should be able to get a firm time tomorrow morning, and I'll call you."

"Okay. Oh…I'd planned to do some shopping. I'll do it in the morning and try to be home by one." She got the lasagna out of the oven.

"I'll make sure the tech works around that schedule." He leaned forward and sniffed the air with appreciation. "Woo-ee, that smells delicious."

She set the casserole on a trivet and admired it.

"The kids aren't goin' to get any of that?" he asked.

"They ate earlier. They're in bed."

"Too bad." He was eyeing the dish. "I just had a ham sandwich a couple of hours ago. No cheese, either." He looked at her.

She jerked her gaze away and popped the foil-wrapped Italian bread into the oven, then wiped her hands on a towel. "Is that all you needed—to tell me about the computer?"

His eyebrows went up. "Yes, I suppose so."

To her relief, he rose and started for the door. Then, his hand on the doorknob, he stopped. "You know, Lindsey isn't the man for you."

It took her a few seconds to process this startling comment.

"He isn't?"

"No, not at all. A woman like you needs a more mature type."

What could she say to this outrageous statement? And what did he mean *"a woman like you?"*

"My first husband was older by fifteen years."

"I said mature type, not necessarily getting on in years."

"I suppose you have come to know me, and Parker, enough in two short weeks to form this opinion?"

"I've been a journalist for a long time. It's a job that teaches you about people. Parker Lindsey isn't up to you."

Up to her? It made her sound like she was a trial.

She gazed at him, with his arm propped on the doorjamb and his body draped there like so much sovereign male.

"Well, thank you for your opinion. You'll understand if I feel I have to make my own decision." He had managed to draw her along where she did not want to be.

"Oh, yes, I suppose you do. Everyone has to find things out for themselves."

"Yes, and now you can leave." Her strong urge to have him out propelled her into incivility. She quite suddenly could not face him and Parker together, and went so far as to step forward, motioning with her hands, as if to sweep him out.

A foot from him, she found herself eye to eye with him.

She gazed at him, and he gazed at her.

She thought for an instant he was going to kiss her, to reach out and take her to him with his strong arm on which blond hairs shone and kiss the fire out of her. She turned her head, in the manner of veering away, knowing she could not, under any circumstances, let him kiss her.

"I have a dinner guest due to arrive any moment." She adjusted the apron around her waist.

He opened the back door and then stopped, saying, "Oh, could I borrow some tea? I meant to ask for that right off. I'd like to have some iced tea, but I don't want to have to go to the store."

She went directly to the cabinet, opened the door and reached in for the box of tea bags. He wanted to know if she had loose tea.

She threw the box of tea bags back on the shelf and strode to the freezer.

As she delved into the freezer for the box of tea, she heard Parker's soft call from the living room and his footsteps approaching.

"Well, good evenin', Lindsey," Tate said. He had planned this.

"Yeah…hi." Parker's eyes went from Marilee to Tate and back again.

"Tate was just borrowin' some tea. He's leaving."

"Yes, you two have a nice evenin'," Tate said, casting a wave before letting himself out the back door.

"Is that guy over here all the time now?" Parker frowned as he rolled his sleeves to wash his hands.

"He has only been over here a couple of times." She got the bread out of the oven.

What in the world had he meant, *"a woman like you?"*

"What is this?" Parker asked, observing the formally set table with surprise and wonder that gave her great pleasure.

Marilee, who was lighting candles, blew out the match and smiled. "I thought we could have a quiet meal and relax. That's all, relax a bit, talk a bit. We need to talk. The children ate earlier. Willie Lee's already asleep. Corrine's reading, or she was. I'll check on her in a minute."

She went to the kitchen for the food, and Parker stepped quickly to help her.

"I'm starved," he said, eyeing the food with an enthusiasm that made her feel she had done a very good deed after all.

So, Tate Hollway…you and your opinion can go jump.

"Here," she said, handing him the bottle of wine. "Please pour our glasses, while I go check on the children."

She left him in the kitchen and went to peek in the children's bedroom, hoping to find both children asleep. They were. Willie Lee was out with his face buried in the pillow, as usual for him. Munro, who had taken to sleeping with Corrine in something of a sentry manner, opened his eyes but didn't move. Corrine had fallen asleep with the book on her chest. Marilee removed the book and turned out the lamp, and could not resist touching each child's head.

Returning, she paused in the hallway. She stood there, with her breath held and time stopped, looking across the living room at Parker sitting in the glow of the candle-light. The wine in their glasses sparkled.

Did she dare tell him she would marry him? It was time. She should not let him get away. She *did* care for him, and her heart swelled with feeling.

She stepped out, determined to follow where the night led.

"Kids asleep?" he asked, eating heartily from his salad.

"Yes. Corrine fell asleep reading. She's been such a light sleeper, but Munro seems to have helped that. She seems to be sleeping through the night since he started staying with her."

"Hmmm." He was eating quite hungrily, in the way that satisfies a woman.

Marilee passed the plate of Italian bread toward him. "Try the bread. I got it fresh at the bakery today."

He bit into a slice of the buttery bread and made an ap-preciative sound. "This is delicious, just delicious," he said, pointing to all the food with his fork.

"Thank you."

Serving herself, she looked at her plate and inhaled the rich aromas of butter and garlic. She looked across at Parker. She realized that she was attempting to feed Parker a full luscious meal in order to make up for denying him an intimate portion of herself. Apparently she was succeeding.

She took up her own fork and began to eat. It was delicious. She had outdone herself. She should have made two dishes of lasagna and frozen one.

Parker lifted his wineglass. "To the cook."

She lifted hers, clinked against his, and then drank deeply.

Attempting to start the conversation off with easy topics, Marilee asked Parker if he'd had any interesting cases lately. He replied that he hadn't had anything out of the ordinary, although he *had* had the tragic case of a mare dying in foal.

"Real nice barrel-racing mare," he said, and he paused in his eating, his shoulders slumping, and sat there with a dark stare at the table. Even knowing the facts of life, Parker always blamed himself a great deal when he lost an animal, and Marilee always felt helpless, because she could do nothing for him.

Trying to retrieve a positive focus, she asked about the mare's baby, and he said, brightening, that it was a healthy filly, that he had secured a wet mare for it from Ray Horn, and the mare had taken the filly immediately. "Ray didn't think the mare would take the baby, but I've done it before. Some mares do, some don't. This one did."

"Well, that's wonderful," Marilee said. "Who owns the baby?"

"Leanne Overton. She's Charlene's cousin. I guess she's livin' out there with Charlene and Mason for a while. Some trouble with an ex-husband, I gather."

Marilee tried to remember Leanne but could not.

Parker offered the information that she was quite a successful barrel racer and that she had three high-dollar horses, another one ready to foal any time.

"Do you suppose that the children and I might come along with you sometime and see a live birth?" Marilee asked, feeling enthused at the idea.

Parker said, "I guess so."

Marilee had the uncharitable thought that she could do with him giving up the word *guess*.

"Aren't they a little young for that sort of thing?" he asked.

Marilee, who found his hesitant tone annoying, pointed out Willie Lee's early acquaintance with his rabbits. "If children are acquainted with the facts of life in a natural way, they accept it as natural, as it should be. And Corrine is already so far advanced in biology. I've been looking at schoolbooks for her for next year. It is amazing what kids are taught these days."

"So you plan to have Corrine with you next year?" He frowned with disapproval.

"I don't know…. I guess I'm not planning anything." Oh, dear, now *she* was using the word. "But I *am* prepared."

She didn't like the feeling of needing to defend herself. Maybe it had something to do with "a woman like her." Tate's phrase repeatedly echoed in the back of her mind— and in his voice, too. She wished she could slap the image.

She drank the rest of her wine and then pointed out that she planned on next year in the same manner that most people planned on next year. "I hope to be alive, and thus far I am given to believe that Corrine will for some time need me to be looking after her."

Parker nodded, appearing to take that in. After a minute, he said, "How is Anita doing? Have you heard from her?"

"She's been sending Corrine cards, and she called twice this week." She felt pleased to give this report. "She has a job at the Tarrant County Courthouse. Secretary, to a judge, I think."

"Sounds encouraging. Benefits and everything?"

"She says so."

"This may be the time she gets her act together," Parker said.

Marilee tore a slice of bread. "Anita has been trying to get herself together for all of her life. Unfortunately, about the time she does, she gets herself hooked on something and comes unraveled again." Marilee was a little ashamed at this bit of sarcasm popping out.

Parker raised an eyebrow at her.

"Okay, Anita is trying and is doing very well," she said more properly. "But past history has me on the cautious side. I don't know if Corrine will still be here for school in the fall or will be able to return to Anita, but it seems prudent, given past experience, to make plans for her schooling and to remain available, just in case.

"The chances are high that I will have Corrine popping in and out of my life. I am, as I have said, a woman with two children. That is how it is, and I'm sorry if it displeases you."

Maybe her sharp attitude answered the question of what "a woman like her" was. *Contentious* came to mind.

"I didn't say it displeased me." He seemed awkward with the word. "I just don't want to see you get hurt, Marilee. Corrine is not your child, and you will have to give her back to Anita when Anita decides to take her. You don't want to look at this. You are gettin' way too involved with her. You are making a burden for yourself that you don't need to have."

"A burden? I don't consider my niece a burden."

"I didn't mean it like that. I meant that you are complicating your life in a way that you don't need to."

"And therefore I complicate your life."

"Well, yes, it does that. And you don't seem to care how it will affect me."

Marilee stared at him. The truth in his words stung, and she wanted to sting back.

"You are an adult, Parker. She is a child. Virtually a motherless child. You condemn me for what I give her? You feel neglected because of it?"

He got all red in the face.

They were now more or less in a good argument. Parker pointed out once again, in different words and with the aid of his fork, that she had no legal claim to Corrine, and that Anita could come and take her at any moment, and there was nothing Marilee could do about it.

"Forgive me if I don't care to see you hurt," he added.

Marilee pointed out that she knew this fact very well, and that Corrine was her niece and would always be her niece.

"I have to be there for her. There isn't anyone else."

It came to her that Parker was an only child of two

rather cool and distant parents. His father had been dead some years, and his mother had remarried and moved to Colorado. It would be difficult for him to relate to feelings for one's sister's child.

"I know this is hard for you to understand, because you have no brother or sister, but Corinne is a blood relative, as close to me as my own child. I was there with Anita when she was born," she added, remembering it all for an instant—the excitement, the wonder, the bit of sadness that the child was not her own and that she had known even then, that Corinne was in for a rough road with Anita, and that she, Marilee, was hopeless to prevent so many painful problems.

She gazed at Parker with her heart full of emotion that spilled over to him.

He pretty well wiped this out, however, by saying, "The best thing you can do for Corrine is to help her with her own mother and quit buttin' in."

She was shocked by her urge to reach across and slap him.

She said evenly, "I am not *butting in.* It was Anita who asked me to come get Corrine, Parker."

Each recognizing how close they were coming to the line, they shut up. Marilee ate her lasagna, which was now sticking in her throat, and Parker mopped up the sauce on his plate.

They finished the meal in comparative silence broken only by occasional overly polite comments, in the manner of two people who are afraid one more cross word might be the last hot straw that ignites a flame to burn down the house.

* * *

Parker helped her to clear away the dishes; then he kissed her neck and cajoled her into kissing him, right there at the kitchen sink.

"I'm sorry we argued. I really am." He gave her his best little-boy grin.

"I am, too." Perhaps it had been more her fault than his.

She kissed him good and wondered what in the world was wrong with her. Pushing lingering resentment aside, she took his hand and led him to the couch, where they settled close together in the low light and talked softly of this and that, all innocuous subjects, while Parker kept getting more and more intimate with his hands, and Marilee kept getting more anxious.

She was annoyed with herself for not coming out and asking, *Do you still want to marry me? Let's get this stuff straight.* She was annoyed with him for not taking the initiative to speak up on the matter.

She could not say any of this. She certainly could not bring up the marriage question. Better to let him bring it up. It was a man thing.

When he did bring it up, she would say yes. That was it. She would say yes. She kissed him deeply with this thought.

And then Parker's mobile phone went off, his answering service relaying an emergency message.

"It's Leanne's mare," he told Marilee, as he clicked off from the service and began punching numbers on the little phone.

He spoke into it and said the name Charlene in a brief

exchange, ending with, "I'll be right out. I'm leavin' from Marilee's."

He clicked off the phone and rose. "After what happened to the other mare, Leanne's real nervous over this one. I said I'd be right out."

"Charlene and Mason's?"

"Yeah. Mason's there…he's 'bout as good as needs be, too."

She hurried with him to the door and out onto the porch. He broke into a trot to his truck. She held on to the porch post and watched as if he were going off to war, sending prayers with him as he backed out and headed off down the road.

God, please don't let anything happen to this mare. It is so hard for him to have that happen.

She went back inside and softly closed the door, leaned against it and fought back sudden tears that somewhat baffled her.

She was struck with the knowledge that she could pray for the life of a mare, but she could not seem to pray about this situation with Parker.

Brushing her teeth, Marilee glanced into the mirror and stared at herself. She bent to rinse her mouth, and then she stared at her reflection again.

Up to a woman like you.

She was a woman who was quite contrary, she thought. Here she had a good man that she really cared for and she kept picking fights with him.

She was afraid of marriage.

This, of course, was only natural, given her experience

with Stuart, and what she had seen with her own father and mother. Marriage was serious business, not to be entered into lightly, so she was showing good sense to be cautious.

It was more. *Some unnamed fear.*

It was fear of life passing by, and of making the wrong choices and being stuck with them.

With a hard tug on the belt of her robe, she pivoted and left the bathroom, stalking into the kitchen, where she made a cup of chamomile tea, sat at the table and sipped it, while alternately staring and looking away from her reflection in the night-black window.

She went to the back door and peered through the window, but all she could see was dark yard. Trees obscured Tate Holloway's house. She wondered about him.

She did not intend to worry about Tate Holloway. Lord knew she had enough to think about, without going *there*.

Seating herself again at the table, she sipped her tea while her gaze wandered in a slow circle from the red-checked tablecloth to her reflection in the window, to the telephone, then again to the tablecloth.

Finally she pushed herself from the table with a deliberate motion and dialed Parker's home number, halfway expecting the impersonal voice of his answering service.

She was startled to hear a "Hello" in an unfamiliar voice. A *woman's voice.*

"I'm calling Parker Lindsey."

"Oh, this is his phone. Marilee? This is Charlene. Parker left his phone here on the table."

"I'd dialed his home phone. I thought his service

would answer, if he wasn't home." Marilee felt confused, but somewhat relieved to recognize Charlene MacCoy's voice. Charlene was a warm person, and her voice was warm, too.

"Well, I guess they've already switched over here. He's out in the barn with Leanne. Do you want me to go get him?"

"Oh, no, it's not important. How is the mare?"

"She's fine. She had the prettiest baby." Charlene's voice became excited. "Not a paint, like Leanne was expectin', but black, with a white star and white feet. A really nice filly. And there was no trouble at all. That mare just popped her out, when she got ready. Parker swore she was holding things up just because." Someone in the background said something, and Charlene said, "That was Mason, and he says that mare was waitin' for the full moon to get up." She laughed.

"Parker was in here havin' coffee just a few minutes ago, and then him and Leanne went back out there to watch the mare and the baby again. Do you want me to have him call you?"

"No...I imagine he'll be tired. I'll call him in the morning."

"Well, Mason's just goin' out there now. He'll tell him you called."

When Marilee hung up, she laid her forehead against the phone and gave thanks for the healthy filly.

And she wished she did not feel so dissatisfied. It made her feel selfish.

Lying in bed, with the moonlight filtering through the window and making patterns on her coverlet, she contemplated herself and her life. She had the strong urge to pick up the telephone and call Tate Holloway, and she wondered at herself.

She simply had too much of a fondness for telephone talk in the night.

Twelve

In Matters of the Heart

Tate jogged along in front of Marilee's house just as golden light shone into the elms that towered over the blue roof of the squatty white cottage.

With relief, he saw that her Cherokee sat alone in the driveway. No sign of Lindsey's truck.

He jogged on over to Main, where his burning lungs and rubbery legs forced him to walk for over half the block. He was getting better, though, because he recovered by the time he got to the police station. When he turned up Church and was past the police station and getting close to the intersection, he began to wonder what might have happened to Lindsey. There was no sign of the man.

What might have happened at the evening's previous candlelit supper? Was the man too worn-out to jog this morning? He did not like that particular train of thought.

He had dropped to something only resembling a jog

and was approaching his driveway when a figure came pounding around the curve in the street half a block ahead, accompanied by a rider on a bicycle.

It was Lindsey jogging, and the blond-haired woman on the bicycle.

"Mornin'," Lindsey said, when he came near.

"Mornin'," Tate replied and gave a wave.

"Hi," the woman said.

"Hello."

Tate watched the two pass, Lindsey jogging and the woman on her bicycle beside him. *Together?*

Tate jogged up his driveway and around to the back door, up the steps and inside and all the way upstairs and into his bathroom for a shower.

He did not think he should jump to hopeful conclusions about the disintegration of the romance between Marilee and Lindsey. Sometimes things were not always what they seemed. A major rule for a journalist was to get the facts.

But he whistled as he showered. By golly, he was showing improvement in the jogging area. Don't count him over the hill yet.

"We'll see you tomorrow, Editor," called Sherry, the waitress who worked the late-afternoon shift at the Main Street Café.

The few other patrons added their friendly goodbyes.

"Later, buddy," from Juice Tinsley, and a wave from Norm Stidham, who had a mouth full of raisin pie.

"Don't forget to send Marilee to cover the Homemakers meeting on Thursday. We're showing the video Ms.

Porter sent from Cairo," said Kaye Upchurch, who was sitting with her mother, Odessa Collier.

"Marilee'll be there."

"Good to have seen you, Tate." Odessa gave her sultry smile.

Odessa Collier had to be pushing seventy but was still hot enough to strip wallpaper, Tate would bet.

He winked at her.

Folding the newspaper beneath his arm, he stepped out into the brightness of a May afternoon.

Thank you, Lord, for this happy minute. He thought of it with the feeling of a man who had been in combat in the jungles of Viet Nam, not to mention all the painful stories he had covered in his life as a journalist. He knew how fleeting happiness was in life on earth.

On this wonderful afternoon he was living what he considered the epitome of his dream. He had formed the habit to head to the Main Street Café at midafternoon each day, where he would get a glass of iced tea and sometimes a slice of pecan pie, and enjoy an informal chat with anyone there. After about fifteen minutes he would head on over to Blaine's Drugstore, where he would get another glass of iced tea or maybe an ice-cream cone, and chat some more with Vella Blaine and whoever came in.

In this way, he got a pulse on the town. He discreetly jotted down the names of people he met, and at night he went over the names and recalled the faces in order to have them handy on his tongue for the next time he met them, or to mention in his editorials. In this fashion, he felt he was making a lot of people happy, and at the same time he built circulation, which was already up by nearly a hundred people. People liked to see their names in print, and he liked to place the names there. It was a happy merging of desires.

This afternoon, upon leaving the drugstore after an ice-cream cone and a chat with Miss Vella, Miss Dixie Love and Gerald Overton of the Citizens Bank, he felt somewhat victorious, as if he'd scaled a tall mountain. He supposed he had only arrived at the first plateau—he had simply gotten moved into town and made some necessary decisions and implemented the biggest one of those, which was keeping the paper going and changing it to a twice weekly. So far he was living his dream and keeping a number of people employed and able to feed their families. Well and good. He tried not to think about the enormous precipice before him in the form of a giant debt, and the somewhat daunting matter of how he would live out the rest of his life.

One day at a time, he reminded himself, as he hopped over the door of his convertible and directed his BMW around the block to drive by Marilee's house and saw only her Cherokee parked in the driveway. His curiosity over what had transpired with the candlelit supper was about to eat a hole in his brain.

Whipping his car on around the corner and into his driveway, he grabbed the bag of groceries out of the seat and went straight to the kitchen, where he made a pitcher of sweet iced tea. He picked up the pitcher and the new box of loose leaf tea he had bought to replace what he had borrowed. Then he stopped and tossed the box of tea back on the counter, before heading out the back door and across the yard to the gate in the fence.

It squealed as he opened it. Late-afternoon sunlight

filtered through the trees down onto the garden patch. Tate looked at it and thought that Marilee needed a plow.

When he reached the back steps of the little bungalow, he glanced upward and saw Corrine gazing out the kitchen window at him. She disappeared, and a moment later the door swung open to him.

"Hello, Mr. Tate."

"Evenin', missy. How are you? Why, is that a new bow in your hair?"

"Yes," she replied with her normal solemness. "Aunt Marilee is in cursin' at the computer you had sent over today."

"Oh, she is?"

He grinned, coaxing a grin in return from the girl, whose eyes looked so much deeper than her years. He had already formed an idea of her situation, a formation based on his instincts about people and bits and pieces of knowledge discreetly picked up along the way about Marilee James, her sister and her family. He, having been a similar child, felt great empathy for this one.

"I brought some sweet tea. Let's see if we can sugarcoat the situation."

She said quite quickly and in a low voice, "Mr. Parker was here, but he doesn't know anything about computers, and she ran him off." She shook her head. "I hope you can help."

"Well, I imagine I can." So Lindsey had been there and had not been a help.

Corrine quietly assisted him in getting the glasses and ice cubes. Then she pushed a package of cookies at him. "I think you'd better add chocolate."

When Tate entered the living room, it was with a glass of iced tea in one hand and a chocolate cookie in the other.

Marilee looked up and saw him and glared. "I don't like this new computer."

He lifted the glass and cookie. "I come in peace, to return your tea...made." And then he determinedly grinned his very warmest grin.

"I had peace until I had to learn a new computer. My old one worked just fine."

"Well, now, you couldn't use the Internet with your old one. It is time to get on the information highway or get left behind."

"I might prefer being left behind."

Feeling a little desperate, he held out the glass and cookie, and she took them very slowly.

He watched her bite into the cookie and then look up at him, her eyes deep blue, and chocolate smearing her moist lips. An immediate full-blown fantasy filled his mind of kissing her until she moaned and writhed like a wild woman in his arms.

"You have a cookie crumb on your chin...let me just...there. Now, let's see how I can help you with this computer."

He pulled a chair over and sat on it backward, right next to her, continuing to look at her lips with anticipation. He knew quite suddenly that he was right where he wanted to be.

The sun was far to the west and the breeze dying down. In the process of deadheading her roses, Vella paused and ran a gardener's appreciative gaze over the spring greenery of her rosebushes and upward into the elm trees. "Thank you, God," she whispered, as she almost invariably did at such a sight.

Then she caught sight of Perry's big black car arriving. Anticipation and an ache slipped across her heart at the same moment.

She hurried up the steps and in the back door and straight to the oven, where she checked the meat loaf. It was good and dark, crusty as she liked it to be. She made a superb meat loaf; Winston always praised it all over when she brought it to the church fellowship supper.

"Got the Wednesday *afternoon* edition of the paper," Perry said as he came into the kitchen. He was a big chunk of a man and seemed to fill the kitchen. Just like every other day of the week, on his way to the sink, rolling up his sleeves, he turned on the little television.

Vella looked over her shoulder at the set that sat on the counter. She had a sudden and disturbing fantasy of herself with a shotgun, blasting out the screen.

"I made meat loaf," she said, showing it proudly as her husband sat at the table.

"Hmmm." He glanced at it, then looked at the newspaper. "That Juice Tinsley's goin' all out with advertisin' for the city council seat. Don't know why anyone in their right mind would want the job."

Vella focused on setting the food on the table. She liked the supper table to be colorful, like a bouquet of roses. There was the browned meat loaf with red tomato sauce on top, light-green-and-gold succotash, steamy ivory potatoes, golden butter and tan-kissed rolls.

Perry, who had been using the remote control to flip

channels on the television until he got to his favorite news program, said, "Looks like we're gonna get in another mess over there with them I-rackees." With one eye on the television, he served himself a slice of meat loaf.

Vella wondered, as she had for years now, how a man as educated as Perry—he had big university education from University of Oklahoma and the pharmacist degree, plus lots of courses every year to keep up-to-date—could have slipped back into such poor grammar.

She looked at her gleaming china plate and then at the array of food. She watched her husband fold open the newspaper and hold it with one hand, while eating with the other, and dividing his attention between the newspaper and the television.

"Perry, how is the meat loaf?" She still had not served herself.

"Hmmm...oh, pretty good," he said, his eyes on the newspaper.

"Perry." Vella, who had not yet served her plate, began unbuttoning the front buttons of her shirtwaist. Her heart began a rapid pumping. It was as if her hand was working all by itself.

Perry was now looking at the television. Vella noted the paleness of his complexion, the blue veins over his nose and at his neck. Yet he still had that little cowlick at the top of his head that she had loved from the very first.

"Perry." She now had the top of her shirtwaist fully unbuttoned.

"Huh?" He did not turn his head from the television.

"Perry!"

In an instant she had pushed to her feet so hard that

the chair scooted back and bumped the counter. Then she yanked her shirtwaist wide open to reveal her voluptuous breasts, full and heavy in their support bra.

"Look at me!"

Perry was looking. He gazed straight at her breasts, with his mouth hanging open and his eyes wide as saucers so that she saw the blue irises, which she had not seen in years.

Vella felt triumphant. She had, at long last, succeeded in getting his attention. She felt, too, that she had gone completely mad, but she could not grab hold of caring.

"I'm alive, Perry! I'm alive and sittin' here with you every night!"

"Well, my god," he said.

"Is that all you have to say?"

He closed his mouth and swallowed.

Letting go of her dress, she swept an arm at the table, sending half the dishes and food crashing onto the floor. Her pendulous bosom heaved and swayed.

"I am sick to death of you actin' like I am dead. Like I don't exist, when day after day I work in your store, wash your clothes, cook your supper and clean your pee drips off the toilet. I am a flesh-and-blood woman who goes to bed with you night after night. I have worn perfume and new rayon gowns and put myself in front of you, and you don't even see." She had begun sobbing. "Look at me! I may be old, but I am not dead. *You* are not dead."

Just then some bit of reasoning sliced into her brain, and she saw herself mirrored in his shocked expression. Covering her face with her hands, she fled the kitchen.

Perry, stunned so exceedingly that he could for some seconds only manage to move his head and watch his wife running away, thought, She's gone crazy.

Then fear pierced his brain enough to propel him into action. He struggled to get out of his chair, but his brain was a little ahead of his body in coming awake, so he had a bit of a time getting going and ended up knocking his chair over.

"Vella?" he said hoarsely, and found the name was not familiar on his tongue.

He went upstairs to find her in their bedroom, grabbing clothes out of her dresser drawers and throwing them into two suitcases that lay wide-open on the bed—the suitcases she had bought when she made that trip to New Orleans to look at roses a couple of years ago and that he thought were way too high priced.

"I am leavin' you, Perry. I can't go on like this another minute."

Perry didn't know what to say. He tried to think of something, but nothing would come. He had a sense of being in the *Twilight Zone* television show.

She wouldn't leave. She was a sixty-four-year-old woman. Or maybe she was sixty-five, he wasn't certain.

The next minute she fastened the bulging suitcases, grabbed each handle with her blue-veined hands, dragged the cases off the bed and past him, and threw them down the stairs, denting and scratching the wall they'd paid big bucks to have painted six months ago, and the banister and the floor at the bottom. One by one she hauled the cases out of the house and threw them into her car and drove off into the hot ball of a western sun.

Perry blinked against the glare. The picture left in his mind was of her enormous breasts in white cotton swaying as she slipped behind the steering wheel.

When Vella flew past in her car and saw Winston in his yard taking in his flags, which he could finally do alone these days, she pressed the accelerator harder to keep from stopping and flinging herself into his arms.

It wasn't until she got to Main Street and passed the drugstore, where her daughter Belinda would be working the counter, that she realized she had no place to go. She could not go in and talk about this to Belinda, for heavensake. Belinda was no more a conversationalist than her father, except with Deputy Midgett, with whom she now lived in sin; thank God she had moved out at last, even if it was to the apartment over the drugstore.

There was Minnie Oakes, but generally Vella found Minnie's brain stuffed with straw. Minnie rarely had an original thought, and their friendship was one of sharing stain removal tips and ice-cream cones, not confidences.

Outside of Minnie, Vella could not name a close friend. At least, not a woman friend. There was Winston, but she could not go to him. She certainly didn't want to be included in his "old lady collection."

She drove on along the highway. Maybe she would just keep on driving clear to California and the ocean, take off all her clothes on the beach and walk right into the water naked.

That she was repeatedly coming back to sensuous thoughts became clear to her. She had been battling them for months, and yet they kept getting stronger and stronger.

Tears streamed down her face. *Oh, Lord, what has happened to me? What have I done?*

About five more miles and the cool air blowing on her breasts brought it to her attention that she needed to pull over and fasten up her blouse.

Tate Holloway *was* flirting with her.

Marilee could no longer dismiss the fact of his flirting, as she had tried to do ever since her very first meeting with the man. Trying, and mostly succeeding, to not let Tate's attention be unduly flattering, she nevertheless admitted to herself that she would have to be dead not to find it quite nice.

And she kept recalling how he had told her, in her own kitchen that Lindsey was not a man up to "a woman like her." She wanted very much to question him about that provocative statement, however, she did not think she would like his opinion. She told herself to focus on his instructions for the use of the new whiz-bang computer.

She knew instantly that she had a fine mind to be able to handle so many conflicting thoughts coming into it at one time, yet she did not overly congratulate herself on such a trait, because science had shown that the ability was present in all women. She thought maybe God had sensibly installed it into the female species as a strategy for survival in a man's world.

"Now, Miss Marilee…you don't have to hit that button. You can just tap this little mouse window you're usin' with your finger."

"Oh, that's right." She liked that.

"Are you havin' trouble seein'? Maybe the screen isn't bright enough. All you have to do is use this button. See?"

"Oh, that *is* better!"

"Who is that in the picture?"

"What? Oh, that's my ex-husband, Stuart." It was silly to feel uncomfortable about being asked about Stuart. She noticed that Tate had blue eyes, like Stuart.

"Devil-may-care fellow."

"Yes...he was, pretty much."

"He looks familiar to me." But his blue eyes were on Marilee's, as if he were trying to see into her mind.

She averted her eyes. "You might have seen his work, or even met him. He was quite a well-known photographer. Lots of his stuff in *National Geographic, Life,* a few in *Time.*" And *he* had been a flirt, too.

Tate frowned thoughtfully. "Maybe I have...but I think he more reminds me of Parker Lindsey."

Gazing at the screen, Marilee typed. The letters came out crazy.

"Your left hand needs to move over a key," Tate pointed out.

"This keyboard is awkward."

"You can plug in your big one. I've got the ergonomic ones on order."

"Oh."

"Want me to plug your big one in now?"

"Yes, that might be a good idea."

He did all he was supposed to, quite efficiently; he apparently knew electronic gadgets. She tried the bigger keyboard and found it worked well.

"Does this little thing do the same as a mouse?"

"Yep."

"It's annoying."

"Your choice."

When they finally closed the computer, Marilee was so relieved and delighted to be able to work it that she not only felt compelled to apologize for her sharp behavior but was actually able to do so.

"I'm sorry for being so snippy earlier," she said, almost choking on the words. She thought of how she had been sharp with Parker and knew that she would probably never master the art of apology.

"Ah, Miss Marilee, I don't think I'd give a penny for a woman without some spunk."

He was looking at her in that way of his, as if thoroughly pleased with every bit of her that he saw. A warm flush fell over her and gathered between her legs.

Averting her eyes, she rose and headed for the kitchen. Willie Lee and Munro had fallen asleep together on the couch, and Corrine was sitting in the big chair, reading an *American Girls* book. Marilee didn't think Corrine should see her in that moment. Corrine was too observant by far; she would understand immediately that Marilee felt an attraction for this man. Good Lord, Marilee didn't want anyone to see her being such a fool.

She poured two glasses of iced tea and turned, intent on taking his into the living room, but there he was draped in the doorway.

"Thank you for bringing the iced tea." She held out the glass, and he came over to take it from her.

Drinking deeply from her own, she thought the best course was to drink the tea quickly down and then tell him good-night. She would not ask him about his comment the previous evening. She was going to ignore it.

"You're welcome," he returned quite happily. "It is my way of returning what I borrowed."

"You borrowed an entire box."

"I know. I'll return it a little at a time, all made up."

Then, without benefit of invitation, just as he had done the previous evening, he pulled out a chair and sat himself at the table, saying, "The important thing to know about brewing good iced tea is to use distilled water. And tea bags are okay, but I prefer to use loose tea—black-and-orange pekoe—and pour the hot water over it. You can't go off and let the tea sit there longer than eight minutes, either, because then you get the tannic acid comin' out, and that makes the brew bitter. 'Course, tea made in the sun can sit longer."

"You are a quite a connoisseur of cold tea," Marilee said, both impressed with a man who would take care with such a small thing and wondering how in the devil she would tell him goodbye now with him sitting himself down.

"Good cold tea on a hot day is the secret of life," he replied.

She gazed at him. "I think I've heard you pronounce about three different things as being *the* secret to life."

"Well, you know, Miss Marilee…"

Tate pulled on his ear and grinned that grin, charming enough to coax bees from their hive, "…I'm still searchin' for that one major secret to life."

Marilee wrapped an arm around her middle and held on to herself, quite possibly to keep from going straight to him, throwing herself on his lap and seeing what the kiss in his eyes would feel like on her lips.

The idea was preposterous. The idea of kissing him scared her pants off.

Thankfully, he quite suddenly quit flirting and led the way into discussing the needs down at the newspaper. He said he had that afternoon hired a new layout man, a young guy fresh from college with a graphic art degree. "With the salary I can pay, my choices of experienced people are limited," he said. "He'll be here the end of next month."

Marilee asked him forthrightly if he intended to let any of them go.

"No," he replied instantly. "I may need to switch people around to different jobs, but I'll find a place for everyone."

"You won't be able to switch Zona to another job," Marilee said and moved to sit opposite him at the table. She had to find a way to make certain Zona remained protected.

But Tate said in an understanding manner, "No, I won't be switchin' Zona," and gave a wry smile. "I've begun to wonder if she sleeps in that office. I don't ever see her come or go."

"She does not intend anyone—especially you—to see her. Give her time, though. She'll thaw a little when she gets to know you. It's just that she has a very hard time with change. And with men."

"What's wrong with her?" he asked bluntly.

"The gossip is her overbearing father. What is known,

however, is that she suffered severe schizophrenia in her twenties. Treatment has helped her, allows her to operate outside a hospital, anyway. After her parents died, she was destitute. Then one day Ms. Porter brought her in and made her the bookkeeper. It turned out Zona is a genius with numbers, and somehow Ms. Porter had discovered this. I think Ms. Porter had been trying to help Zona all along."

"Muriel was always like that," he said with a thoughtful nod. "She doesn't look like an altruistic pudding heart, but she is."

Marilee watched his eyes drift down to the table and saw emotions flow across his face. She looked at the tender spot where his hair curled behind his ear. It was white hair there, mingling in with the sun-streaked blond.

Then he was looking back at her, cocking his head. "How many know that Charlotte is in love with Leo?"

Marilee, quite struck by this further proof of his powers of observation, said, "Well, I know, and now you know. I'm not certain Leo knows. He is so used to women doing for him that Charlotte getting coffee for him each morning isn't going to mean much. And Charlotte may be denying it to herself. She's so hungry for a romantic relationship and scared to death of it at the same time."

"That's a common place to be," he said.

"Yes, it is."

She thought his eyes most remarkable, and then she realized he was gazing at her in that way that was sizing her up.

"I read your piece on the detention center," he said. "You did a very good job of keeping to the middle ground."

"I can take that as approval?" She decided to size him up in return.

"Oh, yes, ma'am...I think your ability to present a story without biasing it with your opinions is very good. I think, too, that when you decide to move people with a feature, like the piece I read in the files that you did about the retirement community the MacCoys are building, or the one you did about the young man getting crazed on drugs and threatening people with an unloaded gun, you're even better. You are good at putting your heart in your work. You should do more of it."

Marilee had not before heard much analytical praise for her writing; Ms. Porter had never been one for even the mildest praise of one of her writers. Either what you had written was adequate or it was not, that was all there was to it. Now Marilee wasn't certain how to respond. She felt decidedly uncomfortable.

Tate said, "I want you to do a feature on detention centers across the state, and how each community has been impacted. I want you to show the good and the bad. Then when you come to your own conclusion, you write a piece reflecting that."

"What if I don't come to a conclusion?" she asked right off.

"Then reflect that."

She nodded, thinking immediately of the children.

As if he heard her thoughts, he added, "It'll mean some traveling, but I believe you can take the children with you." He raised an eyebrow.

"Yes," she said slowly. "I can take them with me, or get someone to stay with them." Her interest was spiraling upward at a rapid rate, but caution sat on it. "I haven't ever done that sort of reporting. I wasn't trained as a journalist. I just answered the ad Ms. Porter put in the paper, and there wasn't anyone else who had the least writing ability, so I got the job. Everything I've written has been set right here in Valentine."

"I got all my journalism training on the job, too," he said. "I went to school to be a Baptist minister. While I was at it, I took a job as a sports reporter for the college paper, and, well, once I saw my name in print, I was hooked."

Marilee was busy looking him up and down. There he sat in cowboy boots, faded denims and a soft khaki shirt. She could not identify what type he looked like, but she did not think it was in any way a minister.

He must have picked up her thoughts, as he then said that had all been almost thirty years ago. "I was infinitely more suited to journalism," he said. "I tended to have a certain type of curiosity about people that was less suitable for a minister but quite well suited for a journalist. And at the time I enjoyed whiskey way too much to be a Baptist preacher." He grinned.

"I'm a farm boy from East Texas, who came up narrow and went wide. I was married one time and divorced some fifteen years ago because I wasn't a very good husband. I gave up drinkin' a long time ago, but I sure can get as high on reading history and sweet tea and good blues music."

He paused, and she was not at all certain what was going on, although she felt certain that something was going on.

"What about you, Miss Marilee?"

"Me?" She straightened her spine.

"What can you tell me about you?"

"I'm certain you know all there is to know about me." She fingered her glass and saw that it was empty…his was, too.

"I know you are a native of Valentine but have traveled some," he was saying. "That Vella and Perry Blaine are your aunt and uncle, and that you are divorced from that devil-may-care fellow in the picture, who I believe you said was fifteen years your senior."

My heaven, the man had a memory.

"You have one son, and now your niece, your sister's child. I know you enjoy motherhood. I've seen that myself in the way you extend yourself for those children. I know you write well, don't like computers, enjoy my sweet tea and are quite addicted to chocolate." He grinned at her. "I'd like to know more."

"Why?"

She remembered quite clearly what he had told her the evening before, and she saw in his eyes that he remembered, and knew she did, too.

He said, "Because we'll be working closely together, and I will most likely have to make decisions that involve you." He paused, then added, "And because, as I have already been trying to get across, I am attracted to you and would like to explore the possibilities between us."

Realizing she had let things go too far, she fixed him with the skeptical eye that she felt would let him know she wasn't in the market for such flirting. "There are no possibilities between us." She got to her feet.

He did not move. "Word on the street is divided about whether or not you are actually engaged to Parker Lindsey."

"Word on the street?"

"Rumor…and I've asked around. Are you and Lindsey engaged? Was that what that little candlelight supper was about last night?"

Marilee wasn't certain which way to go with this. "Nooo…but Parker and I…we have an understanding."

"Ahhh…an understanding. Is that like 'going together'?"

When he said it, it sounded childish. "Yes. We've been dating for a number of years, and we are considering being engaged."

"I see." He frowned. "And you still keep your ex-husband's picture on your desk."

Marilee felt the barb sting. "*If* it is any of your business—which it is not—I keep my ex-husband's picture there so Willie Lee can see a picture of his father."

She took their glasses to the sink, thinking that he would take the hint to leave.

But all he did was scoot his chair back and slouch down more comfortably. She looked over her shoulder. His gaze was on her, and he seemed to be doubling something inside himself that perhaps she had better prepare to rebuff.

Maybe she would ask him to explain his term: *a woman like her.*

At that rather intense moment, however, the doorbell rang, causing Marilee to jump and just about holler "Ohmygod," which was a word not far from her thoughts at that minute. Thank goodness she held herself in check enough to say politely, "Excuse me just a minute."

She hurried for the front door, a part of her not thinking so much of letting someone in as of letting herself out. In her mind, she was practically running down the street.

Corrine had already answered the door, with Munro right at her heels. Willie Lee remained on the couch, as normal for him, fast asleep.

The door swung wide to reveal the caller to be Aunt Vella. On sight of her aunt in quite a disheveled state, Marilee knew instantly that some disaster had occurred.

"I've left Perry," were Aunt Vella's first words.

It was a sight Marilee had never in her life seen, nor expected to see, her aunt crumbling before her eyes. She reached out and took hold of the older woman, who burst into sobs.

"I don't have anywhere to go!" Aunt Vella cried.

Marilee, struck to the core, said instantly, "Oh, yes you do, Aunt Vella. You have right here!"

Putting an arm around her aunt, she led her into the kitchen and sat her at the table, where Tate immediately poured her a glass of sweet iced tea. Aunt Vella took up the glass and knocked the tea back as if it were a shot of whiskey.

When Vella had not come home by the time the late-night news program finished, Perry called his daughter, Belinda, who had finally moved out on her own three months earlier. Likely, he thought, Vella had shown the first signs of going crazy on Belinda's thirty-first birthday, when she had packed all of their youngest daughter's things and told her to move out to the apartment over the drugstore.

"Let me speak to your mother," he said when his daughter's voice came on the line.

"What? Daddy?" Belinda had never had a phone call from her father.

Perry, gripping the receiver, listened to his daughter say that her mother was not there. She had not seen her mother. She wanted to know what had happened, and Perry told her that her mother had gone crazy and driven off.

Belinda, who had little capacity for alarm, said, "Well, if she shows up here, I'll let you know. Did you check out by her roses? Maybe she's out there on the bench."

Perry hung up and padded in his sock feet to peer out the back door window. Vella had planted solar lights in the ground at the edges of her rose garden. They had cost a mint.

He peered hard. The lights lit things up considerably. The bench was bare.

He went back and telephoned Belinda again and told her that her mother was not on the bench.

"Well, I imagine she'll turn up tomorrow mornin', Daddy," said Belinda, with obvious impatience at being again interrupted. "If she doesn't, I'll have Lyle put out an APB."

Belinda hung up and relayed the information about her mother and father to Lyle, who lay beside her in the bed. "They had a spat. Must have really been somethin' this time. Usually Mama just quits talkin' to him," she said, welcoming Lyle's hard body against hers, which was the one thing in life that she had found could sustain her interest for any length of time.

"Mama isn't gonna leave her roses. She'll be in the kitchen makin' breakfast in the mornin'." Then she focused her thoughts on what Lyle did for her.

Tate, his reading glasses on his nose, folded up the yellowed newspaper he was reading and threw it atop the others in a pile on the opposite side of the bed, old editions of *The Valentine Voice* from the archives on the second floor of the *Voice* building. At least the newspapers provided a weight, something in bed with him.

Experiencing a wave of loneliness, he thought of Marilee and imagined her in bed with him.

Immediately he swung his legs to the floor. He rubbed his eyes and checked the clock—1:33, and sleep still wouldn't come.

He got up and dressed in sweatpants and a shirt and running shoes and headed out for a jog. He figured Bubba would be asleep somewhere, but the cat streaked out from beneath the lilac bush and fell in behind him.

Once again, Tate headed along the street in front of Marilee James's house. He saw with some comfort that Marilee's Cherokee was alone in the driveway. He slowed, peering to see if there was a light in the rear bedroom. There was, a low glow. Either Marilee was awake or she slept with the lamp on.

Dragging himself from the sight, he continued on around to Main Street, where he was surprised to meet up with Winston Valentine walking, with his cane tapping, from the opposite direction.

"Winston?" he said involuntarily.

"Hello, Editor."

"Can't sleep, either?"

"Old people never sleep, son." Winston did not stop his slow strides.

Tate kept on going, too, turned at the police station and jogged along Church Street toward his own house. On the opposite side of the street another jogger, a woman whose silver-bright leotard glowed beneath the streetlight, gave proof to hidden lives going on throughout the night.

Marilee gave up trying to sleep. Reaching into her nightstand drawer, she pulled out half of a Hershey bar kept there for emergencies. Punching her pillows, she sat up against them, broke pieces of the Hershey bar and stuffed them into her mouth.

She knew exactly what was wrong with her. She wanted a man. *Yes, Lord, it was true.*

Lying there, listening to her Aunt Vella's snores reverberate from the other room where she slept in Willie Lee's bed, Marilee wished for a man to hold her and fill her with wild feelings that took her away from the loneliness that struck so deeply this night.

She admitted this to herself, hoping to get rid of the desire, trying to give it up to God, but she kept holding on to it, thinking maybe some miracle of a perfect life with a perfect man would appear before her. The lonely yearning tugged ever harder, giving her fantasies of both Parker and Tate, which was about as foolish as could be.

Taking the telephone on her lap, she called Parker. He answered in a sleepy voice.

"Parker, it's me, Marilee."

"Oh…what time is it?"

She told him it was almost two o'clock and that she couldn't sleep. "I need to talk to you for a while," she said, choking so badly on the words that her voice broke.

"What?"

"Could we just talk?" she whispered.

"Okay." His voice was way too sleepy to be satisfying.

"Parker? Parker are you awake?"

"Barely."

He explained that he had been busy that night with an epileptic dog and a horse cut by barbed wire.

Marilee listened, then told him about Aunt Vella, who lay in Willie Lee's bed, snoring louder by the minute. "They've been married forty-five years. I doubt either of them has had a full week apart in all that time."

"I imagine she'll go home tomorrow," Parker said.

Marilee, whose mind seemed to be jumping all over the place, wasn't thinking about Vella any longer. "Parker…would you come over?"

"Now?"

"Yes." She had gone out of her mind. "Come over and sit on the couch with me."

"Okay," Parker said with questionable enthusiasm, despite how he had been after her.

Marilee hung up and stared at the telephone. Good grief. How did she get herself into such nonsense? She slipped into her bathrobe and went to open the front door a crack, so that Parker wouldn't make any noise coming in.

Turning, her gaze fell on Willie Lee. She had forgotten about leaving him sleeping on the couch. She was truly losing her mind. With him here, that left her bed as the only empty place in the house. She imagined herself and Parker falling into her bed.

Propelled by a bit of panic, she hurriedly lifted Willie Lee and carried him into her bed. He never woke up for anything until he was ready, and likely that would probably be when Parker arrived.

On her way back to the living room, she saw Munro come out of the bedroom where he had been sleeping with Corrine. He gave her a curious look.

"Come lie with me," she told him, sitting on the couch and patting the space beside her.

After a few seconds of debate, he came and hopped up beside her, circled twice and lay against her. He felt nice, warm and comforting, and a peace began to steal over her. She thought that she should have thought of Munro before. Sleeping with a dog could have true advantages over a man; a dog wasn't going to make all those demands and then run off and leave you.

She fell asleep and didn't know until morning that Parker had never come. He telephoned while she was having coffee with Aunt Vella.

"Did you call me last night?" he asked.

"Yes," she said, paused and then added, "I was just wantin' to talk, but you were too tired."

"I sure was," he said. "You didn't ask me to come over there, did you?"

"No, you must have dreamed that."

The Valentine Voice
Sunday, May 14

Today's Highlights:

—Detention Center again at the center of conflict. One injury, one arrest as a result of an altercation at Thursday's city council meeting. Story on page 1.

—Identity confirmed of man found dead in his car. Local woman makes a positive identification. Story on page 3.

—Sinkhole repair falls short. City Works loses dirt down hole. Story page 3.

—Valentine High School seniors prepare for graduation. Largest graduating class in school history. Story page 6.

Thirteen

A Fine State of Confusion

She had made a poor decision in not arranging for a sitter for the children or leaving them with Aunt Vella when she went on a research trip to a juvenile detention center up near Oklahoma City. As a result, the three of them, plus Munro, had endured almost six hours of structure and confinement, and were now hot, tired and cranky.

With a pounding head, Marilee felt great relief to see the outskirts of Valentine up ahead. She also saw a bunch of vehicles parked off the road and a group of people clustered around the Welcome to Valentine sign.

"There is Aunt Vel-la." Willie Lee, disobeying the rule by being out of his seat belt, was on his toes and peering over the front seat.

"It's the Rose Club," Corrine put in.

Marilee, slowing down, saw Reggie taking pictures. And there was Tammy with her notebook, talking with Winston for the article in the paper.

She pulled off the road, and she and the children, and Munro, who'd had to wait in the car at the detention center, tumbled out of the Cherokee with great relief to move after the long drive. Munro was apparently doubly glad; he went directly to hike his leg on a tree.

"Hello, Mis-ter Win-ston," Willie Lee said, approaching the elderly gentleman who was directing the work of his younger fellow Rose Club members, frequently pointing with his cane, from a lawn chair in the shade of a big elm.

"Hi there, Mister Willie Lee."

The two shook hands.

Marilee bid Winston hello, as well as his two lady boarders, Mildred and Ruthanne, who sat on either side of him. Mildred was eating jelly beans out of her purse, and occasionally Ruthanne would ask for one, throwing each orange one she received into the grass.

The Rose Club members, the eight who were retired and therefore not at jobs, were busy planting Madame Isaac Pereire rosebushes at each end of the sign and smaller polyanthas, Excellenz von Shubert, in the middle. When Winston and Vella had not been able to find the varieties at any of the local nurseries, the club had been forced to order from a grower in Texas. Aunt Vella had coerced her fellow members of the Rose Club to agree to this, mainly by bowling everyone over with her knowledge of the varieties. Just then, dressed in a lightweight, blue sprigged cotton dress, wide straw hat and purple gloves, she at once directed and got right into the dirt of the work to make certain her fellow members did the job right, which meant according to her specifications.

Marilee marveled at how her Aunt Vella did not sweat and could come away clean from digging in the ground.

"We got a late start," Aunt Vella told her, shaking dirt off her gloves. "We still have to plant the east sign, but now that everyone knows what they're doin', it ought to go faster."

Seeing how vibrant her aunt appeared caused a little panic inside Marilee, who would have preferred a little more pining for her husband on her aunt's part.

Aunt Vella said, "Winston and I are takin' Mildred and Ruthanne out to pizza tonight. We can bring some home for you, so that you don't have to cook," she added quickly, her expression so eager to please that Marilee's heart constricted.

"That will be lovely, Aunt Vella. I need to get a rough draft done up from my notes on this detention center as soon as possible." If she didn't get it down before other situations took command of her mind, she tended to forget the passionate point she wanted to make with a piece.

"Let the children stay and help us. Oh, do say yes, Marilee. We'd love to have them, and then we can take them to get pizza with us, and you can focus directly on your write-up."

"Well, I don't know...." The strong reluctance to let the children out her sight swept Marilee; she was getting to an irrational point of reluctance with this.

Her gaze went quickly to locate her little people. Willie Lee was on hands and knees helping Doris Northrupt tamp dirt around a small bush, and Munro lay sprawled a foot away in the shade of the city sign. She looked down at Corrine, who looked up at her.

"Would you like to stay and play here?"

Corrine nodded somewhat hesitantly. A smile was on her heart-shaped face, if not quite on her lips.

Taking herself in hand, Marilee kissed the children, got back behind the wheel of her Cherokee and drove away, although she looked in her rearview mirror several times. She reminded herself that they were all in the same town, that it wasn't the same as being separated by one hundred miles. And she really was very glad to have a few hours to herself. Even if it was a bit strange to be on her own.

She pulled swiftly into the driveway, went into the house, dropped her leather tote on the couch and carefully put her keys on the desk. Since Corrine wasn't there to help her find her keys, she had better keep track of them.

Pausing, she listened. There was the ticking of the small clock on her desk, a gurgle from the refrigerator.

She had not heard it this quiet in months. For the past five nights, Aunt Vella's snoring had filled the air. Heaven knew Marilee didn't want Aunt Vella to feel as if she were in the way. Aunt Vella had been trying so hard not to be an inconvenience, which was why Marilee felt like a rat wishing she could see an end to the situation of her aunt snoring every night in one of the children's beds. The snoring did not concern soundly sleeping Willie Lee, but Corrine could not sleep in the same room with Aunt Vella. After two mornings of waking up and finding Corrine on the couch, Marilee had insisted Corrine share her bed; she did not believe the couch was good support for a child's growing little body. With Corrine came Munro. As much as she had enjoyed the first nights of her niece and the dog sharing her bed, Marilee now found herself needing breathing room.

Aunt Vella meant one more adult sharing a house with only two bedrooms and one bathroom, and one coffee-maker. Marilee simply wasn't used to it. It gave her a disconcerting glimpse of how set in her ways she had become, and the adjustments that would be required if she married Parker.

She and Parker still had not settled the question of marriage. For the past five days they had hardly seen each other. He had stopped in for supper several times, but had rushed out again on emergency calls. He had not made any further mention of his proposal of marriage. She was not only too hesitant to ask, but too stubborn, too.

Right this minute there was no need to think of that, she told herself, yanking open the refrigerator and staring into it, right at the latest glass pitcher of tea bestowed upon her by Tate Holloway.

The man was true to his word about returning her box of tea all made up, she thought, carrying the pitcher to the counter, where she poured herself a glass of the sweet, invigorating brew. In fact, her editor seemed to have developed the habit of popping in her back door each evening to bring her a pitcher of tea and ask if she needed his help on the new whiz-bang computer, or question her about one or another person he had met in town. Tate definitely had the journalistic quality of being curious about people.

She had not been alone with him, though, to have the opportunity to ask him what he had meant by *a woman like her*, the phrase still echoing in her mind. Although tempted, she resisted the urge to seek time alone with him. That did not seem like a good idea. Every time she came face-to-face with the man, she imagined what it would be like to kiss him, which was foolishness in the highest extreme.

She took the glass of tea—which had just the right amount of lemon; the man sure knew how to make iced tea—to her desk, where she sat with firmness and turned on the little whiz-bang computer that she had grown to appreciate…mostly. She had forgotten her notes, so she had to get up to get them. She sat back down and adjusted herself on the chair. Sometimes adjusting herself in the chair helped her to think.

With determination, she took up a pencil and made a hasty outline. She didn't find it an adequate outline; she couldn't seem to get things lined in her mind. She sipped the tea, thinking it would stimulate thought.

Then she realized she was staring at the photograph of Stuart. She picked it up and looked more closely at the smiling face. She did keep it for Willie Lee…but she supposed she kept it for herself, too.

Gazing at her ex-husband's image, she wondered where he was now.

He could be dead, for all she knew.

But she did not believe he was dead. She had felt him a lot in her heart these last weeks, for some strange reason. She wondered, in the way a woman does when remembering snapshots from the past, if he had changed radically from the dashing young man he was in the photograph— he had been thirty-eight then. He would be almost fifty-five now.

She firmly set the photograph back in place.

With a frustrated sigh, she ran her hands through her hair. She found it ridiculous that she could not keep her thoughts in place. She had a story to write. She adjusted herself in the chair again, looked over the scribbled outline, then sat staring at the computer screen.

She found it ridiculous that the house seemed too quiet.

With that uncomfortable thought, her mind went zinging back to the children and Aunt Vella. She had the sensation of being bereft, and had the very odd urge to race right down and get the children and her aunt.

Almost before realizing it, she was on her feet, taking up her keys and purse, and heading out to her car.

She did not go to get the children. She *could not* go get them; they were having a perfectly wonderful time with Aunt Vella and Winston. They would all think she had lost her mind if she went and got them.

And Marilee really wanted this time alone. That she felt a little afraid of being alone was, she concluded, to be expected, since she had not experienced the alone state in quite a while.

While thinking all of this, she homed directly like a carrier pigeon to the drugstore. Realizing this, she thought that she could have walked down and gotten out nervous energy, at the same time having an argument with herself, demanding that she go back home and get to work. She would do that, she decided, after a hot-fudge sundae.

She came to a bumping halt head-in at the curb. She got out, slammed the Cherokee door, walked swiftly into the drugstore and ordered the sundae from her cousin Belinda, who had, since her mother had left both husband and store, been working the day shift and leaving the evenings to two high school teens.

"Just go ahead and get it yourself, okay? I've been on my feet all day. I'm beat." Belinda said this from where she sat on her mother's tall stool, reading the Sunday edition of the newspaper. "Would you refill my Dr Pepper, while you're there?"

She pushed forward a glass of ice on the counter. What told Marilee that the person behind the wide-open newspaper was indeed her cousin were the pink fuzzy slippers.

Marilee snatched up the glass, thinking that it was a good thing Aunt Vella wasn't there. Aunt Vella despised her youngest child and only daughter going around in bedroom slippers.

Marilee herself often had trouble believing Belinda had come out of her aunt. Aunt Vella had once been a raven-haired beauty possessed of ten-carat diamond style, which she had still. Belinda, on the other hand, was a dishwater blonde with a style no higher than five-and-dime glass. That Belinda took after her father was the explanation in Marilee's mind, most especially as she glanced toward the pharmacy window.

She could hear the murmur of her uncle's television and imagined him back there slouched in his old chair. The thought annoyed her. She felt her uncle should not go on as if his wife of forty-five years had not up and left. She did not expect Uncle Perry to suddenly turn into a Lothario, but the least he could do was pick up the phone and call Aunt Vella.

"I left your mother a little bit ago out at the west welcome sign. She's out there with the Rose Club planting roses." Marilee plopped the refilled soft drink on the counter.

"I know," Belinda said from behind the paper. "Minnie Oakes stopped in here on her way out there to take cold drinks. She made sure to tell Daddy where Mama was."

"What did he say?" Marilee got a vintage sundae glass from the shelf.

"I don't know. I didn't hear. Jaydee is sure chewing at this detention center like a dog with a bone. I heard the mayor will probably have to have plastic surgery on his nose."

"They won't know for sure if it is broken until the swelling goes down." She fought the cellophane covering of a new box of chocolate brownies; apparently the wrapping was designed to keep the brownies safe for a century.

"Well, the detention center is comin'. Socking the mayor doesn't seem like a big help."

"Jaydee didn't really mean to sock the mayor, and it wasn't really over the detention center. He was just frustrated in general, like he can get."

Marilee felt similarly frustrated in that instant by the cellophane covering on the brownie box. She had the enormous urge to throw the package on the floor and stomp on it. And suddenly she realized that she was irrationally angry. It seemed like she had been falling into irrational anger for weeks.

"Then what was it about? I heard it was the detention center. Paper says detention center."

With deliberate calmness, Marilee got the scissors from beside the cash register. "Jaydee was pretty worked up about the detention center, but he was aiming to sock Juice Tinsley, because he made a smart remark about Jaydee's wife possibly ending up in the juvenile detention center, so it would be easy for Jaydee to visit her. Walter got socked when he stepped in to keep the peace." With careful control, she cut the cellophane at the end of the brownie box.

"Jaydee's wife?" Belinda peeked around the paper. "Did he marry that twenty-one-year-old girl he's been goin' around with?"

"Uh-huh. A week ago Sunday."

"Welll…he's at that age for men."

Marilee frowned at the comment, which she found highly sexist. She also found Belinda highly lacking in her attitude about the situation with her parents. She was tired of being the one to shoulder all the care about all of this.

"This is pretty much of a surprise about that dead guy being Fayrene's first ex-husband, isn't it?" Belinda again peeked around the paper. "How many husbands has she had?"

"Three, I think." Marilee plopped a brownie in the dish and licked her fingers.

"Well, it sure is a good thing Fayrene read that back issue of the paper, isn't it? If she had just thrown it out, no one might ever have known about that guy bein' her ex-husband."

Marilee leaned back against the chrome cabinets. "Belinda, we need to get your father to call your mother.

The longer they stay split like this, the harder it will be for them to make up."

"I don't know what we can do about it."

"What if your mother does not go home, Belinda? What if this turns out to be a permanent split?"

Belinda peered around the paper. "Well, I told Daddy that I'm gonna hire somebody to come in here to work this counter during the day. Just because he had Mama doin' it for thirty-five years, doesn't mean I'm gonna. I'll work four nights a week, like I have, and that's all." She disappeared back behind the paper.

Marilee stared at the wall of newspaper, and then her gaze went to the pharmacy window. She thought of her aunt's face whenever speaking to or about Winston Valentine. She looked down at the box of brownies, took a second one and plopped it into the dish.

Belinda said, "I knew all this about Fayrene's ex-husband. Lyle was over there at the station Friday afternoon when Fayrene came in, waving the picture of the car in the paper. He went with the sheriff to take her up to identify the body. He said when she saw the man, she went nuts, just flipped right out. I guess she had really been countin' on seein' this guy, and not dead."

Dropping an enormous scoop of vanilla ice cream atop the brownies, Marilee thought that people counted on so much in this life, such as finding a mate and staying in love. Being able to find happiness. Being able to at least know what life was about. High expectations that appeared to be a mistake.

"It sure is funny about this guy using an alias. John V. Smith… Wonder what that *V* was for."

"It was a made-up name," Marilee pointed out with an energetic tone she felt necessary to combat Belinda's one-way train of thought, as she scooped warm fudge over the ice cream.

"Well, that was the whole trouble with why they couldn't identify him. They were runnin' searches on a John V. Smith, not a Dan Kaplan," Belinda said, as if the fact needed stating. "Lyle said the sheriff mentioned right off that it was strange this guy just had a driver's license and no credit cards or anything. What did Fayrene say about her husband using a fake ID?" She peeked out with a raised eyebrow. "Lyle never saw her after she flipped out."

"I only talked to her a minute. She wasn't in any shape for me to ask questions." Marilee said, taking up the can of whipped cream, shaking it. "I got what's in the article from the sheriff."

She aimed whipped cream at her sundae and thought that it would be a waste of effort to talk to Belinda about her mother's probable infatuation with Winston; Belinda would not be able to bring her head out of the newspaper.

Fluffy cream spurted out, and then only a dribbling stream. "Are you all out of whipped cream?"

"I don't know."

Marilee walked to the refrigerator in the storeroom and returned shaking a fresh can of whipped cream, the ball inside clinking like a piston.

Belinda was saying, "Lyle says fake drivers' licenses are real easy to get. You can get 'em at a lot of flea markets, if you know who to see. I don't know why any of us bother to go get a real driver's license, if that is the case."

Why, indeed? The whipped cream shot out of the can with a velocity that caused her to jump.

"Well, Fayrene will be sittin' pretty," Belinda said, "if she gets the fifty thousand."

"What fifty thousand?" Marilee paused in the act of opening the jar of cherries.

Belinda peeked around the paper. "The fifty-thousand dollars that was in the guy's trunk. You didn't know about it? I thought maybe you knew but the sheriff didn't want you to put it in the article. Lyle says he wants it kept quiet right now."

"No." And if the sheriff wanted it quiet, he shouldn't have told Lyle.

"Oh, well, I guess Neville is still lookin' into it. I don't think they've even told Fayrene. Lyle just told me this mornin'. Lyle thinks Fayrene could end up gettin' it, since her ex doesn't have any relatives. But that's only if it isn't stolen. This Dan Kaplan could have just robbed a bank or something."

Belinda disappeared behind the newspaper again.

Marilee stood there with the jar of cherries, wondering if she ought to go down there and get the scoop from Neville.

But she really didn't want to. Lord knew she had a story she was supposed to be writing right that minute, and here she was making a gigantic sundae. She wanted to sit down with the sundae and eat every scrap of it. Besides, there was little need for a write-up in the newspaper; with Lyle knowing about the money, likely half the town would know by the end of the day.

She twisted the top off the jar of cherries and fished out a stem with her fingers, while Belinda commented on the sinkhole.

"Wonder where all that dirt went?" she said. "Maybe it fills up the hole where they have pumped out oil somewhere else. Holes do have to be filled."

Marilee plopped the cherry in her mouth, twirling the stem and tying it in a knot with her tongue. Stuart had taught her that trick. It took concentration and settled her mind.

Fourteen

Chocolate Sundaes

The bell over the door rang out. It was Charlene MacCoy. She came over to the soda fountain and ordered two barbecue sandwiches and three fountain Coca-Colas to go.

"The sandwiches are for me and Oralee," she said. "Dixie doesn't touch barbecue. I wish I wouldn't," she added with a sigh.

"Marilee will make the sandwiches for you." Belinda sat where she was. "You're already workin' around, Marilee."

Marilee reached for the container of buns. While she began making the sandwiches, Imperia Brown came in to discuss another month of weekly Blaine's Drugstore ads in the newspaper with Belinda, since Vella, who usually handled the store's advertising, wasn't available.

Belinda refused to do anything about the advertising. "I'm not takin' on that job. You'll have to talk to Daddy."

Imperia, who never minced words, said, "Girl, talkin' to Perry is like talkin' to a stump." Then, "Marilee, that barbecue smells good. Would you make me one?" Imperia was a big-boned woman who deemed worrying about eating schedules and calories and cholesterol harmful to health.

Marilee got out another bun.

Imperia, who sported fire-engine-red fingernails, admired Charlene's manicure, and Charlene said that it was the work of the new nail technician who had just begun that week.

"I'm getting too old to be doin' nails," Charlene sighed. "It is a young woman's job."

"Oh, listen to you, girl," Imperia said, waving her away. "Age is a matter of mind."

"Age is a matter of eyes, too, and mine are starin' down the barrel of the far side of forty-five. You can do all sorts of things to look thirty-five forever, but there is just no way to make your eyes see like they did at thirty-five."

Imperia, who was in her midthirties, cast Charlene a startled look.

"I don't imagine you need to work, anyway, bein' married to Mason MacCoy now," Belinda said, not at all concealing envy.

"Well, I still have a life," Charlene pointed out. "I've gone back to school for a license in therapeutic massage. I'll do that in a dim room anyway, and we're planning to put in a salon at the retirement community. Iris is going to finance it, and Dixie and I are goin' to run it, and we're goin' to offer massages and all sorts of herbal treatments."

Marilee, who had been listening idly and who now handed Charlene her sack of sandwiches, thought how lovely Charlene was. Attitude, she concluded. Since marrying Mason, Charlene seemed to get younger every day, which was a mark in favor of marriage, Marilee thought, her gaze drifting to the mirror to check out her own appearance.

There were deeper than normal circles under her eyes, and her hair was limp. She was just about ready to fall off the vine, and then who would want her? Would she bloom, as Charlene had done, if she married Parker?

Just then Charlene said, "I got your note last week, Marilee, and I meant to call and tell you that we'll be there for Parker's birthday party on Saturday. I'll bring my sour cream dip."

The party was a casual affair that Marilee had somehow fallen into organizing each year for the past five. She had sent out the reminder notes to Parker's small group of friends at the beginning of the month and then forgotten about it. She started just a bit when Charlene mentioned it.

"I have to get the cake," she said, checking the calendar. "I forgot about it."

"How old is Parker gonna be?" Belinda wanted to know.

"Forty-three."

"Has he ever been married?"

"Once…for six months when he was twenty." Marilee wondered why she always answered Belinda's intimate questions.

Just then Iris MacCoy entered the store and came

forward with rapid steps, even in platform shoes. She gave Charlene, her sister-in-law, a kiss on the cheek like she always did, whether she saw her once a week or three times in a day, and showed them all a poster she wanted to put in the window, announcing the grand opening of the Green Acres Senior Living Community.

"See…we are emphasizing the word *Living*. The chamber is putting advertisements in national magazines, too."

Going gung ho on working with her husband Adam on building a full-service retirement community, Iris had taken a position on the board of the chamber of commerce. It was widely agreed that Iris could get men to do what they had set their minds not to do. In point of fact, her husband Adam had told everyone he did not intend to build a community for retired old farts, and a week after Iris worked on him, he was contacting architects.

"Iris designed the poster herself," Charlene pointed out.

Each woman made appropriate compliments over it. Iris really had a flare for color and design. She was herself very much of an eye-catcher. Her personal style of bimbo pretty much camouflaged the fact that she had an intelligent brain. Marilee, who had known Iris moderately well for eight years, had an idea that both libertine and intellectual existed inside the woman, and she envied Iris for being able to contain such conflicting natures with apparent peace.

Marilee put Imperia's barbecue sandwich in front of her on the counter. She saw Iris, setting herself on a stool, eyeing the plate.

"Do you want one?" Marilee asked her.

"Well…what I'd really like is one of those hot fudge sundaes." She pointed her silvery-nailed finger in the direction of Marilee's carefully constructed sundae.

Marilee stuck a stainless-steel spoon in the ice cream, now softened just the way she liked it, and plopped the dish in front of Iris. She wondered if she might get some tips.

Belinda was up and leaning on the counter, reading aloud the list of activities for the opening. "All day buffet…bingo…pinball…pool tournament…golf tournament…poker…gospel and country music bands and dancing in the evening." She looked up. "You sure better have paramedics on-site…you are gonna kill these people with all this activity."

Marilee watched Iris stick a spoonful swirled with vanilla and chocolate into her mouth. Turning to the shelves, she took down another sundae dish.

Outside on the sidewalk, Tate Holloway looked up and saw Parker Lindsey approaching from the opposite direction. It was plain that both of them were headed to the drugstore.

Tate stepped up his pace, ducked into the alcove just ahead of Lindsey and got a drip on the top of his head from the air conditioner just as he pushed open the door.

"After you." Tate motioned Lindsey onward. He also got another drip, as he was standing in the correct place for it.

"After you." Lindsey stood his ground.

"No, please…" Tate gestured magnanimously.

Lindsey kept standing there, so Tate gave in and

stepped forward to enter, but Lindsey picked that second to move, too, so they ended up jostling themselves through the door.

At the bit of commotion at the door, the women at the counter quit talking, and Marilee lifted her eyes from the box of brownies to see two figures entering. With the glare from the bright light through the glass, it took her several seconds to recognize Tate Holloway. Then, with surprise, she saw Parker step out from behind Tate.

Marilee took in the two men. Tate Holloway whipped off his hat, saying, "Good afternoon, ladies," and his blue eyes met hers. She jerked her gaze downward, pulled a brownie from the box and plopped it into the sundae dish.

"Hello, gals. Havin' a conference?" Parker asked.

Each of the other women said hello.

Marilee, occupied with arranging two brownies in the dish and avoiding the temptation of stuffing a third directly into her mouth, did not realize she had not offered a greeting until well after the time to do so had passed. Her lapse, however, obviously had not been noted, possibly because of the welcome so evident in the other women at the counter.

It was as if an energy swept them, each woman coming just a little bit more to life as a female will when confronted with powerful male energy, and in this case, it was two very vibrant men suddenly dropping into their midst. Even Belinda, who had been about to lower herself onto her stool, stood straight, brushed a hand through her hair and hid her slippers by tucking them beneath the front counter.

Charlene, moved by the disruption and possibly by

Tate Holloway addressing her as "The most beautiful Miss Charlene," suddenly remembered that she had to return to the salon. "My gosh, Oralee wants this sandwich!"

She cast a wave. "Marilee, bring the children out to see the ponies. Parker, I'll see you on your birthday. Bye, y'all."

Tate was sprinting to open the door, and this set Imperia into motion. She jumped to her feet, leaving her half-eaten sandwich on the counter, saying for Tate's benefit, "I have customers to visit," and hurried after Charlene.

Like a knight from a storybook, Tate bowed to each woman as she went through the door. Observing, Marilee thought that there was not a single man around Valentine who behaved as Tate Holloway did. His antics had Iris laughing gaily of course. Iris laughed quite easily anyway. Men just loved the way Iris laughed, with her head lifted and her hand sometimes touching her bare neck, or them. Marilee noticed Tate wink at Iris, not that it was any of her business, and she focused on building herself another sundae.

Parker, who thought Holloway a stupid show-off, nevertheless determined to show off in his own way. He rounded the counter and went about getting himself a Coke out of the fountain machine. He wanted Holloway to see this, to see that this was Parker's place first. Parker had been here for years and years, and Holloway was a latecomer.

"Would you like somethin', Tate?" Parker wiped drips off his foaming glass.

"Thank you." Holloway had sat himself on a stool next to Iris. "I came in for the wonderful iced tea. I miss Miss Vella, but the cold tea is still good."

"Yes, it is, because it comes from the iced tea maker," Belinda told him. "It's made from packets. The only thing Mama did was put the packet in the machine."

She pushed the button that opened the cash register drawer with a ding and counted away the money Charlene and Imperia had left. Belinda liked to count money. She didn't like to make food for customers and was inclined to encourage anyone to help himself. She reminded Parker that he needed to pay for his Coke, though.

Parker scooped ice into a glass and poured the tea from the pitcher, then plunked the wet glass in front of Holloway, who said, "Thank you. I appreciate you servin' me. Pay the lady, too, will you?"

Annoyed to find himself being treated like a servant, Parker grandly told Belinda, "Put the editor's drink on my tab."

"I'm not runnin' a tab like Mama did. I'm not keepin' track of it."

He pulled a couple dollars from his pocket and passed them to her outstretched hand.

"Thank you, buddy," Holloway said with that annoying grin of his. "Could you hand me a slice of lemon there?"

Parker got the lemon slice and threw it so that it plunked with a splash into the man's glass. "Hey, I'm sorry, *buddy*." He used Holloway's term back at him. "Let me wipe up that mess I made." Parker grabbed a cloth, lifted Holloway's glass and, with elaborate motions wiped the counter, setting up to accidently dump the glass in Holloway's lap.

The next instant, however, Holloway reached for the glass. "Thank you, sir. That's just fine now."

Parker, feeling thwarted, stepped back and sipped his Coke a couple of times, and then his eyes lit on Marilee, who was busy shaking a can of whipped cream, and thus causing her neat bottom to shake in a nice manner.

Stepping close behind her, he put both hands on her waist and bent his lips near her ear. "That sundae is lookin' awfully good. Think you could make me one?"

He was thinking: See this, Holloway. This is my place.

Marilee wriggled away from him, saying, "You are perfectly capable of gettin' it yourself."

Parker stood there, his back to those on the other side of the counter. Thank goodness Marilee had spoken in a low voice that only he could hear. *What in the hell was wrong with her?* He reached for his soft drink glass and casually turned, checking the faces of those at the counter. He was relieved to see that no one was looking his way. He looked again at Marilee, wondering what had gotten her back up. He was getting darn tired of her prickly manner.

This thought caused an uneasiness inside him, and he drank deeply of his soft drink, then ran his gaze down Marilee's profile. He found himself caught between being afraid of her breaking off with him, and being afraid she would say she wanted to marry him. He kept hoping if he left it alone, it would all work out somehow.

Marilee plopped a cherry on the top of her sundae. She wished for more, but by eating them and putting them on sundaes, she had used them all up, and she didn't want to risk this sundae by taking time to go get another jar from the storeroom. She felt certain that she had annoyed Parker—and she didn't know why she had done that, except that she didn't like him putting his hands on her in front of everyone, as if he had ownership.

Of course, surely he did have some sort of ownership, with their pending engagement. Although it might not be pending. Parker had not said one more word about it. Maybe he wanted to just forget he had ever asked, and that he did not tell her this annoyed the living daylights out of her.

The problem was that she felt guilty for not making a decision about marrying Parker and telling him one way or the other. That still hung over her, even if he had not mentioned it again.

She sprinkled pecans atop her sundae, then sprinkled a second helping. She had the feeling Tate was watching her and told herself this was foolishness on her part. She glanced up to check this out and saw him in conversation with Iris and Belinda, his eyes fully on Iris. Parker leaned over on the counter and joined in the conversation. They were talking about the merits of jogging.

Good Lord, Iris said she jogged six miles four times a week.

Again Marilee looked over at Tate, and this time his eyes came swinging around to hers.

Marilee averted her eyes and reached for a cloth to wipe her hands. The next instant, while getting a long-handled spoon from the container, she succeeded in sending two dozen stainless spoons clattering to the floor.

She had to get down on her knees to gather them up. Parker helped, and she thought that was nice of him, after she had behaved so sharply to him. This fact deepened her guilt.

She saved a spoon for herself and threw the rest into the dishwasher. When she turned around, she discovered Parker was helping himself to her sundae.

Snatching it from beneath his next scoop, she sat herself on Belinda's stool and began to eat.

She had sampled one lovely taste of sweet cream and chocolate when Belinda, who had not noticed a body in her stool, backed up to sit herself down. Marilee saw it coming and let out a warning, but Belinda, intent on telling about the fifty-thousand dollars found in Fayrene's ex-husband's car, did not hear and ended up squashing the sundae all over Marilee's bosom.

It was lucky that Aunt Vella was staying at her house, Marilee thought, observing the chocolate stains on her blouse in the filmy old rest room mirror. Aunt Vella was good at getting stains out of clothing. That mirror had to be the first one hung in here, probably at least sixty years old.

With a sigh, she threw the paper towel in the trash and emerged from the rest room. Looking down the narrow hallway, she saw Tate and Parker and Belinda at the soda fountain, silhouetted by the bright light through the big front window. Iris was just leaving.

She stood there a moment, staring.

Then she looked left, at the door leading to the rear room of the pharmacy. The drone of her uncle's television came through the door. After a moment's hesitation, she quietly turned the knob and entered. She apparently wasn't going to get a sundae, but maybe she could have an influential word with her uncle.

"Uncle Perry?"

Her uncle's eyes opened, and he made a mild effort to straighten himself. He nodded at Marilee.

"Are you doin' all right?" she asked. He looked a little too pale to her, but admittedly, she had not paid her uncle any attention for quite some time.

"Yep. Fine. Somebody need a prescription?"

"No. I just wanted to say hello."

He nodded and straightened some more. His gaze moved back to the television, as if drawn there by a string.

Marilee noticed that the early edition of the news was just going off, so it was about five o'clock. She needed to get on home if she was to get anything done on her newspaper article before Aunt Vella returned with the kids. She would be embarrassed not to have any writing done.

"Uncle Perry, aren't you gonna call Aunt Vella?" Aggravation at thinking about being embarrassed had caused her to get short-tempered.

He looked at her. "I guess not," he said, his jaw getting tight.

"Why not?" Marilee pressed.

"Vella's made her decision. Don't see any need to argue with it."

"Don't you miss her?"

"Nope." He focused his eyes on the television screen.

Marilee looked at him and thought she was carrying on

the stupidest conversation in the world. She saw, too, that her uncle's life had not changed one iota with her aunt not here.

Annoyed with the entire situation, Marilee said smartly, "You might want to know that while you're sittin' in here all day and half the night with the television, Aunt Vella is seein' Winston Valentine. She is serious about going off in a new direction. You can sit here if you want, but you're likely to be losin' your house and a part of this store."

While she said that, she searched his face for some reaction, no matter how small. But she did not see any. Her uncle sat there and looked like the lump Imperia had called him. An old man, as her Aunt Vella had said.

Marilee, feeling defeated, left him there and walked out, closing the door quietly behind her.

Pausing, she looked into the front of the store to see Tate and Parker and Belinda, still silhouetted against the light of the big front window.

Stepping out with purpose, Marilee glided out to the soda fountain.

"You're not wearin' a sundae anymore," Parker said.

"No, it didn't fit." She cast him a grin because she felt it rude not to, then picked up her purse from the rear, saying, "I need to go home to write. Good evenin', y'all," and was out the door almost before she realized how coolly she had breezed out.

Whew.

She paused on the sidewalk to take a good breath. The air had become quite humid and heavy, indicating coming storms.

Then her gaze fell on Munro, sitting in front of her Cherokee.

"My goodness, where did you come from?" She had left him with the children and Aunt Vella.

She glanced quickly up and down the sidewalk, looking for familiar figures, wondering if some sort of emergency had happened.

The dog was regarding her with quiet eyes, and she seemed to hear him say, *I came to keep you company.*

"Well, come on, and we'll go home," she told him and opened the door of the Cherokee for him to hop into the seat.

Munro was with her when she entered the empty house, and he curled beneath her desk, while she chewed on a fingernail and dredged up from memory the point of her article for next Sunday's edition.

An hour and a half later, in a T-shirt and sweatpants and bare feet, Marilee had a rough draft written. She had written it in spurts between glancing at the clock and out the window, looking for her family, and then forcing herself to sit in the chair and put words down for ten minutes at a time. She was exhausted and well ready for Aunt Vella and Winston and the children to blow in with the rising wind of an evening thunderstorm. She greeted everyone with happy hugs.

"Well, he *is* here," Aunt Vella said, upon seeing Munro. She stopped with the pizza box high in the air. "I was afraid I was going to have to tell you I had lost him."

"I told them Mun-ro said he need-ed to come be with you," Willie Lee said in his practical tone.

* * *

There came a knock, and Parker poked his head inside. "Anyone home?"

Marilee looked up from the computer screen to see him glancing around, still with only his head poking in the front door. His gaze found hers, and he regarded her uncertainly, no doubt because of her sharp behavior that afternoon. She felt immediately contrite.

"Come in." Marilee rose and went to greet him warmly with a smile and swift kiss, and to more or less haul him inside.

His grin grew broader. "Just passed Winston. He said maybe I could get some pizza here."

Willie Lee came racing in dog-fashion, on hands and knees, barking.

"Why is he doing that?" Parker asked.

"He's pretending to be a dog."

Willie Lee followed along, barking the entire way into the kitchen, where Marilee heated the last two pieces of pizza in the microwave.

"He's really into this, isn't he?" Parker said of Willie Lee, who was now sniffing at his shoes.

"Pretending is a normal part of childhood." Marilee liked to point that out whenever Willie Lee was being perfectly normal.

"Uh-huh." Parker raised an eyebrow and whispered, "I hope he isn't gonna pee on my leg."

Then he said to Willie Lee, "Have you had your rabies shot? I need to get Munro's shots, I can get you one, too."

Willie Lee raced away on hands and knees. This

tickled Parker, and his amusement pleased Marilee. For an instant their gazes met, and the fond look in his eyes caused warmth to wash over her.

"Sit," she said, moving him to the table and setting the slices of pizza in front of him. Then she took the chair next to him and propped her chin in her hand and watched him eat. She could hear Aunt Vella in the children's bedroom, reading them a bedtime story. Parker commented that the pizza was delicious and that he would starve if it wasn't for microwave ovens and Marilee's kitchen. She accepted this compliment graciously, and passed the credit on to Aunt Vella.

"It really is nice for me, having Aunt Vella here to help with the kids and meals and things," she said.

"I'm surprised she hasn't gone back to Perry," Parker said.

"I am, too." She thought of it sadly.

"Do you think she will?"

"I don't know…I really don't know."

The situation confused and frightened her. If her aunt and uncle could get divorced after forty-five years of marriage, then it seemed there was no certain thing in life at all.

Possibly Parker was thinking along the same lines, as he was frowning and staring at the table. Marilee studied his face and thought how he was not only handsome but a good man who would help in a crisis, even if he had a little trouble with mundane, everyday living.

And he needed her to keep him decently fed. To give him a place to call home. A family, such as he had not had before. He needed that, even if he wasn't aware of needing it. The memory of their lovemaking once upon a time sliced through her mind and right down to her belly. Their lovemaking had been very good, and they had been close once.

Of course she should marry him. She should snatch him up. She almost popped out with, "I'll marry you, Parker," but hesitated, suddenly overcome with self-consciousness that maybe he had changed his mind.

She rose and took his hand. "Come on."

"Wha…" He met her gaze and dropped his last bite of pizza, letting himself be dragged out on the back stoop, going with her with a growing grin.

Marilee closed the door behind them, putting them in the dimness of the step, where the only light was reflected through the window curtains. In a bold advance, she brought Parker's head down, parting her lips in invitation to his very apparent enthusiasm.

"Parker…"

She whispered his name with longing and pushed her hands through the opening of his shirt at the base of his neck. His skin was warm and silky. His tongue tasted like pizza. She wrapped one leg around his.

In seconds they were all heavy breath and wet lips and tugging hands. Parker made her wild by kissing her neck and shoving a warm hand between her legs. He whispered for them to go to his truck, and she said she could not do that. In fact, in an instant her fertile imagination drew up a picture of them both, old enough to know better, getting caught right in the middle of the act by a curious neighbor coming to investigate the rocking truck. Added to that was the sudden thought that Tate could come through the back gate and catch them making out on the back step.

Both mind pictures cooled her ardor a considerable amount, and she began to pull away, but Parker held her fast and kissed her deeply, seeking to draw her back into the passion.

Just then, as if coming to her aid, a loud clap of thunder reverberated, causing Marilee to jump and just about sending Parker backward off the stoop. He recovered and attempted to get back to business but was not able to overcome the rain that suddenly came in a downpour, as if someone had unstopped a sink.

"Damn!"

"Ohmygosh, Parker, you're gettin' soaked!"

Her hand fumbled with the screen door, which proved stubborn, but then she got it open, along with the inner door, and they threw themselves inside.

"Here…" She tossed Parker a towel from a fresh pile atop the dryer.

He rubbed his head, and she, with her own towel, dried her face. Then, clutching the towel, she looked at him.

He looked at her.

"Parker, do you still want to get married?"

His eyebrows went up. "Yeah."

The answer was not fully satisfying.

She breathed deeply, summoning words to her tongue.

But then Willie Lee's voice calling "Ma-ma" and running footsteps approaching abruptly ended further discussion. The next instant there came a loud thump, and then a pain-filled wail.

Marilee raced into the kitchen and found Willie Lee

had fallen against a kitchen chair and put his bottom teeth into his upper lip. She scooped him up, calling immediately for a cold cloth.

She sat and pressed Willie Lee, sobbing, against her, instinctively seeking to absorb her child's pain.

Parker put a cloth in her hand.

Willie Lee cuddled close and sucked on the wet cloth. After a minute, Marilee had to pry his head from her bosom and force him to allow her to examine the wound. Then the others—Parker, Aunt Vella, and even Corrine, who seemed to have a great curiosity for bloody wounds—gave Willie Lee's cut lip a thorough examination. Parker pronounced it not serious. Marilee finally concluded that Willie Lee did not need stitches, but he did need her to hold him and rock him back and forth.

She was still holding Willie Lee when Parker bent to kiss her good-night.

"Parker…"

He paused and looked at her. But with Willie Lee in her arms and Aunt Vella in and out of the kitchen, there was no room for privacy. "I'm glad you stopped by tonight."

He nodded. "I'll call you tomorrow."

"Yes. Do."

Then she was alone in the silent kitchen, Willie Lee dozing against her breasts, where not so long ago Parker's ministrations had been working her into wild passion.

The house was quiet. Aunt Vella was not snoring. Marilee tiptoed to the door of the bedroom and looked in, wondering if she should put a mirror underneath her aunt's nose to make certain she was alive. She did not know which she found more disconcerting, her aunt snoring like a character in an animated cartoon, or her aunt not making any noise at all.

At that particular moment, Aunt Vella let out a ragged breath, proving she was alive. With relief, Marilee glanced at Willie Lee, who was sprawled in a perfectly relaxed manner. She smiled. She might worry a great deal about his future, but his present was quite blessed. The swelling on his lip was marginal, and he had fallen back into his secure, easygoing ways.

She then looked into her own bedroom, where the bedside table lamp glowed dimly. Corrine, with Munro lying beside her, had fallen asleep, once again with a book lying on her chest. Under Munro's watchful eyes, Marilee removed the book and turned out the light.

"You are a good friend," she whispered to the dog and touched his head.

Still gazing at him, she wondered where the dog had come from. She wondered at how he had come into their lives seemingly at just the right moment.

Tender mercies, her mother had once explained in a particularly uncharacteristic thoughtful moment. For an instant, warm memories of childhood fluttered over Marilee like a delicate butterfly. There had been good times, but the memories of these times seemed to have been clouded over with the hard, stormy ones. She wished she could find a better balance between the two.

Going into the kitchen, she got out the pitcher of tea—Tate's round pitcher that she needed to return to him. There was one full glass of tea left in it; he had not brought fresh that evening, and she wondered at this. She missed him.

No, she did not, she told herself.

Oh, she liked Tate, and that was good and natural, too. Tate was a likeable man. But she could not make more out of it than was there. There was not a "thing" between them. Parker was hers, what she needed.

Parker was what she could deal with. Tate was way beyond her capabilities.

She thought this as, carrying along her glass of tea, she went to the back door, opened it and peered in the direction of her editor's house. It was perfectly black in that direction; the trees blocking any lights that might shine from his windows, if Tate was reading or doing some strange thing, like making another pitcher of iced tea in the careful manner he liked to take with it.

Inhaling the warm, humid air of coming summer through the screen door, she thought how summer edged upon them this time of year, one night humid as July and the next cool again. As if trying to sneak up on them, or accustom them to what was coming, one day at a time, until all their days were summer, hot and dry and so long sometimes she thought she would burn right up.

What else had her mother said? *The good news is that you can get used to anything. The bad news is that you can get used to anything.*

She paused and listened for a moment, hearing the first click of an early cicada far out beneath a tree…the rustle of leaves…light rain pattering through the leaves and onto the roof. Aunt Vella had begun to snore gently, and the refrigerator purred beneath this.

Thank you, God, after all, even for the hot and dry when it comes. Thank you for my family, for my children all safe in bed. Thank you for the safety of this house. Look after my sister, Lord. And Mama…yes, and dear Mama.

The gratitude came out of nowhere, and she embraced it as the precious emotion it was. This was something she could cling to. Something that anchored her and erased, for brief moments, anyway, the anxiousness that seemed to plague her soul.

She remained there at the door, as if she could keep the gratitude by not moving. As if it had come to her on the night air.

Yet then, inevitably, came a cool, swift breeze.

With a shiver, she closed the door and carried her now empty tea glass to the kitchen sink.

Glancing in the night-black window, she saw the reflection of the telephone on the wall behind her.

She turned and went to it and dialed Parker's number.

The answering service came on the line. The doctor was unavailable at the moment. If Marilee would give them the emergency message, the woman would relay it to the doctor. "He'll return your call as soon as possible."

"Oh, no, this isn't an emergency." Marilee looked at the clock. It was after eleven. Parker might already be asleep. "I'll catch him tomorrow during office hours. Thank you."

She didn't suppose saying, "I'll marry you," was something she should blurt out on the telephone, not to mention waking up Parker to do it.

Fifteen

Toss Up the Heart, See Where it Lands

Tate came out into air heavy as wet wool. The weather-man on the radio predicted high temperatures and possibly more storms that evening. It was enjoy the morning and get in out of the heat by afternoon. Summer was here.

Jogging down the porch steps, Tate felt a sense of power infuse him. This was an atmosphere with which he had full familiarity. By golly, Houston had mornings thicker than this on a dry summer day.

He went past the lilac bush fast enough to cause wet leaves to flutter. Bubba popped out from beneath it and jumped high. Tate sprinted over a puddle at the curb; when his Nikes hit the street, they seemed to be carrying him along all on their own.

Down Porter he went at a pace to warm him up. No one stirring at the James house. The young UPS man did only one quickie on the porch beam and plopped to the ground.

Tate lifted a high five to him and headed on around the corner, his legs and arms and heart all picking up the pace and going with the same strong rhythm. He nodded and called "Mornin'," as he sprinted passed the walking ladies, who were strolling this morning, one fanning herself with her hat.

On Main Street, Bonita Embree was entering her bakery. As she unlocked the door, she dropped the bag in her hand, and Betty Crocker box mixes spilled out on the sidewalk five feet in front of Tate. With the grace of a ballet dancer, Tate bent and swept up the boxes, deposited them in Bonita's arms and proceeded on, having done it all with only a pause of three heartbeats.

"Please don't tell," Bonita's voice followed after him.

"Not a word," Tate tossed over his shoulder and kept on going in his groove.

There was Charlotte across the street, poking the flag in its holder out front of the *Voice*. He waved, but she was already going back in the door.

Then it was around the corner of the police station—was that a mocha aroma in the coffee this morning?—and onward up Church into the first rays of the sun breaking through the morning mist, jogging all the way and still not slowing down.

Good morning, Life! Good morning, Lord! I am ready for whatever comes this day. Thank you for that.

Woo-eee! See me now, Lindsey.

But Lindsey was nowhere in sight.

Tate slowed his pace. He jogged up his driveway and back down again, checked his watch and slowed down as his chest began to burn. He did leg-stretching exercises there at the end of his driveway, keeping an eye out up the hill.

Lindsey did not appear. Of all the mornings for Lindsey to skip jogging, this had to be one of them.

Silly to be wanting to show off, anyway, Tate thought and took himself in hand, jogging on around to his back door.

Ha! Likely Lindsey could not take the thick humidity. Whereas Tate was rather pleased to see that he thrived in it.

He sure wished Lindsey had come along to see.

Through the open door of her editor's office, Marilee saw Tate on the telephone. He was reared back in his chair, his feet up on his desk, every bit the big editor, which everyone had taken to calling him.

Intending to slip in and lay her current detention center piece on his desk and slip back out again, she moved quietly and didn't look at him, but Tate jumped up and grabbed her arm, stretching the telephone cord, which pulled the telephone along the desk at an alarming rate.

His hand was hot and firm through her sleeve.

"Well, I look forward to meetin' the congressman, too, Mayor," he said into the phone. "Sure do. Seven o'clock. I'll see you then, and we'll talk some more. Goodbye."

He let go of her arm and leaned over to drop the receiver into its cradle, causing his shirt to stretch tight over his firm shoulders.

Then he was facing her, his blue eyes dancing. "It's a delight to see you, Miss Marilee." His gaze went to her hair, in that way he had of always seeming to *observe* her.

"Hello." She held out the papers and disk. "I brought the

disk with my detention center piece, and a printed copy, too."

"I like your hair up like that. It gives you a very elegant neck."

"Oh…I wear my hair up when it gets so humid." She was smoothing at her hair before she realized it.

"Well, you are lovely as a summer day with it like that." He slipped his rear onto the edge of his desk.

"Thank you." She felt foolishly self-conscious. Charm was Tate's way, like water from a faucet. "Well, that's all I had." She turned to leave.

"I think Lindsey must not compliment you enough."

That stopped her in her tracks. "Why do you say that?"

"Because you were surprised at me doing it. You always seem a little surprised at my compliments."

"Anyone would be surprised. You say things that almost no other man on earth says. And I really don't believe that Parker complimenting me or not complimenting me is any of your business." She was instantly ashamed at both her bold statement and tone of voice. She didn't know what got into her.

He smiled at her, though. "The secret of life…*one* secret of life," he corrected, "is to know when to make things my business." Without giving her time to comment on that, he added, "You could have sent the file directly to my computer from yours," and picked up the typed pages she had brought him.

"I wasted twenty minutes attempting to do that. Bringing it over seemed a whole lot easier." That was where her temper had come from; dealing with the new computer was wearing on her last nerve.

"This is just fine. No problem at all."

"Good." She nodded at him and stepped toward the door.

"Wait a minute." In a swift movement, he slipped off the desk, reached the door in two strides and surprised her by closing it.

He looked at her, and she looked at him. Was he going to kiss her? She stepped back before she realized, taken by a little panic.

Then, folding his arms, he said. "You are a lovely woman, Miss Marilee, and your hair like that gives you a definite exotic air."

She could find nothing to say to that.

He smiled a smile she had come to recognize as seductive. "I would very much like you to go to dinner with me Saturday night. I'm supposed to have dinner with the mayor and his wife, a state congressman, and a few other people I've already forgotten. Would you accompany me, so that I can have a really good time?"

His eyes were intent upon her, blue as the summer sky, and with a hint of something that caused her to hold her breath for a fraction of a second.

Then she shook her head. "I'm sorry, I can't. I already have dinner plans."

"Well now…there's always another night. How about Sunday night? What's your preference—steak, chicken fry or Mexican?"

"No, I don't think so." She brushed at imaginary stray hairs and looked at the door.

"I suppose this is because you have a standing date with Lindsey."

"I am dating Parker at this time, yes." Which he well knew. She moved a half step toward the door, indicating that she wanted to go.

Her editor, however, leaned his shoulder against the door, fully blocking her in with him.

"Just what is goin' on with you and Lindsey? I have it from him that you two are engaged, and I have it from you that you two are going together and considering being engaged. Which is it? Engaged or not engaged?"

"Parker's and my relationship is not any of your concern." She felt trapped.

"I have the concern of being attracted to you."

She gazed at her boss, and he gazed at her. A certain glint came into his eyes.

"You've known Lindsey for many years, I take it, both of you livin' here in this small town. Since Lindsey is the one who told me you two were engaged, and you are the one who has said you're goin' together and considering engagement, I'm assuming you aren't wild about accepting the man's proposal. It seems to me that your behavior could be considered a little on the rude side. Just how long do you intend to keep the poor man in suspense?"

"It seems to me that your training as a journalist has caused you to do a lot of supposin' into private lives that are none of your business." She reached out and took hold of the door handle.

His jaw tight now, he moved aside. She jerked the door open and left.

When she was halfway to her desk, where she had left the children with coloring pens, a loud banging came from behind her in Tate's office. She, Charlotte and June, who was nearby at the copy machine, turned. Nothing could be seen through the partially opened door.

Charlotte immediately marched herself into his office and seconds later returned and said, particularly to Marilee, "He kicked his trash can across the room."

She had provoked him, she knew it very well, but was too wrought up to feel remorse. He pricked her in the wrong places. She hoped she did not get fired.

The only car in the lot of the Lindsey Veterinary Clinic was a blue Honda that belonged to Deedee, the receptionist. It had white silhouettes of different breeds of dogs stuck all over its rear window.

Marilee pulled to a stop beside the Honda. Munro needing shots gave her the perfect excuse to stop by. Parker had mentioned the shots from the very first day and had kept forgetting to give them to the dog.

Why would she need an excuse to stop by?

Whipping down the visor, she checked her face in the mirror to make certain she didn't have mascara smudges. *Come to supper tonight, Parker.* No, that wouldn't do. She needed to speak to him alone, which meant going out.

Her lipstick had faded, but she would not freshen it and appear so obviously after a man with Corrine looking at her. Good heavens, what was happening to her? She flipped the visor back up and grabbed her purse.

Let's go out to supper, Parker. She didn't think she should be the one to ask. She had asked him last night if he still wanted to get married. It was his turn to speak of the matter. He had said he would call her, but he hadn't.

Although he might have called that morning, after they had left the house.

I'm sorry about the interruption last night. The rain wasn't her fault, though. Her son busting his mouth open and needing her attention had not been her fault, either. Why in the world did she feel so at fault?

She realized then that Corrine was out and walking to the clinic door, while Willie Lee remained sitting in the back seat. She opened his door.

"Why aren't you and Munro getting out?"

"Mun-ro doesn't want to go in there." His blue eyes blinked behind his thick glasses.

"Oh. Well, he has to, sugar. He needs to get vaccinated so he won't get sick. Parker will give him a shot, so that Munro won't get rabies. He could get rabies from a skunk that might bite him." She gazed at both her son and the dog, who sat with his chin as if permanently stuck to Willie Lee's thigh. "Besides that, honey, you and Corrine both have flea bites from Munro sleeping with you. We need to get something to help Munro with fleas…so he can continue to sleep with you," she added in a deliberate and measured tone.

She waited, gazing at him.

Willie Lee gave a big sigh and inched out of the seat. "Come on, Mun-ro."

Marilee followed her son and the dog to the building. *I am ready to talk about this thing, Parker. Are you?* She was ready to get this thing settled between them. *I'll marry you, Parker.*

She took hold of the glass door and they all entered; Corrine in the lead, Willie Lee trudging inside, and Munro slinking with his tail dragging.

Marilee, stepping into the waiting room that smelled of disinfectant, didn't think right this minute, in front of the children, was the place to have any sort of marriage discussion. But if she didn't, maybe neither one of them would have time to get together to get it said. Maybe she should just say it, and they could work out the details later.

"Doc's not in," Deedee told them immediately.

"Oh." She had not given this possibility a thought.

Deedee popped chewing gum. "He's out on a couple of calls." She stood and looked over the counter at Munro, who had lain down, his paws on the floor, trying his best to sink out of sight. "I can page him if this is an emergency."

"No…it's not an emergency. We were just going to get Munro his shots."

"I don't give shots, but I can sell them to you, and you can do it to your own. Lots of people do."

Marilee looked down at Munro, whose eyes popped wide and stared at her.

My thoughts exactly. "I think I'd better wait for Parker."

Munro got to his feet, ready to go.

Aunt Vella was asleep and snoring in the big wing-back chair. Willie Lee went straight to the chair, leaned on the arm and watched her with fascination.

"Willie Lee, come away from there. Don't wake Aunt Vella."

Marilee spoke in a hushed voice, but Aunt Vella's eyes popped open. "I'm not asleep. I was just restin' my eyes."

"You were snor-ring," Willie Lee said.

"Oh, you're a little wild boy."

Willie Lee gazed at his great-aunt, judging the truth of what she said, not grinning until she poked him in the side with her finger. "I am," he said, giggling.

"Has Parker called?" Marilee asked.

"You had some phone calls, but I didn't answer them. Two came while I was hanging clothes on the line, and I wasn't about to run in here from the yard. It's a lot easier to let the answerin' machine get them. That way I won't mess up and forget to give you the message."

Marilee saw the light blinking on her machine. Three blinks. She punched the button.

"Marilee, this is Charlene. I wanted to let you know we'll be bringing my cousin Leanne to Parker's barbecue on Saturday. I don't know if you know, but she's livin' with us for a while. That's why her horses are here. Oh, Jojo will be coming, but Danny J. won't, so really we'll be the same number as expected. Leanne's makin' her salsa recipe and bringin' it. It's really good. Bye."

The machine beeped, and a deep male voice said, "This is Rick returnin' your call, Marilee. I got the steaks for Saturday. All set."

One more beep. "If you are thinking of siding your house, call Martin's Home Siding. We're runnin' a special. 555-2323."

That was the end of the messages. Nothing from Parker.

In the kitchen, Aunt Vella was making peanut butter and jelly sandwiches for the children. Marilee poured glasses of apple juice and asked Aunt Vella if she would be available to watch the children that evening.

Aunt Vella said she would love to do so, and Willie Lee, grinning, said, "You will watch me, a wild boy."

Aunt Vella poked him and got him giggling, then she asked Marilee, "Where are you going, dear?"

"I think I may have a date with Parker, if I can get ahold of him."

A couple of hours ought to be enough time to find out if Parker still wanted to get married, and to tell him that she would. She would like to be back home in time to put the children to bed.

Marilee, sitting at her desk and writing club reports on the new whiz-bang computer, cocked her head to listen to the voices float from the kitchen.

"Hello, missy."

"Hello, Mr. Tate."

Marilee's heartbeat fluttered. *Which is it—engaged or not engaged?* She recalled his blue eyes, so intense when he had asked.

He was her boss, the man who paid her salary, the man who irritated her and who she found too attractive by far.

"How are you today?" His voice could charm birds from trees.

"Fii-ine."

Marilee found herself leaning forward, as if to see around the door. Ridiculous. She got up and went to the kitchen, where her boss stood in the middle of the room. Corrine was beside him, looking at Marilee with deep, dark eyes.

"Peace." Her boss and neighbor held up offerings—a fresh pitcher of tea with one hand, and a small square bakery box with the other. "Cake…a double-chocolate from Miss Bonita's. She puts pure chocolate chips in them, she assured me."

She gazed at him, trying to get perspective on this thing. He wore his enticing, although at the moment reserved, grin.

Turning, she went to the counter and picked up the clean pitcher waiting there. "Here's your other pitcher. You sure have a lot of them."

"Muriel left her dishes. When she left her old life, she really left it."

He set his offerings on the table. "I apologize for my behavior this mornin', Miss Marilee. You are right—your relationship with Lindsey is not my business. I behaved rudely, and I'm sorry." He looked her in the eye.

It took her several seconds to find a response.

"Apology accepted." She took a deep breath and then went for it. "I believe I owe you an apology, as well. I perhaps have not been clear about where I stand. Parker and I have a long-standing relationship that is precious to me. It's not that I don't find you an attractive and charming man. It's that I am committed to the relationship I have with Parker." The statement, once given voice, gave her a clear focus.

"I respect your choice." His summer-sky-blue eyes met hers without wavering.

"Thank you."

Then his grin came soft and sweet, and he opened the bakery box, saying, "If you would go ahead and cut this cake, I could help y'all polish it off."

Tate Holloway not only could make an apology, he could sweep everyone along with him.

At that moment Vella and Willie Lee came to the door and spied the cake. Corrine was already leaning across the table, putting her finger in the icing.

"I have vanilla ice cream for those who want it," Marilee said.

They all sat round the kitchen table, where Tate regaled them with stories of being a boy in East Texas and eating homemade ice cream laced with overripe peaches salvaged after the pickers had finished with an orchard.

"We cut off the bad places. Mmm-mm…nothin' sweeter than overripe peaches. They're one secret to life." He bestowed his wonderful grin upon the children, casting a side glance to Marilee.

Marilee took a bite of rich chocolate and thought that she would not have any appetite for supper with Parker.

The television flickered black and white—the old movie channel which was showing the musical *42nd Street*—although Marilee was too busy obsessing about how Parker had not called her to be following the movie's story line. There really wasn't a story line, anyway, just excuses for dancing that was nice to watch.

When the telephone at her elbow rang, she jumped six inches, then snatched it up before it could ring again. The hands of the mantle clock read 10:55.

"Hello," she said, clicking off the television at the same time. Aunt Vella's snores continued with rhythm from the front bedroom.

"Hi, Marilee." It was Parker—at last.

"Hi." After all the waiting, she was now uncertain of what to say.

"I got your message, but I just got in. I've been out on calls all day."

"Oh. You must be pooped."

"I am."

A pause.

She plowed on into it. "I called because I was going to suggest we go to dinner. Aunt Vella was going to watch the children for a couple of hours." Explanation seemed in order. "We need to talk, Parker. We've kept getting interrupted, I know."

"Yeah. I'm sorry I didn't get back to you earlier."

"Oh, I understand. I know you're busy."

She wished she did not feel so annoyed at hearing him say yeah. Yeah had no sense of positiveness about it. She really needed some positiveness from Parker.

He said, "Yeah. It's been one of those weeks, I guess."

She clamped her mouth shut.

When she had not said anything for a full minute, he put forth, "Do you think you could get Vella to watch the children tomorrow night? We could go to Rodeo Rio's."

Whew. He had spoken slowly, but at least he had taken part.

"Vella has her Rose Club meeting. But I'll see if I can get Jenny. And let's go up to Michelina's. It's quieter there."

There she went, taking charge again. That was a major problem between them. But Parker simply did not think of things like atmosphere in a restaurant.

Main Street in Valentine shut up by nine o'clock on weeknights. Now, at eleven, a few flags that shop owners did not take in remained, seeming to have lost color in the lights from the old-fashioned pole lamps. Fred Grace, who had been balancing his accounts, wearily closed the door of his florist shop and got into his car and drove away, leaving a totally empty street.

Belinda, gazing out the open window of her apartment over the drugstore, watched Fred's car turn left at the Church Street stoplight. Behind her, from the bathroom, Lyle called "Ba-lin-da," in a tone that struck her as being very much like her father's. He wanted to know had she bought him any new shaving cream. She always insisted he shave before they went to bed. The one good thing she felt she had was her complexion.

Over at the newspaper, Tate turned off the light in his office. A security light in the rear of the big room cast a dim glow, illuminating his way to the front door. He stepped out onto the sidewalk and made certain the door had caught, then stood there for some seconds giving *The Valentine Voice* sign a look, before shoving his hands into his pockets and heading home.

A big red one-ton truck coming down Church rumbled to a stop at the red light at the intersection of Main. He saw the barrel-racing logo on the door and then recognized the blond woman jogger behind the wheel. He had learned her name was Leanne Overton. She turned right, heading out of town, and he crossed the street.

At the police station, light flowed out through the glass doors, and officer Dorothy Jean Riddle could be seen inside, standing at the reception desk.

Tate briefly considered stopping in and chatting. Coming back to his office and working had not been able to banish his blues. Maybe what he needed was some good conversation.

Deciding that the last thing he wanted was idle chitchat, he headed on up Church Street in long strides.

I am mad, God.

He had done the right thing in going over and apologizing to Marilee. It had sure been hard. He had thought that by now he would find apologizing a little easier, having been obligated to do it so many times in his life.

I let her go, God. I let go of this woman, but I don't seem to be able to let go of the desire for her.

He kicked at some pebbles as he crossed the alleyway running behind the row of Main Street buildings. He kept on walking and found his hands were fists in his pockets. He pulled them free and began to jog lightly.

Whatever is meant to be or not be with Marilee James is in Your hands. I give it all over to You, right along with all the other parts of my life.

There. He had done it, yes-sir. But there was no way he would like it.

The Valentine Voice
View from the Editor's Desk
by Tate Holloway

Next week, our good congressmen and women up at the state house take up a discussion about whether or not to change the law so that coffins can be purchased at places other than funeral homes. Although this idea has been kicked around for a long time in private circles, this is the first time it has made it to the state house. I predict this first official discussion will be quickly tossed aside; however, the idea is not going to go away.

As far as I know, every single person who dies is buried in a coffin purchased from the funeral home that handles the funeral. There is cremation, but discussion about that is better saved for another editorial. Now, one may call different funeral homes and shop around for price, however, the only place to get a coffin is at a funeral home. The point I am bringing forth is that what we have is a monopoly on coffin sales by funeral homes, and when there is a monopoly, higher prices are generally the result. It seems to me that corporations in this country have been broken up because of just such situations.

What if one could purchase a coffin at any number of stores? What if, say, one could shop for a coffin at Kmart or Wal-Mart? No doubt a person could save considerably on the cost of the coffin, maybe as much as half in comparison to private funeral home prices.

It is this editor's view that not only would one save quite a bit of money, but I suspect the selection would be greater should coffins be readily available in regular stores. Also, anyone who is forward-thinking would be able to watch for a sale, buy the coffin and keep it in their garage, right on hand, and save their loved ones a lot of expense and trouble when the inevitable time comes. I think this sounds like a good deal all the way around.

Send me your views on this subject, or any other matter, and I'll print them. Call up there to the state house and let your congressmen know how you feel. Participation is the key to good government.

On another note, I'm happy to report that the mayor is acting on Winston Valentine's idea of placing benches about town. He said he would use his limited power of purchasing as needed and would start with four benches. Now it has to be settled on where to put them, so call over to city hall and give them your preferences.

Don't forget, I'm handling the petition to get trees on Main Street. Come on by and see us. The coffee is always hot.

Charlotte was shocked by Tate's editorial. After she had proofed it, she had to question him about the wisdom of printing it. He thought it was fine, of course, just like he thought everything he wrote should be spotlighted with a beam from God.

"We're gonna get a lot of calls." She had to say it.

To which he replied, "Of course we are—and we're gonna sell more papers, too." He winked. That man was a caution, for sure.

"You have one hour to think about it. I'll pull it if you come to your senses." Adjusting her glasses and focusing on the computer screen, she set the piece in place in the layout, knowing he wasn't likely to change his mind.

Twenty minutes later, she picked up the phone and called over to Montgomery's Funeral Home to set up an appointment for making plans. She needed to be prepared for her mother and to take care of her own arrangements. God knew her mother wouldn't be able to handle anything, should Charlotte be the first to go.

Sixteen

Lives Unseen

Lindsey was back jogging this morning, if about five minutes late. Tate met him coming around the curve of Church and down the hill, as Tate jogged up. When he saw the figure coming toward him, Tate's chest seemed to quit burning and his legs to become iron and carry him along like a marathoner.

"Good mornin', Doc," Tate called gaily, his breath even.

"Mornin, Editor," Lindsey replied, certainly a little surprised at the sight of Tate continuing up the hill.

And possibly a little surly? Maybe missing a day's jogging caused Lindsey some discomfort.

Tate kept on jogging up the hill, halfway expecting Leanne Overton to come jogging along, or maybe riding her bike.

She did not appear, and he slowed, finally taking a glance over his shoulder to make certain he was out of sight of Lindsey. He stopped in the street and fought for breath. Lindsey had it easy, going down the hill every day.

Just then music blared out and about knocked him off his feet. It appeared to come from opposite directions— *The Star Spangled Banner* from his right and *Dixie* from his left. Winston Valentine and Everett Northrupt were raising their flags.

Tate, who had done a ten-month stint on an aircraft carrier during Viet Nam, stood straight in the middle of the street and joined the older men in patriotic salute of the flags and a new day.

Munro padded along beside his boy's sneakers through a door into a delicious-smelling place. The smell triggered the memory of the mornings he had spent with the man, when the man would give Munro warm biscuits or sometimes a sweet roll.

There was a long counter with glass that everyone was looking into, but Munro could not see. Finally he rose up, propped his paws on the glass and looked into the wondrous display, spying piles of what he knew instantly were the sweets the children sometimes shared with him. He wondered how he would let his lady know he wanted one. The next instant, however, a shriek aimed directly at him sent him down and ducking behind his boy's legs.

"Good Lord! He was up on the glass." And then, "I'm sure there are ordinances about dogs not being in places that serve food." This was said by a tall woman who stared down at Munro.

"Mun-ro goes with us ever-y-where," his boy explained.

"I'm sorry, I didn't think," his lady said. "Willie Lee… honey, you'll have to take Munro outside. Corrine, you and Willie Lee wait outside while I get Parker's cake ordered."

His boy dropped to hands and knees beside Munro and barked like a dog.

"Willie Lee, not now. Take Munro outside."

"I'll take 'em, Aunt Marilee. Come on, Willie Lee dog and Munro."

His boy continued on all fours right beside him to the door that his girl held open.

Munro, feeling uncertain and annoyed with the tall woman, cast her a reproachful glance and then followed behind the boy.

On the sidewalk, his girl stood near the building, while his boy got to his feet and walked to the curb. Munro felt a little torn. He liked to keep very close to his charges. Finally he went to the curb with the boy and sat where he could keep an eye on both children.

Seeing his boy, who was now hanging an arm around a pole, shade his eyes to look at a gleaming car passing slowly, Munro looked, too. A face behind the tinted window seemed to stare right at them. Munro, sensing a high curiosity from this human in the car, moved closer to the boy.

The car disappeared behind a parked truck, and the bell over the door of the store rang out.

"Here, y'all…sweets for my sweets. Here's a snicker-doodle for you, too, Munro."

Munro thought how wonderful it was that his lady had heard him thinking. The treat, however, caused him some difficulty in that his humans, who could eat while walking, headed on down the sidewalk, leaving Munro behind. He wolfed down the sweet food, took half a second to lick the crumbs from the sidewalk, then raced to catch up to his humans.

He reached them at the vehicle, where he looked up to see two strangers appear on the sidewalk. He saw that the gleaming car was parked right next to his lady's, and understood that these people had come from that car.

He looked at them, and he caught a whiff of familiar scent. He *knew* these humans. They had been with his former man, the one he had met in the bright-shining parking lot.

The woman, whose eyes were covered by black sunglasses, had her face and attention pointed at him.

"Come on, Mun-ro," his boy called.

Munro dove off the sidewalk and jumped through the door the boy held open. Immediately he rose up with his paws on the back of the front seat and looked through the windshield. The strangers remained on the sidewalk, side by side, with both their heads turned toward his lady's vehicle, which was backing out onto the street.

A shiver went down Munro's spine.

His boy rose up beside him and put a hand on his back. "Ma-ma…who are those peo-ple?"

"Who, honey?"

"That man and la-dy. They were look-ing at Mun-ro. He does not like them, he told me."

"Oh, honey, they are strangers, and probably just lookin' at a lot of stuff. They didn't mean anything by looking at Munro. Now put on your seat belt and get Munro down on the seat with you."

"Mun-ro needs a seat-belt," his boy said.

Munro quickly got down and laid his chin on his boy's leg to show how good he was all on his own.

Tate, having just gotten the details of Deputy Lyle Midgett's apprehension early that morning of twelve suspected illegal aliens, parted with the young, proud deputy just outside the glass doors of the police department.

"The report'll be in this afternoon's edition," Tate promised. He would have to hurry to get it in there.

"I'll tell Belinda," the young man said eagerly, casting a wave and hotfooting it toward the drugstore.

Tate had heard rumors of wild passion between Belinda Blaine and Lyle Midgett; it was a concept somewhat hard to imagine, given the innocent apple-pie face of the deputy and the careless, dim demeanor of Miss Blaine. He recalled the cake mix boxes falling out of Bonita Embree's shopping bag. One never knew about the deep secrets of ordinary lives.

At that particular moment, he caught site of Marilee driving past. If she saw him, she did not indicate it but kept her eyes focused straight ahead out the windshield. He stood there on the sunlit sidewalk and watched the white Cherokee pass through the intersection, heading on to somewhere other than home, maybe to the IGA or the post office, or maybe out to Parker Lindsey's place.

Then he realized that he was still staring after her vehicle and pictured what he must look like, standing there on the sidewalk, drooling after a woman.

With a disgusted sigh, he stuffed his hands into the pockets of his khakis and turned to head on over to the newspaper, when his attention was caught by a man and woman who passed with swift steps.

No one walked that fast in Valentine without a good reason.

And these two were a type that stood out as much as the twelve Mexican men Deputy Midgett had come upon driving through town in a Ford Bronco. The man's blond hair was slicked back in the old-new style of the current sophisticate from L.A. or New York; he wore a crisp white shirt, colorful tie, dark-blue sport coat and pants, and shiny wing-tipped shoes and dark glasses. The woman wore a classy raw silk suit that neatly hugged her tight body, with the skirt a good three inches above her knees, and heels that made her legs go on forever. Her gleaming brown hair was carefully a mess, and her eyes were also hidden behind dark glasses. The pair seemed right out of a made-for-TV cops-and-robbers movie.

Tate watched over his shoulder and saw the two turn into the police station. Immediately sensing a story, he pivoted and followed. As he came through the double glass doors, the two were at the reception desk, telling Lori Wright that they wanted to speak to Sheriff Oakes.

"We're from Tell-In Technologies. He's expecting us," the tight-suited woman said.

Lori, as if blown back a step by the force emanating from the woman, said, "Just a minute," picked up the phone and punched the button for the sheriff's office ten feet away, door shut.

The man turned and looked curiously at Tate, who stuck out his hand. "Tate Holloway…I'm editor of *The Valentine Voice.* Can I be of any help?"

At that he found himself given a once-over by two pairs of sunglasses.

"I don't think so," the woman said and turned her back, dismissing him.

Tate, who as a journalist had plenty of experience hanging around in oddball fashion, just stood there.

The next moment the door of the sheriff's office opened, and Neville, a big man with a correctly creased uniform, filled the space. He nodded at the visitors, "'Lo," and stood aside for them to pass through into his office. As he closed the door, his gaze met Tate's and he gave a nod that said, "I'll tell you later."

"Who are they?" Tate asked Lori when they were alone.

"That dead guy—Fayrene's first ex-husband—he worked for their company, I guess. Tell-In Technologies. He was some sort of computer genius or something."

"Hmmm. I imagine they're here about the money."

"I guess…but I don't know. Sheriff Oakes isn't one to talk around, and even if I knew what-all it was about, I couldn't be talkin' about it to the press without his okay," she added, as if feeling it should be stated.

The telephone on her desk rang, and in a manner indicating her complete readiness for any possible crisis, she snatched up the receiver, saying crisply, "Valentine P.D."

It apparently wasn't a crisis, though, as Tate saw her slim shoulders instantly relax. He left her helping the caller with what apparently required computer searching and wandered back to the drink machine.

He and Lori were the only ones in the rather crowded office space. Valentine only had four people on the police force: Lori, their receptionist during the day; Sheriff Neville Oakes, who had taken over when his father had retired; Deputy Lyle Midgett; and Deputy Dorothy Jean Riddle, a young woman fresh out of the police academy up in Oklahoma City, who had joined the force two months ago. Behind the wall the drink machine sat against was a single jail cell, used for rare overnight stays by drunks or disturbers of the peace. Any true criminals, who might show up once a year, were taken up to the county jail.

Tate punched the button for Orange Crush. It was in the can, not the bottle he preferred, but this was the first drink machine he had seen in years with Orange Crush in it. Orange Crush reminded him of when he was a boy.

Minutes later, the door to the sheriff's office opened, and the three people came out, Neville leading the way.

"Lori, get Fayrene on the phone, please."

"Yes-sir."

Lori immediately picked up the phone. The three people, the sheriff leaning his tall frame on the counter, waited. Tate looked at the out-of-towners, and they looked at him.

Lori spoke to Fayrene and then handed the receiver to the sheriff, who said, "Fayrene, honey, I've got those people from Tell-In here, and they'd like to talk to you. Are you feelin' up to it today?"

Tate's ears pricked at the sheriff's warm tone. He

studied the man's face, and then he drank deeply from his Orange Crush. All sorts of things went on in people's lives.

"Okay, honey, thanks," the sheriff said into the phone. "We'll be over there directly."

Tate watched the three people leave through the glass double doors, then downed the last of his Orange Crush, dropped the can in the recycling barrel, and walked quickly back across the street to get Deputy Midgett's story written up in the next half hour before the deadline. He wouldn't want to disappoint the boy.

Belinda was on her knees, straightening magazines on the wide wooden shelf and reading any headline that caught her interest. It was the lull time in the morning, before the lunch crowd, which she dreaded. She kept thinking she could hang the closed sign on the door. Her father, who never came out from the pharmacy, wouldn't know. Unless someone telephoned him.

The bell above the door rang out, interrupting her. Well darn, was the first thing she thought. Knowing she was hidden by the comic book rack, she kept still, thinking maybe whoever it was would leave and she wouldn't have to wait on them. She was darn tired of waiting on people.

The footsteps and voices told her it was two people.

Just then she realized that they were arguing.

"I know that was the same dog." A woman said this. Belinda tried to place the voice but could not.

"There must be a lot of dogs like that in the world." This was a man's voice, and unfamiliar, too.

"How many dogs could there be that look exactly like that mutt Dan Kaplan picked up in the head office parking lot, and now right here, where he ended up?"

Dan Kaplan. Wasn't that the dead guy, Fayrene's first ex-husband? Belinda cocked her ear attentively.

"There have to be thousands of mutts like that in the world. And so what if it is the dog?"

"I don't know…but we still haven't found the chip, and we have found that dog."

"*Maybe* it's that dog. And we don't know we haven't found the chip. It's most likely in the car or the briefcase, and we'll get at those when Frank gets us the court order. At least it's all safe right now. Man, I've got a devil of a headache—I'm gonna get some Motrin and something to drink, if anyone shows up to wait on us in this hick place."

Belinda, who thought it was a hick place, too, took no offense, nor did she feel prodded to do anything about waiting on them. She peeked around the bottom of the revolving comic book rack and saw the slim, nylon-covered legs of a woman in dark pumps and the dark-trousered legs of a man in shiny loafers disappear behind one of the drugstore shelves.

She sat back on her heels, wondering about who the people were. Somebody to do with that dead guy. What dog?

The man called, "Hey, anyone back there?" and Belinda, opening a hairdo magazine, heard her daddy come out and wait on them.

A minute later her daddy called, "Baa-linda? Ba-linda, we got some people here who want somethin' to drink."

"All right, Daddy," Belinda said, pushing stiffly to her

feet. Her legs were numb from sitting on them. She scrambled around to slip on her flip-flops.

The man and woman looked a little stunned to see her come out from behind the magazine rack. They ordered Cokes to go and didn't even sit while she made them. They threw the money on the counter, where she had to pick it up. She watched them walk out, and she thought of the looks the two had exchanged upon sight of her.

Well, she thought as she edged herself onto the stool and opened the hairdo magazine again, she would get it out of Lyle that night who these people were, and what it was all about with that Dan Kaplan and some chip and a dog.

Vella missed her home. She couldn't say she missed Perry. Maybe she missed who Perry used to be. Maybe that was part of old age—missing everything as it used be. It had just seemed to slip away so fast. All those years. Where had they gone?

She pulled her champagne-colored Crown Victoria into the driveway, shut off the ignition and looked around to see any neighbors who might witness her arrival. There was not a sign of anyone, as usual during a weekday morning in the old neighborhood. Which did not mean that Doris Northrupt wasn't peeking out from behind her window curtains. Likely nosy Mildred down at Winston Valentine's house was, too, unless she was eating or watching television.

Her purse strap over her arm pressed to her middle, she walked quickly across the side yard around to the back to her rose garden, where she slowed to a stroll, enjoying whiffs of fragrance.

Pulling a pair of all-purpose scissors out of her purse, she cut blossoms for a bouquet. Again and again she reverently touched the leaves and sniffed the wide blooms. When she was full of the scent, she walked slowly to the house and let herself in the kitchen door that had not been locked in the forty years she had lived there.

She put her bouquet in a mason jar of water and sat it on the table and admired it. Then, noticing food stuck to the table, she got a wet cloth and scrubbed it clean. Next she cleaned the coffeemaker and made a fresh pot.

The window drew her, and she looked out toward the Valentine home, wishing for Winston to come across the pasture. He had visited her at Marilee's, but they had not been alone since she had left home.

She washed the cup and glasses left in the sink and cleaned the counter that had food and coffee stains on it. She went on to wipe over everything and sweep the floor. She looked toward the Valentine house again, then sat at the table to drink her coffee. Halfway through it, she began sobbing. The suddenness and depth of the sobbing frightened her. When she managed to stop, she wiped her eyes and blew her nose.

Then, swept along on a wave of fresh desperation, she took up the telephone and dialed Winston's phone number.

Winston himself answered the phone. *A sign from God.*

"Winston, I'm over here in my kitchen. Could you come down? I'd like to talk."

After what seemed a very long moment, during which Vella worried what Winston must think, he said he would come right away.

Fairly flying around the kitchen, she got Winston's favorite blue mug from the cupboard, wiped it shining, then poured it full of coffee and set it on the table along with sugar and cream. With the roses and her cup there, the table looked inviting.

She glanced out the window and saw Winston coming across the small fenced pasture between their houses at an encouraging rate, even with his cane.

A man hurrying to her. Tears sprang to her eyes at the wondrous sight. She whirled and, with the heart of a young woman, she raced to the back door and opened it before Winston had time to make it up the few stairs.

"Are you all right, Vella? You didn't sound very good on the phone." His expression was filled with concern as he came stiffly up the stairs.

"No…no, I'm not all right." The words poured forth, and then she burst into tears and had to avert her face in shame.

Winston, whose ripe age and experience with women had accustomed him to tears, reached out, drew Vella against him and let her cry into his shirt. She leaned on him a bit, and he had to balance with his cane, and after about a minute, he began to worry that Vella might push him over. He didn't want to break a hip here in her kitchen and have the paramedics have to show up and everyone know he was alone with her.

"Vella…here, gal. Sit down and drink some coffee. That will help you feel better."

He got her sat down, and then he sat himself down and felt greatly relieved at having averted breaking his hip. Old age was a pain in the neck, as well as the hips, elbows and knees.

He poured coffee for both of them. After a few sniffs, Vella took up her coffee cup with both hands and drank. Winston drank his, and for a couple of minutes there was silence, broken only by the hum of the refrigerator and Vella's sniffs.

"This is really good coffee," Winston told her. "I've missed it."

Instantly he realized he had said a wrong thing, because she began to cry again. He decided to retreat into the safety of silence, drink his coffee, and wait her out and hope she stopped crying before Perry came home.

Keeping silent did the trick. Before he had finished his coffee, she managed to get ahold of herself and, as so many people did, slipped from sadness into anger.

"Oh, Winston," she said with some vehemence. "I miss my house, and I miss my roses."

Winston nodded, biting back the comment that she should just come home. There was no telling what might set her off again.

"I feel so foolish…leavin' my house and Perry like I have. At my age, Winston."

Winston nodded again.

"It's just that…well, I'm all confused. I don't seem to fit. It's like all the rules have changed…like there just aren't any rules today."

Winston said, "Things are sure different," and nodded.

"My heaven…even my menopause was later than most."

Ohmygod. He sure hoped she did not continue on that subject.

She didn't. She snatched up a magazine from a stack

atop the microwave oven and shook it at him. "Just look at all the people they are puttin' on the cover of *Modern Maturity* these days. Movie stars. Do we all have to compare ourselves to movie stars? Do we have to have advice from people who get their faces and Lord knows what-all lifted and tucked? I can't look at the thing anymore."

With that, she tossed the magazine to the floor with force enough to send it sliding through to the dining room. Winston laid his hand firmly on the table to hold the cloth if need be.

"I look in the mirror and there's this old woman," Vella said with passion, "but I don't feel that in my heart."

Winston watched her press her hand in the middle of her very ample bosom. Something stirred inside him, a natural curiosity to see her lovely bosom. He was pleasantly surprised at his reaction.

"Perry has not touched me in so long, Winston."

Winston, who definitely did not want to go any deeper with that, said quickly, "You are a lively woman, Vella. And you are not so old. I'm old," he added, heavily.

"I'm sixty-six."

"You are still in the youth of old age," he volunteered, thinking of how he was in the old age of old age.

Vella said, "I don't look forty…but I don't feel sixty-six."

"You are a handsome woman, Vella."

She regarded him in a way that made him feel uncertain.

"At my age," she said, "my mother was a really old woman and didn't do anything but sit on her porch and talk about eating. She talked about what she had for breakfast and what she was going to have for lunch and for supper. Minnie Oakes talks about that, and what she plans to watch each night on television. She marks it all down in the *TV Guide.*

"The only other woman my age that I think may have my same feelings is Odessa Collier, and she's...well, it is understandable for Odessa to be a little wild and loose, because she has always been wild and loose. She's artistic," she added pensively.

"You're artistic," Winston volunteered. "Just look at how you grow your roses and then arrange them." He gestured at those in the mason jar.

Vella looked at the roses. Then, feeling an urge to move, she got to her feet and stepped to the counter. She now wished she had not started pouring her heart out to Winston. But since she had started, she might as well continue. She had so thoroughly tossed everything to the wind, what did she have to lose?

"I am not like Odessa. I'm just not like anyone, and being my age is not like I had imagined at all. I don't know what to do with myself. I still want to do so many things. I still *feel* so many things."

She sighed then, a sigh that hovered between exhaustion and desperation. She felt herself in a precarious balance between sobs and screams.

Winston got to his feet. He had begun to worry a little about Mildred coming down to check on him, and his bones pained him when he sat too long. He thought it time to look for an exit.

"It's a good thing to feel, Vella. It proves you are alive.

And I guess being a little mixed up is a big part of livin'. It is better than the alternative," he added.

This was a phrase he had been telling himself a lot of late. He wasn't believing it so much anymore, though. Death had come to look pleasant, an end to many aches and pains and annoyances.

Vella lifted her head and looked at him. He was startled to find it was like she was aiming at him, and the very next moment she moved right up against him and kissed him. He saw it coming and couldn't do anything but stand there and take it.

"Thank you, Winston, for your kindness to me," she whispered with her lips still brushing his.

Her kiss had not been a thank-you sort of kiss. It had been an invitation, and she remained against him, looking him in the eye with that invitation that kindled a surprising feeling inside him.

He further astonished himself by encircling her with his free arm and kissing her with a passion he had not known he could summon. He wasn't dead yet.

The sun was far to the west when Vella turned the Crown Victoria into the alley at a high enough rate of speed to cause the front to bounce precariously, but without slowing, she shot on past behind the police station and came to a jarring halt at the back door to the drugstore, right behind Perry's dusty Lincoln parked in his space. She jammed the shift lever into park, left the engine running and propelled herself out from behind the steering wheel.

Rounding the hood, she stalked to the rear passenger

door and pulled out two suitcases. She started dragging them on their wheels; they fell over on the gravel, and she didn't bother to right them, but dragged them on their side, until she got to the door, where she hefted them inside, making a lot of commotion in the endeavor. She was, after all, a sixty-six-year-old woman throwing around suitcases that each weighed half as much as she did. The thought brought her strength, and she threw the second case halfway across the storeroom.

Belinda appeared in the doorway from the front. "What in the world…?"

"I'm bringin' your daddy's things."

"You are *what?*" Belinda took a wide stance and put her arms akimbo on her hips, as if to block Vella's entry.

"I brought your daddy's things from home," said Vella, who had righted both cases and started tugging them forward. "He is down here from dawn to dusk anyway, he might as well move on down here. I'm movin' back home."

"You *aren't!*"

"Yes, I am." Vella was heading for the rear pharmacy door. She yanked it open. "I made that home for forty years. I worked down here, too, but I'm choosing the house. Your father already chose this pharmacy years ago. Perry!"

There wasn't any need to yell his name. Her husband was struggling to get himself out of his old chair. His eyes were wide, and his mouth open.

"What in the world are you doin' now, Vella?"

"You heard me, I'm sure. Here are your things." She did her best to swing the cases forward, and in the process she almost toppled herself and had to grab the doorjamb to keep from falling. Breathing deeply, feeling her heavy breasts move up and down, she added in a more controlled manner, "I'm movin' back home. You can stay here. I'm seein' Jaydee about a formal separation."

She turned and headed out of the store, and Belinda followed, saying hysterically, "Mama...don't do this. Don't do this to me...leavin' Daddy with me!"

Vella was listening for Perry, God help her, but she listened in vain, because her husband did not call to her.

With her vision blurred by tears, she got back into her car and headed on down the alleyway, bumping out on the other end.

Seventeen

Situations Unfolding

"Marilee?" Vella called out as she entered the house and tossed her purse onto the couch. She breathed deeply, feeling depleted and therefore totally calm.

The house was warm. Marilee had not put on the air-conditioning. The windows were wide, and late-afternoon sunshine shone across the porch and through the front screens.

"In here."

Vella followed the sound of the voice to the back bedroom, where she found Marilee sitting on the foot of the bed, which was covered with clothing and shoe boxes and various other paraphernalia. In fact, the entire room was covered with a wide variety of paraphernalia.

"It looks like a tornado hit this room."

"What? Oh." Marilee, who had been reading something, looked around as if seeing for the first time. "I was picking out a dress to wear tonight, and then I got to lookin' for the box with my birthday stuff…tryin' to find the candle for Parker's birthday cake on Saturday. Pretty soon I had so much out, it seemed a good time to clean thoroughly." She paused. "I had a keep pile and a give-away pile, but now I don't remember which is which."

"You have a certain candle for Parker's cake?" Vella shifted a pile of clothing to make room on the corner of the bed, sat and slipped off her shoes. Her big toes were becoming arthritic and suffered in shoes, although it struck her now that this was the first she had thought of it all day. That seemed a good sign of how alive she felt.

"The number four," Marilee was saying. "I've been savin' the four and just buy a new number to go after it. I used it on my cake last year. We blow it out real quick, so it's like new." She twisted and reached a hand to the windowsill, bringing back the candle to show Vella. "See…just a little bit melted there."

"It looks fine." Vella thought that her niece could sure be thrifty.

The two sat there a minute, as if both out of breath. Vella found the room dim after the afternoon brightness outside. Golden light beams filtered through the trees and the window screen. A faint breeze brought the sound of the children's voices in the backyard and gently stirred the drapes. Watching the drapes move, Vella thought, not for the first time, that her niece showed a marked fondness for a forties look; the draperies were of a large flower pattern similar to one Vella herself had in her living room way back when. She did not care for it now.

Perhaps for a while the young got old, and then the old got young again.

Her gaze came around to her niece, as if to see herself at that age. She then noticed Marilee's disheveled appearance.

"Have you been crying?"

Vella had long ago given up expecting Marilee to be truly happy. It was a set of mind that Vella, too, had struggled with when in her forties. Maybe she was just now coming out of it, she thought.

"Oh—" Marilee wiped her eyes "—yes, and it's silly really. I just got to reading some of Stuart's old letters." She fluttered one and indicated the shoe box filled with folded papers and envelopes. "I kept them…heaven knows why, but I did. I just now found the box in the back of the closet."

She looked at the letter she held, and Vella did, too, recalling the tall, handsome man who had swept her niece off her feet, and for whom Vella had never cared. She had known Stuart James instantly as a childish philanderer, without an ounce of giving anywhere in him.

"We wrote a lot of letters to each other, even when we were together. We were both writers." Her niece smiled wanly, looking in that instant so very young.

"Of course you kept them. We like to go back over things like that so we can cry all over again." Then, more gently, "They are memories that are important. They deserve to be kept."

Vella thought perhaps she was speaking to herself. She automatically reached to take out a letter.

"You can't read them!" Marilee pushed Vella's hand away and gathered the box to her lap.

"Oh, I wasn't thinking. Of course I can't read them."

She had simply been following curiosity, with the box right in front of her. Her escapade of the afternoon had her thoughts all awry.

"Well, some of them you could read." Marilee's expression was apologetic. "Most of them, in fact. We did a lot of discussing of theories in general, like love in general. Most of them were written when I was in college and indulging in an intellectual phase that is so far removed from reality. I was profoundly impressed with Stuart's mind. I guess I thought he knew everything there was to know about life. He'd seen so much, done so much traveling to exotic places, and he presented such a wise philosophical figure. He was like a guru. He loved that, gathering all of us admiring students around him. Look, here's a picture of our little gang."

"Where are you?" Vella pushed her glasses down her nose to sharpen the bifocals.

"I'm…this one, here's my head."

"Oh." She recognized her niece's face, in the rear of the picture and half-hidden by hair. Marilee in those days had been quite introverted, hiding her feelings and her entire self, if possible. She still hid her true self to a great extent, Vella thought.

"Reading the letters now, I see that I put a lot of intentions into them that were never there. I built Stuart and our love up into some great fantasy that it never was." She paused. "Maybe I didn't love him as the man he was but as a fantasy of him in my mind. Then, when he was the human man he was, I got mad at him for disappointing me."

"Oh, everyone does that when they fall in love," Vella

said. "None of us would ever get married if we saw our lover as human. We have to be blinded by love and then grow to accept the reality. By the time we do, we're a little more used to it."

What had happened to her being used to Perry? Maybe she simply could only take so much reality of him.

"Well, it was a great disappointment when I could suddenly see. Stuart didn't want a wife. He wanted a perpetual cheerleader."

"Don't most men?"

Marilee laughed at that. "Yes, but most do grow out of it by the age of forty."

"Hmm, maybe." Vella, whose spirits were sinking by the minute, thought that it would be nice if Perry wanted anything more than someone to mop up after him.

Marilee stuffed the letters back in the shoe box and put the lid on it. "I'll need to go ahead and get rid of these. I doubt Parker would take very kindly to me hauling my former husband's letter along into our marriage."

"You're goin' to marry Parker, then?"

"Yes. And here's the dress I'm going to wear tonight to tell him. What do you think?"

"It's lovely."

Holding the dress before her, another one that reminded Vella of the forties, Marilee observed herself in the mirror. "I've been rude and thoughtless to Parker," she said to her aunt and to herself. "Keeping him waiting all this time. I didn't mean to be…. I just don't want to make another mistake." Marilee's eyes were dark and had that bit of worry that seemed always to be there.

"Oh, honey…you are human, and the plain fact is

humans make mistakes all over the place. Don't be so hard on yourself, and don't expect to escape making mistakes. Every mistake makes us smarter."

Marilee turned to face Vella and said, "We won't be getting married immediately. We'll have to make plans, get Parker's house ready for us…but you can come with us, Aunt Vella. There'll always be room for you with us."

Vella had not realized that she had fallen into a thoughtful state, which Marilee had read as pensive. "Oh, honey, how very thoughtful of you." She supposed she *had* been pensive, thinking of living alone. "But I won't need to go live with you and Parker. I'm going back home."

Marilee looked startled. Then she smiled broadly. "Oh, Aunt Vella, I'm so glad. I know you've been disappointed in Uncle Perry, but you two can work this out. You should be together."

"Well, I don't know about shoulds," Vella said, touched by her niece's emotion and sorry to disappoint, "but I know what I had to do. I went to see Jaydee Mayhall and started separation proceedings. I've moved Perry out of the house, so that I can move back in."

Marilee, in a stunned state, followed her aunt into the kitchen, where Aunt Vella began opening cabinet doors and asked, "Do you have anything planned for supper for the children?"

When Marilee said she did not, Aunt Vella suggested macaroni and cheese. "I can eat with the children before I go to the Rose Club meeting, and then all Jenny has to do is get them bathed. I'll be moving back home tonight, too."

"I'm going to bathe them before I go." Marilee was following her aunt around the kitchen. "Have you really thrown Uncle Perry out? How can you do that?"

Vella said, yes, she had thrown Perry out, and it had been easy. "I just packed him two suitcases. He really doesn't have much. He can get all his televisions whenever he wants."

"How can you throw away forty-five years of marriage? Aren't they worth anything?" Marilee wanted to know.

To which Aunt Vella replied, "Yes, they are worth a lot, and I'm not throwing them away. I am honoring those years. They have made me the woman I am…a woman who isn't so stupid that she wants to spend her remaining, relatively few, years being tied to an unfeeling dolt. Here, grate this cheese."

Marilee grated cheese and chopped up carrot and celery sticks, all the while saying in ten different ways: "Are you sure, Aunt Vella? Are you really sure? Do you not care at all for Uncle Perry anymore?"

Vella replied, "Yes, I do care for Perry. I wish him well. I want him to be happy. But the first person I love is myself. God gave me a life, and it is my responsibility to honor and live this life. My husband no longer takes part in our marriage. He doesn't even see me, so I see no reason to hang around and be ignored. I cannot live with that level of indifference.

"I also love my house," she added. "I picked it out, I decorated, I've kept it all these years, and I see no reason to give it up just because I've given up my marriage."

All of her aunt's confident explanations dried up

Marilee's questions. A heavy sadness at the situation and at life in general settled over her. It appeared in that moment that life was a most uncertain and lonely business.

When Marilee gave voice to this depressing sentiment, Aunt Vella said, "Of course it is. Those who think differently are fooling themselves with unreasonable expectations. There are no hard and fast answers anywhere, except to keep moving on and trusting God to guide, trusting Him be there with you, as well, through both wise and foolish actions."

Marilee could not seem to grasp this concept. Foolishness seemed too risky to trust even to God. When she stated this opinion, Aunt Vella said, "Why, honey, foolishness is the human condition and exactly what God handles best."

The IGA was a major place of running into neighbors and holding conversations. Tate wasn't much in the mood for holding conversations, but he didn't seem to have a choice in the matter.

Minnie Oakes came up to him in the produce aisle and told him in no uncertain terms that she would not at all appreciate walking through Wal-Mart and coming upon a bunch of caskets. "If they did stock them, I'd expect a separate room, with the door closed. That's my opinion, for the paper."

"Yes, ma'am. Thank you, Miss Minnie."

Tate noted her comments on an index card. She gave a quick nod and went off toward the bread, her tiny back ramrod straight. He turned to choosing bananas and some very aromatic nectarines, laid the bags gently in his cart and pushed on to the meat section. He hated grocery shopping.

The store was having a beef sale, and Norm Stidham had a cart full of steaks and rump roasts. "Got a passel of grandkids comin' in this weekend," Norm explained, then gave the long list of names. "Oh, and I been meanin' to give you my opinion on this casket monopoly, Editor. I think maybe we ought to have a tax and all funerals paid for by the government. Just my opinion. Do you know how to spell my name?"

Over in the condiments aisle Tate ran into the mayor's wife, Kaye Upchurch, who asked his choice for the appetizer for Saturday night's dinner party: cold artichokes or green bean vinaigrette.

"Green bean vinaigrette," he said.

"Oh, really? I was leaning toward the artichokes."

"Then artichokes are wonderful." He did not know how he would stand several hours of this woman's demanding company, on top of his disappointment over Marilee not being with him.

"Oh, and, Tate, please don't bring up the subject of coffins at the party."

"No, ma'am, I won't."

"And if anyone else brings it up, change the subject."

"Yes, ma'am." His mother had taught him well.

She gave him a quick nod and went on her way. With a deep breath, he lifted a bottle of ketchup off the shelf, then headed on around to the next aisle. As he went around the corner, he almost bumped right into an oncoming cart. It was Leanne Overton, and the first time he had seen her in other than her jogging clothes. She wore a crisp white shirt and turquoise jeans that hugged her slim shape in about the same manner as her spandex pants.

"Excuse me," he said. "They need traffic lights in here."

"Yes…" She smiled and headed on.

For an instant Tate thought of engaging her in further conversation. Perhaps he should open himself to other women, since he had given up on Marilee James.

He had no heart for the idea, though, and pushed on to the end of the aisle and the tea section, where he stood gazing at the array of colorful boxes of herb tea. His low mood might profit from his cutting his caffeine intake.

"Marilee is still havin' his party. Juice said that no one has canceled the order for steaks."

Tate's ears immediately pricked.

"Maybe Leanne had an emergency with one of her horses," said another voice. "Her horses have had problems lately."

The vaguely familiar voices were coming from around the corner of the aisle, from women hidden from Tate's view by the bulging end shelves of Little Debbie snack cakes and cookies.

"I imagine they have," said the first voice in a knowing fashion. "But what kind of emergency could it have been that she was comin' out of Parker's driveway at four o'clock in the mornin'?"

Whoa, buddy. Tate became very still.

The voice continued, "I had brought Juice to work, since his Jeep was in the shop, and I was goin' home to get some sleep before I had to get to the post office. Tuesday's my late mornin'. I should get a whole day off, but since Alice has been down in her back, I can't get that."

It was Julia Jenkins-Tinsley, postmistress and Juice's wife, speaking. She came pushing her cart around the corner and down the aisle, followed by a rather plump woman who Tate recognized although could not name.

After a quick glance, he focused hard on the teas, more or less trying to blend in.

"Well, I've seen 'em joggin' together in the mornin's. They come along about the time Everett raises his flag." Ah—he placed the woman now—Doris Everett. "They don't come together…they've been meeting up there where the path comes out in the field the other side of Blaines'. Sometimes Leanne rides her bike…and all the way in from MacCoys', too. That's maybe five miles. Usually when she comes back she stops at Winston's, and Charlene'll get her and take her back, or I guess she goes down to the beauty shop and has Charlene get her from there."

Tate, still focusing on the array of tea, saw in his mind's eye Lindsey and the shapely Miss Overton jogging along together.

"She come out of his driveway without her headlights on," the postmistress said. "Maybe she thought she couldn't be seen, but there's that pole lamp right there at the edge of the parking lot for the vet clinic. I mean, really, plain as day. Oh, shoot, I got to go on back and get biscuits. Mama's comin' to supper this Sunday, and she just loves those Grands biscuits."

Tate was again in the aisle alone. He snatched a box of Lipton loose-leaf black-and-orange pekoe and dropped it into his cart. He liked Grands biscuits, too, but he kept himself from continuing to eavesdrop on a conversation he could not truly qualify as having journalistic merit.

What was he going to do about this thing?

He hardly knew when he had made it to his kitchen, he was stewing so hard over the situation.

Tuesday morning, the morning Lindsey had not shown up jogging, Leanne Overton had been coming out of Parker Lindsey's driveway.

He set his grocery bags on the counter and put the kettle of water on the stove over the flame.

Leanne Overton had not shown up that morning, either.

Of course, the two had been jogging together a lot, but not every morning. Leanne Overton generally did three mornings a week, while the Doc did all five…until that Tuesday.

He had seen Leanne Overton's truck heading in the direction of the veterinary clinic last night. She could have been going anywhere, though. He had no way of knowing the truth. What he had heard at the grocery store was idle gossip, not fact.

Yet Julia Jenkins-Tinsley had been speaking of a first-hand sighting.

I am committed to my relationship with Parker.

There was no way he could go to her and tell her about this, he thought, spooning tea leaves into the china pot without even counting. It dawned on him that he had about five spoonfuls in the pot, and he had to empty it out and start over.

It wasn't his business. Except that he cared for her. Somehow her welfare did seem his business. Heat swept over him as he thought about Lindsey messing around on her.

Then it came to him: she had said that about her commitment to Lindsey yesterday evening. He had not spoken to her today at all. Maybe she and Parker had broken up since then.

He got rather excited about the idea for a couple of seconds. But he hadn't heard anything about it, and surely he would have heard if they had broken up. People would have been talking about it already.

Still, it was possible it had happened late in the day, and he might not have heard. He didn't hear every single thing that went on.

If Lindsey expected to keep his liaison secret, he was the biggest kind of fool.

He had to find out about this thing. That was all, just find out where Marilee stood.

Quickly, he fixed up a pitcher of tea with lemon and sugar, and ice cubes clinking around, and went across the backyard into the deepening evening shadows of the trees and through the gate.

Marilee opened the door for him. Her eyes popped wide, as if she were surprised. "Oh, hello. Come in."

Tate himself was pretty surprised. Marilee was dressed in a black slinky dinner dress, a silver bracelet on her wrist, a silver earring in one ear, and she was trying to get the other earring in the other ear.

He gave a whistle. "Goin' somewhere?"

"Yes." Her cheeks turned pink, and her gaze flitted away. "Parker and I are going out." She strode into the kitchen. "I'm sorry I don't have time to chat."

He followed, going to the refrigerator and shoving the pitcher of tea inside, which was the only thing he could think of to do at the moment.

"You don't have to keep bringing me iced tea. I'm sure you've repaid me a number of times over."

"Don't you like it?" he demanded, feeling suddenly quite annoyed.

"Oh, yes. I do, very much, it's just that I don't want you to feel obligated."

"I don't do things out of obligation." He realized his anger was out of all proportion.

"Here...let me help you with that." He motioned toward her earring, which she still had not gotten into her ear.

"That's okay...I'll go to the mirror."

"Just let me have it." He fairly snatched the earring out of her hand.

Her eyes met his, and then she leaned her head over and pulled back her hair. He focused on the pierced hole in her lobe. Her flesh was warm to his fingers.

She said, "Aunt Vella has moved back home."

He saw her blink rapidly. He couldn't see well enough to get the wire through the hole. "Let's move over to the light." He fairly dragged her by the ear. "So Vella and Perry are gettin' back together?"

"No...Aunt Vella threw Uncle Perry out."

"Well, dogged." He got the wire through the hole and let go of her ear. "It will be all right with Vella and Perry. Things do work out."

She gazed at him. "I don't know. I hope so."

They stood there gazing at each other. He wanted to haul her against him and kiss her senseless. Kiss her and show her what she needed.

The sound of the front door opening broke their gaze. Marilee stepped around him and away into the living room. He heard her voice welcoming Lindsey.

Tate stepped into the doorway to the living room, and at that same moment the telephone rang, drawing Marilee away from Lindsey's embrace.

Tate looked full into Linsey's face. The veterinarian frowned at him.

"So you and Marilee are goin' out to dinner," Tate said, coming forward.

"Yes."

"That's nice." Should he bring up what he had heard?

"Yes, it is. What are you doin' here?"

"I brought some iced tea. Marilee likes my iced tea." He wanted to knock the guy's teeth down his throat.

Something in Marilee's voice had them both looking over at her.

"Yes…thank you for calling, Ruth. I hope Jenny gets feeling better very quickly."

She replaced the receiver. "Jenny's sick with the stomach flu. Just started throwing up twenty minutes ago. She can't come baby-sit."

She sighed, and Lindsey said, "Oh, great," in thorough disgust.

"What about Vella?" Lindsey wanted to know.

"She's already gone to get Winston. It's her Rose Club night." Then she added, "And she's moved her things back home. I don't want to disturb her."

Lindsey made an irritated sound this time.

"We can stay by ourselves," Corrine said. She had come silently, as always, to the hallway and stood there looking small but brave. "I can look after Willie Lee."

"Oh, honey, I know you can look after you and Willie Lee, but I wouldn't want you here by yourself." Marilee went to Corrine and pressed the small girl against her legs.

"You can give her my mobile number, Marilee. She could get us if she needed us."

"No."

Lindsey was a fool to think she would go for that. Not Marilee, who did not care to let the children out of her sight.

"I'll stay with the kids." Tate spoke before he even knew he was going to. Was he nuts? Why should he help Lindsey?

Marilee and Lindsey looked at Tate. Marilee's eyes were wide, Lindsey's searching.

"I think I qualify as an adult. I'll stay with them. What do ya' say, missy? You and me can handle it, okay?"

Corrine grinned at him, tentatively, and then her grin widened as Marilee looked down at her. She nodded at Marilee.

"Well, I guess that would work." Marilee spoke slowly, still uncertain. "If you're sure you wouldn't mind? You don't have plans?"

Her eyes, smoky and beautiful, were on Tate.

"No, I don't have plans. You two go on with yours." He did what he felt was required of him.

She had to make certain with Willie Lee, before agreeing to the plan. For two minutes Tate stood five feet away from Lindsey.

"You've been a busy man lately, I hear," Tate said.

"Yeah…a little bit."

No time to go further with it, because Marilee came back and got her purse, at the same time thanking him all over the place. She kissed the children good-night, and walked out the door on Lindsey's guiding hand, and Tate kept all of his words inside himself. He had made a pledge to God to let go.

Marilee and Lindsey returned three hours later. She had an engagement ring on her finger. Tate congratulated the couple and kissed the bride-to-be on the lips, but quickly.

He did not leave, but stood there while Marilee went to the bedroom to check her children, who were now asleep.

The instant she was out of the room, he said in a low voice, "I trust that this engagement means you have cut off your fling with Leanne Overton."

Lindsey about jumped out of his skin. "What do you mean?" he said in an equally low voice.

"You have a small problem in that Leanne was seen driving away from your house at four o'clock in the morning." He let that sit there while Lindsey stared at him about like a deer caught in headlights. "Marilee is bound to hear about it sooner or later, so I would suggest you be the one to tell her."

"There isn't anything between me and Leanne."

"Tell Marilee, don't tell me."

Marilee came back into the room. "Thank you, Tate, for watching them."

She was relaxed now, and pleased, and this pleased him. "It was my pleasure. I got to be a kid again for a while."

He would have kissed her again, but something held him back, some unnamed, fearful caution.

Then he shook Lindsey's hand, squeezing it as hard as possible.

It was not his place to tell people how to live their lives. Each one had to find his own way. He hated that. He was reminded how Lucille used to tell him that he liked to think he knew everything, that he thought he was God. He had learned a thing or two since then, one major lesson being that people did not like tale bearers. Marilee would not thank him for telling her the truth about this man she had decided to marry.

Eighteen

Rough Day

Marilee just about put her eye out with her engagement ring the following morning, when she awoke and flopped her hand backward over her eyes to shield them from the fresh light of morning spilling through the windows. She had forgotten to pull the shades.

Extending her hand, she squinted at the ring. The diamond caught the light, blinding her further, and she dropped her hand to the bed, thinking, Ohmygod.

She had been stunned when Parker had produced the ring from his jacket pocket and proceeded to put it on her finger. It had been his mother's. It looked like something his mother would wear. It slid all around on Marilee's slender finger.

Pushing herself out of bed, she shuffled her way to the kitchen, where Corrine had a pot of coffee ready and waiting.

"Bless you, my child," Marilee said, kissing Corrine, who sat at the table, already dressed and reading a book.

Marilee sipped the dark coffee from the mug she held with both hands. Where was Willie Lee?

"He's out in the garden, moving worms," Corrine informed her.

"Moving worms?"

Corrine nodded. "He wants to make certain there are lots of worms around his flowers."

Marilee looked out the window to see her small son, his pale hair spiked in all directions—a haircut was in order—digging with a trowel in the garden, in a very concentrated manner. Munro lay beside him, his head upon his paws, watching.

Just then the front door opened. "Hey…anybody awake?"

Parker? Well, my goodness.

"In here." Her voice came out a croak, as his footsteps came jogging through the house.

There he was, fully awake and jogging lightly into the room, wearing a muscle shirt that showed his tanned, hard frame, shorts and bright-white running shoes.

"Mornin', beautiful." He smiled and kissed her cheek, with barely a pause in jogging.

"Good morning." Her voice was still croaking like a frog. She hated chipper people first thing in the morning. Hadn't she told Parker that sometime in the past years? Surely he would have figured it out by now.

"Just thought I would drop by." Obviously. He was jogging in place now. "What do you think about me and your aunt gettin' married?" he said to Corrine.

Corrine's eyes shifted uncertainly to Marilee.

"I haven't talked to them about it yet, Parker. I just got up, and they were asleep when we came in last night."

Parker's jogging was causing the floor to vibrate. She had the sudden thought to grab the iron frying pan off the stove and smack him to get him to stop.

"Oh." He kissed her cheek again. "I'll call you later." He turned and jogged away. Marilee's eyes lingered on his hard-muscled back until he disappeared. His shoes thudded through the house, and then the front door shut with a near slam.

Marilee drank another good swallow of the thick black coffee, and then she showed Corrine her engagement ring. Corrine said it was pretty.

Marilee couldn't figure out what else she could expect Corrine to say.

She poured her coffee cup full to the brim and took it into the bathroom and a shower. Peace and quiet and aloneness for twenty minutes.

Parker was a morning person and a jogger; she was *not* a morning person, and definitely *not* a jogger. They were going to have to make some ground rules first thing.

Tate, making a good pace up from Main Street, saw a jogger come from right on Porter Street. Lindsey…from the direction of Marilee's cottage. Well now.

Tate slowed as he entered the intersection at the same time as the veterinarian.

"Stopped by to see Marilee this mornin'," Lindsey told him.

The man had at last begun to protect his investment, Tate thought. Giving a nod, he kept going, jogging up the hill of Church Street. He had liked participating in the raising of the flags and thought he would keep it up.

Parker, who was mildly surprised to see the editor bypass his own house and head on up the curving hill of Church Street at a fair rate of speed, took note that thus far the road coming down was empty. Relief swept him, followed by determination that gave him a fresh burst of speed, sending him along Porter and in the direction of home. He had started out early in order to miss running into Leanne. He didn't want to risk her catching up with him now.

They sat on the couch in a line: Corrine, Willie Lee and Munro. None of their feet touched the floor, and three pairs of eyes regarded Marilee, Willie Lee's large and blue behind his thick glasses, Corrine's black as drops of crude oil, and Munro's the golden-brown of a fall leaf.

The children were obviously not surprised about her announcement of impending marriage to Parker. Marilee had not expected they would be, although one could never be certain of children's thoughts, and she had been a little anxious about the matter.

Corrine appeared pleased—or as close as Corrine could ever get to pleased—but she still held her wariness, as usual. Willie Lee, quite reluctant to have been pulled away from his worm moving, had the only concern of being reassured that Munro would go with them to Parker's house.

"Of course Munro comes. We are a family. Munro, too." Munro looked relieved, and she smiled at him. "And you and Corrine will each have your own room. Parker's house is a lot bigger than this one."

She was very pleased to tell the children this fact. This

marriage would be good for all of them, a bigger house, wider yard, greater financial security. She had made the right decision.

Willie Lee frowned. "I will need Mun-ro to sleep with me, if I have to sleep in my own room." He made sleeping in his own room sound like a punishment. Tilting his head, he told Corrine, "Mun-ro can go sleep with you after I go to sleep, o-kay? O-kay, Mun-ro?"

Then it was, "Can I bring my worms with me to Parker's house?"

Marilee, who was thinking of sleeping with Parker, said, "Honey, Parker's yard will have worms in it."

She came out of her thoughts enough to see her son regarding her very seriously from behind his thick glasses. He said, "Yes…but I want my own worms."

"You can bring your worms, honey."

Her mind was not on worms, but on wondering how she would handle sleeping with a man, after so many years alone. This concern mounted with lightning speed. It had been many years since she had shared a mattress and covers with another adult. What if Parker snored? She did not know this about him.

There would be many adjustments to getting married. She had known this, but she had obviously not known it in the same capacity with which the knowledge now came to her on a rising tide of revelation.

She supposed they were all going to be bringing worms, of a sort, with them into this union.

As she made up her bed, she wondered if Parker liked his sheets folded over the mattress in hospital corners, or if he preferred them loose, so he could stick his feet out. He had a king-size bed, and she would like that. There would be plenty of room for Willie Lee or Corrine, if they needed to sleep with her because of a nightmare or sickness or thunderstorm.

Parker might not like the children to sleep with them.

As she got a glass from the kitchen cabinet and poured herself some cold tea from Tate's round pitcher, she thought of Parker's cabinets full of dishes. All mismatched.

She loved her dishes, which were heavily accented with cobalt blue. Hopefully Parker would be agreeable to pitching his dishes in the trash and using hers.

She would be asking Parker to make a lot of changes.

The ring would have to be sized down for her. She had said she would take care of it, and now she was vexed at herself for taking on the responsibility. Shouldn't Parker have said he would do it? It was, though, her finger that would have to be present. They should make plans to do it together. That was probably going to be one of their major adjustments, learning to do things together after each of them had lived so many years alone.

The setting on the engagement ring would also need to be worked on. It snagged in her hair, and on the rough fabric of the desk chair, and on the kitchen hand towel.

Finally she took the ring off and laid it in the little dish of paper clips on her desk. Wearing it would take some getting used to.

Just then the telephone rang. Marilee reached out to answer and then withdrew her hand.

The phone rang again, and then again, while Marilee sat there, gazing at it.

At the third ring, Corrine came in from the bedroom.

"We'll let the answerin' machine pick up this morning," Marilee told her. "I have things to do and don't want to be distracted. Unless it's Parker," she added hurriedly, as the answering machine clicked on.

Her mother's voice came through the speaker. "Just checking to see if my eldest daughter is still among the living," her mother said. "I haven't heard from you. I wanted to let you know that Carl and I are going away to a sales conference in Las Vegas this weekend. We're flying out Friday afternoon. Well…I guess that's it."

Marilee felt guilt wash over her for not picking up the phone. She felt more guilty because Corrine had witnessed her avoidance of speaking to her mother.

In the following moments of reflection, however, Marilee decided that she was perhaps glad to have displayed for Corrine her choice to have quiet time for herself. She had made a great leap by engaging herself to Parker. She had to catch her breath.

Parker stopped by at just after noon to give Munro his shots. Marilee had to quickly run to her desk and get the ring, then slip it on her finger, before he noticed she didn't have it on.

He shoved his chair away from his desk, refraining from putting his fist through his computer screen.

Why could he not come up with an editorial that pleased him? Where had all his brains gone?

Stalking from his office, Tate went to the coffee station to find that the coffeepot was empty, and so was the coffee can. Why hadn't someone thrown it out? Silly to have an empty can sitting in the cabinet. He tossed it into the trash and looked through the cabinets for a new can, slamming doors with increasing annoyance when he found no coffee.

When Charlotte ignored his slamming doors, he called to her, "We are all out of coffee."

"Yes?" she called back. Her brown eyes regarded him in an unconcerned manner that annoyed him.

"Who is responsible for maintaining the coffee?"

"Whoever is drinking it. Today that is you. A lot."

Tate sighed. "We need to keep coffee ready to offer to visitors." He didn't want his office to seem skimpy on anything. And doggonit, he wanted a cup of coffee.

Charlotte simply looked at him.

At the moment, the only other person in the offices was June, who proceeded to keep her head down and to scribble on paper. Tate contained himself. He had learned not to raise his voice to June. She got teary.

He glanced at the closed door of their comptroller's office. Zona had her own coffeemaker, and the absurdity of his employee having her own coffeemaker and him not having one struck him. He could go in and request a cup from her, but he would have to knock on the door and wait for her to unlock it. This was definitely a deterrent.

"I appoint you in charge of purchasing coffee supplies," he said to Charlotte, as he strode back past her desk. "I want you to make certain we have cans of coffee, filters, cups, anything else we need."

Maybe he would get his own coffeemaker. He should

do that as the editor-publisher. But then he would be the only one to make it, and he liked other people to make the coffee. He got tired of getting his own food all the time, which was the bane of being single.

"Who's going to brew it?" She rose and reached for her purse.

"I'll be in charge of brewing it." Since he apparently could not get anyone else to do it. "We'll rotate the weeks of who will brew it." The idea came to him, and he liked it! With rotation, he would only have to do it every six weeks or so. "But you will be fully in charge of stocking it." There, that settled it.

"Yes, *sir*. But I think in your mood the last thing you need is some more caffeine." With that, she whipped open the door and strode out in her long-legged fashion.

He was in a mood. A rare one for him, but he was in it, by golly, and that was it. He did not think having coffee was too much to ask to console him in such a mood.

The door had not fully closed behind Charlotte when Sheriff Oakes appeared through it. Tate was still standing there just outside his office door, dealing with his confusion between being in a bad mood and feeling guilty for not being able to correct himself.

"Just passed Charlotte. She said you were in, but that you were in a wicked mood."

That washed away his guilt and shoved him completely into his mood. "It's a rough day," he said, more sharply than he had intended.

"Yep. For me, too." The sheriff's drawn expression caught Tate's attention. "I came over to fill you in about these Tell-In Technologies folks."

"Come on in." Tate waved toward his office. "I'm sorry I can't offer you any coffee. I got an Orange Crush, in a can. It's hot, though." He had not gotten the six-pack into the refrigerator. What he needed was a good private assistant.

The sheriff, wisely declining the warm Orange Crush, lowered himself into the leather chair across the desk from Tate. He produced a toothpick from his breast pocket, stuck it in his mouth, wet it well and then began. "I got those Tell-In folks buggin' me from one side, and my wife chewin' at me from the other."

"Oh?" Curiosity swept Tate, improving his mood.

"Here it is from the start. What these Tell-In folks put forth is that this Dan Kaplan stole a computer chip he had invented for them. Something for increasing memory…I don't understand all this computer stuff. Anyway, he turned around and sold it to some Japanese outfit, and that's where the money comes from. Those Tell-In folks therefore claim that the money is theirs."

"That seems to be reaching a bit far." Tate found himself rather fascinated by Neville's use of a toothpick, which he chewed on even when speaking, whipping it from one side of his mouth to the other, as if to emphasize certain points.

"That's pretty much my opinion." He shifted the toothpick again and chewed rapidly. "What they're also claimin' is that this chip, or plans for it, or what-have-you, was in Dan Kaplan's possession and could still be in his things."

"I imagine it's small and hidden," Tate offered.

Watching the sheriff's mouth maneuver the toothpick, he tensed, ready for action, in case the man choked. He was not certain what he would do, though; likely normal procedures would be ineffective with a toothpick that might have to be surgically removed if stuck.

"So they say. What I gather is that they had some sort of informant who leads them to believe...*hope* is probably a better word...that Kaplan had only partially been paid and was in the process of deliverin' the chip and full plans, at which time he would receive the final payment. Fayrene does say that Kaplan told her that he was supposed to meet some people in Dallas, that he was headin' there, and was stoppin' here on his way down, and wantin' Fayrene to go down with him to Dallas." He slid the toothpick to the left.

"Anyway, to my mind, just because the chip once belonged to these Tell-In folks—and they haven't really proved that part, yet—I don't see how they can lay claim to the money. And I'm sure not givin' it over to these two yahoos on just their say-so, nor am I givin' over Dan Kaplan's stuff. That's what I told 'em, too."

"I imagine they were not too happy about that."

"No...no, they weren't." The toothpick went back and forth at a rapid rate. "That woman offered me five hundred dollars, if I'd give over the case and the money."

"Huh." Now here was a story stirring.

"Yep, and when I turned that down, she offered me a thousand."

Tate, who was not surprised, shook his head. The big man shifted in his chair, broke the toothpick in half with his tongue and spat it out.

"I just about threw her butt in jail, but I didn't have a witness…and besides, I wanted rid of them.

"I'll tell you what…those people do not understand that money doesn't call the shots around here. Justice and legality call the shots, and I uphold them, as is my sworn duty. The money and the briefcase and all of Dan Kaplan's effects are evidence in my jurisdiction, and until this is all sorted out, and with them producing some proof of their claims, what I got is a man who died clean of a heart attack, no report of theft from anywhere, besides what these Tell-In people are sayin', and everything paid up and no relatives, so his ex-wife has right to inherit by virtue of she was his only wife, and he left some letters stating plainly his intention to legally marry her again."

"Will that stand up in court?"

"Well, I don't know. But that's how I see it, and I figure until some judge tells me different, I'm in charge. My sworn duty is to protect and serve the people of this town, and that means Fayrene, not some strangers from outta state."

Tate nodded. They didn't make a lot of dedicated sheriffs like the one sitting before him.

The next instant the big man's shoulders slumped. "My wife isn't happy about any of this."

"She isn't?" Another wrinkle.

The sheriff shook his head and, in an obviously nervous habit, brought another toothpick from his breast pocket, as he said, "Maybe I am goin' out on a limb for Fayrene, but she's a good friend. When I was just a kid, seventeen, Fayrene sixteen years older, she and I…well, she showed a boy a big part about bein' a man." A softness came over his face. "Man, I was scared for my first time, and she showed me all about it. I guess she was my first love, but there wasn't anything either of us could do about it—you know, another time, another place, maybe."

The big man's face was filled with emotion that he obviously revealed to few people. Tate felt humbled.

He also thought about how still waters hid surprising matters. And about how for some reason people had always confided in him the deeply private details of their lives. Even as a teenager, other boys and girls would seek him out and confess all this stuff that he would rather they had kept to themselves. Back in his hometown he had known whose parents beat who, who was pregnant and unmarried, who was cheating whom out of what. His mother had said it was his demeanor and that he was meant to be a preacher;

his brother had said he was perfect for journalism, that all the stories would seek him out.

He recalled overhearing the women gossiping yesterday at the grocery store.

Neville jerked him out of his wandering thoughts by saying, "My relationship with Fayrene was never anything like how I love my wife, and all of it was years ago, anyway. The only way it pertains to today is my friendship for her. A man doesn't leave his friends just because he gets married."

"No, can't do that."

"My wife can't seem to see it any other way than that I'm strayin', though." Back and forth again went the toothpick. "Ever since she found out about Fayrene and me, she's been jealous, even though it happened years before she and I ever met. I've explained my head off, but nothin' I say can seem to change how she takes it." He shook his head. "I tell you, women can make a mountain out of a molehill."

Tate figured that each person viewed a molehill from a different perspective. If said molehill was in a neighbor's backyard, it was never so important as when it was popping up in your own backyard. Mighty hard to be unconcerned with your own backyard torn to pieces.

He had just seen the sheriff out the door when Charlotte came blowing in, and she looked madder than a wet hen.

Without a word, she slammed her purse on her desk and, still standing, proceeded to sort through the stack of mail she had brought with her.

Tate debated whether or not to ask her what was wrong. He did not feel up to handling another confidence or problem. He did, however, want his coffee, and he did not see that Charlotte had brought a can.

"Where's the coffee?" he asked.

"What?" She paused in her mail sorting to frown at him. "Oh, shoot. I went to the post office to get the mail first, and I got to talkin' to Julia and clean forgot I had gone out for coffee."

She had spoken to Julia Jenkins-Tinsley. He wasn't going to question that.

"I'll go get the coffee," he said and walked out the door.

He wondered if the main secret to life might be minding one's own business, and if this might not be the hardest thing in the world for a human being to do.

* * *

That evening Marilee experienced certainty in her decision to marry Parker. She was, in fact, finding her effort to love him worthwhile, because he was responding with equal effort to be agreeable. He got them both Coca-Colas, pouring hers into a glass, and brought the drinks to the dining room table, where together they discussed wedding plans.

Actually, it was not a discussion. Parker asked Marilee what she wanted to do about getting married. Marilee, wondering at the expression, cocked her head.

"Do you mean what to do about the wedding?"

"Yes," he said, and she noted the positive yes.

She wanted a small church wedding, with Pastor Smith officiating, and the children and her Aunt Vella present, and her mother would want to be included, of course. She got carried away with hopeful thoughts that maybe Anita would come up for the ceremony. And she would like enough time to get a new dress for herself, and new clothes for the children. And flowers.

"Whatever you want," Parker said.

"Well…I think it will take a couple weeks, at least, to get it together. We'll have to work around Pastor Smith's availability." She began a list, putting contacting the pastor first.

Then there was the question of a honeymoon. Marilee thought it would be a good idea for them to get away, and Parker exhibited more eagerness for this idea than for the wedding. The first question was where to go.

"Wherever you want," Parker said.

She wasn't certain where she wanted to go. "Charlene and Mason went to Cancun. They liked it." However, the prospect of distance and time between her and the children unnerved her. She did not say this, however.

"If that's where you want to go, that's where we'll go," Parker said. Then he added, "I'll have to see if Morris can come down from Lawton, or maybe get Dr. Swisher to come out of retirement. I'll let you know what week one of them can stand in for me, and we'll go anywhere you want. Your call."

Later, with the children in bed, they sat on the couch. Parker kissed her deeply and suggested that he stay the night.

Marilee pushed his hands from her breasts and told him gently, "I would rather we not go sleeping together until we are married. I think this is best for the children. We need to take one step at a time, Parker. I want to present the children with a secure environment."

Parker was quiet, and then he said, "All right."

Having focused on the children, which was easiest, Marilee said she was concerned about having to leave their garden behind. They all enjoyed it so much. It was too late to plant an entire garden in Parker's yard now, but she and the children could plant flower beds. Then there was the combining of their households to be considered.

"It'll take me time to sort through all our stuff. We can move over to your house gradually. Okay?" She was suddenly struck by a great reluctance to leave her cottage, no matter how small and cramped.

Parker said, "Sounds good."

"I'd like to buy Corrine a four-poster bed and make her room up really pretty."

Parker nodded and said, "Fine."

He kissed her and pushed her down upon the couch and began slipping his hands up beneath her shirt. Marilee felt the great confusion of desire and restraint. She wished she could explain to him how she felt about her position as a mother of small children. She could not speak to other times of her life, neither years before nor years ahead, but only to that particular time right then, when her choice was to wait. When, in fact, she felt a panic at the thought of sex. She fairly pushed him on the floor.

He did his little-boy frown, and she stroked his temple hair back around his ear with her fingernail. "I'm tired, anyway…and you said you were, too."

"Yep. Got a dog I need to check when I get back." He got to his feet.

She closed the door after him and went to clear away their coffee cups and clean up the sink. She paused, staring at her reflection in the night-black windows.

Parker had been most agreeable all evening. Why, then, did she feel such dissatisfaction?

She wished he wouldn't keep going after her body like a wildcatter determined to bore for oil. And that he would have been more forthcoming in making mutual decisions. He seemed unwilling to take part in planning, content to leave it all to her.

She sighed deeply, feeling as if she were a very hard woman to please.

Maybe that was the correct answer to *a woman like her.*

Marilee was just slipping into bed—and almost guiltily glad of having it all to herself again—when the telephone rang.

It was Belinda, who said, "Well, you are gonna have to do somethin' about Mama and Daddy."

"What do you mean?"

"Now I have got Daddy up here in my apartment, in front of my television, sleepin' on my sofa, and strewin' his stuff all over my bathroom. This is just not gonna work. You are gonna have to do somethin'. You have got to talk to Mama and get her to take Daddy back home."

Marilee said she had talked to Aunt Vella and had gotten nowhere. "I talked to your daddy earlier, too, and didn't get anywhere. I'm sorry, Belinda, but there doesn't seem to be anything I can do." Marilee was also thinking that Belinda should have been more concerned before everything had gotten to this point.

"Well, somebody is gonna have to do somethin'. I can't stand this," said Belinda, as distraught as Marilee had ever heard her. Then the line clicked dead.

With thinking up things to do to get her aunt and uncle back together, worrying over how the upheaval of moving from their house to Parker's would affect the children, and trying to work up enthusiasm for leaving the children to go on a honeymoon, Marilee lay awake a long time.

Nineteen

The Engagement

"**W**ell, congratulations." It was Charlene, telephoning just before nine. "Parker was just here to worm Leanne's horses, and he told us about giving you a ring. So it is finally going to happen—you and Parker are going to get married."

"Yes."

She really could not postpone another day telling people of the news. The first one she needed to tell was her mother, and she had better catch her before she got off to Las Vegas. Right there, with her hand still on the receiver after hanging up from Charlene, Marilee dialed her mother's number.

"Hello, dear. I'm packing.... I had to go out and get new luggage last night. Our other set was just so old, it looked tawdry. I didn't think it would look good for Carl's store for us to be lugging that stuff around. I still need to get Carl's shirts from the cleaners.... He's back at the store, and I'll pick him up on the way to the airport. I'd just as soon he stayed at the store and out of the way. He just hates to travel…. He gets all wrought up, and there won't be any food on the short flight down to Dallas. It's that awful prop plane. I sure hope it isn't rainin' down in Dallas, when we have to change planes. I have the hotel number around here somewhere…we're stayin' at the Grand. Oh, you won't need us anyway. It's just the weekend." Her mother finally paused.

"Mother, Parker and I are engaged."

There was no answer. The line was silent.

"*Here* it is! Whew, what a relief. It is such a nice packet from the travel agency. The itinerary isn't quite as detailed as usual. Dotty didn't do it, she's havin' her gallbladder out, and this young girl did it. She doesn't half know what she is doin'. Here's the confirmation number for the hotel. We sure need to have that. Last time the hotel was way overbooked and they wanted to put us across town, but I had my confirmation number, and I just refused. That's what you have to do, just refuse. I have the girl's name from the travel agency, too, just in case. Now, I have to get off here, honey. I have to get this packin' done. Carl doesn't like me to keep him waiting."

Marilee said quickly, "I wanted to tell you Parker and I are engaged."

"You are? You and Parker?" She sounded as if it came as a complete surprise.

"Yes. He gave me an engagement ring. We haven't set the date, but we plan sometime next month, as soon as Parker can get a fill-in vet, and I can schedule Pastor Smith."

"Well, I'm glad you have come to your senses on this thing. You are darn lucky to get Parker. Have you called Anita to tell her?"

"No…not yet."

"Well…oh, there's another call…it may be Carl. You can tell me all about your plans when I get home. Goodbye, dear."

Marilee hung up and breathed deeply. She thought Parker might be a little lucky to have her, too. Except that she felt so short of temper these days. She hoped she was not turning into a shrew.

She sat there for a full two minutes with her hand on the telephone, considering telephoning her sister. Anita would be at work, but maybe she had an answering machine hooked up now. Marilee thought she would just leave a message. That seemed the easiest.

In the end she decided to telephone her sister on Sunday and tell her everything. She was just too busy with doing Parker's birthday and telling everyone in town about the engagement.

Charlotte's reaction to Marilee's news was curious. Granted, Charlotte was not an effusive woman at the best of times, but Marilee found her manner, when told of Marilee's engagement, quite lacking.

Everyone at the newspaper was happy for her, of course. She made her announcement, and they all, except Charlotte, gathered round and repeatedly oohed and aahed at her ring. June began to cry, and Reggie went into that really annoying bit of making an announcement into a pen and then singing "There Is Love." She tugged Leo to his feet and danced him around. They really were a handsome couple. Tammy poured canned cola into paper cups and proposed a toast. Imperia thought to go call Zona to come out to see Marilee's ring and join them in celebration. The small accountant came forward and said, "I hope you two will be very happy, Marilee," in her amazingly sweet voice, lifted a paper cup of soft drink in good wishes, and then turned around and slipped right back to her office.

Marilee kept glancing at Tate's open office door. He was not at his desk, and she concluded he was not in at all. Disappointment swept over her, which was totally silly, of course. It was so much easier for her without him present.

Charlotte had quickly returned to her desk and focused on her computer screen. Marilee was a little taken aback by this distant behavior. Of everyone at the paper, Charlotte was her closest friend. She and Charlotte had worked there the longest, watching many others come and go. Both she and Charlotte knew the workings of the paper and could do everyone else's job, too, and they had done it all on numerous occasions. This expertise gave them a certain camaraderie born of facing crises together. So many times getting the *Voice* out had hung by a thread that Marilee and Charlotte had knitted up together.

It struck Marilee that perhaps the woman was jealous. Marilee's heart swelled with feeling. Charlotte was thirty-six and had never been married; she read scads of romance novels, saw every romance movie, and had displayed quiet crushes on a number of men passing through her life, Leo, Sr. being only the latest, yet as far as Marilee knew, Charlotte had not even had a date in ages. There were few single men in town who met with her approval, not to mention her height, which tended to scare men away.

Marilee sauntered over to Charlotte's desk and said in a low voice, "We're just going to have a tiny ceremony, no fancy dressing and not a lot of guests, just Mama and the children, but I was hoping you would stand up with me…be my matron of honor."

Charlotte regarded her solemnly from behind her thick glasses. "Okay. What day? Don't forget the grand opening of Green Acres on the first weekend of the month. We'll have to cover that, and I have a dental appointment the next Friday—on the ninth."

Marilee absorbed this rather halfhearted reply. "We haven't set a day yet," she said. "I'll work around those dates."

Across the street at the soda fountain of Blaine's Drugstore, Deputy Lyle Midgett enjoyed a Coca-Cola and barbecue sandwich made by Nadine, the new girl Belinda had hired, and told Belinda all about the goings-on down at the police station, where the people from Tell-In had returned with a third person, a thin, silent man who was some sort of search expert. Armed with a court order that gave them access to the dead man's effects, although not possession, they began an immediate and thorough search of Kaplan's luggage, briefcase and car. Lori was given custody of the fifty thousand dollars, stuck in a paper sack that she put under her desk at her feet.

"Judge Watkins signed the court order. They can't take

nothin', but they can search it right here, and they sure are doin' it," Lyle told Belinda, his voice muffled by a full bite of barbecue sandwich. "This is good." He smiled at Nadine, and Belinda did not like that much. She shifted herself to be right in front of him.

"Have they said how big the chip is?" Belinda already knew all about Kaplan being the inventor of the chip and having stolen it, as she had gotten the full account out of Lyle days ago. "Do they need a magnifyin' glass to see it?"

"Shush," Lyle whispered. Glancing around furtively, he lowered his voice. "I heard them say it is about the size of a dime, I think. Or maybe it was a nickel. Somethin' like that. I said he could have mailed it to the Russians, since it wasn't no bigger than that. I don't know why he wouldn't have done that."

"Russians? What would they want with it?" Lyle did not keep up with commerce, whereas Belinda read a lot of magazines. She read *Today's Money* just about every month. "Maybe you mean the Microsoft people."

Lyle shook his head and said it was some foreign country, only he couldn't remember which one. China, he finally decided, after thinking hard on the matter.

"I don't think anyone ever sends stuff like that through the mail," Belinda offered. "But I don't know why not. Maybe they do, and they just don't make movies about it, because that would be boring. I wonder where the dog fits into this."

"I haven't heard anything about any dog." Lyle shook his head.

"I told you about the dog," she reminded him, and he

said he knew that. "You said there was a dog dish in Kaplan's car."

"Maybe it was a dog dish, but there wasn't any dog food or anything. Might have just been some old dish." And Lyle had not been about to ask the sheriff about the dog, either, because questions might reveal to the sheriff that he told Belinda a lot of stuff he wasn't supposed to be telling her. He didn't know why he told her. Somehow he just found himself doing it. She was the first woman to ever really listen to him, for one thing.

The bell over the door rang, and Marilee and her children came in. Marilee called over for the children to be given whatever they wanted. "I'll be there in a minute. I'd like a chocolate shake."

Belinda, watching Marilee disappear behind one of the shelves of the pharmacy, wondered how Marilee could keep drinking chocolate shakes like she did and not ever get any fatter. Probably it was that Marilee was too nervous most of the time. Marilee was always doing or planning something. Belinda had observed that having kids tended to do this to a woman, which was why she had no desire for any. People were all the time asking her when she and Lyle were going to get married and have children. She replied that she knew when she was well off and could read an entire magazine when she wanted.

Her gaze flowed over the two small figures approaching the counter and lit upon the dog walking at Willie Lee's heels. A multicolored dog, with spots.

The children came and sat on stools to Lyle's right. Lyle, upon seeing the dog said, "I'm not sure dogs are supposed to be in an eating establishment. I think there's an ordinance."

Belinda, who came around the counter to get a better look at the dog, told Lyle, "Don't look, then."

Corrine twisted her stool back and forth and stared up at the lighted menu, obviously trying to make up her mind. Willie Lee wanted an ice-cream cone, one scoop of vanilla on a sugar cone. Belinda had found that Willie Lee generally knew exactly what he wanted.

"Mun-ro wants a dish of water, please," said Willie Lee, who always knew what his dog wanted, too.

Marilee came over with a gift box set of men's after-shave and cologne. It was the expensive brand Belinda's mother ordered from Germany, and she had managed to get a good business going with it among a number of the women seeking to spruce up their husbands. Belinda preferred regular stuff on Lyle; she saw no need to waste money.

Lyle told Marilee that he thought there might be a fine for bringing a dog into an eating establishment.

Marilee replied that they would leave, just as soon as they got done with their refreshments. "I'd like to buy a gallon of the vanilla ice cream, too, Belinda—for Parker's birthday tomorrow."

"You can get it out of the freezer before you leave," Belinda said and added, "It's gone up to seven and a quarter." If the ice cream was so special that Marilee wanted to buy it, she might as well pay well for it.

While Belinda rang up Marilee's charges, Marilee introduced herself to Nadine, who said, "Hiya'" and instantly turned around to wipe up all around. Nadine was proving a hard worker, who did not care to talk and cared even less to eat. Belinda was pleased.

As Marilee wrote out her check, Belinda saw the ring on her finger. "Is that an engagement ring?"

"Yes. Parker and I got engaged."

"Huh. Nice ring. When's the wedding?"

"We haven't set the date yet. Next month, though."

Belinda's attention was distracted from any comment on the matter, however, when the bell over the door chimed and in came the tall blond man—one of the Tell-In people. He stood there with the door open a moment, the air conditioner dripping behind him, all straight in clothes crisp and shiny, as he removed his sunglasses and seemed to scan the store. Then he came forward to the soda counter.

"I'll take a packet of the Motrin," he said, speaking to Belinda and motioning with his hand. "And a Coke, to go."

"You should try the headache powders," Lyle offered.

The man's head spun as if on a pivot, and his eyes observed Lyle, who added that headache powders went to work a lot faster. Lyle could be overly friendly, and Belinda could understand the man's frown, while Lyle just kept on. "It's 'cause they don't have to dissolve like a pill."

The man, not replying to Lyle's recommendation, paid Belinda with exact change. She put the money in the cash drawer and closed it with a snap. As she turned back to the counter, movement caught her eye, and she saw Nadine bending down…she was petting the dog that had slipped behind the counter.

The man walked out of the store, with his Motrin and Coca-Cola, without a word of polite goodbye.

Nadine said, "I would guess that guy is not from around here."

"He's one of those Tell-In people; and he has head-aches," Belinda said, informing Marilee that she knew things. "The sun probably gets to him. They're down there searchin' that Dave Kaplan's car out back of the police station, lookin' for a computer chip."

"Belinda...you aren't supposed to go tellin' ever'-body," Lyle objected.

"I'm not tellin' everybody. Just Marilee, and I think she probably should know, bein' a member of the press...and she is my cousin."

"What computer chip?" Marilee glanced from Belinda to Lyle and back.

"That ex of Fayrene's stole a computer chip from his company. He invented it, but that doesn't matter, it was still the company's chip, and he took it to sell to the Chinese. That's where he got the fifty thousand. But his company hopes he didn't have time to get it to the Chinese, and they came today with a court order to search his stuff. The sheriff hasn't told you any of this?" She leaned forward on the counter.

Marilee shook her head. "Tate is probably doing the story. All I did was speak with Fayrene and do the initial write-up."

Belinda did not think Marilee was sufficiently im-pressed with what Belinda was telling her. "They're takin' that Mercedes apart. They must figure that chip is hidden in there somewhere, or in that briefcase. A computer chip isn't very big. This is computer espionage."

Marilee, getting the children up from their stools, said she would make certain Tate knew to investigate for a possible story. Lyle asked her not to say where she heard about the matter.

As Marilee went out the door, Belinda looked at the dog walking behind Willie Lee's feet. It sure seemed that dog had made certain the Tell-In guy had not seen him.

"You are gonna get me into trouble, tellin' everything all over," Lyle said in a dispirited voice.

Belinda, ignoring the comment, leaned across the counter and said, "Parker is havin' an affair with Leanne Overton."

Lyle blinked. "But didn't Marilee just say she and Parker were engaged?"

"Yes."

"I guess Marilee must not know about Leanne, then," he said.

Belinda sighed. "Well, of course not." Lyle could be so dense.

After a minute, Lyle said, "How do you know about Parker and Leanne?" as if she couldn't possibly know anything and had gone and made up the story.

"That Julia Jenkins-Tinsley saw them," said Belinda in a what-for manner. "And she is tellin' it all over. She is such a gossip."

Fred Grace had installed a mechanical pony ride out front of the florist, sandwiched in between racks holding buckets of bouquets beneath his awning. Willie Lee saw it instantly when Marilee headed to the florist to get flowers for the party.

Marilee thought the ride a fine ploy to draw more mothers and grandmothers to the store.

"You aren't too big to ride yet, are you, Corrine?"

Corrine smiled shyly in answer. Marilee put a quarter in each child's hand and allowed them to remain outside and ride the pony while she went inside to get a table arrangement.

Corrine said, "I'll watch Willie Lee," as if to earn the quarter.

"I know you will, honey. Thank you."

Marilee entered the florist and stood for a minute to let her eyes adjust to the much dimmer interior. The first thing she saw clearly was Tate Holloway standing back at the counter. She heard his familiar voice, too.

"Have it delivered this afternoon," he said to Fred Grace.

Marilee had a little panic about seeing him, one that she did not understand at all. She couldn't just turn around and go out, though, and she wondered who he was having flowers delivered to.

She went toward the counter, and Fred Grace saw her and greeted her, and then Tate turned her way.

"Hello, Miss Marilee."

"Hello."

"I hear you and Parker are finally gonna tie the knot," Fred Grace said. The adam's apple in his thin neck bobbed whenever he spoke.

"Yes, we are. Next month sometime." She really needed to get a date set; she was getting tired of saying *sometime*.

Fred Grace, holding up an order paper, said, "I'll be

right with you, Marilee…let me get Tate's order in the works," and disappeared through the rear curtain, leaving Marilee and Tate standing there, alone.

It was perfectly silly for her to feel nervous about being alone with Tate. She launched immediately into telling him about the articles she had left with Charlotte, and the entire time she spoke, she tried to figure a casual way to ask about who was to receive Tate's flowers.

Willie Lee rode the pony first, and he laughed and laughed. Corrine liked watching him. She felt excited and happy about playing with the electric pony. This was a feeling she did not fully trust. Her past experience had been that she could not trust having fun. Somehow she usually had to pay for it.

As if to prove this point, suddenly here came the school principal, Mrs. Blankenship. "Hello, children."

Corrine said hello, and Willie Lee did, too.

Then, right there in front of Corrine's wide eyes, the principal said, "Here, let me treat you to another ride," and immediately she put a quarter in the slot for Willie Lee, and then gave Corrine a coin, holding it out until Corrine took it. With a smile and a nod, the principal disappeared inside the florist's store.

Corrine stared at the glass door and figured that the principal was in a good mood because school was out. Willie Lee was laughing and saying, "Yeee-haaa," and Corrine found she could begin breathing again.

It came Corrine's turn, and she rode, feeling a little self-conscious, since she was eleven years old. With her second coin, she said, "Willie Lee, ride with me." That way, if any classmates from school should come along and see her, it would look like she was helping Willie Lee.

"O-kay!"

He scrambled up behind her and put his hands around her waist. She quickly put the coin into the slot, and beneath them the metal pony began to gyrate. Willie Lee called out, "Yeee-haaa!"

Corrine had to laugh.

But then there was Munro in the middle of the sidewalk, backing up and wrinkling his nose with a growl.

Corrine blinked, taking in everything that was happening. It was the man who had come into the drugstore earlier—the man Belinda had said was a Tell-In man and had headaches—and a woman was with him. It came suddenly to Corrine that these were the two people who had stared at them on the sidewalk earlier that week, and they were heading for Munro.

The woman was saying, "Here, doggy."

"That is *my* dog," Willie Lee said, speaking with alarm.

Corrine felt Willie Lee let go of her waist. She reached back to grab him, to keep him from falling off the pony that was still bouncing.

"He looks like the dog that belonged to a friend of ours," the woman said.

"He is *my* dog," Willie stated again.

Corrine wished the pony would stop.

"How long have you had him?" the woman said, even as she moved toward Munro.

Just then the man jumped at Munro, to grab him, but Munro quick as a flash scooted under the front bumper of a parked car.

Willie Lee launched himself off the pony, yelling, "That is *my* dog!"

Corrine scrambled off the bouncing horse, toppling onto the concrete.

The next thing she saw was the man and the woman running into the street, and Willie Lee after them. Somehow she got to her feet and ran after Willie Lee, catching him right in the middle of the street and dragging him back to the sidewalk, her heart pounding clean out of her chest. There had been only one car far down the street, but it could have reached Willie Lee. And she was supposed to look after him.

Willie Lee was crying. Corrine put her arm around him and tried to think of something to say.

But then suddenly Munro appeared from behind the stand of flower buckets.

"Mun-ro!" Willie Lee went to the dog, while Corrine looked over her shoulder to see the two strangers going down the opposite side of the street.

"Shush!" She grabbed Willie Lee, and shoved him and the dog back against the stand of flower buckets, crouching there herself.

"I am go-ing to tell Ma-ma." Willie Lee made a move toward the florist.

"No," said Corrine, who believed it better to never tell anything. "If they do own Munro, your mother will make us give him back."

Willie Lee gazed at her from behind his thick glasses.

Just then Marilee came out of the florist shop, and Mr. Tate was with her. Right behind them came Principal Blankenship. Because the grown-ups were all talking, no one noticed that Willie Lee was sniffing. Corrine shook her head at him, and he pressed his lips together.

Aunt Marilee bid goodbye to Principal Blankenship, and Mr. Tate walked them along to the Cherokee, which was only a few yards down the sidewalk. Corrine kept an eye out for the two strangers but didn't see them. It was hard to see over the cars, though.

They got into the Cherokee, and Munro lay down with his head on Willie Lee's leg. Corrine and Willie Lee remained perfectly quiet while Aunt Marilee talked with Mr. Tate some more through the driver window.

As Aunt Marilee headed the Cherokee home, Corrine caught a glance of the man and woman at their dark car in front of the police station. She squished down in the seat.

"Corrine? Honey, what's wrong? You feel okay?"

"Yes, ma'am…I'm just a little tired. I think I want a nap. Willie Lee does, too."

"I will not tell, Cor-rine," Willie Lee said from over in his bed, where he lay with Munro.

"I won't, either," Corrine said. "And we'll have to watch out for a while, make sure we don't see those people again."

After a minute, Willie Lee asked, "Why?"

"Because they may be the real owners of Munro. They will take him." Corrine was puzzled about this entire thing, but she did not see anything to do but hide. In her experience, grown-ups rarely cared what little kids wanted.

* * *

Marilee turned off the whiz-bang computer, where she had written two small pieces for the paper, and rubbed her eyes. She should see about glasses.

Her gaze fell on Stuart's photograph. Should she put it away? Willie had long ago quit asking about his father. She had explained that Stuart traveled away, finally ending that he was gone from their lives. Willie Lee was such an accepting person. She wished she could be so, she thought, finally tucking the picture into the top drawer of her desk.

Rising, she turned out the lamps and walked softly to peer at the children on her way to bed. The light from the hall lamp fell softly into the room. Her gaze fell on Willie Lee, asleep all spread out, and then onto Corrine, who was facedown into her pillow, with Munro pressed to her side.

Corrine was crying softly.

"Oh, honey, what is it?" Marilee pulled her niece up into her arms.

"I…I had…a bad dream."

"Oh, it was only a dream. You are okay." After another minute, "Come on and sleep with me." She took Corrine's hand. Munro hopped from the bed and up beside sleeping Willie Lee.

Marilee snuggled Corrine into bed, got into her own gown and slipped in beside her niece, whose hands were formed into balls.

"I'm sorry, Aunt Marilee," Corrine whispered.

"Whatever for, honey?"

"Because I know you like to have the bed to yourself."

"Oh, sweetheart…yes, I do," she said, knowing honesty was in order. "But I also like to have you come in here sometimes, and Willie Lee, too. I like to hold you both close. You are a comfort to me, too."

Gradually she felt her niece relax, and gradually Marilee relaxed, too.

Some time before dawn, Marilee awoke to find Corrine on one side of her, Willie Lee on the other, and Munro at her feet. It occurred to her that it was quite possible that Parker would object to such crowded sleeping arrangements.

In that moment, however, thus surrounded by her children, with Corrine's hand knotted in Marilee's hair and Willie Lee breathing upon her chest, Marilee was supremely contented and fell immediately back into a deep, lovely sleep.

Twenty

Nick of Time

Marilee got up early, squeezing carefully out from between the children and the dog, succeeding in not awakening them. She went to the kitchen, made coffee as strong as Corrine's, and set about throwing her mind into the accomplishment of Parker's birthday party.

Sometime between the first and second cups of strong coffee, she began to go at it in an all-consuming manner that fully occupied her mind and kept her from perturbing thoughts about her pending marriage. She would deal with those concerns later, after she had finished with Parker's party.

She had the children's breakfast made when they came into the kitchen; Corrine was quite surprised, of course.

Leaving them eating and dawdling, she dashed around, gathering everything to take to Parker's house. She got herself into a chambray shorts sunsuit she had been saving for the occasion and that showed her bare shoulders to good advantange, applied her face in the thorough manner of the unmadeup look, and carefully pinned up her hair to appear careless.

While tying on canvas wedge sandals, she caught a glimpse of herself in the long mirror. She stood and observed her appearance and decided that she had made her decision about marrying Parker in the nick of time, while she still had something to offer and a man would even consider her. Her breath seemed to grow shallow with these thoughts, and she strode out the door and onward into the day.

At ten-thirty, they were each carrying boxes and bags out to the Cherokee; Marilee was somewhat surprised at the amount of the supplies, now that she tried to fit them all into the rear of her vehicle. As she was going about this, Tate came driving past, the top down on his car, his pale hair catching the sunlight. He stopped in the street and wished them a good day.

Marilee called back, "Good day to you, too," and the next instant, she turned, slammed the rear door closed, headed for the driver's seat and told the children to get in. Slipping behind the wheel, she wrenched the rearview mirror around, as if to look at herself, but really to watch Tate drive on.

She breathed a sigh of relief as his car disappeared, and then felt perversely annoyed.

Jerking the shift lever into reverse, she backed out into the street and then took off with the windows open. Willie Lee and Munro stuck their heads out their window, their faces to the wind for the drive to Parker's house. Willie Lee began singing "Happy Birthday," and Corrine and

Marilee joined in. They were singing "Happy Birthday" when they rolled down Parker's long driveway.

She was a bit startled to note the neglected landscape. The house could be deserted, in fact, with no other attention than mowed grass. She thought it odd that she had never noticed the lack of care before. Surely it had not been that way when she had last visited, which had been all the way last fall.

Parker came out the front door, and they all tumbled out of the car, yelling, "Happy Birthday!"

His smile was like that of a delighted boy. It made Marilee's heart ache and fill at the same time. "Here… you can take this helium bottle and this box," she said, pressing him into service to help empty the Cherokee of all the party paraphernalia.

"Wow!" Parker said when he saw his cake.

Marilee, very pleased, shifted the cake out of its box and onto the middle of the breakfast bar. She stuck in the candles, while Parker snitched a fingerful of icing and the children laughed as Marilee shoved him away.

Marilee saw immediately that she had not anticipated correctly the work necessary to have the house in order for a party. She was a little shocked at Parker's house, again pointing up the fact that she had not been there in some time.

While Parker was generally clean, he exhibited no thought to the finer points of home decoration. The house looked as if it was a stopping off place and nothing more, and his every-other-week housekeeper was obviously less than dedicated. This was the week that the housekeeper did not come.

The job of readying the house for the party was an endeavor that properly required days, but Marilee dove right in to accomplish the task in two hours. Like a veteran general, she gave everyone their assignments, setting Parker to work filling balloons with helium and Willie Lee to helping him. She gave Corrine the duty of arranging the patio furniture, table and dishes, and directing the males on how to hang the ribbons and balloons.

Tying an apron over her sunsuit, an addition that made her feel like a pinup girl, and armed with a basket for collecting strewn items, a bag for trash, several sizes of dusters and the vacuum cleaner, Marilee swept through the house in the manner of a guerrilla single-handedly reclaiming lost territory.

She first attacked the kitchen, the room that would receive the most use during the party, and had it in acceptable order, if still lacking in identity, in forty-five minutes, with numerous detours to answer questions from the crew on the patio. In a similar manner of pointed concentration, she proceeded on into the dining room, through the living room, and into the rear of the house and the two bathrooms and master bedroom. Pacing herself, she broke into only a light sweat; she had turned the air-conditioning thermostat down to an extravagant level.

All the while she cleaned, Marilee made mental notes of necessary decorating changes for when she and the children moved in. The carpet throughout would have to be changed from a deep blue that didn't go with anything. The bathrooms required new wallpaper and total decoration; the walls were currently some off-orange, and there was not one stick of pleasantry in them. She had never noticed that Parker had no taste in home decor colors. Marilee pictured towels of complementary colors, rather than selected at random, as Parker's appeared to be. She wanted linens in colors to match the towels, too, and she preferred the muted, earthy colors of sea green, lilac and blue that she employed in her own home. This would mean brand-new sheets for Parker's king-size bed, so enormous in comparison to her own standard double. Spreading up the covers, she wondered how Parker slept on such sheets—bright yellow and orange and green stripes. Surely such colors would tend to keep one awake.

Pausing, she stared at the bed, and then she sat down on it, testing the mattress by bouncing lightly. She quite liked it, although she would prefer to move it to the opposite wall, where there would be more room and the bathroom door would not keep hitting the left nightstand.

Parker liked mints and threw the wrappers on the nightstand, along with various brochures about animal medications, pairs of socks, a spare key, his pocket knife and loose coins. Marilee opened the drawer to brush the stray items inside, all except the socks. She snatched them up to toss into the basket of dirty clothes.

Something dropped to the floor.

An earring.

Picking it up from the carpet, she looked at it closely— a dangling earring of silver and turquoise and black onyx. And there, on the night stand, lay a matching earring, underneath where the socks had been.

Placing them in her palm, she gazed at them, then looked at the pillow right beside the nightstand, and then back again to the earrings, while all manner of thoughts twirled in her head, all of them on the same theme: what woman had been in this room?

"Marilee?" Parker poked his head in the doorway.

She jumped. "Yes?"

"Are you 'bout ready? Rick and Vickie just got here…. Rick's firin' up the grill." Parker looked happy and expectant, and very handsome.

"I'm coming."

She slipped the earrings into the pocket of her sunsuit, picked up her cleaning supplies and hurried to the kitchen. Parker was there getting cold drinks. She told him she wanted a Coca-Cola, and while he got it for her, she put her wrists beneath the faucet of cold water.

Of course, there could be any number of reasons why the earrings that were not hers were on Parker's nightstand.

He could have found them somewhere. This was the most reasonable explanation. Maybe the owner of one of his patients had left them at the clinic. This line of thought presented the image of some lunatic woman who took off expensive handmade earrings, maybe bored while awaiting her appointment, and just threw them on the floor or over the counter. Maybe she was hysterical because her pet died, so she ripped them out of her ears and tossed them down, and Parker had not yet discovered to which owner of which deceased pet the earrings belonged. He'd had a few deaths recently.

Marilee realized her imagination was running wild. There were, in fact, a lot of indecipherable thoughts running around in her head, which she kept shoving aside and which kept popping back at her, so much so that she found herself going to the kitchen to get a basting brush for Rick and ended up staring into the refrigerator, picking a grape tomato out of the big bowl of salad and eating it. What she really wanted was a piece of chocolate. The birthday cake caught her eye, and she had to resist the urge to cut herself a piece; it was rich chocolate underneath the vanilla icing.

Why did she not simply ask Parker where the earrings came from?

That was out, with Parker standing at the grill with Rick and the doorbell giving out a chime.

Ted and Wendy Oakes came without their three children. "I need a break," Wendy said, putting her hand on her round belly. "I'm trying to get all the rest I can before this one gets here. Here's Parker's present. It's a...oh, my gosh, is that an engagement ring on your finger?"

Marilee told her it was and ushered her out to the patio, where the big bowl of chips and guacamole caught the very pregnant woman's attention.

Ray Horn, who was recently divorced, brought his new girlfriend, Heather. Everyone was polite and didn't stare at her. She was a dark-haired, dark-eyed knockout, and looked at least fifteen years younger than Ray. She had brought her son, Bobby, a very pretty, shy dark-haired boy who was determined to remain on her lap. The two really were a lovely sight.

The Macombs, Jerry and Mary Lynn and their daughter

Sarah, drove up in their minivan, followed immediately by Charlene, Mason, Jojo and Leanne Overton in a brand-new Suburban. The people came pouring out of the vehicles, laughing and talking and bearing gifts and covered dishes. Charlene had cut her hair again; she looked stunning, walking beside Mason. The two's happiness was breathtaking. Mary Lynn, always in a hurry, was urging Jerry, who probably couldn't hurry from a fire, to get up to the house.

Marilee led the way to the patio, directed where to set dishes and offered cold drinks.

Charlene grabbed Marilee's hand and took a look at the engagement ring. "My heaven, that is a gorgeous ring. Congratulations, Parker!" she called across the patio to Parker, who apparently had taken up residence next to the grill with Rick. Parker, giving a shy grin, raised his beer in acknowledgment.

The women oohed and aahed appropriately at the engagement ring, each taking hold of Marilee's hand. She glanced over to observe Parker.

"Oh, you two haven't met," Charlene was saying. "This is my cousin, Leanne…Leanne, this is Marilee, Parker's fiancée and the official hostess of the annual Parker Day barbecue."

Leanne was pretty. "Hello." She stuck out her hand.

"Hello."

Marilee shook the woman's hand. Good blond frosting job, polished silver earrings, the makeup of a fashion model and bright smile…and a necklace crafted of fine silver and turquoise and black onyx.

"It's nice to meet you." Her gaze stuck on the necklace.

"You, too. I've heard so much about you."

"Oh?" The earrings burned a hole in her pocket. She refrained from whipping them out and asking the woman to lean over so she could compare.

Charlene, dipping a large corn chip into a red mixture, said, "Leanne brought her simply-to-die-for salsa. You have to try this, Marilee."

Marilee complied. "Oh, yes, it is good, really good."

"I want some," said Wendy, who came armed with a chip in each hand. "Vitamins A and C and almost no fat. I need to eat a lot of it."

"Go for it," Marilee said, then turned away. "I'll get more ice."

She took up the ice bucket that was still half-filled and retreated to the kitchen, where she stood for a moment gazing at nothing. Then she went to the window that looked out at the patio of people—Heather was whispering something in her son's ear. The two girls, Jojo and Sarah had commandeered the glider and were swinging. Corrine sat alone, watching them. Was Willie Lee still okay? Yes, there he was beneath the rose of Sharon, digging for worms.

There was Leanne, her profile turned toward Marilee. Marilee realized the younger woman had her blond hair pinned up in almost the same way Marilee did. Parker was over in the male knot beside the grill, as if this were their domain. She watched him tilt his head in the manner he used when listening, this time to Ted, who seemed to be telling a joke.

Marilee fished the earrings out of her pocket and gazed at them.

Returning them to her pocket, she then filled the ice bucket and returned to the patio to smile and serve as the gracious hostess.

Things might not be as she thought. She should not jump to conclusions.

The moment came, totally unplanned.

Marilee was loading the dishwasher with the first load, Parker was filling the ice bucket from the freezer, and Leanne appeared, bearing an armload of dirty dishes.

"Here's the last of them, I think." Leanne set the dishes on the counter and wiped her hands on her shorts.

"Thank you."

There they were, just the three of them.

"Oh, Leanne…I think I have something that belongs to you." Marilee reached into her pocket.

Leanne, who had already turned to leave, paused and cast Marilee a curious look.

Marilee held out the earrings on her palm.

"Oh." Leanne said. Her face lit with recognition, and her hand reached out, then stopped in midair, as her eyes cut to Parker.

Parker, who had turned to look, averted his eyes.

"I found them on Parker's bedside table. I believe they match your necklace, Leanne."

She knew the truth of it, the same as if it had been stated aloud, although no one said a thing.

Leanne's pale eyes studied Marilee, and Parker looked at the floor. She wondered if she had expected him to say anything. Surely she knew him better than to expect him to take his part.

Laying the earrings on the counter, she stepped past Leanne and went out to the patio to gather the tablecloth off the table that Ted and Ray were moving, in order to have room to dance.

Marilee and Parker danced and mingled and gave no indication there was a problem between them, other than that they did not say a direct word to each other, a fact no one seemed to notice. Leanne kept to herself, but no one seemed to notice that, either. A good time was had by all.

Afterward, after everyone had left, traipsing out to their respective vehicles and going away down the gravel drive in a cloud of dust rising in the evening heat, Marilee gave Parker back his ring.

He said, "It didn't mean anything, Marilee…it just happened, and you and I weren't engaged then. You wouldn't even sleep with me. Leanne doesn't mean anything to me. Don't take it like this."

She said, "It isn't because of you and Leanne. I understand…I know it wasn't anything. It is just that I suddenly realize we are not suited. I apologize that I just now see this. I should have seen it from the beginning. We are great as friends, but not as mates. We'll kill each other in six months, if we live that close. I can't stand it that you put up with mismatched colors."

He was staring at her, possibly, she thought, because she had never dared speak so directly to him. She had never dared to speak so directly to herself.

Gathering her purse and the last bag of her stuff to take home, she headed for the door. He followed close behind her.

"Marilee, let's talk about this."

She was running away, she realized, but did not stop. "Let's talk later, when we've thought this all out," she tossed over her shoulder. That would have to do.

She strode out the door and down the walk to the Cherokee, where Corrine, given the keys, had the engine and air-conditioning running. She got behind the wheel, took a last look at Parker, standing there at his front door, and then turned the car and drove away.

Great emotion welled up in her. It was a great epiphany that seemed to ring out from above and wash all over her.

The incident had given her an out, she realized, experiencing relief. This was followed closely by seeping guilt, because she had basically led Parker on. She had led herself on. She had allowed the fear of loneliness, the desire for physical and financial ease, as well as desire for her mother's approval, plus who knew what-all other motives, to make a fantasy out of a relationship that could be only what it was: friendship. Nothing more.

She had been trying to make herself fit where she was not going to fit, and further, she had been trying to make Parker fit into her image of what she wanted.

She caught sight of his neglected yard in her rearview mirror.

In the nick of time, she thought. In the nick of time.

It was dusk. Marilee walked with Aunt Vella in her aunt's rose garden, where lights stuck in the ground emitted a soft glow. The children chased the first fireflies of the season across the lawn.

"I'm so ashamed," Marilee told her aunt. "I was

making my relationship with Parker into something it just couldn't ever be. I was trying to make him how I wanted him to be." She shook her head. "I just saw myself getting older, and I didn't want to be alone, I guess."

"Ah, honey, I know." Aunt Vella put her arm around Marilee and squeezed her tight. "There is nothing to be ashamed of. You had to go through this experience to learn…. That's what these things are for. We learn, and we press on ahead, without looking back.

"And as for being alone, well, we all are really, for all of our days on this earth. We are all in this alone together."

Moths were batting around streetlights when Marilee loaded the children and Munro into the Cherokee and headed down the street and around the corner to home.

The Porter house—Holloway house—was dark, the portico where Tate parked empty. He had his dinner with the mayor, she remembered.

And then she was turning into her own driveway. Home. Her porch light shone warmly. She unlocked the door and thought that she could never again enter her house and not be glad to be home. It might be small, but it was so very pleasant, and all the colors matched.

The Valentine Voice
Sunday, May 20
Today's Highlights:
—More people spending their money at home. City sales tax revenue up by 3 percent. Debate as to how to spend money. Story on page 1.
—Tuesday election for city council seat vote. Over-

view of two candidates: Mayhall versus Tinsley. Story page 1.

—Sinkhole on First Street causes dilemma for City Works Department. Story page 4.

—Majority of Valentine citizens want easier purchase of caskets, but not at discount department stores. Your views on page 3.

Twenty-One

Filling in the Holes

Tate waited until nine o'clock to telephone Charlotte. He was afraid he would either catch her too early and wake her up, or miss her if she went to church. He felt relief when she answered on the second ring, her voice as competent as ever.

"No, it isn't too early. I do sleep in on Sunday mornings, don't get up until seven."

Tate could imagine. "I'm going out of town," he told her. "Down to Houston to see some folks, and then on to Galveston to visit my mother. I'll be back Friday or Saturday at the latest. I finished up my editorials for the next two editions, plus a couple extra pieces, and left them on my desk. I'll be in touch by phone and e-mail. Oh, and tell Marilee not to worry about feeding the cat. I'm takin' him with me."

There wasn't much to that, he thought, as he hung up and finished packing.

He threw his two bags in the back seat of the BMW, with its top down. Then he got Bubba and put him in a cat carrier he had found in the laundry room, and put the carrier in the front seat.

Bubba wasn't happy. He growled. Continually.

A man and his cat. It appeared it had come to this, Tate thought, throwing a towel over Bubba, who then quit growling.

He turned the key, backed out of his drive and started away, thinking that his mother was probably at some healing revival or bridge tournament, and he would end up alone with Bubba, lying in her spare bed with a ceiling fan to look at for the next three days.

No matter. He needed a long drive. He could not stay and see Marilee engaged. Maybe getting away would give him a better perspective. He would come to accept what he could not change.

The sun was bright and warm when Marilee and the children and Munro walked to church. Out front of the parsonage, the sinkhole was still cordoned off with the yellow City Works tape. Holding securely to both children's hands, Marilee took them over to join the small knot of observers. The hole had grown; the engineer at City Works was still working out the best way to deal with it.

Marilee looked at the hole and thought of her life.

Munro accompanied them up the steps and into church and into the back pew. He was accepted as routine now.

Marilee, sitting there gazing at the light playing on the altar and determinedly keeping to her no-worry status, was suddenly jerked to awareness by whispers. People were whispering and looking at the group who had just passed Marilee's pew.

It was Winston, with Ruthanne and Mildred on his arms, and Aunt Vella following them, sashaying in a bright floral dress and an enormous sweeping hat. Ramona Stidham, who sat with Norm and an entire pew of grandchildren in front of Marilee, turned and said, "Marilee, I don't care what people say, Vella has sure gotten a life since she and Perry split up."

Getting a life was an apt phrase, Marilee thought, watching her aunt's filmy dress sway as she slipped into the pew beside Winston Valentine. The poor man was somewhat squished, with Mildred leaning toward him on one side, and Aunt Vella smacking him with her hat on the other every time she turned her head.

They stood for the opening hymn. Willie Lee, standing on the pew, leaned on Marilee's arm, his eyes on the hymnal while he tried to sing along as if reading the words. Corrine stood straight, holding open her own hymnal, singing in a faint voice. "'His eye is on the sparrow…'"

Tears of gratitude filled Marilee's eyes. She looked with her blurry vision at the cross on the altar. *I'm sorry, Lord, for all this mess with Parker. I behaved poorly with him. Running on fear, not faith. Show me the way, Lord. I can't do it on my own.*

Just as Pastor Smith was giving the closing blessing, there came the sound of a crash from outside. Before he had properly finished, people were exiting the building, intent to see what had happened. Marilee guarded Corrine and Willie Lee, to keep them from being trampled.

"Well, look at that."

"My Lord."

"Marilee, you'd better get over here for a story."

The pastor's wife's little green Toyota, which had been parked several yards distant from the sinkhole, was now sitting very nearly nose first in the hole that had widened in all directions.

"This is good," said Winston, causing people to look at him. "This thing has probably hit bottom, so there's nowhere to go with it but up."

It was a daunting thought that now she would have to go tell everyone that she and Parker were not getting married after all. She managed to get away from church without one person asking her about it, and her Sunday was spent blissfully alone with the children, but on Monday, the prospect loomed over her head.

"I do not want to go down-town," Willie Lee stated, when she told him they were going down to the *Voice* offices.

"You don't?" she said, surprised. Willie Lee was always so agreeable. "I need to take some articles to the paper, honey, and afterward I will take you to get ice cream. Wouldn't you like that?"

"Yes. I like ice cream."

"Then come on. Let's get your shoes on."

Willie Lee shook his head. "Mun-ro and I want to stay home." He climbed on the couch and sat there, looking at her from behind his thick glasses.

"Are you sick, honey?" She felt his forehead. It felt fine.

He looked at her. "No. I am not sick. I want to stay home."

Marilee looked over at Corrine, who sat in the big chair with a book. "I want to stay home, too," Corrine said.

Marilee called Aunt Vella, who readily and eagerly agreed to come stay with the children. "They are probably tired of you draggin' them around everywhere with you," Aunt Vella said.

Likely this was true, Marilee reflected. She needed to find a way to get them interacting with other children.

She decided to walk downtown, and along the way she rehearsed several ways of nonchalantly telling Tate, "Parker and I are not engaged. We have called it off."

She had seen Tate only once since the night she and Parker had gotten officially engaged, when he had taken care of Willie Lee and Corrine. He had kissed her quickly, in congratulations. She was disappointed that he had not come to her house with a pitcher of iced tea since then. Perhaps he had found some other woman upon whom to bestow his tea. And of course that was just fine. She did not want anything special to do with Tate Holloway. In fact, thinking of it further, she was torn between wanting to tell him that the engagement with Parker was off and being quite reluctant to admit it. Tate had been the one to be adamant that Parker was not the one for her. Now she would have to admit he had been right.

Tate's office door was closed, she saw first thing upon coming into the newspaper offices. She had not seen the door closed in some time. Perhaps he was having a private meeting, maybe with Leo, who was the only one not in evidence.

She went to her desk, plopped down her tote and purse, and stated in a loud voice, to get it over in one fell swoop, "Parker and I are not getting married. We have called it off."

There were the expected surprise and condolences. Reggie, bless her heart, came over and hugged Marilee hard and long.

"I'm here, if you want to talk," Reggie said.

"Thank you, Regg." Her heart warmed. Reggie gave her another quick hug, Imperia kissed her cheek, and June laid a handful of Hershey's chocolate Kisses on her desk.

She looked at the closed door to Zona's office; she did not want to leave the woman out of the goings-on, so she went over and knocked.

When Zona's faint, "Come in," sounded, Marilee poked her head in the door and said, "I just wanted to let you know I won't be marrying Parker after all."

"Oh." Zona blinked behind her glasses.

Marilee withdrew and was closing the door, when Zona said, "I'm sorry for your disappointment, Marilee."

She put her head back in again. "I'm okay."

"Good."

Marilee withdrew again, and Zona said, "Maybe you had better leave the door open…just a crack."

"Oh, okay. How's that?"

"That's fine. Thank you."

Marilee stood there looking at the crack in Zona's door, the crack in her secure wall.

Then she went back to her desk. Well, she had dispensed with a necessary responsibility, and everyone was back to work at their desks, evidence that her private life had little effect on others.

Her editor's door was still closed. She debated about whether to go knock on it.

She took the update on the sinkhole and the obituary write-ups to Charlotte's desk and said in an offhand manner, "His door is closed. Is he in some sort of meeting?"

Charlotte shook her head. "Nope. Gone for the week, be back Friday or Saturday."

"Oh."

When she recovered enough from this surprise to speak, she said to Charlotte, "I guess you're off the hook for standin' up with me at my wedding."

"I never felt on the hook. I just wasn't too thrilled about you marrying Parker." Charlotte sat back and turned her computer screen to the side.

Marilee looked into the woman's dark eyes. "You knew about him and Leanne."

"Yes."

"Does everyone know?"

"Not everyone, but enough people. Julia Jenkins-Tinsley knows and told."

Marilee let out a large sigh.

"I didn't think it was my place to tell you," Charlotte said, looking apologetic. "Telling just never seems to make anything…well, work out."

Marilee nodded, at once touched by Charlotte's caring, and hurt that the woman had held such a secret about her life.

"I never thought you two were suited. You don't match. You are a woman who…" Charlotte paused, as if thinking.

"A woman who what?" *A woman like you.*

Charlotte shrugged. "A woman who needs someone different than Parker."

That did not at all satisfy, but Marilee decided she would rather let the subject drop. "I guess I'll go over to the post office and let Julia know the engagement is off. If I tell her and Belinda, I won't have to tell another soul."

"Well, you're probably right there," Charlotte said. Then, as Marilee went out the door, she called, "Oh…you don't have to feed Tate's cat. He took it with him."

"Well, my goodness, he must have gotten fond of it."

"A man and his cat," Charlotte said, casting a wave and picking up her glasses to again focus on her computer screen. It was wearing to be involved in people's private lives; she preferred books that she could put down at will.

The phone on her desk rang. Without taking her gaze off the computer screen, she reached to answer. It was her boss.

"Hi, is Marilee there? I just called her house and Vella said she was down there."

"She's already gone…just this minute." Charlotte spoke loudly; there was a lot of noise coming across the line.

"Oh." Pause. "Well, how is everything there?"

"The same as always…too much for the few of us to do but none of it earthshaking. Oh, except I suppose the sinkhole is earthshaking—it just about ate the pastor's wife's car yesterday morning." She was again raising her voice over background noise on her editor's end, and this made her peevish. "Where are you? What's all that noise?" People should know trying to talk and listen over noise was impolite.

"That's just some friends…we're at a bar for lunch."

Now Tate had raised his voice, and Charlotte's mind went into visions that caused some disapproval, and worry. Maybe, because of all the strain of changing the *Voice* around, their editor was going to stray into all manner of irresponsible behavior. He'd just up and left on this trip, like he was running off.

The noise abated. "There, that's better," he said. "Put Reggie on the sinkhole. Tell her just to take a picture and write a caption. No need for an article. We'll begin following it with pictures."

"Marilee took care of it."

"Oh, okay." Pause. "Then everyone is fine."

"Yes, everything is going along fine." Then, because he sounded a little disappointed and she wanted him to feel responsibility, she added, "But you've only been gone a day. You never can tell what emergency might happen. You'd better stay ready."

The visit to Julia Jenkins-Tinsley was short. Marilee poked her head in the door, saw Julia at the counter and said, "Julia, Parker and I have broken off our engagement."

Julia's eyes went round. She opened her mouth, but Marilee pulled her head back out of the doorway and headed down the sidewalk for the drugstore. She required an enormous chocolate sundae.

Just as she entered the store, the door opened and there came Winston, being hustled out the door by Uncle Perry. Marilee had to back up.

"I'll thank you to go use the new Rexall out on the highway," said Uncle Perry, who then shut the door.

Winston straightened himself, smoothing his shirt and adjusting his belt.

"Are you all right, Winston?"

"Yes." He smiled quite happily. "Yes, I am. I stirred him." With a nod and "Good day" to her, he smacked his cane on the concrete and started away.

Marilee went in and checked on her uncle, who she found sitting in his chair, like always, although his face had color in it for the first time in years. She asked him if he was okay, and he said, "I am as okay as any man could be who has been thrown out of his home by his wife gone insane and havin' an affair, and who has a daughter who doesn't want him, either."

For a moment Marilee worked on finding some positive comment to refute the statements. At least she should contradict the accusation of Aunt Vella having an affair. But could she?

What came out was, "I'm sorry, Uncle Perry," and by the look he gave her, she knew she had fallen far short.

She made a retreat to the soda fountain, where the new girl, Nadine, looked at her over the counter.

"I'll have a chocolate..." She paused, reconsidering. "I'd like a glass of iced tea," she said. She was ready for a change.

"Sweetened or unsweetened?" Nadine asked.

"Sweetened." She watched the girl turn to fill the order.

She had to stand on tiptoe to get the glass. "Where is my cousin this morning?" she asked.

"Upstairs…said she was goin' to put a cold cloth on her head."

"Oh." Marilee sat there, her eyes coming around to see her image in the long mirror on the wall.

Nadine set the tall glass, with a slice of lemon on the rim, in front of Marilee and plunked down a spoon beside it, then turned back to her compulsion of wiping every bit of stainless steel in sight.

Marilee sipped the tea and occasionally looked at herself in the long mirror on the wall. She made no effort to figure out anyone's life, not even her own. For those minutes she sat and relished the cold sweet tea in a tall glass, and it was enough.

When she finished, she put the money on the counter and said to Nadine, "Please give Belinda a message for me. Tell her that her cousin Marilee and Parker Lindsey broke off their engagement."

Then she left and walked home, thoroughly refreshed.

It needed to be done. A full apology and explanation were in order. If he did not want to speak to her, he could say so.

She telephoned Parker and asked if he was free to come by that evening.

He said, "Yeah…I guess I can."

It was dusk when he arrived. She met him on the front porch. "The children are watching a movie on television. Let's sit on the steps."

They sat side by side. Parker didn't say anything; he

sat rubbing his hands together as he often did when uncertain. Marilee reminded herself that she was the one who had requested the meeting. She had rehearsed what she was going to say and still had great difficulty getting the words to her tongue. "I'm sorry, Parker, for how I've treated you."

He looked surprised, but said nothing.

She took a breath and went on to say that she had been attempting to make more out of their relationship than was there all along. She had done this by having the wrong motives, and said she had not seen the reason she kept putting off sleeping with him was that she was not as committed to the relationship as she believed. She explained that she was just not ready to be married. Finally she quit talking, because she doubted that Parker got any of it anyway. She doubted she had made a lot of sense out of something that even she did not fully understand.

"I do hope we can be friends. We always were good friends," she ended.

She wondered about Parker's motive for wanting to marry her, but decided not to ask. If he said he loved her, she doubted she would believe it. She suspected he had wanted to marry her simply to get her into bed again, which seemed really strange, so perhaps it was that added to someone to keep house and cook for him. Parker did seem to need taking care of.

The extent of what Parker said was, "Yeah…I guess we're pretty good friends."

Marilee looked out at the streetlight where it pooled on the sidewalk. Yep, nick of time.

Twenty-Two

Family Matters

Corrine was reading in the big chair when she heard a car pull up in the driveway. Her Aunt Marilee was working at her desk. She sat there staring at the computer, with her chin propped on her hand, looking like she did when she was frustrated. Willie Lee and Munro were watching cartoons on the television.

Corrine, as if her antenna were tuned to any change, rose up enough to see out the window. The car, sleek and dark, was unfamiliar; an unfamiliar man was getting out from the driver's side.

With a gulp, Corrine slipped down beside Willie Lee and whispered in his ear, "Somebody's here. Take Munro in the bedroom."

He cast her a puzzled frown, and she made wide eyes at him. "Hurry up…they might be here for Munro." Ever since that day when the two people downtown had tried to get Munro, she had been on the lookout and ready.

Willie Lee scrambled to his feet, causing Aunt Marilee to look over from the computer. Corrine heard voices coming up the walk and shook her head at Willie Lee, to tell him to keep his mouth shut. He and Munro went on to the bedroom, and Corrine looked at the door. Someone knocked.

Corrine went to the door and slowly opened it, peering around it with half an idea that she could shut it again if need be.

It was her mother standing there. Her mother with a smiling face.

"Hello, hon. Are you gonna let me in?"

"Mama!"

Marilee, in something of a daze, walked across the room to greet her sister, taking in the man standing behind Anita with a cursory glance, before her gaze fell totally on her sister's head bent against Corrine's. Two dark heads together, two at last.

Then Anita looked up at Marilee, her expression so hesitant and doubtful of her welcome, that Marilee instantly opened her arms, and the two of them fell together, embracing and crying, "Ohmygosh, it is good to see you!"

It was strange how the burst of warm closeness could quickly fade to one of caution.

Marliee made coffee for her sister, who had come, out of the blue, not even calling first, taking for granted, of course, that Marilee would be right here where she always was—good ol' Marilee—just waiting to see Anita and entertain her and the man who had brought her, Louis

Alvarez, a man so handsome and full of sex appeal that he could probably get women to drop their pants with one glance of his smoldering eyes.

Marilee, after the initial surprise, told herself she had been awaiting such a visit. Anita was given to showing up when she felt like it. Listening to Anita's and Corrine's voices, softly talking, coming from the dining room, she felt a stab of fear. *Was Anita going to take Corrine away?*

Parker had been so right; she had not wanted to deal with this happening. For an instant she felt as if her brain were sizzling and she might just go all to pieces.

With a deep breath, she straightened her shoulders and put the hot pot of coffee on a tray, with cups and saucers, cream and sugar, glasses of juice for the children, and her best cloth napkins. She carried it all in to the table.

"I'm sorry I don't have a coffee cake or anything. I planned to go shopping this evenin'." It was lunchtime. She could not feed them peanut butter and jelly, which she had planned for her and the children. "Would you two like pizza? I could order it in."

"Oh, we don't need anything, Marilee. Don't fuss." Anita flashed a smile bright as a camera bulb. Anita was as beautiful as ever, thoroughly and expertly made up, hair shining, clothes as if they came from Neiman-Marcus, which she had always managed, even when unemployed. She laughed gaily. "Louis doesn't eat sweets anyway."

Louis, who drove a Jaguar and wore a large diamond ring on his little finger, looked like nothing softer than well-done steak ever entered his mouth.

Marilee passed out the cups of coffee and tried to

ignore that her hair was pulled back in a band, and she wore a T-shirt and sweatpants.

"My car would never have made this trip," Anita said. "But I wanted to see my baby—" she stroked Corrine's hair "—so Louis said he would bring me. We can't stay…just this afternoon, and we have to get back. Louis has a court case tomorrow, and I've got to be back at work."

No mention of taking Corrine with her.

Marilee studied her sister's face, then looked over to see Corrine's dark eyes moving anxiously back and forth from Anita to the dark-haired, totally impassive Louis.

Willie Lee came and showed his Aunt Anita his dog and his fresh bucket of worms dug just that morning. When she asked how he kept the worms alive, he told her he let them go every night in the garden. "But I keep Munro with me. He sleeps with me. He is my dog. Some people tried to take him away, but they did not get him."

"Well…that's good," Anita said.

"Who tried to take Munro, Willie Lee?" Marilee asked, puzzled about the comment. She could not recall any such incident.

"Oh, it was the dogcatcher came by," Corrine put in, "while you were in the florist…remember? We told them that Munro was our dog."

"Yes, they were try-ing to catch my dog," Willie Lee said.

"I'm hungry," Corrine said, sliding off her chair. "I'm going to make us sandwiches, okay, Aunt Marilee? Willie Lee can help me. You all stay there and talk."

She and Willie Lee, followed by Munro, went into the

kitchen. Marilee saw Anita leaning over, following her daughter with her eyes, until the swinging door came swinging closed. Then Anita and her Louis and Marilee all looked at each other, in the manner of wondering what in the world to talk about now that they were left on their own.

Marilee picked up the pot of coffee. It was still warm; she had made it strong, and now it was thick as sludge, but Louis pushed his cup forward. He did not use cream or sugar. He had yet to say a full sentence, she realized.

"So you are an attorney, Louis?" Marilee asked, surveying him, wondering what sort of bad habits were hidden beneath his fine clothes and appearance.

"Yes," he said, his eyes coming up and meeting hers in a surprisingly straightforward manner. "I work for the county prosecutor's office."

"Ah. Sounds interesting." She experienced a sort of attack of liking for the man. It came from his steady gaze and steady tone of voice.

"You're not wearing a ring," Anita said, as Marilee spooned sugar into her warm coffee.

At Marilee's look, Anita said, "Mama called me last Friday and said you and Parker are gettin' married. Where's your ring? Didn't Parker give you a ring?"

Bingo. This was the reason for the sudden visit, and for hauling up here with her Mr. Stud-man.

"Parker and I called it off," Marilee said.

Anita looked startled. "Called it off? But didn't you just get engaged last Thursday?"

"Wednesday. And we called it off Saturday, after his birthday party. We realized our error quickly." She did not know what possessed her, but she looked straight at Louis and said, "So, Louis, are you and Anita getting married?"

He shook his head, and it was his turn to surprise her, when he said, "I'm already married."

Marilee, who had just sipped her coffee, almost spat it out.

They had long been separated by Anita's bent for the "high life," and Marilee's bent for the quiet side. Anita, in anger, went her way, and Marilee, in anger, went hers, and every once in a while, when Anita needed Marilee, the two got together. Why was it Anita never seemed to think that maybe sometimes Marilee needed her? Maybe she did think it and didn't care, and this caused Marilee's stomach to knot.

She was not surprised that Anita intended to leave Corrine with her indefinitely. She *was* a little surprised that Anita was moving with Louis to New Orleans.

"He's takin' a position there with a private law firm…a big, important firm," she said, and reached up to break a leaf off a low-hanging branch of the elm tree.

They were out in the yard, walking around the garden, just the two of them alone. Standing there, with a slice of late-afternoon sun playing on her dark hair, there was about Anita the air of a woman on the edge. Marilee could not put her finger on it. Her sister had always been too much, she thought. Too beautiful, too sensitive, too wild and passionate, all too much for her small body and unstable spirit.

"And what will you do?" Marilee wanted to shake Anita. "You're going to up and leave your good job at the courthouse?"

"Louis will see if I can get on at the firm." Anita, withdrawing from Marilee's annoyance, played the leaf around in the air. "I have experience now in the legal field, and offices always need experienced secretaries. If the firm doesn't want me, there'll be somewhere I can work."

"You are not going to marry him, but you are going to base your life on his. So, where does his wife fit in?"

"Oh, don't be so righteous, Marilee. His wife has left him but doesn't want a divorce and will make it real nasty if he tries it. Is your life any better? Stuck here in this one-horse town, workin' like a dog to keep this little cottage. Lordy."

"This little cottage is apparently good enough for your daughter."

Anita's eyes flashed at her. "I'm not you, Marilee, and I never will be."

"Thank God" hung in the air.

Anita's eyes were pinpoints. "I need a man in my life, Marilee. I don't want to be a woman alone. I don't see any future at all in that. At least, not a future worth livin'."

Marilee, gazing into her sister's sultry countenance, thought that she agreed a lot with the sentiment, if not fully, but that it would do no good to discuss her views.

In an instant Anita turned all sweetness, as if turning on a faucet, and went on about how the cottage and Valentine really were most suited to raising children, and how Marilee was a much better mother than she herself could be. Marilee realized that whenever anyone wanted her to do something, they would praise her as being so much better at it than themselves.

"I need time to catch up," Anita said. "I'm going to

keep saving, and in another nine months or so, maybe I can have a proper home in New Orleans for Corrine. Until then, I'm so grateful to you, Marilee. I know Corrine is well taken care of…much better off than she would be with me trying to get my life established."

Marilee, who had been doing some figuring of her own, said, "*You* tell Corrine your plans."

"Oh, won't you? You are so much better at it than I am." She cast her sweet, little-girl smile.

"No." She did not feel guilty for her stance, either.

Anita and Corrine went for a walk to have a talk; Willie Lee went out back to put his worms to bed in the garden. This left Marilee to entertain Louis. Neither of them knew what to say to the other, although this did not seem to bother Louis. Possibly not much at all could bother Louis.

Just then there came the sound of the ice cream truck. Marilee said, "Would you like a fudge Popsicle from the ice-cream man?"

A look of delight bloomed on the man's chiseled face. "Yeah…I haven't had one of those in years."

Marilee grabbed her purse and ran outside to wave down the colorful, slow-moving van that came along sounding its gay tune. It occurred to her that her world was beginning to revolve around food. It did seem to soothe the savage beast.

When she came back in the house, Louis stood at her desk, the telephone to his ear. He thrust the receiver at her. "It's for you."

"Thank you." She handed him his fudge Popsicle, said

into the phone, "Just a minute," and went to put the other Popsicles she had purchased into the freezer.

Back again at the phone, she was startled to hear Tate's low drawl come across the line. "Hi, Miss Marilee, this is Tate. Who was that who answered the phone? He said his name was Louis."

"Yes. Louis." She had the perverse inclination to not explain.

"Who is Louis?"

She was being silly. "My sister's boyfriend." She looked over to see Louis licking his fudge Popsicle like a little boy. It was an arresting sight. For an instant Marilee could clearly see Anita's point about wanting a man.

"Oh. So your sister is visitin'?"

"Yes. She came up for the day."

He paused. She thought to say: *Parker and I are no longer engaged.*

Good grief, she could not say it straight out. And why should she tell him? She would feel the biggest fool. He had told her that Parker was not for her. She hated to admit that he had been right.

"How is the city council election coverage coming?" he asked.

"Tammy is doing the coverage today, and I have interviews with both candidates in the morning, after the firm results. We'll get it in the Wednesday afternoon edition. Are you having a nice vacation?"

"Of sorts." He did not seem thrilled. She was glad, and felt silly.

He said, "So everything is goin' along all right up there—no hitches?"

"None that I know of." She supposed her called-off engagement was a hitch in things going along. At least a change of direction. She could slip it in now.

She didn't.

She never did say anything about it. She and Tate, both obviously at a loss for words, said goodbye and hung up. That she had not told him about her canceled engagement was annoying. It really was not so big a deal, though. Why would he care?

But she did think he would care. She hoped he would care, and this hope made her quite annoyed.

Louis was over at the table eating his fudge Popsicle with great concentration, probably in the same manner he would grill a defendant, or perhaps lick a woman.

She went and called Willie Lee and got their Popsicles and joined Louis, all three sitting there having a pretty grand time licking when Anita and Corrine came in the door. Corrine did not want her Popsicle. Anita ate only a bite of hers before giving hers over to Louis, who licked it like a boy.

Standing at the bottom of the porch steps, Corrine watched her mother drive away. Aunt Marilee stood beside her, with a hand on her shoulder. Her mother called from the car, "Love you, honey," and waved and acted like she was about to cry. Corrine stood there and did not cry. She would not cry about it.

When the car was gone, she felt her Aunt Marilee looking at her. She hated her aunt looking, and she hated everybody.

"Come on, Willie Lee." She did not hate Willie Lee.

Willie Lee was the one person on earth she loved, and in that minute it was like every bit of love she had inside focused on him to such a degree she just about lost her breath. "We'll finish putting your worms to bed."

She turned and went straight through the house and out the back door, with Willie Lee and Munro following behind. She got down on her knees in the dirt. Put her hands in it. It was just about too dark to see any worms, but she wanted to dig. She could feel Aunt Marilee come to look out at them every now and then.

It was understandable that her mother would leave her here with Aunt Marilee. Her mother said she wanted to get them a nice house in New Orleans. Her mother was moving very far this time; usually it was just across town, leaving because she couldn't pay the rent, or was embarrassed because of one of her boyfriends. Corrine wanted to stay with Aunt Marilee; she liked it here. It was okay what her mother did. She didn't care. It didn't matter.

Marilee was at the kitchen table, jotting a grocery list; actually, making up a grocery list was something to do to let her sit at the table and do nothing. Her energy seemed at a low ebb. It was as if Anita had taken it all away. She kept trying to figure out what she should say to Corrine, if anything. Corrine seemed perfectly contained, not upset at all. Perhaps Marilee was blowing things all out of proportion.

Corrine, all bathed and in fresh pajamas, came into the kitchen and asked if she could have a juice drink from the refrigerator.

"Sure, honey." Marilee, trying not to appear to stare, noticed Corrine had dark circles under her eyes.

Corrine got the juice, uncapped the bottle and threw the lid in the trash. Marilee went back to trying to make a grocery list.

Then, "Aunt Marilee, why doesn't my mother want me?"

Marilee's head came up to see Corrine standing there, her bottom lip trembling.

In an instant Marilee had Corrine in her arms, and she held Corrine, until Corrine pushed away, choking somewhat and gasping for breath. Possibly, Marilee thought, she had been holding her niece way too tight, in her great urge to absorb the child's pain and make everything all right with a hug.

Wiping the tears away, Corrine turned and took up her juice. "I'm sorry…it doesn't matter."

"Oh, yes, it does matter." Marilee spoke so forcefully that she startled both herself and Corrine.

All right, God, tell me what to say.

She took Corrine's hand. "It is not that your mother does not want you. That's not it at all. As a single woman, your mother is in a difficult position. She does not have the skills to earn a salary that can support you and her at an adequate level."

Corrine's dark eyes were on her.

Marilee closed her mouth and searched for elusive honesty. "Corrine, it isn't about wanting you or not wanting you. It is about your mother being your mother. None of it is about you. It is about your mother and her needs, and what happens is that you are caught in that. You have not caused your mother to make this choice, and you cannot change it.

"And really, your mother is making a decision that benefits all of us. God knew I wanted more children, and this is His way of letting me have a daughter. It is perfect. Your mother wants you to have a good solid home, and I want you to be here with me. I'm so glad you are here, Corrine."

She tugged her niece to her again and attempted to hug everything right, but trying not to do so with quite as much force. Corrine accepted this.

Feeling as if she had yet not gotten everything said that needed saying, just before Corrine went to bed, Marilee gave it another go.

"I want to tell you something important, and that is that every feeling you have matters. When you are angry, it matters. When you feel hurt, it matters, the same as when you are happy. We matter because we are human beings who are children of God. You matter, I matter, Willie Lee matters, Mr. Tate matters...each person on earth." Suddenly, with startling clarity, Marilee knew that she was saying this to herself, to the little girl who still lived inside and who had to hear the words. "Don't ever again say that you, or how you feel, does not matter."

"Yes, Aunt Marilee." Corrine's dark eyes blinked impassively.

Marilee, persistent for her own need as much as for what she thought her niece needed, again hugged Corrine, and after a brief hesitation, Corrine hugged her back.

Later Marilee thought of how upset Parker would have been at the turn of events. And how happy she was at it.

She felt a little guilty, for it meant she was glad Anita had abdicated her role as mother. That was the truth of it, Lord. Forgive me. I am glad.

It had to be done. Marilee had put it off as long as she could. She telephoned her mother to tell her that she and Parker would not be getting married after all.

"Hi, Mom. How was your trip to Las Vegas?"

"Wore me out. We had a good time, but it wore me out. We didn't get home until noon yesterday. We decided to stay over Sunday night, because Carl and Charlie Linford got to playing slot machines, and Carl got on a roll. He just started winnin' and winnin'. I played, too, and I won three hundred dollars, but Carl won two thousand, so he told me to go change our plane reservations. I didn't want to do it, but I did, and when I came back, Carl had won another five thousand dollars, at the slot machine. His machine hit some premium number. When that happens a light goes off on your machine, and a guy will come over and give you a ticket for the money. When I got there, a crowd was all around where Carl had been playing, and I thought at first that he'd had a heart attack."

When her mother paused for a breath, Marilee, quite impressed, said, "That is just wonderful, Mom."

"Well, you know Carl had to keep on then. He gave me five hundred of it, and he took the rest. I played the machines for a while, but then just went up to bed, and Carl played way into the night, until they wouldn't let him play anymore, because he'd had too much to drink. He had won another four thousand, though."

Marilee was amazed. "Carl won eleven thousand dollars?"

"Yes, he did. He didn't know how much he had won by the time he came up to the room. He had a bucket, but he had chips stuck all in his coat and pants pockets. I pulled one out of each of his shoes, even. Heaven knows what he was thinking, but he had tucked them in his shoes.

"I took all of those out of his clothes, and I went downstairs and cashed them in. There was nearly fifteen hundred dollars from just in his clothes. He never knew when he woke up. He just remembered about the bucketful. And then, while we were waitin' for our cab, he went in there and lost that entire bucket at the blackjack table."

"Oh."

"I never did tell him about that fifteen hundred dollars I got out of his clothes. He remembered the five hundred he'd given me and wanted that, but I wouldn't give it to him. I told him I had paid it on his drink bill." Her mother's voice dropped. "I want you to help me get it into the bank down there in Valentine. Carl won't know about it there. I want you to help me choose a CD."

Marilee sat there a minute. Then she said, "The bank will help you choose a CD. I wanted to tell you that Parker and I are not getting married."

She did not know why every conversation with her mother seemed as if they each spoke a foreign language.

Twenty-Three

Seize the Day

He spilled his guts to his mother, in her kitchen at 6:00 a.m., over morning coffee. His mother had already had her meditation and yoga workout, and having slept very little, he had lain in his bed, listening to her stir.

He had, he realized, come running to her just as he always had, despite being a man of a certain age. He was also quite amazed at his level of heartache. He simply had not known what was going on inside him until he had arrived at his mother's house and found he didn't want to bathe or shave.

Now that he had poured out his difficulty of wanting a woman he could not have, he didn't feel any better, either. If anything, he felt worse.

His mother's response was not a great deal of help. When he had finished with his sad tale of love rejected, she said, "So she got engaged, and you ran off."

Tate did not appreciate this take on the situation. "I let

go. I quit tryin' to make it be my way. She's made her choice. I'm not going to beat my head against a brick wall to change things I cannot change."

"Oh, pshaw…all she did was get engaged." She sipped her ginseng tea. "You can let go but still stay around to see what happens and see if things are eventually going to go your way. What you did was more like giving up. Two different things entirely."

Tate was stung. He had not expected this criticism.

"People often change their minds, most especially about being engaged," his mother continued. "You don't know that she might not have changed her mind the next day. You were too busy runnin' off because of your hurt pride."

As Tate saw it, a man did have his pride.

"You're down here, so you aren't goin' to know what is goin' on up there. You say this Parker fella isn't right for your Marilee. Well, it may take time for her to realize this. What if she realizes it while you're down here pitying yourself?"

"I am not pitying myself." Tate did not appreciate the picture his mother painted of him. He smoothed his hair and got up to refill his coffee, real coffee, not some health-nut stuff his mother wanted to palm off on him.

Grudgingly, he could admit to slogging around in a bit of pity. Maybe ankle deep.

"You wanted my opinion, and I'm givin' it. Get back up there and see what develops."

"I didn't ask for your opinion," he clarified. "I just wanted you to listen…and to make me feel better." He was disappointed and annoyed, and felt very childish.

His mother got up and came over, kissed him and hugged him hard. "There you go."

Just before noon, the door opened and Charlotte looked up to see a man enter. Young, in his twenties, thin as a rail, and wearing his slacks high at his waist. Her mother would have told him to jerk his trousers down where they belonged. It was, however, his great height that arrested her attention; she found herself looking at his thighs, and then her gaze moved upward, higher and higher, to six and a half feet at the very least.

"Hello. I'm Sandy Conroy."

"Hello…Mr. Conroy," Charlotte said, as she slowly stood, until she was straight as a rod. Finally, at long last, she was looking upward at a man. "Can I help you?"

"I'm here to see Mr. Holloway."

"I'm sorry. Mr. Holloway is out of town. Was he expecting you?"

"Well, no…well, yes, ma'am, but he was expectin' me next week. He's hired me to do layout. I was supposed to be in next week, but I decided to come on down."

Charlotte saw his blush and instantly drew the conclusion that there was a story behind his coming early. The most likely scenario would be a breakup with his girlfriend.

"I should have called, I guess." He looked at a loss.

"I can show you to your desk," Charlotte said so quickly that he blinked. She suddenly was not going to take a chance on him leaving.

"Oh, I'm Charlotte Nation. I'm the receptionist and general do-all person."

She put out her hand, and he shook it with some eagerness. "Glad to meet you, ma'am." At his touch Charlotte thought something happened to her. She seemed to lose coherent thought.

Seeking to regain her poise, she strode firmly back to the office cubicle that had belonged to their former layout artist, gesturing along the way at the empty desks—"The paper is put to bed, so everyone sort of scatters, and Leo has taken the disks to the printer…he'll see to the deliveries later."—and Zona's office, telling him the names of his new colleagues. She was thrilled to be walking beside a man who stood a full head taller than herself.

She had to knock dust off the desk. Only then did she notice he carried a bulging case with him, likely a portable computer. "This space hasn't been used much since we lost our layout man, several months ago now. June uses the long table some."

He placed his case on the desk and looked around. He was shy, and quite suddenly Charlotte felt very shy. It was such a foreign emotion that she didn't know how to handle it. She had no idea of where to lay her eyes, because she found she could not meet his gaze.

"There's the coffee machine," she said gesturing. "Oh, only there isn't any coffee made, since the editor is out. But you can help yourself to the cold drinks in the refrigerator…if there are any. I don't know. I haven't looked today. I like mixed juice drinks, but I haven't brought any down this week. Sometimes the editor puts Orange Crush in there. Do you like that?"

She was rattling and just came out with the question, while what she was really thinking as she gazed into his soft brown eyes was: Are you free and open to an older woman, and would you possibly like Chinese food, which is my favorite?

"Yes, I like Orange Crush," he said, seeming a little surprised at the question.

"Well, help yourself. Look around. I'll leave you to settling in." She was backing up. "If you need anything, let me know."

She beat a retreat to her desk, sat herself squarely, and sought to find her familiar composed, even cool, self. Goodness. She was shy. This was quite a surprise. It had never happened to her before. She did not care for the feeling.

As she struggled to bring herself into some order, she attempted to focus on her computer screen, while her eyes were repeatedly drawn back to the young man moving around in his glass cubicle. The ringing of the phone was a welcome interruption.

"Charlotte?" It was the editor.

"Yes. It's a good thing you called."

"It didn't sound like you. Why? What's happened? Is there trouble with the Wednesday edition?"

She was a little surprised at his rapid-fire questions. Her boss did not usually speak so fast. He sounded almost as if he wanted trouble. "No trouble with the paper. It's a light edition, already gone to the printer. But the layout artist you hired—Sandy Conroy—has shown up."

"I wasn't expecting him until next week."

"That's what he said."

"Well, make him welcome. You can show him his desk and stuff."

"I did." Did he think she'd thrown him out? "He's at his desk now. Do you want to speak to him?"

Her editor said he did want to talk to the "young man." Charlotte called back, "Mr. Conroy, the editor is on the phone for you," and punched the button.

Sandy Conroy was looking wide-eyed at her through his window. Then his phone rang, and he answered it. Charlotte sat there thinking that he wasn't all that young. He had just taken a responsible position at a newspaper.

The two men conversed for some minutes, and then Sandy Conroy lifted his head right over his cubicle window and hollered, "He wants to talk to you again, Miss Charlotte."

She snatched up the phone and pressed the button. Her editor told her the young man was starting immediately and to have Zona cut him a check for a week's pay. He then wanted to know who won the council seat, and she told him it was Jaydee Mayhall by a landslide. "He was embarrassing going on about it, and then him and Juice got into it so bad that Sheriff Oakes hauled them in for disorderly conduct last night. Marilee interviewed them both at the jailhouse, right after they were let out. Reggie got a picture, too."

"I've missed some excitement," he said. "Where is Marilee? I called her house, but no one answered. She didn't go get married today, did she?"

"Oh, no. Marilee and Parker broke up."

"They broke up?"

Her editor fairly yelled, and this got her attention. She had been concentrating so hard on an unobtrusive way to ask about Sandy Conroy's age that she had not fully processed his question, which, now that she thought of it, was a very telling one.

"When?" he demanded.

"Well…they were broke up on Monday." She had not asked Marilee when, and she didn't think it really mattered, although she clearly saw the situation now.

"Why didn't anyone tell me?"

"You weren't here, and I did not know you particularly wanted to know." Okay, that dealt with, she said in a hoarse whisper, "How old is Sandy Conroy?"

"Uh…twenty-five. And, Miss Charlotte, don't let Marilee get back engaged to that idiot before I get there."

"I don't think I can do anything about what Marilee does." Her editor was getting carried away.

"I put you in charge of it—and in charge of helping Sandy Conroy find a place to live, so you owe me. I'll be there tonight." And the line clicked dead.

She sat there, wondering how she could have been so blind to her editor's inclinations toward Marilee, but then her gaze slipped over, and she was looking through the window of Sandy Conroy's office again. It was only an eleven-year difference. That wasn't so much. And he was taller than she was. He was so tall that she could once again wear high heels.

What she thought was something along the lines of: Seize the day. She had spent too long mooning after Leo, Sr., and many others before him, men who were too short to be fully satisfying, and usually married or otherwise beyond her reach. She had done this because she was afraid to reach out. Now, here before her, was a real chance, and she was going to go forward and take it.

She pushed her chair away from her desk, took up her purse and walked back toward the young man's office. On the way she poked her head inside Zona's cracked door and said, "Zona, Editor says cut a week's check for Sandy Conroy. We'll pick it up later. I'm leaving for the day. You are now in charge."

She proceeded onward so quickly that she caught the barest glimpse of Zona's shocked expression.

"The editor said for me to help you find an apartment. Would you like to go check out some places, and then possibly have supper?" She was no longer shy. She knew what she wanted. Her ship had come in.

"Well…yes, thank you." His grin was shy but wide.

As she walked beside him out the door, she dared to slip her arm through his, and she stood straight and tall.

After some minutes, Zona came to her door and peeked her head out, looking around at the huge empty room. Slowly she opened her door wider and left it that way. Everyone was getting too lax in the workings of this paper, and the responsibility to hold the fort apparently had fallen to her. She could do this, for Ms. Porter.

Tate told his mother, "Okay, you were right."

She did not ask what about but said simply, "I won't ever say I told you so."

In twenty minutes he had his bags packed, Bubba stuffed into his carrier, and was loading his car. His mother brought him a mason jar of cold tea with lots of ice, just like the ones she would pack in the old days, for working in the cotton fields. For an instant, memory of how cool and sweet the tea would be on his tongue and going down his hot throat washed over him.

"Thanks, Mom," he said and kissed her cheek.

"You're welcome, and now remember: everything will turn out how it is supposed to, and in its own time."

"That isn't what you were saying this mornin'."

"I could not say it then, because you were running away, upsetting the flow of life. Go back up there and get into the flow."

She was standing in her little yard, watching after him, as he drove away with the salty air of the Gulf blowing around his windshield. He gauged that he could get to Valentine in less than seven hours. And he supposed he had within his reach the best secrets of life: cold sweet tea and a high heart.

When Perry came driving down the street, Vella was sitting on the front porch, drinking iced tea flavored with her own mint leaves. She had not wanted to start sitting on her porch; that was something her mother and other old ladies did. However, she had been taken with a new set of wicker furniture on sale up at the Home Depot, really pretty, newfangled wicker that went through anything and never molded, so the brochure said.

Her front porch was beautiful with it, and once she had sat down in the chair, she found it rather relaxing, sitting there, gazing out at the street, watching the birds and rabbits, a blue jay harass a cat. Certainly it wasn't as bad as she had anticipated. She didn't feel any older or more depressed sitting on the front porch than she did sitting anywhere else. In fact, it did seem to soothe her.

Sitting there, she was quite surprised to see Perry's black Lincoln approaching in the middle of the morning. She did not think she had ever seen him go anywhere outside the pharmacy before five o'clock in the afternoon, not in a decade, since they had buried his brother in a morning service. She felt a flicker of anticipation. Of hope, and it ran along the lines of her husband dashing up in the driveway and saying he had come to be the man she had married.

Watching the black Lincoln more or less crawl along the street at an incredibly slow pace, however, she squashed that fantasy down in the manner of swatting a fly. Get real, Vella. The black Lincoln turned into the driveway so slowly that it looked like it might just roll back out again. Vella found herself tensing, as if trying to give the car a helping hand. Somebody needed to tell Perry that if he couldn't drive with more conviction, he needed to get off the road.

When he got out of the car, he hitched up his pants and gave a look around, then started up the walk. About halfway along, his head came up and he saw her for the first time. He sort of jumped, his eyes widening.

"It's me," she said. Who in the world did he expect to find here?

He did not reply, and she might have known he would not.

He came up the walk and stopped at the foot of the stairs. Lord, he looked awful. Her gaze moved back and forth from her husband to his car, which she noticed had stuff piled inside it at the same time that she took note that his shirt looked as if he had deliberately squashed it into a ball before putting it on. He needed a haircut, and his pants were sagging. He looked generally wrung out. How would anyone confidently accept a prescription filled by this man?

"My television took out down at the store." He squinted at her. "I came for the one in the kitchen." He squinted at her.

"It isn't in the kitchen anymore. I put it in the closet under the stairs. You're welcome to it."

He stood there a moment more, then started up the stairs, holding to the handrail, his head bent, as if to watch carefully his footsteps that trudged.

Oh, Lord, oh, Lord. Vella felt emotions, like bubbles, erupt from deep within her and move upward: pity, resentment, regret, guilt.

She sat very still. Perry opened the door and went inside. The storm door closed after him. Shifting her gaze to his car, she saw shirts hanging at the back window. It looked like clothes were lying over the front seat. Panic mounted. Was he living in his car? Had he come to this? Whatever would she do?

She was not responsible for him; he was a man grown. If he could not take the initiative to go to a motel or do his laundry, so be it. She was not his mother. She picked up her glass of tea, drank deeply and wrestled with her demons, trying to bring out her better self, but uncertain as to just what that entailed. She had been uncertain about this for some time. *Lord, help!*

Perry, standing with the door of the closet open, cocked his head, listening for his wife to come inside. He wished she would come inside and start a conversation.

Moving slowly, still listening, he bent into the closet and hefted out the television; it was a little heavier than he had anticipated. He wondered at Vella having hauled it into the closet. He felt like a wimp, and he jerked it up, got it out of the closet, and then he felt stuck with a kink in his back. He had the fleeting thought that maybe in carrying it he would suffer a heart attack. Vella would not be able to boot him out then.

Pretending to be ill had been Winston's suggestion, as if that were the only way he could get his foot back in his own house. Truth was, he had been thinking along the same lines, and then Winston had gone and suggested it, which made Perry furious. He could not go and follow a suggestion from Winston.

It did not appear that Vella was going to come in to see what was taking him so long, and the television was getting heavy, just standing there holding it. He went to the door and realized he could not open it and carry the television at the same time. He banged on the door.

"All you had to do was ask," Vella said, opening the door for him. "You don't have to bang down the house."

"Open the dang door wider, then."

He got out on the front porch and with sudden decision veered over to the porch rail, where he set the television. He pulled a handkerchief out of his pocket to mop his face.

"How did you get this dang thing in the closet?" he had to ask.

"I put it on the towel it was sittin' on and dragged it in there. I couldn't carry it."

He felt silly. Of course, he wouldn't have been able to

drag it across the living room carpet. And he felt good that he had carried it.

"Are you livin' in your car?" Vella asked.

"My wife threw me out of my house." She ought to know what she was putting him through. "And there ain't room at Belinda's for my clothes."

"Don't you know how to go on out to the Motel 6 and get yourself a room? Don't you know how to find an apartment?"

"Maybe I don't want to." That answer did not suffice. He felt he had never been clever with words.

He had sat down before he knew he was going to. Suddenly his legs would not carry him farther. The thought of leaving the porch made him feel that all would be lost.

And unless he asked Vella to go down there ahead of him and open the door, he would have to go down there, set the television on the hood, open the door and scoot clothes out of the way to make room for it. If she did go down there and open the door, she would see the mess of his car, and she would have a great comment on that. He did not think he could stand up under her comments.

Vella sat down in the other chair, on the other side of the door. She kept looking at the car and feeling guilty, mad at herself for it, and mad at Perry.

"Where's your boyfriend?" Perry asked. "I thought you two were a hot combo?"

"If you mean Winston, he is where he is every afternoon, at home takin' a nap. And no, we are not a hot combo…except maybe compared to you and I. Two dead people are a hot combo compared to us. And Winston and

I do converse. We have not burned our brains away with the television."

The truth was that Winston had proved a disappointment to Vella. She had gotten carried away with a fantasy there. Winston was not up to her fantasy. It could very well be that *she* was not up to her fantasy.

Just then, at the same instant, they each let out great sighs. Vella looked over at Perry, and he looked over at her.

"I'm not up to this, Vella."

That his words so closely mirrored her thoughts startled her.

"I'll help you carry the television," she told him, and slid to the edge of the wicker chair.

"No, I don't mean that...I mean startin' a new life somewhere besides here. I'm not up to gettin' out there by myself, and I don't think I'm up to anything you want from me, either." His voice cracked, bless his heart. And then he said in a worn-out tone, "I think the only thing I am up to is sittin' on this porch."

The idea came to him that he was going to sit on the porch and not leave. Vella would have to call the police, and they would have to forcibly remove him. Sitting still was one thing he could darn well do.

He realized just then that the chair was brand-new. "I like this chair." He had always found fancy outdoor chairs lacking in strength to hold his big frame, but this one felt solid.

"I bought it this week up at Home Depot."

"Well, I like it. I could enjoy sittin' here."

"You always enjoyed sittin'," she said, then added, "but I'm not havin' a television on my porch."

"I don't think I'd need one here. It's nice just to watch the street and things around."

They sat there in silence, Perry halfway waiting for Vella to tell him to leave. He was a little disappointed that she did not, and that it was unlikely the police would be called to break him out of his sit-in. The entire idea had enthused him, and now, knowing it wouldn't happen, he dipped deeper into discouragement.

After about fifteen minutes, Perry said he could use a glass of something cold to drink.

"Go get it, then," Vella told him. He needed to realize that she was not his maid. "There's Coke and iced tea in the refrigerator."

After a minute, he got up. He extended his hand, and she wondered what in the world.

He said, "Would you like me to freshen yours?"

Could have knocked her over with a feather, but she refused to let on. "Yes, thank you." She handed up her glass.

He went inside and was gone so long that she was just about to go in and see what had happened when he came out with two full glasses. He handed her one and sat back down in his chair.

Vella thought how it really didn't matter whether he was in the house or not. She did not need to kick him out to have her life. The only thing stopping her from having the life she chose was her own choices. She could only find another man without Perry hanging on to her, but maybe the most startling thing she had come to know was that any man her own age would be unable to keep up with her, and she did not have the constitution, nor the opportunity, to take up a man fifteen years younger.

"Could you look at me in the mornings and thank me for your coffee?" she asked, without looking at him.

"I could do that." His voice cracked, and he cleared his throat. "And I could take you out to dinner once a week."

Knock her over again.

"No more television in the kitchen. We will talk while we eat."

There was a long pause, and Vella felt her fury rising. She was just about to whip around and give Perry a what-for about the television when suddenly he was on his feet, and he leaned over and gave the television a shove off the railing. It landed on the ground with a loud crash.

Vella, who had involuntarily gotten to her feet, stared at him. Slowly, stunned, she moved backward and sat down.

"I still want my one in the living room, though," said Perry, who was pleased to have shocked her as she had shocked him the day she had left him with half her clothes hanging open.

He sat back down and mused, in the silence between them, that knowing he had shocked her really seemed to get his blood pumping, and he had the most surprising thoughts to follow. Thoughts of a sensual nature.

Vella, after some twenty minutes of silence, said, "I guess we'd better get your clothes inside. I'm not doin' them all up, though. We can send them to the laundry. I have lots of other things I want to do."

The sun shone far from the west, casting long shadows, when Marilee looked up from the book she was reading about learning disabled children to see it was past their normal supper time. Then her gaze fell on a clay giraffe Willie Lee had fashioned. She picked it up and looked at it, marveling at the craftsmanship. There was a part of Willie Lee that excelled.

The children's shouts and laughter floated in from the backyard. She got up from her desk and went to the back door, looking through the screen. Corrine and Willie Lee were playing tag with Munro again. The dog would chase them, pulling on their shorts, tripping them, and children and dog rolled across the grass.

Since her mother's visit, Corrine had been withdrawn again, no laughter, nor even much of a smile. Now, thanks to the dog, Corrine was running and jumping and laughing. Surely the dog was a gift from God, healing the child where Marilee could not.

Both children were sprawled in the grass now, exhausted. Marilee opened the door and hollered for them to come help her with supper. In they came, running again, Munro bringing up the rear. It was fruit drinks for the children and a fresh bowl of water for the dog.

It was pleasant, all of them in the kitchen together. While she put spaghetti noodles and canned sauce on the stove, Corrine and Willie Lee set the table.

"Summertime, and the livin' is easy," Marilee began to sing, and the children joined in. They repeated the verse over and over, as it was all any of them knew.

The doorbell rang out, loudly, as if someone might have pushed it more than once before they could hear it over their rather raucous singing. Corrine went to see who it was, and when Marilee turned around again, there stood Parker in the kitchen doorway, looking both hesitant and hopeful.

"Hello, Parker."

"Hi." And then, "I wondered if there might be a place for a friend for supper."

Marilee smiled. "Set another place, Corrine."

Parker went to the sink to wash his hands. He said with feeling, "A person can get tired of eating out, or cookin' just for himself."

Twenty-Four

Opening Doors

Tate came hauling down the state highway past the Welcome to Valentine sign, and suddenly he saw red blinking lights behind him. As he pulled off the road, he recognized Lyle Midgett's wide-brimmed hat behind the windshield of the patrol car.

"You need to slow down, Editor."

"Well, yes, I guess I do. I'm a little anxious to get home." Sitting at the top of a hill, he saw Valentine in the valley, washed in the golden glow of a setting sun.

"I thought I'd missed seein' you around." The deputy propped himself on the windshield frame. "Where you been?"

"Galveston. I went down to see my mother for a couple days."

"Your mother lives there? My uncle lives in Galveston. Isn't that a coincidence? I haven't seen my uncle in years, since he moved down there." The young man wanted to chat. Tate, one hand on the wheel, one on the stick shift, kept himself from running out from beneath him.

The deputy was saying, "The fartherest I've been from Valentine is up to Oklahoma City and down to Dallas. Ever'body goes to Dallas. I'm thinkin' about goin' over to Tunica for my vacation this fall, though. You know, to those gambling casinos. The sheriff and his wife go over there least once a year. He says you don't have to pay for any food."

"It's good seein' you, Deputy," Tate stuck in, "but I need to get home. This cat has had about all the travelin' he wants."

"Oh...sure. He is startin' to growl pretty loud, isn't he?"

"Do you want to give me a ticket?"

"What? Oh, naw. Just don't you be—"

But Tate was already away, and the deputy's words were snatched by the wind.

He came down Main Street and then turned up First and onto Porter, to pass by Marilee's house.

Right there in her driveway sat Parker Lindsey's blue pickup truck, big as life on a bad day.

She had just served up four plates of spaghetti and sauce when the back door opened and in came Tate.

"Hi, I'm back," he said immediately.

Marilee was so surprised that she stood there holding the empty saucepan in one hand and the spoon in the other. She was alone in the room, the others having gone to watch television until she served.

He came forward. "I've brought iced tea." Ice cubes clinked as he lifted the colorful pitcher.

"Uh...thank you."

Then they were face-to-face, Tate having come along the counter and set the pitcher down next to the lineup of glasses. Marilee set the pan and spoon aside.

"I heard that you and Lindsey were no longer engaged." He spoke in a manner she did not quite appreciate.

"Yes." She was annoyed at herself. He did not need to know her business. But she wanted him to know.

"Yes, you are not, or yes, you are?"

"Yes, we have broken our engagement, if it is necessary for you to know," said Marilee, who thought he just had to twist everything that was said.

"Good."

She did not respond to that. In fact, her attention was tuned to the other room and listening for footsteps coming this way. For some reason she felt acutely self-conscious at the thought that at any moment the children or Parker could walk in.

"Parker is here, but just for supper." She felt the need to tell him that, and the inclination annoyed her.

"I'd sure like supper, too. I've been drivin' all day. I'm starved."

He gave her a provocative look. How could she have forgotten how luminous his eyes were?

"I guess I could stretch it," she said. She looked at the plates wondering how in the world she would do that, and at the same time knowing she was darn well going to accomplish it.

"Great. I'll fill the glasses."

It was only supper, she told herself, as she stole part

of Parker's spaghetti. This made her think of her mother, stealing money from Carl's pockets. Not the same, she told herself, and took some from her own plate, and then a little from Willie Lee's. He never ate all of his. And she could make more garlic bread; she had another small loaf in the freezer. Only supper. That was all. No need to make a big deal out of it.

Parker came in, and immediately Tate said, "Hey, buddy, how are you tonight?" There never was anything subdued about Tate Holloway.

"Hey, Editor," Parker responded in a flat tone of voice.

Tate said an effusive hello to the children, who responded in kind.

Willie Lee said a very curious thing. "I am glad you are not the dogcatcher."

"I'm glad, too." Tate said, setting himself down at the place Parker usually took at the table. "Why would you think I was the dogcatcher?"

"You might be," Willie Lee said, quite logically. "But you are not."

Parker stared down at the plate she put in front of him. She had tried to disguise stealing from it, but her efforts could not fully be concealed.

"Here's the Italian bread," she said, setting the basket on the table. "There'll be more in a few minutes.

She saw Parker looking from his plate to Tate's.

Marilee said, "Shall we bow our heads for grace?"

"I like the end of Italian bread," said Tate, taking up the end slice.

"A lot of people use the ends of the loaf to feed the

birds, or as fish bait," said Parker, taking a slice from the middle.

"Then I'm easily caught," Tate said, "because these hard ends suit me."

"I guess I have a taste for the finer things in life." Parker smiled as he tore his bread in half.

Marilee, her gaze going back and forth between the two men, felt a food fight might be imminent. Further, Corrine was closely observing both men.

"Does anyone need a refill of tea?" Marilee asked, getting to her feet, which seemed to be required. She felt more in command on her feet. And, in fact, the two men looked up at her, and she gave them her best stop-it-this-instant-you-are-not-fooling-anyone expression.

As she sat down, it occurred to her that she should be flattered, two men fighting over her. Although, on second, deeper thought, it had little to do with her and was about the men themselves. When the two came together, it was like flint hitting a rock.

Willie Lee, who was busy passing pieces of bread underneath the table, said, "Mun-ro likes the end *and* the middle."

"Well-rounded dog," Tate commented. He was a man to have the last word.

He was more the rock, Marilee thought.

Tate found himself left with Parker. That was how he thought of it, as if left with a difficulty. Marilee was getting the children bathed and ready for bed. In his estimation, she had thrown herself into that activity to avoid him and Lindsey. He wasn't certain what he had expected when he got back to town, but he had not expected to drive six hours and have Marilee avoid him. The least she could have done was tell Lindsey to go home.

"You had your meal," he said to Lindsey, who had taken root on the sofa, remote control in hand, watching the news. "You can go on home now."

Lindsey looked up at him. "*You* can go on home. Don't let me stop you."

Realizing then that he was the one on his feet and therefore in a less-rooted position, Tate went over and sat himself at Marilee's desk, definitely a more solid position than Lindsey on the sofa. He looked over her desk, which was neat as always. There was a small clay giraffe. He picked it up and looked it over, and then looked over at the stack of books to the side, all which appeared to be on children and learning dis- abilities. Hmmm.

His gaze slipped to the telephone, and he looked from it to Lindsey, who was staring at the nightly news. He experienced possibly the greatest idea of his life, and he got so enthused in thinking of it that he had to force himself not to chuckle out loud.

"Well, I need something to drink," he said, speaking a little loudly and toning himself down. "Would you like something—tea or cola?"

Lindsey looked over with a frown. "I'm fine, thank you."

Tate shrugged and went into the kitchen. Immediately through the door, he slipped to the side and over to the phone on the wall. His heart beat rapidly. Did Marilee have the number on her speed dial? There it was. Yes! Thank you, God!

He experienced an instant where he questioned God's

part in this, but quickly put the thought aside, punched the number and listened to the ringing come over the line.

"Lindsey Veterinary Clinic. This is the answering service."

Answering service. Hallelujah! He cupped the speaker. "Hey, this is Sheriff Oakes, and we got an emergency out here. A horse has been hit by a car—out on Highway Six, a mile north of Rodeo Rio's. Tell the doc to get out here pronto and I think we can save him." Tate thought he imitated the sheriff quite well.

"Can you give me your number, Sheriff?"

"I got a situation here. Just tell the doc to get out here."

He hung up and moved quickly from the phone. He should be ashamed of being so pleased. But he wasn't.

As he poured his glass of tea, he heard Lindsey's mobile phone go off. He heard the veterinarian's terse tone, if not the exact words.

Tate, seeing Marilee's reflection in the kitchen window as she entered the living room, went to the doorway. Lindsey was on his feet and talking into the telephone.

"Yeah, I got it. I'm on my way."

He snapped off his phone and told Marilee, "I got an emergency. Horse hit by a car on Highway Six."

"Oh…my."

He kissed her cheek and thanked her for supper, and headed for the door.

Marilee followed and called after him, "I hope it goes well."

She shut the door and turned to look at Tate across the low-lit room. She looked so worried that he felt a stab of guilt.

"I hope the horse isn't hurt too badly," she said and then continued on about how Parker had such a hard time whenever he lost a patient. "And it is even worse on him when he has to put one down."

"Ah…" He wrestled with his conscience. "There isn't really an injured horse."

"What?" She cocked her head to the side, regarding him.

He felt quicksand beneath his feet. "Well, I put in the call to his answering service. I pretended to be the sheriff and said there was a horse…hit by a car," he finished slowly as he saw his own image reflected in her incredulous expression.

"How could you do that? Parker—" she was getting wrought up and gestured with her arm swinging out "—is fully committed to saving animals' lives. He is racin' out there now, committed to doing all that he can to save a horse. He could be in a wreck because he's hurryin' out there to save a horse that isn't even there!"

Tate had no answer to that. The full import of his actions came to him, although he did not see them in quite the disreputable light Marilee painted. Obviously she believed he had crossed over the line of integrity.

"I wanted time with you," he said. "Lindsey is a big boy, and he will deal with this."

Marilee heard what he said but could not absorb it. She was too taken up with hurt for Parker. She felt horribly guilty, knowing she was the cause of him being falsely called out.

"He can't stand to see an animal die," she told Tate, as she went to the phone on her desk and snatched up the receiver. "He will go to great lengths to prevent that." In her mind, she saw him colliding with another vehicle in his race to get out to find and save the injured horse.

"Marilee—" he took hold of her forearm "—he will get there and realize what happened. He does not need you to be his mother."

She looked at him. "You have sent him off on a fool's errand. I can't let him be drivin' all over creation, lookin' for a horse that isn't there. He'll feel a fool when he realizes what you've done."

"That's it." Suddenly she was facing Tate's fury. "Focus on Parker, mother Parker, because you can't face your own life as a woman. When I found out you had broken off with Parker, I came drivin' up here at break-neck speed for six hours to see you. I don't see you getting all worked up about my welfare. I'm tired and lonely and wearin' my heart on my sleeve here. What are you gonna do about that? About this man—" he jabbed his chest "—not a boy, who is crazy about you."

Marilee stared at him and felt a type of paralysis come over her emotions and her body. She could not seem to put down the phone. She could not seem to stop her course, even if she wanted to.

"I have to call him. You don't know how these things hurt." She did not think she could bear the consequences of not calling Parker, not that she knew what those consequences would be, just that she needed to cling to making the call. She felt compelled to cling to the course she knew, because to abandon it would mean she would be lost.

"Do you think he is too stupid to figure out what happened when he gets out there and there isn't any horse, nor any police cars?" He flung her arm away in disgust. "Do you have such a low opinion of his coping powers? He'll figure it out, and he'll be mad as hell, but he'll be wiser, and someday he'll use this same little trick on somebody else. That's how I learned it—it was played on me, to get me out of the way of somewhere I never belonged in the first place."

"I can't," she said, anger flaring because he was pressing her for something she did not feel capable of giving.

"I'm not going to stand here and beg for your attention. I wouldn't want to interrupt your motherin' of Parker. Apparently you need that more than you can appreciate some attention from a man."

He stalked off to the kitchen, and she called after him, "Go ahead. I never asked you to come around here…and that is what men do—they leave. Better sooner than later." She shut her mouth then, afraid she might have awakened the children.

The sound of the back door shutting caused her to just about double over, as if from a blow.

What Tate said was true, she realized, her spirit sinking to depths so dark she ached with despair. She simply could never seem to get herself out of mother mode. She had always been a mother, from the age of nine, when she'd had to be a mother to Anita, and on to becoming a mother to her own mother. It was all she knew.

Likely she attracted men who needed her to mother them—like Stuart and Parker—and repelled men, like Tate, who did not require her mothering talents but wanted her to be a full woman and mate, which was something she could not seem to grasp. She could not be a woman to a man, because she did not know how. Probably she did not have some sort of gene required to be a woman to a man. It was as if she were learning disabled in this area, the same as her Willie Lee was in the rest of life.

A voice came from the receiver: "If you'd like to make a call, please hang up and dial again."

She was still standing there, holding the receiver. She stretched a finger to depress the button and start again, but her inclination to call Parker had faded. Suddenly she did not think she could speak, she was so totally discouraged. Likely Parker was close to figuring out that there was no emergency with a horse, anyway. Surely another ten minutes and he would know this. He would be furious and feel the fool, and she did not feel up to taking on his emotions.

Tate, at the back gate, stopped in his tracks. It was as if a hand had come down on his shoulder and turned him around, and he distinctly heard a command to get back in there.

He had come too far to give up now. And he wouldn't leave her his tea, in any case. By golly, he was not wasting any more tea on the woman. He would just march right in there and get his pitcher. He went up the stairs and burst in the doorway.

Marilee, hearing the back door open, threw the receiver onto the hook and hurried to the kitchen doorway, from which she saw Tate stalking across the room toward the counter.

"I forgot my tea." His tone and manner were furious.

He snatched up the pitcher sitting there. "I'm takin' it back." He had lost his mind, he thought.

Marilee, standing with her hand on the door frame, tried to drag herself from her odd paralysis of emotion, a course she had seemingly been on all her life. *He had driven six hours for her...for a woman like her.*

The phone rang, and this jarred her into motion. Two steps and she lifted the receiver.

But then Tate was there, taking hold of her and jerking the receiver from her hand. He said into it, "Go away," then let it drop, where it bobbed and banged against the wall, while Tate took her by her shoulders and looked deep into her eyes.

"Let me in, Marilee. Open up and let me in."

His eyes entreated her; his voice commanded her.

"I can't.... I don't know how." Crying, shaking her head, trying to avoid his lips, but still he went to kissing her cheeks and her eyes. She hit his chest with her balled fists. "I don't want to be married...I can't go there again...it hurts too bad...I don't know how."

He found her mouth and stopped her words with his kiss, which caused an immediate and enormous response from deep inside of her. Quite suddenly she found herself kissing him in return, with the passion of a woman come to life, full of desire that burned away the fear. They became all hot breath and pounding blood and passionate bodies. When finally Tate lifted his head, so that she could see his luminous grey eyes, she could not stand up and had to hold on to him.

"That's how," he whispered against her lips, and then

kissed her again, having to hold her up against him to do it.

When at last the kiss ended and she was staring up at him through dazed eyes, she said what popped into her mind. "I've wanted to know what it would be like to kiss you from the moment I saw you."

"I've wanted to know, too," said Tate, with a ragged chuckle. Then, "Let's do it again."

And he kissed her again.

When at last he raised his head, she gasped for breath. "I won't," she managed to say, meaning she would not sleep with him, she would not marry him, she would not go any further.

He merely chuckled again and gave her yet another kiss, deeply and expertly, making her know in that minute that she would follow the delicious passion wherever it led. He kissed her, and she kissed him, until they were both about to burst into flame.

She had never in all her life been so thoroughly kissed, so that she felt it in every cell in her body.

"Now, what were you sayin'?" he whispered in her ear, his breath warm and moist upon her tender skin.

"I can't remember." She felt helpless. Never had she felt helpless with a man. She did not know if she liked the feeling.

"The phone's still off the hook." The recording was speaking about hanging up.

"Leave it."

"Okay." She could not think a coherent thought.

Tate scooped her up into his arms and carried her

through to the living room, where he sat in the big chair, holding her across his lap.

"Why not the sofa?" she asked, as getting down into the chair proved to take some doing.

"You and Parker used to be on the sofa."

"Oh." She laid her head on his shoulder and nuzzled into his neck. "I cannot have sex with you. I have two children in the other room."

"Quit blaming it all on the children. I'll wait until you are ready." He stroked her head, and she felt ready.

"I want to marry you," he said. "That's what I want."

She realized that Tate was a little struck silly by passion, too. "I don't know if I can marry you. I don't think we should even try to think about it right now." Heaven knew she could not think.

She added after a moment, "I don't know if I can ever marry anyone."

"I'll wait for you to find out."

"I don't know how to be a wife. I'm a good mother, but I am awful at being a woman with a man."

She began to cry. She could not figure out her emotions. They were no longer paralyzed but now felt as if they were fighting to go in all directions. She cried harder, so hard that she soaked his shirt, while he held her to him and kissed her hair and murmured that she was just the sort of woman he needed.

"What sort is that?" she asked, sniffing. "What did you mean—a woman like me?"

It seemed a very long time before he answered. She pulled back and looked at him. He looked puzzled, and at last he said, "That you are a full and passionate woman who demands that a man stand up on equal footing. I have to be a better man when I'm around you. I have to be all the man I can be."

"Oh, Tate." Had ever a woman been so complimented? Her heart felt as if it had cracked in two. She kissed him full and hard.

After that kiss, he said, "Will you be my girl?"

"Yes." At first the word would only come in a whisper. She tried again. "Yes, I'll be your girl. But I am not making any further promises."

She lay back in his arms then, and he kissed her softly, and then held her. They sat there, and it was both sensual and comfortable. She listened to his heart beating and inhaled his scent, imprinting it on her mind, imprinting the feel of his body through their clothing. He stroked her leg, and it was in such a tender and worshipful manner that she began to cry again.

Tate did not say so, but he had a feeling that Marilee had never known a man to truly make love to her. Obviously she had experienced sex, but quite possibly never experienced having a man make love to her as a woman enjoyed by a man. This thought excited him, but it made him a little nervous, too. He hoped he would be up to the job. It would take a hell of a man to give Marilee what she needed. Maybe he would need to study books or something.

He was thinking so hard on this matter, that it was some minutes before he realized she had fallen asleep. He sat there, for that space of time, as if he had opened wide the door and was staring into the full secret of life in his heart.

Twenty-Five

Life is Good

The night lifted, and the light of a new day dawned on the roofs and trees of town and across the land, west to where a long, white limousine turned off the interstate and onto the state highway, gliding past the sign that read: Valentine, 10 miles. The driver, commanded by his employer, who did not like speed, went at a slow pace.

In town, garbage trucks started their run, the City Works crew were gathering to make another attack on the sinkhole, and Winston Valentine, putting on his glasses, looked out the kitchen window at the thermometer; the needle pointed already at eighty degrees.

"Summer's here," he said, and turned, heading through the long hall, where he took up his flags from the hall table and went out the front door. He was early, and this seemed prudent, with the heat coming. Everett had apparently made the same decision; he was just coming out his door, too.

As Winston went to his flagpole, his gaze focused in the distance at the Blaines' driveway across the meadow, and Perry's black Lincoln sitting there, still. That seemed a promising sign. Vella had called Winston last night to say that Perry had moved back in. He would go down there later and see how things had gone. He had not felt up to being all Vella wanted of him, but he was a little sad to lose her attention. Oh, well, aggravating Perry would give him something worthwhile to do.

Down on Porter, Tate, minus Bubba, who was sulking, jogged past Marilee's cottage; it was quiet. He knew better than to stop in, because he knew Marilee was not a morning person.

At the house on the corner, the young UPS man was coming down his front walk. He had a black eye.

"Woo-ee, that's a beaut," Tate said, admiring, but not breaking stride.

"You should see the other guy." The young man grinned and then winced.

Tate, sweat already beginning to wet his hair, turned left instead of right on First, and jogged down to where a burly City Works employee was guiding a concrete truck into position some feet away from the sinkhole site. Apparently they were going to run a tube from the truck, so as to not take a chance of getting the truck stuck in the hole.

Tate took a second look at the big elm tree in the front yard of the Methodist Church parsonage; it seemed to be leaning toward the sinkhole.

"We got a handle on this thing now, Editor," the burly City Works worker told him. "We are fixin' to pump thirty-five yards of concrete into this sucker. That's gotta stop it."

Tate gave the worker Reggie's phone number and requested the man call her immediately on his cell phone, so she could get a shot for the Sunday paper. Then he headed back along to Main Street, waving at Bonita Embree through the bakery window. The flag was not yet flying at the *Voice;* Charlotte was much later than usual this morning. He wondered what that was about. Turning the corner at the police station, he headed up Church, keeping an eye out in the distance.

There came Lindsey down the hill.

They met at the intersection. Tate was prepared to defend himself. He had not had a fight in a long time, so he hoped he could come out of it in decent shape.

Lindsey stopped to stretch his legs, and Tate followed suit.

"Guess you think you're pretty funny, don't you, Editor."

"*Clever* is the better word. Actually, I think it could be considered outmaneuvering." He was warming to the descriptions, yet still keeping a watchful eye on Lindsey's demeanor.

At that moment, there came Leanne Overton, flying down the hill on her bicycle. She cast a nod directed at both men as she zipped between them and curved around to Porter heading east, the cheeks of her lovely derriere moving in rhythm as she pedaled.

"If you hurry, maybe you could catch up with her," Tate suggested, a little puzzled at how Lindsey was just standing there, as if out of energy.

Lindsey shook his head. "Her looks hide some other stuff. You know?"

"Ah, well, that's not too good." Tate felt a twinge of pity for the guy.

But suddenly Lindsey straightened his shoulders and looked straight at Tate. "I'm goin' to get you back, Editor. It may take me a while, but I'm goin' to pay you back for last night."

It was a firm promise, and with that, the veterinarian swung into motion, heading away east on Porter at an easy jog with his powerful tanned legs.

Tate decided to cut his jog short and went on around, entering through the back door. The phone was ringing.

"Would you like to come to breakfast?" It was Marilee!

"Do you know your voice is very sexy first thing in the morning?" he said. "And I'll be over in fifteen minutes."

Life is good, he thought as he hurried upstairs to shower. He had a woman who liked to cook, and who had a sexy voice, too.

He ran his shower quite cold.

The long white limousine glided to a stop in front of the James house. The neighbor across the street saw it and kneeled on her couch to get a better look out her front window.

Marilee was putting homemade biscuits in the oven when the doorbell rang. Corrine was setting the table.

"Now, who could that be so early in the morning?" It was too quick for it to be Tate.

Marilee brushed her hair back from her face, and then

realized her hands were coated with flour. She asked Corrine to go see who was at the door. She was annoyed for being interrupted in cooking biscuits and gravy. She had not cooked both from scratch in a long time, and the effort required all her concentration.

The doorbell rang again. Corrine, skipping through the living room, saw a head peering in the front window.

"It is the dog-catch-ers!" said Willie Lee, who had come from the hallway and had his shirt buttoned crooked over his pajama pants. He raced back into the bedroom, calling Munro with him, and slammed the door.

"What in the world?" Aunt Marilee came from the kitchen. "Who is it, Corrine?"

Corrine, who had made it to the door but was hesitant to open it, gazed at Marilee and blinked her deep-brown eyes.

Marilee went to open the front door herself. A man with a shock of thick and rather long white hair, and dressed in a crisp, pale-blue suit, smiled at her.

"Hello. Do I have the pleasure of addressing Mrs. James?"

"Yes."

"Do you have a little boy who has a rather splotchy type of dog, an Australian shepherd, I believe?"

"Well, yes…what is this about?"

She did not know the man, but she recognized the tall, slick blond man, the one Belinda had said was from Tell-In Technologies. He stood behind one of the white-haired man's shoulders, while a very sophisticated woman stood behind the other shoulder. All three were gazing at her.

"I'm Thomas Gerard, president of the Tell-In Technologies. May I have a few minutes of your time? If you would not mind, I would like to come in and sit down, and explain in detail."

The man and woman behind him were now peering around his shoulders, as if looking at something behind Marilee.

"Well, okay." She opened the door for them to step inside.

Quite slowly, the man went to sit on her sofa. Marilee wondered how old he was. His face was not old, but he was stooped. Corrine, who was stuck to Marilee like glue, squeezed herself down in the big chair beside Marilee, and Marilee put an arm around her niece. Glancing downward, she saw she had streaks of flour on her dress.

"You are familiar with the facts of our case?" The man spoke slowly and in a very gentle manner. "That a former Tell-In employee died of a heart attack just outside of town?"

Marilee said she was familiar with the incident, and that the former employee apparently had some sort of company property.

"Yes." The man nodded. "We believe your son now possesses a dog that belonged to that former employee, and we have reason to believe this dog may be the key to us locating…something…our former employee stole from our company. Could you please tell us—was the dog wearing a collar when your son found him?"

"Yes. It had his name on it."

"And is he still wearing that collar?"

"Well…yes."

The man nodded some more and said, "We need to see that collar. It is possible that what we are looking for is in the collar, or may even be implanted in the dog itself."

"Implanted in the dog?" Marilee repeated. She looked at Corrine, as if to make note of the child in order to be certain she was not imagining this conversation.

"Yes, possibly," said Mr. Gerard in his distinctive manner. "Could we see your son's dog? I promise that we mean the dog no harm. We do not want to take the dog, only to examine him."

When Marilee sat there, thinking and gazing at the three sitting on her couch, he added, "This means a great deal to my company, Mrs. James."

"I have no doubt. As my son means a great deal to me, and for some reason, he is afraid of you." She added, "Let me speak to my son."

Marilee went to Willie Lee's bedroom door. It was locked. "Willie Lee? Honey, I need to talk to you."

Corrine was right beside her. "He thinks they want to take Munro." At Marilee's questioning gaze, she said, "They tried to, one day in town. Munro ran away. He does not like them," she added in a pointed manner.

Marilee called to Willie Lee again, but there was no answer.

Then Tate came from the kitchen. "What's going on over here? Willie Lee said the dogcatchers are in his house." He looked from Marilee in the hallway to the people on the couch and back at Marilee.

"You've seen Willie Lee?" She looked back at the door and realized her son must have gone out the window.

"Yes, but I told him I wouldn't tell where he and

Munro are." He turned a questioning eye on the three strangers, who were now getting to their feet.

"Ah," Tate said to the younger man and woman. "I believe we have met…in the police station. You were waiting to talk to the sheriff. I'm the editor of *The Valentine Voice,* who you said couldn't help you. I might be able to now, it seems."

Tate went out to talk to Willie Lee.

Corrine stood guarding the closed swinging kitchen door, while Marilee, watching through the window, saw Tate go across the yard to the tree containing Willie Lee's tree house. He looked upward, speaking, and there was an exchange for some minutes, after which an object came dropping out of the tree. Munro's collar, which Tate brought back in to the people sitting on Marilee's couch.

The blond man reached for the collar, and all three on the couch bent their heads to look at it. Marilee and Tate and Corrine hovered, trying to see, too.

"There it is," the blond man said with triumph. "Oh, and here's the—"

Whatever it was, was gone from sight in an instant, as the blond man pocketed the collar.

Thomas Gerard, getting to his feet, said, "I would like to thank your son personally. I owe him my company's future. I'd like to give him a reward."

Willie Lee, assured that Munro was still safely his dog, came back inside and into the living room and right up to Thomas Gerard, holding up his hand for a shake. "Hello, Mr. Ger-aard," he said very carefully when introduced.

"Hello, Mr. James. I thank you for taking such good care of this dog."

"He takes care of me, and Cor-rine, and Ma-ma," Willie Lee interrupted.

"Ah, so he does." The man's pale eyes fell on the dog sitting at Willie Lee's legs. "I had a dog such as this once, when I was a boy. A long time ago. I wish so much to have another."

"Ask God. That is what I did."

"Ah…I shall." Thomas Gerard pulled a paper from his inner suit pocket. "Here you are, Mr. James. Please accept this with my gratitude for returning to me something very important. Good day to you all."

Marilee saw the three people to the door and watched a moment as the white-haired gentleman went carefully down her porch steps. There was no rushing or excess of movement in Mr. Gerard.

When she turned around, she saw Tate examining the paper the Tell-In president had given Willie Lee. "Stock," he told Marilee. "Looks like Thomas Gerard just gave Willie Lee thirty-thousand dollars worth of stock."

Marilee had to sit down. She looked at Willie Lee. *He will have something for when I'm gone.* Tears came into her eyes. *Thank you, God.*

Suddenly the smoke detector started going off, and all of them raced to the kitchen to see smoke rolling out of the oven. Her biscuits had burned right up.

Tate told her. "Well, get yourselves fixed up. I'm takin' us all down to the Main Street Café for breakfast. I'd like to start showin' everyone that you're my girl."

She jerked her head up and looked at him, and his

luminous eyes smiled a deep smile at her. Slowly she returned the smile. Maybe she could be a woman to him.

Maybe for her to be the right sort of woman for a man, she needed the right sort of man to bring her out. And maybe she had at last found him.

The Valentine Voice
Sunday, August 6
View from the Editor's Desk
by Tate Holloway

Tomorrow another school year begins, so be on the lookout for children darting in the road as you are driving around. The Valentine School Board finds enrollment up again this year. This growth in population is becoming a serious concern for the school board.

Principal of our elementary school, Gwen Blankenship, has reported that this year she has some classes with over thirty students. Classes this large are a difficulty for both students and teachers. Folks, we are looking at the definite need to expand our schools and increase the number of teachers.

My hat is off to the school board for hiring two more assistant librarians. Our libraries are our greatest resource. This brings me to the proposition that if there is an increase in tax revenue this coming year, we need to establish a town library. I want to hear your views on this. Drop by the offices, or stop me on the street.

My hat is also off to the school board for establishing for the first time in the Valentine schools a program for the learning disabled. We have a lot of promise in these young folks, and it is to our own benefit to provide the best education for them we can. You can thank our own Marilee James, who worked hard all summer to bring this program into our schools, and who saw to getting a teacher with the right requirements. You can read a profile of this class on page 4.

And lastly, Norm Stidham caught me on the street and took me to task for not writing about anything controversial for several weeks. Norm, I'll work on it, and I'll be happy to take suggestions. Come on in and visit.

Charlotte was still not happy with Tate's bent for inviting all and sundry in to visit them. She deleted the last sentence, thinking Tate would not notice.

"Put that back in there," he told her, just before she sent the disks to the printer.

Twenty-Six

Moving On

"Tate's here," Corrine called.

Marilee grabbed her purse and her tote. "Okay, let's get movin'."

"We are mov-ing, Ma-ma," Willie Lee said, as he walked with deliberate motion out the door ahead of her, Munro at his heels.

They piled into Tate's car and drove to school, where children were pouring out of buses and cars, and streaming across the yard and up the walks. Marilee kissed Willie Lee, who then walked away with Tate, Munro walking right along with them, to his classroom. Then she walked Corrine to her classroom.

Outside the door, Marilee said, "Do not hesitate to call me if you need me."

"I won't."

"I'll miss you."

"I know…but you will be all right."

Marilee breathed a deep breath, wondering at who mothered whom. She kissed her niece, who, her shoulders straight and stride easy, went into the classroom. Corrine had grown taller, and her grace of movement was arresting. Marilee, still gazing in the doorway, saw a number of boys turn their eyes to her dark-haired niece. Oh boy, more hurdles. Corrine would be equally as beautiful as Anita.

It was so hard, leaving them. As she walked out of the school, she felt she left her heart behind.

"How'd he do?" she asked Tate when they met back at the car. She had resisted the urge to go peek into Willie Lee's classroom, afraid she might be spotted, afraid she might go in there and jerk Willie Lee back out.

"Very well. He seemed to accept that Munro is show and tell just for today."

Tate directed the car from the curb, and Marilee sat there, looking straight ahead. She breathed deeply. She would be okay. As long as her children were okay, she would be okay.

Tate drove to the *Voice* offices, parked at his space in the rear, and gave her a quick kiss before getting out of the car. They went inside together, Tate into his office and Marilee to her desk, where she worked for two hours, her eyes repeatedly checking the clock and thinking the day so very long.

Finaliy, almost not realizing she was doing so, she took up her purse and tote and headed out the door, telling Charlotte, "I need to go home for some things that are on my computer there."

She walked out the door into the hot August day,

across the street and up the long block of Church. She was wet with perspiration by the time she got to the corner of Porter. Her pace picked up, though, heading for home. She went into her house and shut the door and leaned against it, listening to the quiet.

She hated the quiet.

Pushing herself away from the door, she went to her computer on the desk, sat down and turned it on.

She wished Munro were there, at least.

This would not do. She had to get ahold of herself and her swirling thoughts.

She went to the back door, more or less just aimlessly moving. The sunlight made speckles through the trees on the back steps. She went out and sat down.

This was where Tate found her. He drove over to check on her when he had found her gone from her desk. It was a little absurd, but he had been worried since they had let the children off at school. He knew it was hard on her, and she had seemed too calm to him.

He got in a little panic when he went in the front door of her house and didn't find her. The house was stone quiet, and he had the thought that maybe she had been abducted. She never did lock her doors. Things could and did happen, even in small towns.

"Oh, here you are," he said, speaking with some relief when he got to the back door and found her sitting there.

"Well, yes."

She moved over to let him out to come sit beside her.

"Someday I shall get new lawn furniture," she said.

"I like sitting on the step."

"I do, too."

They grinned at each other.

She looked away quickly, suddenly sad and afraid to reveal herself. Then she dared to say, "I miss them."

"I do, too."

"I'm really glad for the summer we had. They came so far this summer. I think Willie Lee has real talent with sculpting, and we wouldn't have known that if I hadn't started tutoring him."

"He really does. No tellin' what can happen there."

"And Corrine's had time to get confidence. She's really growing up. She's becoming a young lady."

"Yes. A lovely young lady."

The entire time Marilee was thinking and chatting of these things, she was becoming more and more aware of Tate's strong thigh touching hers. More aware of the fact that they were there alone, for the first time in months. Her brain seemed to whirl, bouncing between her awareness of Tate and her sadness at missing the children that had by now caused a lump in her throat and the need to cry, which she really did not want to do.

"They don't need me like they used to," she said. "Oh, they'll always need me, but it's changing. I feel like there's a sinkhole right underneath me, the sand just runnin' out." Tears began to roll down her cheeks. "I'm so tired of adjusting. You know that's what life is, adjusting time after time, and sometimes I just don't want to adjust any more."

"I know." Tate put his hand on the back of her neck and pulled her against his chest. "I sure miss them, too."

"You do, don't you?" This fact somewhat amazed her. Tate had so fully involved himself in the children's lives.

"Yes. Makes me feel old without them."

"Oh, you're not old." She tried for a smile for him and to dry her eyes, but then a fresh wave of discouragement came over her. "I feel old, too. My babies are growin' up. What will I do?"

With that she went to sobbing against him. He rubbed her back and whispered soothing whispers. Gradually she became very aware of his hand caressing her back, of his strong chest, of the scent of him.

Then he was nuzzling her neck and said, "Let me make you feel better…let me…"

She lifted her head and met his kiss, eagerly and completely.

Tate's response to this kiss, when he lifted his head, was to say, "Good golly!"

They made love in her bed, slowly and without nervousness. They had been together for months now and discovered, with delight, that they knew each other very well.

He was a miracle, Marilee thought, pressing her cheek against his chest and hearing the beating of his heart.

"Nothing is awkward with you," she said.

"Don't know why it should be," he replied. "This is most natural between a man and a woman who are attracted to each other."

He kissed her in places all over her body, and he caressed her with abandoned pleasure, and he made her laugh, and made her cry, and made her shout his name with searing ecstasy.

Afterward, they lay in each other's arms and talked as they had not talked in the past two months.

"I guess when two people have done this," she said blushing, "it is easier to say some things."

He grinned at her and kissed her and whispered that she sure did something to him that was great.

She told him she was afraid, and then she told him something about when she had grown up, how she realized where she got the mothering talent. "I'm afraid I won't be able to be a woman as a wife. I've messed it up for two relationships now."

"But you've learned. We learn from our mistakes. And I'm not the same as Stuart and Parker."

"No, you aren't."

He told her about his growing up, about a father who drank until he got run over by a train, and his mother, whom he described as beautiful and with quite strong spiritual ideas, as he put it. Marilee liked watching the light in his eyes as he spoke. He told of his failed marriage, and how he had not been able to be married, had not really wanted to be.

Then he said, "But I want to be married now. And I want to marry you. Will you?"

Immediately all sorts of questions popped into her mind. Fears.

"Yes," she managed to get out at last.

He laughed aloud. "It is sure a good thing I'm a secure man."

Then he kissed her in the way every woman wants to be kissed and only a few get to experience.

They went to pick up the children together, as they had taken them to school. Marilee could not wait, and they were in Tate's car at the curb in front of the school ten minutes before the children were let out.

Marilee jumped out and went to meet them and kiss them both. "Oh, I missed you so much!"

Willie Lee said school was okay, but that Munro did not want to go anymore.

Corrine said she would like a special planner notebook. "In lavender, if I can," she added.

Tate said, "We need to celebrate today," and cast Marilee a private smile. "Let's go down to Blaine's."

They were greeted by Aunt Vella, who was once again manning the soda fountain, but only four days a week, with Fridays off. She said, "How are my shu-gahs today?" and kissed each of them, even Tate.

Willie Lee wanted a cherry ice-cream cone, and, "Mun-ro wants a dish of van-il-la, please."

Corrine, after much deliberation, chose a dish of pecan ice cream.

Tate ordered a glass of iced tea, and Marilee, who had been about to get a chocolate shake, changed her mind. "I'll take iced tea, too."

The bell above the door rang out, and Parker entered. Tate welcomed him over. "Let me buy you a cold drink, buddy."

Parker went behind the counter and got his own drink, then leaned on the counter to visit with all of them, the children telling about school, Parker telling about one of his patients, Aunt Vella talking about her latest rose catalog. Soon here came Uncle Perry and Winston from back in the pharmacy. The two, to everyone's amazement, had taken up playing chess. They sat in chairs with glasses of lemonade and discussed the television channel that featured a chess instruction program.

Marilee's eyes chanced to look up in the long mirror on the wall. She saw herself and Tate, sitting side by side, in the midst of her family and friends.

Quite suddenly she realized she was looking at today, herself as a full woman, the haunting of yesterday's child nearly faded clear away.

Tate's gaze met hers in the mirror. He leaned over and gave her a kiss, then said, "Good company, good tea…it doesn't get any better than this."

The Valentine Voice
Wednesday, August 23
Local Boy Struck By Fortune
By Tammy Crawford
Staff Writer

Willie Lee James woke up to find himself rich this morning, when the stock he owns in the Tell-In Technologies Corporation split two for one late yesterday afternoon.

It was reported early last week that Tell-In Technologies Corporation, a computer firm, had released a revolutionary new computer containing a more accurate and faster processor, in part powered by a chip developed within the company. Since that time, the corporation's stock has been climbing in value.

Last spring, Tell-In suffered a theft of the new chip that enables their revolutionary processor. Willie Lee James was instrumental in finding the chip, and the president of Tell-In, Mr. Thomas Gerard, personally rewarded the boy with a gift of stock.

In the past weeks, beginning with rumors of the new computer, the young James found his stock already nearing triple its original value. With this split, and as of this report, his stock's value is in excess of 115,000. The stock is expected to keep rising for some months to come.

When asked for comment, Mr. Willie Lee James said, "I am going to buy Munro a new collar. A gold one."

Young James's mother said they did plan to sell some of the stock and begin a trust fund for her son, as well as endow a learning-disabled program for the Valentine school district.

Tell-In president, Thomas Gerard, has said he is going to join in spirit with Ms. James by establishing an endowment for the learning-disabled nationwide.

Tate, upon making his normal rounds of town that afternoon, made certain everyone saw the article on Willie Lee. He said, "Just when you think it doesn't get any better, by golly, it always can!"

* * * * *

Turn the page for an advance look at
CHIN UP, HONEY
by national bestselling author Curtiss Ann Matlock
coming in May 2009
only from MIRA Books

"Berry Enterprises offices. Shelley Dilks speakin'."

"Hello, Shelley. This is Emma. Is John Cole in?"

"Well...yes. Just a minute and I'll see if he can get the phone."

And why would he not get the phone for his wife? Emma thought, squeezing her eyes closed. *If Shelley Dilks knows and spreads the word about me and John Cole, I will snatch her baldheaded.*

"Hey. Emma?"

At John Cole's voice, her eyes flew open.

"Yes...hello." She thought his tone actually seemed welcoming, which was gratifying, considering their situation. Although maybe she imagined it. She had not felt at all certain about anything with him for a long time.

"Are you in your office?"

"Yeah. Why?"

"Are you in your office alone?"

"Yes, I am." He was a little testy, and she didn't think he needed to get that way.

"Well, I have somethin' important to tell you. I don't want you distracted by Shelley or somebody, or stuff goin' on. Why don't you close your office door?"

"It *is* closed, Emma Lou. What is it?"

She opened her mouth, then closed it. Suddenly the fact of Johnny's engagement was too big and tender for words. She pressed a hand to her chest, as her memory flashed back through the years and she recalled telling John Cole of having gotten pregnant at last, after their years of desperate trying. She had done this same thing, gotten him on the phone and not been able to say a word.

"Emma?" he said with a bit of alarm.

"It's good." She reached for a tissue.

"O-kay."

She imagined that familiar patient expression he got when he settled in to outwait anything and everything. John Cole could have the patience of Job. It was annoying.

She swallowed, took a deep breath and got it out. "Our John Ray is gettin' married."

"He is?" His tone was more confused than surprised. It generally took John Cole some time to absorb news of such magnitude.

"Yes, he is."

"I just saw him yesterday mornin'. He didn't say anything about gettin' married." He still sounded confused.

"He talks to you about money and business. He talks to me about life and love. Besides, I don't think he had asked her then. I kinda' got the idea it all happened last night...that he got the ring just yesterday."

"He just bought a car."

"I don't think there's a limit on these things."

The line hummed with disapproving silence.

She said more gently, "Our son is a man grown and fully capable of makin' good decisions for his own life."

"Yeah, I guess so." Then, "Who is he marryin'? Is it the one with the long dark hair—Gracie? Is that her name?"

"Yes," Emma said, with some impatience at his question. Who else could it have been? He just didn't pay attention to anything that wasn't work related.

"She is the only girl he has been datin' for the past six months, at least. But I think he's known her since way last fall. He's brought her out here twice this spring to Sunday dinner...oh, but the second time you were gone to the NASCAR races down in Dallas."

That her son had brought Gracie only twice, now three times, in all those months seemed a telling commentary. Other girls he had brought quite often, but this Gracie was special.

"I've seen them together a number of times," John Cole said in a defensive tone. "When I dropped by his place, and I took them to lunch once. She seems a nice girl."

"Gracie is a woman, John, not a girl. She's a lovely, intelligent and solid young woman. I knew from the first time I saw her that Johnny was ready to settle down. I told you that, remember? Johnny never had a girl like her before."

She went on to tell him that the kids wanted the

wedding sometime in the middle of September, but were in consultation with Gracie's mother and all their friends about the exact date and location.

"We've got the big Convenience Store Expo up at Oklahoma City in September," said John Cole. "The second week in September."

To which Emma instantly replied, "I don't think that is near as important as John Ray's wedding. You can miss it one year."

"I was just mentionin' it, Emma Lou."

She bit her bottom lip.

Then she said, "We'll know more about everything on Sunday. The kids are comin' for dinner—we're gonna have a little family engagement celebration and talk over the wedding plans. I think it would be good for you to be here on Sunday, if you can."

"I'll be there," he said instantly.

"Well, good." Then, "John?"

"Yeah?"

"I think it would be a good idea for you to come on home. We just can't do the divorce now. It would tear Johnny's world apart at a time that is supposed to be filled with joy—his and Gracie's special time. We need to just drop the idea and make everything seem normal, at least until after the wedding. Don't you think so?"

She squeezed her eyes closed.

"Yeah, I think you're right."

Everything just melted inside her. While she had often felt dissatisfied with John Cole as a husband, it was pure truth that she had always been able to count on his excellence as a father.

It was a lot to take in. First she was getting divorced from her husband of thirty-two years, then her son was getting married, now her husband was coming home.

John Cole was coming home that night.

What about sleeping arrangements?

She entered their bedroom and gazed at the bed—king-size, solid cherrywood. She had bought it back when they got their first house. John Cole never had paid much attention to the interior of the house. Every time she bought something, he would grouch about her spending money on it, but then, when the piece was in the house, he really liked it.

Going to the enormous chest, she opened the two doors, revealing the television and stereo system that had not been turned on in the days since John Cole had left. There, too, was his collection of small metal antique cars.

There was no way John Cole could manage sleeping in the guest room. He would end up making the family room and his recliner his bedroom.

She entered the walk-in closet, where one side still contained most of his clothes, with a line of boots and shoes below. She gathered up her nightgown and robe and slippers, carried them down to the guest room and threw them over the end of the bed. She wasn't going to move her clothes, because she could not have anyone know that she wasn't still in her own room. Then she returned with two large wicker baskets to the bathroom, where she swept her things off the counter and out of the drawers, carrying them down to the guest bath and tucking the things in the cabinet.

Subterfuge was going to be a lot of work.

Return to Virgin River with a breathtaking
new trilogy from award-winning author

ROBYN CARR

February 2009

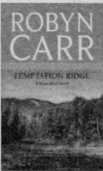

March 2009

April 2009

"The Virgin River books are so compelling—
I connected instantly with the characters
and just wanted more and more and more."
—#1 *New York Times* bestselling author
Debbie Macomber

A riveting novel from acclaimed author

DIANE CHAMBERLAIN

When Janine Donahue arrives to pick up her daughter Sophie after a weekend group camping trip, she discovers that somehow, along the route, Sophie has disappeared.

Suffering from a rare disease, Sophie cannot survive long without her medication. All her instincts tell Janine that Sophie is alive, but time is running out.

Deep in the Virginia forest, Sophie finds refuge in the remote cabin of Zoe, a woman struggling to save her own daughter from the law—and Sophie's presence jeopardizes that. Zoe is as determined to save her daughter as Janine is to save Sophie...and only one of them can succeed.

The Courage Tree

Available wherever books are sold.

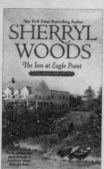

Let Sleeping Dogs Lie
SUZANN LEDBETTER

CRIME DOESN'T PAY...ENOUGH

Private investigator Jack McPhee has a two-word
business philosophy: No partners. Rules are allegedly
made to be broken, but Jack didn't expect a contract to
nab the so-called Calendar Burglar would force him to
team up with a ten-pound, hyperactive Maltese.

Or that he'd fall deeply in like with Dina Wexler, a
groomer whose definition of a P.I. comes from watching
w-a-y too many detective shows.

Or that his absolutely genius idea to catch a thief would
make him the prime—and only—suspect in a cold-
blooded, diabolical homicide.

MARCIA PRESTON

Marik Youngblood left her father's ranch—and the child she gave up for adoption—years ago. Her father's death brings her back to a pile of debt and a haunting need to find the child she left behind. Leasing the land for wind towers solves one problem, but creates another— hostility from her neighbors, Burt and Lena Gurdman.

Lena Gurdman may be poor and uneducated, but she knows she and Marik have more in common than the property line between them. When the bones of an infant are uncovered nearby, both Marik and Lena are left with questions about secrets they thought were buried long ago.

The Wind Comes Sweeping

REQUEST YOUR FREE BOOKS!

2 FREE NOVELS
FROM THE ROMANCE/SUSPENSE
COLLECTION PLUS 2 FREE GIFTS!

YES! Please send me 2 FREE novels from the Romance/Suspense Collection and my 2 FREE gifts (gifts are worth about $10). After receiving them, if I don't wish to receive any more books, I can return the shipping statement marked "cancel." If I don't cancel, I will receive 4 brand-new novels every month and be billed just $5.49 per book in the U.S. or $5.99 per book in Canada, plus 25¢ shipping and handling per book plus applicable taxes, if any*. That's a savings of at least 20% off the cover price! I understand that accepting the 2 free books and gifts places me under no obligation to buy anything. I can always return a shipment and cancel at any time. Even if I never buy another book from the Reader Service, the two free books and gifts are mine to keep forever.

185 MDN EF5Y   385 MDN EF6C

Name	(PLEASE PRINT)

Address	Apt. #

City	State/Prov.	Zip/Postal Code

Signature (if under 18, a parent or guardian must sign)

Mail to **The Reader Service**:
IN U.S.A.: P.O. Box 1867, Buffalo, NY 14240-1867
IN CANADA: P.O. Box 609, Fort Erie, Ontario L2A 5X3

Not valid to current subscribers to the Romance Collection,
the Suspense Collection or the Romance/Suspense Collection.

Want to try two free books from another line?
Call 1-800-873-8635 or visit www.morefreebooks.com.

* Terms and prices subject to change without notice. N.Y. residents add applicable sales tax. Canadian residents will be charged applicable provincial taxes and GST. Offer not valid in Quebec. This offer is limited to one order per household. All orders subject to approval. Credit or debit balances in a customer's account(s) may be offset by any other outstanding balance owed by or to the customer. Please allow 4 to 6 weeks for delivery. Offer available while quantities last.

Your Privacy: Harlequin is committed to protecting your privacy. Our Privacy Policy is available online at www.eHarlequin.com or upon request from the Reader Service. From time to time we make our lists of customers available to reputable third parties who may have a product or service of interest to you. If you would prefer we not share your name and address, please check here. ☐

BOB08R